here there be monsters

Republica Helvetorum #1

ec garrett

The story, all names, characters, and incidents portrayed in *Here There Be Monsters* are fictitious. No identification with actual persons (living or deceased), places, buildings, and products is intended or should be inferred.

Copyright © 2024 by Midnight Pages LLC

All rights reserved, including the rights of reproduction, in whole or in part, in any form.

No part of this publication may be reproduced, distributed, or transmitted in any form or by any means, including photocopying, recording, or other electronic or mechanical methods, without the prior written permission of the publisher, except as permitted by U.S. copyright law.

Cover Art and Design by EC Garrett

Cover Model & Photographer by Варвара Курочкина

Interior Formatting and Design by EC Garrett

Map by Shepengul

Editing & Proofreading by Havoc Archives

eBook ISBN: 979-8-9890690-7-1

Paperback ISBN: 979-8-9890690-6-4

Hardback ISBN: 979-8-9890690-5-7

*For anyone who has ever looked in the mirror
and seen a monster reflected back.*

*Embrace the chaos.
Let the monster out.*

be warned

This book isn't for the faint of heart.
Here There Be Monsters is a Gothic book in that it features horror elements, psychological mind-fucks, and grief. This story is set in an alternative early medieval universe that is just coming out of a Dark Age. The world is dark, cruel, and grotesque. The characters walk the line of consent and engage in taboo, extreme kink acts like bloodplay, verbal degradation, humiliation, and more. These are done consensually, but the situations are extreme.
If HTBM was a movie, it would be UNRATED.
Proceed with caution and review the trigger warning list below before you dive in. If it all sounds good? Then get ready for a *monstrous* time.

Triggers that are frequent are in **BOLD** and triggers that are extremely frequent are in **<u>BOLD AND UNDERLINED.</u>**

<u>HATE, DISCRIMINATION, & OPPRESSION</u>
Bullying, **Classism,** Lesbomisia, Poverty, Racism, **Religious Persecution,** and **Sexism & Misogyny**

<u>SEX & ROMANCE</u>
Airtight, Anal Sex, **DVP (double vaginal penetration), <u>Barebacking</u>, <u>Begging</u>, <u>Biting</u>,** Bisexuality, **<u>Bloodplay</u>, <u>Blood Consumption</u>, Breeding Kink, Bondage,** CNC (Consensual Non-Consent) Sce-

narios,D/s Power Dynamics, **Degradation,** Demisexuality**, Dubious Consent Situations, Exhibitionism**, **FF Sex, Graphic Language**, **Group Sex, Humiliation, MM Sex, Oral Sex (F & M),** Pansexuality, Pet Names, **Rim Jobs, Sex Furniture, Sensory Deprivation, Snowballing, Spitting, Switching,** Vaginal Fisting, and **Voyeurism**

MENTAL HEALTH
Depression, Dissociation & Dissociative Episodes, Intrusive Thoughts, Post-Traumatic Stress Disorder, Self-Harm, and **Suicidal Ideation**

SUBSTANCE USE
Alcohol Consumption

INJURY & MEDICAL
Amputation, **Blood & Gore Depiction,** Body Horror, Cannibalism, **Dead Bodies & Body Parts,** Decapitation, Dismemberment, Drowning, **Emesis, Eyeball trauma, Loss of Limb,** Medical Experimentation, Paralysis, **Physical injuries,** Physical illness, **Poisoning,** and Scars

DEATH & LOSS
Death of a Friend, Death of a Parent & Guardian, Death of a Partner & Spouse, and **Grief & Loss Depictions.**

VIOLENCE & CRIME
Abuse of Power, Building Collapse, **Captivity & Confinement, Corruption**, Cults, **Electrocution,** Explosions, **Fire & Arson, Imprisonment & Incarceration,** Knife, Sword & Axe Violence, Murder & Attempted Murder, **Physical Assault, Poisoning,** Torture, **Vitriolage,** and Whipping.

<u>WAR & GENOCIDE</u>
Colonialism, **War Themes & Military Violence**

<u>ANIMAL DEATH & CRUELTY</u>
Animal Attack, Animal Death, and **Hunting.**

ANGLORUM TERRA
THUN
BIENNE
THE HELVETAS MOUNTAINS
THE AIVE
THE GLADE
THE KLEINBASEL RIVER
SCHOLLEN GORGE
INTERLAKEN
REPUBLICA HELVETORUM

n
w
e
s
THE MOUNTAIN GODS TERRITORY
THE REPUBLIC

the language

characters

Aegidus – *ah-gih-dis* – He/They

Albrecht Bucher – *all-brech-t boo-hair* – He/Him

Aleksander – *ah-lick-san-der* – He/Him

Balthazar – *bal-tha-zsar* – He/Him

Daphne Bucher – *daf-nee boo-hair* – She/Her

Elsing Wylder – *el-sing wild-er* – She/Her

Heidi – *high-dee* – She/Her

Lythe – *lee-thee* – She/Her

Nerethus – *nere-uh-thus* – He/Him

Noctis – *nock-tis* – He/They

Pennios – *penny-oh-ss* – They/Them

Pertcha – *perch-ah* – She/Her

Rhaeta – *ray-ta* – She/Her

Sälva – *sael-vuh* – She/Her

Tante Inga – *taunt-uh ing-ga* – She/Her

Trystan – *trys-tan* – He/They
Uri – *yur-ee* – They/Them
Uriel – *yur-ee-el* – She/They
Willem Tell – *will-em tell* – He/Him

places

(The) Aive - *aye-v*
The home of the Mountain Gods

Alamania - *all-mon-ee-uh*
The land to the north of Republica Helvetorum. The entire Republic used to be Almania but the land has gotten smaller and smaller every year as the Republic pushes further north.

Anglorum Terra - *anglo-rum terra*
Country to the Northwest of RH

(The) Below - *bee-low*
The Underworld, which consists of three parts: the Beneath, the Between, and the Beyond.

Bienne - *bean*
town south of Thun

Interlaken - *in-ter-lah-ken*
Elsing's home, a small village on the southwest side of the Helvetas

Kleinbasel - *klein-bah-sel*
River

Midgard - *mid-gard*
Realm of the Gods

Ostmark - *ost-mark*
Country to the northeast of the Helvetas. Actively at war with the Republic.

Republica Helvetorum - *ree-pub-lick-uh hell-veh-tor-um*
Also known as "the Republic"

Schollen Gorge - *shh-oh-len gorge*
A dangerous rocky area with waterfalls in the southwestern Helvetas.

Thun - *thoon*
a town to the northwest of the Helvetas

terms

Apothe - *uh-poth-ee*
A potion maker and healer.

Aureus - *or-uhs*
1) The monetary unit of Republica Helvetorum 2) a gold coin with Paul II's image.

Basilisk - *bas-sil-isk*
A Dragon egg that was cursed by a Witch, so when the beast hatches, it doesn't have legs and is evil.

Deprimierend - *deh-prim-ear-end*
"Depressing" in Almanni

Erbreche - *ear-brech-uh*
(*pull the "ch" in "brech" into the back of your throat"*
Verb, singular, I, "to vomit"

Frau - *fr-ow*
"Ms."

Gottverdammt - *gott-ver-damm-t*
"Goddamnit"

Heilige Hölle - *hell-lig-guh hule*
(*pull the "u" in "hule" into the back of your throat)*
"Holy Hell"

Heilige scheiße - *hell-lig-guh shyy-sUH*
"Holy shit"

Ja - *yah*
"Yes"

Jäger - *yay-ger*
The Family Name of a very powerful line of Witches known for hunting other monsters. The Jägers can also "cast" without speaking aloud, which is why other Witches hate them so much. It's speculated the Jägers are descended from Pertcha Herself.

Kotzbrocken - *cot-ss-broch-en*
(*pull "broch" into the back of your throat)*
"Pile of puke"

Maleficer - *mal-if-fiss-er*
A derogatory term for magic users

Primatori - *prim-uh-tory*
Equivalent to an Emperor, chosen by "God" to lead.

Scheiße - *shyy-sUH*
"Shit"or "Fuck"

Shauptmann - *shau-pt-mahnn*
Governor

Sommer - *zo-mer*
Summer

Traurig - *trau-ig*
"Sad"

Vampir - *vam-peer*
"Vampire"

Vielen Dank, Mutter - *vee-len dah-nk, mooter*
"Thank you, Mother" [Mother being Pertcha, the Mother of Magic]

Verdammter Idiot - *ver-damn-pt ih-dee-oht*
[a] goddamned idiot

Werwulves - *where-wol-ves*
Werewolves

Wintar - *win-tar*
Winter

Wintarberries - *wintar berries*
A poisonous berry native to the Helvetas

Witch - *witch*
A human with elemental powers that can be channeled through "casts,"
which are spells said aloud. Witches often have a familiar. Lifespan,
500-1,000 years.

*Almanni spells are translated and spoken in the you/you all (formal)
conjugation.*

Atmen - *auh-t-man*
"Breathe"

Aufwachen - *owf-vach-en-see*
(Pull the "ch" in "vach" into the back of your throat)
"Wake"

Freischalten - *fry-shalt-en*
"Open"

Heilen - *hail-en*
"Heal"

Hitzen - *hit-zz-en*
"Heat"

Schützen - *shoot-zen*
(Pull the "oo" in "shoot" into the back of your throat)
"Shield" or "Protect"

Stärke - *shh-tar-k (Pull the "a" in "tar" into the back of your throat*
"Relax"

Stormschlagen - *storm-shh-lag-en*
"Shock" or "Electrocute"

author's note

If you didn't already know, I'm a bit of a Medieval History nerd. I received my Bachelor's degree from the University of Nevada, Reno in 2016 in Medieval and Early Modern Literature and a minor in Medieval History. Specifically, I have always been very drawn to the later Roman Empire and the Christianization of early medieval Europe. I could spend hours analyzing the Roman Empire going from a polytheistic religion (multiple gods), to a state-mandated monotheistic religion (Christianity), and the subsequent effects of this change; many of which we still can see to this day.

The Holy Roman Empire proceeded to conquer and colonize western Europe, which, once upon a time, was known as Germania. Germania was made up of many different Pagan tribes. You might have heard of one of these tribes: the Vikings. The tribes of Germania went as far north as the area that is now known as the Netherlands.

Each tribe had a different language and held different beliefs. In the name of the Christian God, the Holy Roman Empire proceeded to colonize these tribes. In the Republica Helvetorum world, you enter an alternate reality of our world but set in an early medieval time period five to six centuries after the Republic (which is the equivalent to the Holy Roman Empire) has begun to imperialize the north.

Before the Republic arrived, this land used to be known as Almania. In the RH world, Almanians hold on tightly to their pagan culture, despite the Christianization of the world around them. Our main character Elsing is born under Republic rule, but she identifies as Almanian, and as such, her spells are cast in Almani, which is based on modern day German. You will see some Norse language as well.

The inspiration for this story came from my delving into my own family history. My family, many centuries ago, lived in Switzerland. I started researching Swiss, German, and Alpine lore specific to the mountainous region in south-central Europe.

This is a world in which magic exists. It is not illegal, per se. Just as it wasn't always specifically "illegal" to not pray to the Empire's God, but it was frowned upon and those people were shunned. The Republic looks for any excuse to target and punish magic users, using propaganda and fearmongering to achieve their goals. It is a world that will feel very familiar to you, except magic exists and humans are aware of it.

Welcome to Republica Helvetorum. The Mountain Gods await.

XOXO,

welcome to the republic

SCAN FOR THE OFFICIAL

here there be monsters

READING PLAYLIST

A Decree From The Republic

Paul II, son of Paul I, Primatori of Republica
Helvetorum, he who is Highest unto the
One True God.

For the eternal reign of the Republic, I hereby warn
that any use of unsanctioned witchcraft or magic,
shall be punishable by death and divine judgment.
I command all Shauptmann of the Republic to
pay diligent attention to these cases, as God
has intended.

The Devil is known for his deceit. You are to ensure
no witch, or magical person thereof, are left alive if
proven to have ties with the Devil. Dispose of them in
whatever manner you see fit. Their magic is a sin and
He commands us to wipe clean the slate of the
Republic, lifting us higher unto Heaven.

Protect the Church.
Protect the Republic.
Protect our Eternal Souls.

Amen.

paul II

the year of our Lord 750

beware
the forest

—that way
monster's lie

then

the trial

chapter 1

"Elsing Wylder, I hereby find you guilty of murder through means of witchcraft! In the name of the one true God, I sentence you to *death*."

The crowd went wild at the proclamation, jumping to their feet to shout insults towards me.

"WITCH! WITCH!"

"BURN THE WITCH!"

"MURDERER—"

"SILENCE!" Willem bellowed, spit flying from his mouth.

The crowd quieted instantly, waiting. Willem Tell, the Shauptmann of Interlaken looked at me with hate in his violet eyes. **"Do you have any last words, malificer?"**

I smirked. "I do. I wish I could resurrect him so I can kill that pathetic fucker again!"

The crowd erupted in shouts again, calling for my death.

"That wasn't very helpful, Elsie," Uri's scratchy voice sounded in my head.

"I will not lie. My fate was already sealed, regardless of my words." I sent the thought back to my familiar who watched from one of the windows, their raven figure hidden between tree branches.

"Your heinous crime deserves a punishment worse than death." Willem paused and the crowd went still. It was an effort to keep my eyes from rolling back into my head. Willem *lives* for the drama. When the air of the room was thick with tension, he took a deep breath and lifted a finger, pointing it directly at me.

"Tomorrow night when the moon is full, you shall be sacrificed to the Mountain Gods!"

The crowd was on their feet a second later. It wasn't angry shouts that erupted—*it was applause.*

Crazed, violent applause.

Fucking assholes.

I twisted in my chair, looking at their excited faces. Willem Tell freed me from my rope bonds long enough to grab me by the arm, dragging me through the aisle of crowded bodies. They flooded around me, grabbing at my dress, scratching my skin in the mania to claim their pound of flesh.

I spat in their faces and bit any flesh that came close. Blood dripped from my mouth as I crunched down on the bone of a pointer finger. The owner of the finger screamed, flailing wildly as the pain overwhelmed them.

They were quickly forgotten in the raucous crowd as we made our way down the aisle and toward the edge of the room.

If I'm going down, I'm taking Willem Tell with me.

"Oh no! Who is going to make your erectile dysfunction draughts now?" I said, loud enough for the crowd to hear.

"You're going to die, *Witch*," Willem hissed in my ear. "All that will be left of you will be a pile of weak, brittle bones."

"Tante Inga can't make a potion to save her life. Will you *ever* be able to get it up again?" I asked, my voice laced with pretend concern. We came to a sudden stop and then pain exploded in my face, a sharp crack blasting my eardrums. Distantly, I heard doors opening. Stars burst behind my eyes and my legs began to tingle.

Uri's voice filled my head. *"Don't pass out, Elsie."*

"I won't," I growled, officially pissed off. *"But that fucker is getting on my last nerve."*

I blinked away the stars as Willem tried to shove me to the ground.

But I held fast, gripping his arm hard enough it would end up leaving bruises.

"The offer still stands to peck his eyes out. I've never tasted violet eyes. Shall I?" Uri squawked with excitement.

I huffed a laugh. *"Not yet."*

"Rude." They sounded put out.

"The last thing I need is you getting hurt too," I reminded them.

Uri made a distinctly human-like sigh, something odd for a raven. *"Fine. I won't eat his eyes... yet."*

"Thank you." I chuckled.

"Eyes are the best part, you know. So gooey and delicious. That moment when I puncture them with my beak is so delectable." They made a happy noise.

I stifled a laugh. *"Bloodthirsty bird."*

"Like calls to like, pretty Witch." They squawked out a laugh.

Willem continued dragging me into the town toward the gallows. There were three pillories in front, meant for holding prisoners awaiting their fate. I was to be held in the pillory overnight and all day tomorrow. When evening came, they would take me to Schollen Gorge and leave me to be eaten by the Mountain Gods.

Such a lovely fate.

Willem shoved me again, so I spit in his face. He lunged, moving to push me to the ground, but I was faster than him—particularly when I was mad.

And I was fucking *seething*.

The townsfolk of Interlaken crowd behind Willem as we emerged into the town square. Willem tried to shove me to the ground again, going to kick the back of my knees. He's a tall man, at least a foot taller than me, but I'm not a short woman at nearly 1.8 meters tall. I easily sidestepped his kick and used his momentum to spin to the left. This gave me the perfect leverage to shove him.

"Stormschlagen," I casted with my thoughts, and a jolt of electricity

shot out from my fingertips, shocking Willem as he fell. I cackled at the high-pitched shriek he let out.

Most Witches can only cast through verbal incantations—with the exception of my mother's line. I've never met another Witch besides my parents who could cast through mere thought, which is why I can easily pass for a plain mortal.

When I moved to Interlaken, I didn't hide my witchcraft. The old Apothe had died, and while potion-making isn't my favorite, I'm proficient enough to do the job. So we took the Interlaken posting, and I sent a prayer to Pertcha that it would go better than the last.

"Aureus for your thoughts?" Uri's musical voice called in my head. I rescued my raven familiar ten years ago. I was traveling from Thun through western Helvetas to the town of Bienne, when a pained *squawk* drew my attention to the poor injured bird. But the second I touched it, our magic connected, and I knew the Goddess finally blessed me with a familiar. Our magic merged and their wings healed instantly. They've been my best friend ever since.

Even if they are a tricky little shit.

"Naughty Witch," Uri's cawing laughter sounded in my head. *"You're in enough trouble as it is! Did you have to curse him, Elsie?"*

"Yes," I deadpanned. There was a beat of silence before more of their cawing laughter. *"At least you can eat his eyes if the curse I just laid on him makes them fall out."*

"Ooh, tasty. Yes, this is a good plan. I haven't had human eyes in so long..." They broke off with a pleased sigh. I chuckled as a red-faced Willem pushed up off the ground and grabbed me, fury in his eyes.

The citizens of Republica Helvetorum are well aware that magical beings exist, and they *hate* it. Witches are tolerated, nothing more. Finding good, steady work is difficult, and when it comes, it's not to be wasted. Most Witches, upon finding a good role, don't quit until they're dead.

But humans are a fickle breed with a complex as big as a giant. To them, the idea that they are not the apex predators is blasphemy. So Witches stay quiet and keep to the shadows.

Or we did, at least. A century ago, the Primatori of Republica Helvetorum announced new punishments against any Witch or magical being found guilty of a crime. After this, more and more Witches began to go missing, their bodies turning up days later. More towns began outlawing witchcraft entirely. Interlaken is the last town in the empire to allow it.

Willem Tell hated me from the moment he looked upon my face the day I arrived in Interlaken.

He took one look at the raven who normally resides on my shoulder and knew he hated me.

Not because I'm a Witch, although that is his favorite excuse, despite the fact that I'm not the only witch in town. Willem and Tante Inga, a witch who looks older than the mountains themselves, are old friends, something that's always confused me.

No, Willem Tell doesn't hate me because I'm a witch.

He hates me because I'm not afraid of him.

I do not flinch when he bellows. I do not back down when he glares.

For every snide remark he slings at me, I have a sharper one to throw back.

The only power Willem has is fear. By refusing to give him the satisfaction of using it to manipulate me like the rest of the town, I became enemy number one.

Unfortunately for me, the townsfolk of Interlaken adore Willem. As our mutual dislike became more apparent, more of the town turned against me.

Too bad for them I don't care.

I don't need to be liked. I need to be *feared.*

So as Willem dragged me over to the pillory, I didn't fight. Instead, when his violet eyes met mine, I *smiled,* andthe rage on his face was fucking delicious.

"Shall I bring you some food, Elsie? I saw a yummy-looking rat this morning that I can feed you." Uri hopped from one foot to the other in front of me.

The moon was high in the sky and the town was finally quiet. For the past few hours, men stood around and harassed me while kids pelted me with tomatoes and other harder vegetables.

Yet I said nothing. I sat there in silence as the town of Interlaken ridiculed me. People I had helped, had healed. Men who needed to get it up for their wives. I helped them all.

Eventually, the men grew tired, leaving me alone and allowing Uri to come down from the trees.

There was no chance of me getting any sleep, not when the wind coming off the Helvetas was so cold I could feel every gust in the depths of my bones. Shivers wreaked havoc on my body for the past few hours, but with the last townsperson asleep in their bed, I could finally do something about it.

"Hitzen," I whispered the word in my head, causing warmth to ease into my bones. An invisible bubble formed around me. Within it, the air rapidly heated, warming me.

"Better?" Uri asked gently, their voice low and scratchy.

"So much better." I exhaled hard. *"Thank you for the rat offer, but you know quite well I like my meat cooked, Uri. So for now, I will pass."*

"Humans are so strange," Uri grumbled, cranky at being turned down.

"I am human as much as you are a simple bird," I reminded them.

"You need to eat, Elsie."

I rolled my eyes, although as my face was pointed towards the dirt, I doubt they saw the movement. *"I'll be fine, Uri. I'm going to get eaten alive tomorrow anyway. I don't exactly feel like being fattened up before I'm supposed to be the supper pig."*

Uri hopped around the pillory, using their wings for balance until they reached my legs. The large black raven nuzzled the small sliver of skin around my exposed ankles where my socks have fallen down.

"A pig sounds lovely. I especially love their livers," Uri commented.

I couldn't help but smile despite the awful circumstances.

Only Uri could make me laugh at a time like this. They made me feel something other than emptiness and anger.

"What are you going to do when I'm gone?" I asked.

Uri went still against my ankle. *"I don't know, Elsie. I suppose I'll fly north to Anglorum Terra. There is a large unkindness there."*

Sadness flooded my heart. *"Will you find another witch?"*

Uri sighed. *"I thought you knew."*

"Knew what?" I asked, confused. *"Uri, what is it I don't know?"*

Uri rubbed their head against my ankle again, their feathers as soft as silk. *"Familiars only happen once, Elsie. If... When one of us dies, there will never be another."*

Oh.

"You're my Witch, Elsie. Mine. Whatever happens tomorrow, you will always be mine," Uri said sadly.

"I didn't know. I would... Fuck, I would have done this differently, Uri. I didn't..." I floundered, mentally trying to find the right words, but the guilt was choking me.

"I know." They cawed, feeling my emotions. *"It's not your fault, Elsie. I would have said something about it sooner. I just assumed you knew."*

Silence formed between us for a moment, both of us lost in our thoughts.

"I will stay with you until the end," Uri whispered. *"Always."*

"If there's anything left—" I blinked furiously against the hot tears now flooding my eyes. *"—place two coins over my eyes, so Pertcha can find me."*

"As you wish." Uri cawed. *"Then I'm pecking out some eyes."*

"Uri!" I scolded. *"Don't risk yourself like that. When this is done, get as far from the Republic as possible. Please."*

Uri responded with a scratchy laugh.

"Close your eyes, I will watch over you until morning," they ordered. I protested but they pecked my legs, shutting me up.

"Fine. Fine!"

Uri cawed lightly before quieting down. A low, vibrating hum began to sound as they purred against my ankle. Or at least that's what it sounded like. It wasn't a purr in the way a cat purrs. But it was a happy, low warbling sound that would cause Uri's little raven body to vibrate. The sound and feeling of their soft feathers always relaxed me.

Uri purred when they were content or when they wanted to calm me down. The first time Uri made this noise, I thought they were dying. Now I recognized the sound as one of happiness and comfort.

"I love you, witch. Always have, always will," Uri whispered in my head. *"I wish things were different."*

"As do I," I sent back, imagining that I was hugging Uri's soft raven body against my chest.

Between the warmth of my spell protecting me from the harsh wind, Uri's soft feathers against my leg, and the low, happy sounds they were making, the world began to fade as sleep wrapped me in its clutches.

the sacrafice

chapter 2

"*W*ake up," a voice said in the distance. *"Elsie, they're coming. Wake up!"*

Something sharp poked me in the leg and I squeaked. I tried to stand but my body wouldn't move.

Oh. Right.

My eyes opened, bringing with them the weight of realization as I slowly regained consciousness.

A groan fell from my lips at the sight that stood in front of me. The men who taunted me yesterday were back, as were the children, their pockets stuffed full of more things to chuck at my head.

My patience has always been thinner in the mornings. Perhaps that's why Uri and I found each other. We're both night owls.

Annoyance sunk into me, twisting through my blood and worming its way into my bones.

"Schützen," I whispered in my mind. The air around me shimmered and the townsfolk blinked in confusion. It was early enough in the day that they'll chalk it up to poor sleep. A few of them rubbed their eyes, wondering if they were seeing things.

But when a child with white-blonde hair and bright blue eyes threw a tomato at me, it was stopped by my invisible shield, hovering in the air right in front of my face before it rebounded back and hit one of the men in the nose.

I laughed as their eyes widened in equal parts confusion and fear. They'll assume I cast it during the night. They'll blame themselves for not being there.

As more children threw vegetables at me, more food ricocheted into the crowd. Someone screamed as the crowd began to whisper nervously.

"Oh! The tip of a parsnip hit someone in the eye. Lots of blood and oh look—" Uri squawked. *"Now someone's throwing up! No one will notice if I sneak in there and grab it. Can't let an eye go to waste."*

"No! Stay a safe distance away please," I replied sharply. *"With all this screaming, you know Willem will be here soon. They'll be forced to put me in the town hall cellar to wait until this evening."*

"Smart," they responded, and at that moment, the crowd parted, letting Willem Tell through. The tall man walked confidently towards me, his beautiful face twisted in a disgusted sneer. His silver hair was still damp from the bath. I dropped the shield just before he hit it. Water drops hit me in the face as Willem leaned over the pillory.

"More witchcraft?" he hissed in my ears.

"I don't know what you're talking about, Wil," I replied tartly, my eyes wide in faux innocence.

"Bitch," he hissed in my ear, spit hitting my cheek.

"That's Witch bitch to you."

His fist hit my ribs and pain exploded through my side. Suddenly it hurt to breathe.

Willem undid the pillory and I fell to the ground, arms clutched around my ribs as pain assaulted me.

The Shauptmann chuckled, reaching over and grabbing my hand so fast I barely saw it. But suddenly something cold clicked around my wrist.

I blinked, my stomach sinking at the sight of an iron bracelet on my arm, a symbol of Paul II and other Republic iconography etched into the metal.

Fuck.

"Heilen," I casted frantically. *"Heilen, Heilen, Heilen!"*

Nothing happened.

"Uri, lend me your magic."

My familiar was within my mind in an instant.

"I... cannot. There's nothing for my magic to connect to. Whatever that metal monstrosity is, it's suppressing your magic completely."

Gott Verdammt! I cursed internally.

I heard rumors the Republic created a magic suppression device. I never thought they'd trust an idiot like Willem Tell with it, though.

Willem stood finally, addressing the waiting crowd. "His Holiness, Primatori Paul II, knew the malificers would do this. God told him they would need to be controlled, for *our* safety." Fake piety oozed out of Willem's every pore. "The criminal is no longer a threat. Her magic is sealed. But I know her sinful presence is bothersome, so she shall be locked in the cellar until this evening, when all shall bear witness as Elsing Wylder is sacrificed to the Mountain Gods."

The crowd cheered as Willem grabbed my arm, dragging me to the grain storage despite the way I groaned in pain.

Admittedly, being locked in some random cellar ended up being quite nice. Despite the fact that I nodded off last night, I remained exhausted, and sacks of grain make quite comfortable beds. I slept the day away on my bed of rice and pillow of bulgar wheat, only to be rudely woken by Willem Tell slapping me awake.

"Wake up, girl." Even if he hadn't slapped me, the snide tone of Willem's voice would have.

"How long will it take for them to realize you're one of us?" I asked, gasping around the pain in my ribs. I hadn't moved much, so I'd been able to ignore it. But it felt as if knives were being stabbed into my body with every spoken word.

The pain was worth it to see the look of raw fury on Willem's face.

"I don't know what you're talking about," Willem said tightly.

"They're going to realize you have magic eventually, and they and your precious Republic are going to turn on you. When will you realize *they* are your enemy?"

Between the otherworldly beauty and the way he used his voice like a Syren, hypnotizing anyone who listens, it's been clear to me since day one that Willem Tell isn't human.

A low-level Dryad, perhaps, or a weak Vampir.

"I said," Willem hissed, leaning in to hover above me, "I don't know what you're talking about. Such rumors will only hasten your demise."

I shrugged, ignoring the pain.

"I'm just sad I won't be here to see the day they destroy you, too. The Republic will kill or push out every magical Almanni, mark my words."

Sharp pain suddenly exploded on my cheek as Willem slapped me, my head snapping to the side. Blood flooded into my mouth, the taste hot and metallic.

"Almania is gone. Don't ever use that word again or I'll drag you into the square and cut off your limbs one by one."

I should have shut up. I should have stayed quiet.

Instead, I flashed him a bloody smile. "How kinky. Tell me, does your God approve of that kind of foreplay, Wil?"

Another slap echoed through the room as pain burst on my other cheek, the telltale crunch ringing in my ears as my cheekbone shattered. My vision blurred and I threw up on Willem's feet.

I gasped for breath when it was over, but the pain overwhelmed me as Willem dragged me up the stairs and out into the town square. The evening turned blurry as my eyes began to swell shut, the pain robbing me of speech.

The blurry outline of people with pitchforks was in the distance, but I was unable to make out their faces.

"I don't know why they even bothered," I whispered to Uri. I felt their

mind connect with mine the moment I awoke.

"Humans are stupid," Uri squawked. *"But their eyeballs are delicious."*

I chuckled internally, too afraid to jostle my aching body to do so aloud. *"I wouldn't know."*

"You're missing out, Elsie."

"Noted."

There was a pause. *"I'm so sorry I can't heal you. That damn bracelet is evil. I want to peck out their brains and shit in their skulls for doing this to you."*

"I know," I responded. *"I can feel your rage. But you promised, Uri. Don't get yourself killed too."*

I could have sworn Uri snarled. *"Fine. But I really want to kill them."*

"Aren't you the one always telling me not to murder people?"

"Well, yes. Humans are so prudish about it. All their laws and rules. But those rules don't apply to me, Witch. Animals are brutal. The only law we follow is survival..." Uri broke off and I felt their moment of realization. *"And I just proved your point, didn't I?"*

"You certainly did." I sent them an image of a hug, imagining that I was petting their midnight black feathers.

Willem suddenly came to a halt, making me crash into his shoulders. I groaned at the pain the movement caused.

"TO SCHOLLEN GORGE!" Willem shouted, and in return, the frenzied mob screamed back. Children were there, dressed in pure white, sitting in stark contrast to my black dress and boots.

I'm dragged to the stables where a large black horse awaits. Willem Tell's warhorse was a mean bastard whose hobbies included biting and kicking people. Many townsfolk have ended up needing healing potions from me due to a horse attack. Yet Willem shoved me up the mounting block, kicking me in the back so I fell onto the black stallion.

The pain made me pass out. The void of unconsciousness was a relief. But it was over with fast as more pain yanked me back into reality. With every step of the stallion's harsh gait, I was thrusted against its side, right on my broken rib. The pain was so great that I was unable to breathe. Panic flooded me.

A distant magic brushed my mind and there was a loud caw as some of Uri's magic reached me. They healed my rib just enough to ease the pain. The ache in my cheeks eased as well.

Then the magic disappeared. All that was left was the feeling of exhaustion from my familiar.

"That burnt out my magic. It will take a while to come back." Uri's voice sounded faint.

"My hero."

"Please let me peck out his eyes, Elsie." Uri's snarl echoed in my head. I could feel them flying above us, watching.

I was surprised when the stallion suddenly jumped over a fallen log. The movement sent me airborne, making me land hard against the side of the horse and knocking the wind out of my lungs.

I threw up, which made the pain worse.

For every one of my groans, Willem *laughed.*

Men who get off on being feared make me want to crush them.

The only problem was nothing he could ever say or do would make me fear him.

All I felt when I looked at him was disgust. Never fear.

A long time ago, I promised myself I would never give anyone or anything the pleasure of seeing me afraid. Not because I'm more powerful. I might've been more powerful than Willem Tell in terms of magic, but there were many beings in this world far more powerful than I.

No, I refused to fear. No one would have that power over me *ever* again.

Willem Tell included.

I wouldn't give Willem the satisfaction of my screams. Even if it killed me—and it was about to.

The forest was dark and murky, the evening air was frigid. Frostbitten leaves crackled beneath the horse's hooves as it galloped down the hard dirt path. The hoofbeats of other horses followed as the townsfolk rode along in tense silence.

No one went into the forest anymore. It wasn't safe. It hadn't been for centuries.

Yet there we were, descending further into darkness.

After half an hour of riding, we came to a halt.

Schollen Gorge was on the edge of the southwestern Helvetas. It overlooked a large waterfall that cascaded down the mountains. It was known far and wide to be the most dangerous part of the southern Helvetas due to the sharp, slippery rocks lining the entire waterfall.

The danger was also due to the fact that Schollen Gorge was right on the edge of the Mountain Gods' territory. No one, be it man, woman, or magical being, may pass the borders. Anyone who tried winded up dead, their bodies only sometimes recovered, but there was usually nothing left.

Just broken bones and piles of oozing flesh.

Everything else got consumed. But in the past 200 years, the attacks outside of their territory became more frequent. They began attacking travelers on the outskirts of the forest.

Nothing was stopping it. It seemed that nowhere was safe.

Until ten years ago, when Willem Tell, a nobody orphan, claimed the one true God spoke to him in a dream and showed him how to save us.

"Twice a year at each solstice, a person from every town bordering the Helvetas must be sacrificed to the Mountain Gods. If we appease their hunger, the attacks will stop."

He wrote down this proclamation and sent it to the Primatori. Permission was swiftly granted to begin God's apparent plan. Interlaken would, for the period of ten years, test human sacrifice to see if it reduced attacks on travelers.

As soon as the sacrifices began, the killing stopped.

The wintar solstice was only three weeks ago. An extra sacrifice such as this has never happened.

Not until now.

"Come here, malificer," a croaking, female voice interrupted my thoughts. "Willem! Kick that stupid horse and get it to walk faster, boy. Bring me my prize."

Tante Inga.

I used to like her. I even asked her to mentor me, once.

Now I understood why she was the only Witch Interlaken would ever accept.

Tante Inga *hated* Witches—despite the fact that she herself was one. Instead, her powers went towards punishing other Witches. Which won her Interlaken's eternal loyalty.

I was still dangling on Willem's horse when two hands pried my mouth open and shoved something down my throat.

I gagged but her hands closed around my mouth, forcing me to swallow. Choking, I forced it down. Whatever it was tasted of sickly sweet berries and rotten trees. Yuck.

"*What did that old flesh suit just do?*" Uri asked.

"*I don't know,*" I admitted. "*Just stay a safe distance away, okay? You don't need to watch what's about to happen.*"

I swear the raven scoffs. "*I'm not leaving you, witch. I will never leave you.*"

My heart warmed. "*I know. I would say I'll never leave you too but...*" My vision blurred, and suddenly it was difficult to talk. "*I guess I have to.*"

"*Elsie?*" Uri asked, sounding far away.

They fucking poisoned me.

"Poison?" I gasped in pain as Willem pulled me off the horse. I landed in the mud, unable to move. He and Tante Inga *laughed.*

So I laughed too. I turned slowly, mud in my mouth and nose as I laid in the puddle.

"How *mundane,*" I spit, and Tante Inga kicked me in the face. Stars burst behind my eyes and blood filled my mouth.

Hoofbeats echoed in the distance as other townsfolk arrived, but I only saw their blurry figures through the corner of my eye.

"B-Bitch," I cursed at Tante Inga.

She spat in my face. "I hope they eat you whole. Your very existence is a mistake. But that gets remedied tonight. I hope you like Hell, malificer, because death and misery are what awaits you."

"F-Fuccckk yooou," I slurred, "youuu old hagg."

The last thing I saw was Willem Tell leaning down into my face, with Tante Inga next to him, when something hard hit my head and everything turned dark.

I hurt everywhere.

"You need to wake up!" Uri squawked in my head, but they sounded so far away. Sleep and pain faded as the weight against my eyelids lessened, allowing me to open my eyes.

Shit.

I was tied to some tree, my hands above my head and I couldn't move. Pain rushed through my body with every *thump* of my heart.

"Citizens of Interlaken!" Willem Tell bellowed, standing next to me. He grabbed my hair and yanked my head back, exposing my neck. "This woman is guilty of using witchcraft to murder one of our own! So we shall appease our Mountain Gods early!"

The blurry townsfolk shouted and clapped at Willem's speech.

Tante Inga hovered at my side, staring at me with disgust written all over her face. Her eyes must have been as blue as the skies, once, but now they were cloudy and terrifying. Her rotten, yellow teeth smelled disgusting as she let out a hot breath in my face.

The odor of carrion and rotten herbs made me want to vomit, but I swallowed it down, grimacing at the flavor.

"Open up, malificer." Willem's hand was suddenly in my mouth, holding it open so Tante Inga could slip more poison down my throat.

He didn't hold my mouth closed long enough, though. As soon as he let go, I spat in his face. With a shriek, he staggered away, covering his eyes.

"You stupid girl," Tante Inga snarled at me.

Willem recovered eventually, but he spoke slower as the poison began to enter his system.

"MOUNTAIN GODS!" he shouted as Tante Inga quickly followed to his side, putting an arm around his waist so he could stay standing.

"WE SACRIFICE THIS WITCH TO YOU! CONSUME HER BODY AND SOUL AS PAYMENT FOR OUR SAFETY! WE HONOR YOU!"

Then, they left. They mounted their horses and retreated back to town. A few people hurled rotten vegetables at me before following the others.

The light began to fade as my eyelids grew heavy.

"No, Elsie. Wake up! Please, stay awake!" Distantly, I heard the flaps of Uri's wings. Something pecked at my wrists and I wanted to groan but I couldn't move my lips.

The temperature dropped suddenly, and the forest went silent.

Unnaturally silent.

"I love you Uri," I whispered in my familiar's head for the last time. *"Now, please. Fly away from here."*

"No, no, no. Hold on, Elsie. Just hold on, please. I love you too. You're my Witch, and I-I need to tell you something…"

Their voice faded and I went limp, unconscious from Tante Inga's poison, only vaguely aware of the shaking trees in the distance.

the glass castle

chapter 3

I thought death would be quiet.

Or just the opposite, if the Republic were to be believed. Their afterlife sounded fucking miserable, honestly.

But it was neither quiet nor full of the sounds of tortured screams.

Instead, the only sound I could hear was that of a roaring, crackling fireplace.

It was warm too, closing in on too hot.

Scheisse—I'm in Hell.

I swallowed that fear whole, opening my eyes, ready to face whatever horrible torment awaited me.

Rows of books crawling up fine wooden shelves was to be my torture, apparently.

I was in a large, opulent library, lying on a velvet settee in front of the fire covered with an iron gate. The library shelves went so high, there was no perceptible ceiling; just books fading into the dark.

"Where am I?" I tested my voice. No soreness from the poison.

My hands traveled over my body, pressing my ribs and the spots I had injuries.

There was no pain, save for my throat. My ribs were broken last I remembered.

The fact that I was healed proved I was dead.

I pushed up on my elbows, easing into a sitting position before slowly rising to my feet.

My blood and mud-caked boots were nowhere to be seen as I placed my bare feet on the thick fur rug beneath me. Without thinking, I curled my toes into it, sighing at the soft warmth.

After giving myself a look over, I was greeted with the same blood-covered outfit I died in.

I couldn't have at least gotten new clothes? I have to be in a dirty frock forever?

Well, that's just *great.*

Annoyed, I turned from the fire to explore the rest of my new ghostly confines—only to run smack dab into a brick wall.

I was nearly knocked off my feet but something caught me.

Not a brick wall at all, but a man. A huge, beautiful man. I'm not short by any means. I've always stood taller than most women in the villages where I've lived throughout my life, but the man *towered* over me.

I had to crane my neck back just to look at him.

He was dressed plainly, but the fabrics were fine and expertly tailored. He wore black fitted pants that hugged his thick, muscular thighs, paired with a simple white tunic unbuttoned at the top, showing off his muscular chest. The tunic threads shimmered faintly in the firelight.

Spidersilk.

One of the most expensive materials known in our world—and nearly impossible to harvest.

Yet he wore the shirt with casual confidence, as if he just threw it on without thought or care.

The stranger held me intimately. Too intimately.

I pushed away from him with a hiss.

"Put me down!"

There was no answer, but he did as I commanded.

I put distance between us, taking a few steps back. The farther vantage allowed me to get a better look at him.

Finger-length short black hair was expertly coiffed, falling lightly against his forehead. The man cocked his head, the movement revealing a deep, red sheen to his midnight hair. His umber skin glowed as if the flames were beneath his skin, burning through his veins with hot vengeance.

"Are you finished staring?" he asked in a rich, accented voice. There was something proper about it. He spoke like a king.

I was frozen. Stunned into silence at the gaze that greeted me. Sparkling ruby took up most of his eyes, but it was the diamond pupils within their centers that made me pause.

Not a *man* at all then.

He was the most brazenly inhuman person I've ever met. Human clothes—albeit fine ones—cannot distract from the truth.

There was no way he was human, it was simply impossible.

One of the Demons from the Republic's horror stories, then?

"What are you, then?" I asked, voicing my thoughts aloud. "A Demon?"

I've never been one for manners. They waste so much time. I'm polite when I have to be, but that was before.

Death was surprisingly freeing.

The Demon flashed a set of brilliant white fangs, and it made my knees weak in equal parts fear and need.

His beauty was staggering. I could feel his presence in the air, hyperaware of how close he was standing.

He motioned to the settee with a nod, inviting me to sit. I sniffed and crossed my arms.

This stranger would not get my subservience.

"As you wish." He shrugged, taking a seat. The Demon leaned back with a sigh, perching one arm on the settee edge. The movement made his arm muscles bulge, making my internal temperature spiral.

Goddess, it's hot in this room. When did it get so hot?

"I might be old and out of touch, but I do know that's a very rude question to ask," the Demon said. "After all, I'm the one who rescued you. I think it is you who owes me some answers."

I sneered. "I owe you nothing, Demon."

He never took his eyes off me. It was unnerving.

"Answer my questions, and I might answer yours. Who are you?" he questioned.

I crossed my arms and went silent.

He won't get anything from me, no matter how handsome he is.

"Well, well. I see our new pet is awake," a new male voice said, drawing my attention. I looked away from the Demon to find the library doorway now full of another giant man.

Scheiße, another Demon? This one had shoulder-length brown hair streaked silver and a slightly paler complexion than the other Demon sitting in front of me, but his eyes were an unnatural yellow-gold.

"I am no one's *pet*," I objected.

The new Demon laughed in response.

"I do love a pet that bites."

"Bite me," I responded, "and I'll rip your balls off."

"Kinky," the Demon winked, and my stomach went tingly in response.

He was equally as beautiful as the other. More rough around the edges. There was a wildness to him that felt untamed, uncontrollable.

It didn't help that his shirt was completely unbuttoned, showing off his muscular abdomen. I lost count at twelve abs.

"Oh but you are, little one. A *pet*." The Demon prowled towards me with purpose.

I had the sudden realization that I was being hunted.

The predator found his prey.

Naturally, he expected me to back away in terror.

Instead, I lifted my chin and met his yellow-gold eyes as he approached me.

Not silver streaks in his hair.

Feathers, I realized. *They're silver feathers.* My hand twitched to touch them, to feel them. But I resisted, my control unbreaking.

"A dangerous lack of self-preservation, too? What a treat." The Demon smirked. "This will be fun."

"Do ignore him," the ruby-eyed Demon on the settee said. "The rest of us do."

"Blow me," the other responded, winking at the red-eyed one.

"If you wanted some wilting, fearful flower," I told them, "then you should have looked elsewhere, Demon. I will never fear you, no matter how you torture me."

The Demon came to a sudden halt right in front of me as he blinked, looking rather confused.

The ruby-eyed one was at my side a moment later. Taking my arm surprisingly gentle, it took every ounce of willpower within me not to react at the hot burn of his hand against my bare wrist.

Wait. *My wrist is bare.*

"What happened to my—" I paused, not wanting to tell them too much. "My *bracelet*. Where did it go? Did you steal my things?"

The ruby-eyed Demon blinked.

"I accidentally crushed it when I carried you here."

My Goddess.

How powerful was he that this Demon could crush metal with his bare hands?

"What is this torture you speak of?" the ruby-eyed one asked.

"Well that's why I'm here, isn't it? Get on with it, then!"

The Demon blinked, looking confused. "Why would we torture and abuse you when we *saved* you?"

Now it was my turn to be confused. "Saved me? What the Hell do you mean you *saved* me? I'm dead, and this is Hell. One of them, at least. You did not save me. You *doomed* me."

"She thinks she's dead and we're Demons," the golden-eyed one said. Then he exploded in belly-roaring laughter. "Oh, Aleks is going to *love* this."

"Who is Aleks? Another hulking Demon?" I asked snidely.

The ruby-eyed Demon sighed and glanced at the yellow-eyed Demon.

The two share a look, and then both abruptly leave the room.

"I asked you a question!" I shouted at their retreating backs.

Then they were gone, leaving me confused and alone.

I had no other choice but to follow. Outside the library was a long hallway, but I was struck by the way the ceiling was made of pure glass. Above me, the moon shone brightly amongst the glittering stars.

Where the Hell am I?

"This way, pet," the golden-eyed male's voice called from the end of the hall.

"I'm not your pet, Demon," I called back. Echoes of wicked laughter was the only response.

The cold stone floor was freezing underneath my bare feet. As I padded further down the hallway, I inspected every inch of the walls.

Strange, macabre artwork in fine gold leaf frames and ornate mirrors lined the walls. Lots of skeletons and scenes of blood, confusing me even more.

Maybe Hell has a moon and stars? I thought.

Finally, I made it to the end of the hallway, which opened up into a large atrium. The two males were sitting in large leather chairs in front of an even bigger fireplace than what was in the library.

But the room itself had no solid walls. Only glass planes, giving the illusion that we were sitting amongst the clouds.

I took a step forward, walking to the edge of the room so I could press my hands against the cold glass.

It was sky as far as the eye could see. We were so high up, I couldn't see the ground. Just distant rocks and the peaks of smaller mountains.

But I knew these mountains.

I turned slowly, my blood turning ice-cold as I beheld the men watching me with their glowing, odd eyes.

"Do you understand now?" the ruby-eyed one asked.

"If she doesn't, she's an idiot." The yellow-eyed one sighed. A pained hiss followed as the ruby-eyed man kicked the other in the foot.

"Play nice, Trystan," the ruby-eyed man snarled, his eyes flashing.

So the one with the silver-streaked hair was called Trystan.

I filed that bit of information away for later.

"I'm no idiot," I said with a shaky voice. Not in fear but in realization. In the stunning realization at just how wrong—and how *right*—things had gone.

"I'm not dead, am I?" I asked them. The yellow-eyed man—Trystan—smirked, but the other, his red eyes curious, shook his head.

"No, you're not dead," the red-eyed one confirmed.

"And you're not Demons?" I asked, and my heart nearly fell from my chest as both of them smiled.

"No, pet. We are not Demons."

The one named Trystan rose from his seat, prowling over to me. He approached me with confidence, cupping my chin with his large hand and tipping my head up towards him. I jolted at his touch and ignored the searing heat that flowed through my body in return. Then the male smiled as I felt his nails shift, growing into sharp, black talons that pierced my skin, nearly drawing blood.

"We're so much worse."

"You are the Mountain Gods," I gasped. "You're monsters."

"Not an idiot after all, then," Trystan chuckled, suddenly leaning forward to lick my cheek. I swallowed my shriek of surprise at the feeling of hot tongue against my skin.

"Mmm. I can taste the fight in you. It's delicious." Trystan inhaled my scent deeply. I fought the urge to fidget and back away, especially when he fixed that yellow gaze on me and smiled, showing off a set of sharp white fangs. "I do love when my prey fights back."

I will not fear them.

I will not give them power over me.

"Welcome to the Aive," the red-eyed one said from his seat, gesturing around with a hand. "Home of the Mountain Gods."

the mountain gods

chapter 4

A hundred different thoughts ran through my head all at once.

I'm not dead.

I'm not in Hell.

I'm in the home of the Mountain Gods.

The home of the monsters who have been terrorizing the Helvetas for centuries.

I was plenty familiar with beautiful monsters.

"What are you, then? Giants? You're tall enough," I asked, sizing them up. As I processed, Trystan joined the ruby-eyed man in the sitting area before pouring himself a glass of some amber liquid. He was in the middle of taking a sip when I spoke, causing him to choke and sputter.

"Giants! She thinks we're Giants." Trystan's head tilted towards the ceiling as he let out a full body laugh. "Gods, I'm so mad Aleks is busy. This is fucking *hilarious.*"

"Be nice," the ruby-eyed one growled. I swore fire flashed within his eyes.

"I do not think you are a Giant," I said to Trystan, crossing my arms. "I just think you're an asshole."

The ruby-eyed man let out a snort, catching my attention.

"You though? You have to be a Giant. You're far too tall to be anything else."

"More like a giant pain in my ass," Trystan mumbled, causing the red-eyed one to glare at him.

They were clearly friends.

The ruby-eyed man was suddenly standing and walking towards me. Hesitantly, I glanced over my shoulder, checking my surroundings should I need to escape. We appeared to be next to some sort of kitchen area.

It was so... modern.

There were no buckets filled with water. No wooden utensils. Instead, everything was metal and glass. Open shelves lined the walls of the kitchen, and various cooking instruments and cups lined the shelves. It was clean. Tidy, even.

"Are you hungry?" the ruby-eyed man's voice said, and I nearly jumped out of my skin. He was standing so close I could feel the heat of his skin. He moved in complete silence.

"No," was my only response. The man ignored me and walked into the kitchen, his fingers grazing my lower back when he passed by.

"You should drink some water, at least. How long were you out there?" He turned a strange looking knob and I inhaled my scream as water shot out of a spout. He didn't react at all, instead he just held a cup underneath the spout and it quickly filled.

Goddess, what kind of sorcery is this?

"Drink," he ordered. I was far too shocked to do anything but grab the offered cup.

The last time someone made me drink something, I was poisoned.

Aufdecken. I casted the spell within my thoughts carefully, keeping my shields up. The water remained clear.

Not poisoned then.

I brought the cup to my lips, taking a real sip. The water tasted crisp and cold, igniting my thirst. I quickly finished the entire cup and the ruby-eyed man grabbed it back, refilling it from his magic waterspout.

"So, you're a God then? Are you the God of Giants?" I wiped my wet mouth on the dirty sleeve of the dress.

"THE GOD OF GIANTS!" Trystan chortled from the sitting area, clutching his stomach as he let out a peal of laughter. "Oh, pet. Thank you. I needed some entertainment."

"Ignore the bird," the ruby-eyed man growled, fire flashing in his eyes yet again before he turned his gaze back to me. At the mention of a bird, the loneliness hit. I missed Uri. It felt so quiet inside my head without them, so empty.

"All who live in the Aive are Gods," the ruby-eyed man said, watching me.

"I thought Gods would be more..." I sniffed. "Shiny. You do not look like a God."

Lie.

A bald-faced lie.

"JUST A MAN!" Trystan broke off into another laughing fit at this. The ruby-eyed man snarled at him, flashing a set of sharp fangs.

"Shut the fuck up or I will throw you off the mountain again," he warned. But Trystan continued to laugh, causing the big male in front of me to sigh.

"I can fly, lizard. Throw me off the mountain all you want. You're stuck with me, remember?" Trystan said, taking another sip of amber liquid from his glass.

The ruby-eyed male sighed and cracked his neck, as if the presence of his friend was a physical strain.

"I am no man."

I felt his voice in my veins.

"I did not think there was a lizard God," I said, trying not to show how much his presence was affecting me. A loud thump followed as Trystan fell off his chair, laughing too hard to sit upright.

The ruby-eyed man stared at Trystan for a few moments, emotionless.

With a tight sigh, he turned to me with a nod. "Excuse me for a moment."

In a single blink, the ruby-eyed man became a blur. There was a loud *whoosh* and suddenly a gust of wind so strong it could lift me into the air hit me as one of the windows opened up, allowing in the frosty wintar air.

The ruby-eyed man blurred again, picking up Trystan and then—

Oh scheiße.

They jumped off the mountain.

I quickly eased over to the open door, careful not to get too close. The wind was so strong it nearly knocked me over. My black hair flew in every direction as I was battered.

There was a loud screech as black nails the size of my forearm gripped the window frame so hard it left a dent. Then two huge yellow eyes stared at me behind a razor sharp black beak.

I nearly lost control over my bladder.

It was a Griffin.

A real-life *Griffin*. A huge one at that.

But the eyes.

They were Trystan's eyes.

The Griffin shoved himself through the open door, his nails clacking on the floor as he spread his wings. Feathers of all shades of silver and brown covered his massive wingspan and all of his body besides his legs. His four legs were scaled, and where he used to have hands, he now had dangerous claws.

"You're a Griffin?" I gasped. Trystan opened his beak and let out another loud screech before blurring and shifting back into a man instantaneously.

"That's the God of Griffins to you, pet." He waved a hand and a gust of wind hit me. "I'm also the God of the Sky."

Trystan was still clothed, but I guess that was the benefit of being a God.

My thoughts were interrupted by a roar so loud the glass vibrated. I braced, ready for the worst as another huge gust of wind hit me. I was knocked to the floor, my knees hitting the hard stone with a sharp burst of pain.

"You look delicious on your knees for me, pet," Trystan purred. I scrambled to stand, ready to punch him when I saw what watched me from outside the glass.

"Oh my Gods," I whispered, looking into the huge red eyes of a massive black Dragon that hovered just outside the glass.

"That's Nerethus," Trystan added with a mischievous smile.

I walked right to the edge of the open window and the Dragon shoved his nose towards me. There's no way he could fit his body through the door, unlike the lean Griffin.

Nerethus in Dragon form was nearly the size of the entire mountain. His form was so massive it blocked out the brightness of the moon. But the stars shone down upon his scaled hide. Each scale gleamed like polished midnight. Two huge black horns curled up from his ridged forehead, meeting the spikes that followed down the Dragon's spine, all the way to a barbed tail.

Huge eyes watched me, those vertical slit pupils noting my every breath.

"You're a Dragon," was all I could think to say.

The beast nodded, flapping his wings once more before flying away.

For a second, he disappeared into the clouds. Then the shadow of his body was back, and this time he was flying directly towards me.

Oh shit.

I must have said this aloud, because Trystan snorted. I backpedaled, scrambling away from the door, ready to meet my death yet again. Just before he hit the Aive, the Dragon blurred. A flash, and he was back to his mortal form.

"Why did you save me? Why am I here?" I asked, suddenly more confused than ever before and needing answers.

Nerethus padded towards me on bare feet. "You've had quite an ordeal. I do not think this is a conversation we should have when you're still covered in blood and poison."

"Yeah, you smell of nightshade *so* bad," Trystan added. They both crossed their arms and looked at me, and I realized there was no use in truly fighting them.

Yet.

"You will answer my questions," I said, chin raised. "You will tell me why I'm here and why you saved me."

Nerethus nodded. "Of course."

"Yeah," Trystan added. "Besides, this is your home now too, pet."

I... what the fuck?

I backed away, my heart beating so fast I wondered if it might give out.

"Excuse me? What is that supposed to mean?" I continued before they could answer. "My *home* is the Helvetas. My *home* is Almania, even if the Republic is trying to erase it."

For the first time since waking up, I felt afraid.

Because the look in Nerethus's eyes was one of pity.

"This is your home now," he told me. "Once you enter the territory of the Mountain Gods—once you pass the borders of our land, you can never leave. You are stuck here. You're cursed."

the curse

chapter 5

"Explain. Now," I bit out. The Dragon blinked. A ghost of a smile appeared on his lips, but it disappeared so fast I wasn't sure whether or not I imagined it.

Nerethus tilted his head to the side as he contemplated my command, although whether he was taken aback at the order itself or simply how he would respond, I'm not sure.

"We, and this place, are cursed," Trystan commented from a few meters away.

I glanced at him, turning my body so I could see them both—and keep track of them. Trystan suddenly turned his neck almost completely around, meeting my eyes with a dark smile.

"Stop that," I hissed. "What do you mean you're cursed? Aren't you a God? Aren't you too powerful to be cursed?"

Trystan smirked, taking one step forward. I mirrored him, stepping back.

With a wicked smile, he prowled towards me. I backed up until cold glass against my dress stopped me. My stomach was in knots as Trystan continued to approach, stepping into my space. He raised both arms, pinning me into place so I was unable to escape.

He leaned in and I slapped his chest, trying to push him away.

"Leave me alone, *bird boy.*"

Trystan let out a chuckle. Then he blurred and my arms were suddenly above my head, both of my wrists easily held within one of his large hands.

I struggled against his hold but he showed no reaction.

"Keep insulting me, *girl*—" he said, leaning down so close that his lips were almost touching mine, "—and I won't hesitate to punish you however I see fit."

"Try it." I bit the air, my teeth clanking loudly as my jaw closed. Trystan jerked back just in time to prevent my teeth from tearing into his lips.

I chuckled at his moment of fear.

"You thought this was Hell?" The smirk Trystan flashed me made me tremble. His thick, muscular thigh was between my legs. I went still, frozen in shock.

Then Trystan *rocked* his leg against me. The friction and pressure against my aching clit sent a shockwave through my body.

Trystan took advantage of my surprise, using the moment to lean forward and suck my lower lip into his mouth. He bit down, not enough to break skin, just enough to hurt. I squeaked, surprised and instantly needing more.

With one last suck on my lower lip, Trystan released me.

"*Hell* can be arranged, pet," he clasped my jaw with his free hand, looking me in the eyes as he licked his lips. Heart racing, I tried to yank my hands away, but he just laughed and rocked his thigh into me again.

Releasing my jaw, Trystan reached down and hiked my dress up, so the only thing between him and my wet pussy was the fabric of his pants.

"Already so wet," he taunted me. I was halfway through preparing a snide remark when he leaned in, running his nose down my neck. "You smell delicious, pet."

He repeated the movement but instead of his nose, his hot tongue landed on my pulse, tasting me. I felt each swipe of his tongue through my whole body. My muscles were light and tingly while my thoughts turned floaty.

Is he going to bite me? Do the Gods drink blood in the same way the Vampir and the Werwulves do?

Each swipe of his tongue sent more waves of pleasure through my body. Beyond reason and consciousness, my hips began to thrust of their own accord, grinding against his leg.

"I get the feeling you would enjoy my idea of torture, pet," Trystan murmured against my neck. Then his hand was around the back of my neck, pushing my face down so I could see where our bodies were pressed together.

"Look at you. Look at that creamy pussy staining my black pants." Then his hand moved, fisting my hair as he yanked my head back.

"If you want to play," he purred as our eyes locked, "all you have to do is ask. But push me again?" Trystan rocked into me again and a needy moan escaped me. "Push me again, and I won't ask permission. Push me—" *Rock.* "—and I will hunt you down—" *Rock.* "—and fuck your greedy cunt—" *Rock.* "—like you're my personal fuck toy. My *pet.* And I don't care who sees. I'll fuck you on the Primatori's front doorstep, pet. Keep pushing me and see what happens."

His hands disappeared and his leg pulled away. I collapsed, falling to the floor, unable to hold myself up without warning.

"Enough." A hand slapped Trystan on the shoulder as Nerethus appeared and pulled him away, shoving the Griffin out of the room. I take a few deep breaths, collecting myself, unable to help the way my hands tremble.

My head said, *"You will not be afraid. Fuck that asshole. Ignore him."*

But my body said, *"Come back and fuck me until I can't remember my own name."*

"Are you alright?" Nerethus asked gently, distracting me from my scattered thoughts. He reached out a hand to help me up. Hesitantly, I placed my hand within his own and he easily pulled me to my feet.

Gods, he's huge.

I wonder if he's huge everywhe— **No. No!** *Don't think about that, Elsing. Get it together!* I shoved the stray thought away.

"Tell me, Dragon, what's the punishment for ripping off a God's cock? Will it grow back eventually?" I asked him.

Nerethus looked to the side, hiding a small smile. He was so serious that for a moment, I was thrown off.

"We are cut off from the other Gods here," he explained, looking back at me. "Which means there would be no punishment. Aleksander would kill you, of course. If one of us didn't. But Trystan likes pushing people. The more you push him back, the more you'll turn him on."

Lust flashed through the Dragon's ruby gaze and I blinked in surprise. "You're lovers?"

Nerethus looked at me with calculation in his eyes. "Yes. Most Gods have multiple partners. Monogamy is a human concept."

"Hm." I just learned more about Dragons than anyone has in centuries.

"Does that bother you?" he asked, staring at me.

"Why would I care?" I responded.

He smiled lightly. "So prickly. It seems Trystan isn't the only one who likes to push people."

I'm glad that's all he sees, I thought.

A monster lurked beneath the Dragon's skin. A monster with scales and claws.

"Humans are so scandalized by sex, let alone sharing," Nerethus answered finally.

They think I'm human then. Good.

"Well, most humans are prudes. But I'm not."

The Dragon watched me closely. I felt his gaze on me.

It was unsettling.

I cleared my throat. "I'm quite tired and overwhelmed. I wish to bathe and go to sleep. Point me in the direction of wherever it is I'm supposed to sleep, Dragon."

Nerethus tilted his head to the side. "Of course. You can stay in my room."

"Fine." I exhaled sharply, wishing the thought of being in his room didn't make pussy throb.

It's been so long since I last laid with anyone, let alone a man.

Being in his presence—in *both* of their presences?

It made me *ache.*

They made me ache, and need, and want.

But that meant attachment. I couldn't get attached.

"Follow me." Nerethus turned, leaving the room. I followed him out of the main living quarters. Eventually we emerged into another hallway on the opposite side of the house that I arrived in.

"You woke up in the library, which is housed in the East Wing of the Aive. That wing also has our weapons room, the entrance to the hot springs, and that's where Aleks stays. My rooms as well as Trystan's are in the West Wing."

He fell silent as we got to the end of the new hallway. The only other door we pass is closed shut.

The walls were a light blue, accented with silver and black framed artwork, all in similarly muted shades.

But as we stepped through an open doorway, my jaw dropped.

Nerethus's room wasn't light blue.

It was *gold.*

I followed him into the huge chamber and spun, taking it all in.

The entire far wall was glass, seamlessly blending into the ceiling. It gave the illusion of there only being three walls, as if you could get out of bed in the morning and walk off into the clouds.

The three remaining walls were black, but the color barely peaked out behind the piles of gold.

Thousands of gold coins were piled around the edges of the room, along with various larger gold treasures, trunks, and jewelry.

"So, the legends are right. Dragons *are* hoarders."

A loud growl was the only response.

I went still, glancing at Nerethus, only to find him glaring at me.

His eyes closed for a moment as he took a deep breath, composing himself.

"We are *not* hoarders." He spoke carefully, leashing his emotions.

I waved a hand, gesturing to the outer edges of the room, "You have more money than the entire town of Interlaken. You're a hoarder."

Nerethus clenched his jaw. "It's not for humans to understand. I am not a hoard-*er,* this is simply part of my…"

He went quiet, searching for the word.

I gave him a cold smile and crossed my arms. "Your what? Your hoard? Hmm? That's what you were going to say. Go ahead, say it, then. This is part of your Dragon hoard."

Nerethus cracked his neck. "Trove, actually. We call it a trove, and that, little human, is all I can tell you. A Dragon's trove is a secret from all but his mate. We do not share any details."

Hm.

A huge bed sat in the middle, big enough to fit five of him. I suddenly was unable to look anywhere else but the bed.

Images of our naked bodies tangled between the sheets flash through my mind.

"I hope this will be comfortable for you." Nerethus interrupted my thoughts, making me jerk. He motioned to the bed. "I will be next door, but you needn't come get me if something is wrong. Just say my name and I'll hear you."

His hearing is that sensitive? Fuck.

My emotions must play on my face because he snorted and gave me another small smile. "Do not worry. I can't read your mind. But as you said, we are monsters. This," he motioned to his current shape, "is merely a choice. On the inside, I am Dragon. I can hear my prey from hundreds of kilometers away, as can Trystan."

Nerethus paused, taking a few steps forward until we were nearly chest to chest. His hands raised and he cupped my face, not aggressively like Trystan did, but with delicate reverence, as if he couldn't believe I was real.

He gently tilted my head up to meet my gaze.

"Your heart," he rasped, "it doesn't race. You've seen my true form, beheld my true glory. You've seen what hides beneath my flesh—and yet, you're not afraid. Why, little human? Why are you not afraid of me?"

"Elsing," I corrected him. "My name is *Elsing.*"

"El-*sing*." He stretched out each letter of my name, rolling it over his tongue. "Why are you not afraid, Elsing? Your heart should be racing, your blood rushing faster and faster—but it's quiet." I stepped out of his grasp. His hands fell to his sides, but I tried to ignore the disappointment that flashed through his eyes.

Stupid, stupid heart.

"Long ago, I feared a man," I said, looking around the room and inhaling deeply. The scent of cypress and sage is subtle in the air. "He saw it, this man. He saw my fear and decided to use it to kill me." I paused, taking a breath and turning to Nerethus, who watched me from a meter away. "So I let him try. Men look at women and see us as weak, defenseless creatures whose only purpose is to serve them and pop out as many babies as possible. This man was no different. So, I decided to teach him a lesson. By the time he went to stab me in the heart with the dagger he had hidden beneath his shirt, the poison I had coated on my lips was entering his bloodstream. I was banking on him kissing me and he didn't suspect a thing."

Nerethus didn't look taken aback as he nodded. "Sounds like he deserved it."

"I was fourteen." My voice didn't waver. "Fear is power, Dragon. I refuse to give someone that power over me. Even a Dragon. Even a *God.*"

Nerethus's gaze remained firm, no shadow of doubt to be seen. "I made my first kill an hour after I was born. I am not a man, Elsing. I do not carry their downfalls. I am every tree on this mountain and every worm beneath the dirt. I *am* the mountain." Nerethus paused. "I do not say this because you should fear me. But when you look at me, you will never see the faults of man."

I crossed my arms. "That remains to be seen, Dragon."

Nerethus held my gaze for a moment before nodding. "You are not what I expected, Elsing."

He turned and left the room, the moonlight casting shadows with his silent step.

"What else did you expect?" I called, but the door shut with a soft click, leaving me alone.

My mind raced. His red eyes stayed with me. The way he looked at me, it was like he was reading every secret carved onto my soul, and for the first time since getting here, I *feared*.

Gods, I wish Uri was here.

the god of
the sky

chapter 6

The Dragon's room felt so much bigger without him in it.

Without thinking, I walked over to the big bed in the middle of the room, my feet sinking into the thick fur rug with every step. I reached for his silky sheets but paused just as I went to touch it.

Blood and dirt were caked on my hands.

Oh Goddess. I was suddenly hyperaware of how dirty I was. My black dress was disgusting, and I smelled like something rotten. The shock of the past few hours wore off.

I'm not dead. I'm alive.

Heilige scheiße. Goddess, thank you.

This changed *everything.* But I still felt disgusting. There was no washroom to be seen, but there *was* an arched doorway on the far side of the room. I padded over, wondering what it would lead to.

As I stepped through the doorway, magic made my hair stand on end as goosebumps formed on my arms. The taste of sage was heavy on my tongue, but not at all unpleasant.

An enchantment.

Magic always had a taste, and it's been so long since I tasted another's magic besides Tante Inga. The minty, spicy flavor of the sage enchantment was a welcome upgrade from sickly sweet berries and rotten trees.

Beneath my bare feet, the ground changed from cold to warm. It was jarring to my senses as I stepped farther through the doorway. It quickly became obvious as to why the floor was heated. A few steps into the mystery hall protected by an enchantment and the room suddenly opened up, revealing a huge system of bubbling, luxurious limestone hot springs.

Oh wow.

It was beautiful—and quiet. Only the slight noise of rippling water and the occasional hiss of warm air. Unlike a normal hot spring, there was no scent of sulfur.

It just smelled like calming sage.

The ground beneath my feet was damp and slick as I walked down to the edge of the largest spring.

Underwater tunnels and walls separated the pools. Some were closed off and smaller, while others looked to be connected.

I've heard of hot springs, but never been to one.

Witches weren't welcome there ever since the Primatori decided that a Witch could curse the water and somehow kill everyone using it.

Trottel.

The ceiling of the cave is far above me. I inspected every inch, noting the stalactites decorating the edge. This was the most powerful enchantment I had ever seen. The Mountain Gods were *bending* reality. Their home—the Aive, they called it—is at the very top of the mountain, and yet these springs could only exist close to the ground. Either the doorway was a portal that took us deep into the earth, or something was pulling heat *up*.

I leaned down and untied my boots, dropping them near the ledge of the springs so I could dip my toes in.

The water was blissfully warm.

I glanced around.

I was well and truly alone.

Sighing, I shed my dirty clothing. The movement released the putrid smell of poison, dried blood, and body odor. It was hard not to gag at the smell.

I dropped my soiled clothes on the wet floor and stepped into the warm water, letting it envelop me. The water turned pink for a moment as dirt and dried blood dissolved instantly.

The taste of patchouli was subtle but present on my tongue, dancing with the fresh sage.

I took a deep breath and quickly dived underneath the water before surfacing again. When I went to untangle my hair and prepare to braid it—something which takes *hours* sometimes—I'm instead shocked when I find it perfectly clean and soft as silk.

The water is enchanted. A cleaning cast, and a damn strong one at that. The strongest one I had ever seen. But a different magic user did this than whoever made the portal.

The Griffin?

Lost in my thoughts as I contemplated, I allowed the magic of the springs to wash away my worries. I floated around on my back, the tension easing out of my sore muscles with every passing second.

My thoughts drifted inward, looking at my own magic.

It was quiet, lethargy making it slow to respond when I tried to draw it to the surface.

There were no stories of any magic user escaping the Republic, so there was nothing to compare it to. I had no idea how long it would take my magic to recover from being suppressed at such an intrinsic level.

The more I focused on my magic, the more I detached from reality, becoming less and less aware of my surroundings. Which is exactly why, when something huge suddenly dropped from the ceiling and plunged into the water, splashing me so hard I got water up my nose, I *screamed.*

"Enjoying yourself, pet?" Coughing up water, I steadied myself and planted my feet, taking in the equally naked and wet Griffin God before me.

"Not anymore, thanks to you," I snarled, pushing my wet hair out of my face. "Were you watching me the whole time?"

"Of course," he said, tossing himself backwards as he sank into the water, splashing and twisting in a very bird-like manner. Then he was standing again, his upper body completely out of the water, giving me an eyeful.

My knees almost gave out as I got a look at his sculpted, muscular body. He looked like a warrior.

He looked like a **God.**

"So much for privacy," I glared, turning from him, although any attempt at privacy was gone. The clear water didn't hide *anything* and I had to stop myself from looking at him. I didn't usually look so closely at men. I didn't usually feel much of anything for them at all, no matter how pretty.

Why the *fuck* was I so shaken by their presence? So hyperware of their proximity?

I had seen the Griffin shirtless already but *scheiße*, Trystan naked was so much different. I could easily see his cock already hard and at full-mast, straining just beneath the surface of the water.

For the first time in perhaps my entire life, I floundered, unsure what to do. I stared a hole into the far wall of the cave, trying to will him away, despite the fact that I wasn't sure I really wanted him to leave.

My wishes were denied as a gentle wave hit me, signaling the approach of the God of the Sky.

"Leave me alone." I refused to look at him, concentrating hard on the texture of the walls.

"Hmm. I don't think you want me to leave though, do you?" His voice was suddenly at my ear as his large hands wrapped around my waist. He placed his palms beneath my breasts, cupping them and gently rubbing my hard nipples with his thumbs. I gasped at the touch. It felt like being struck by lightning.

It took me a moment to realize he had pulled us to the shallower side of the springs. Water came to my mid-thighs. I didn't notice because of his hot hands against my skin. It warmed me where the air turned cool.

"I do." My words didn't match the crack in my voice or the way I was panting with need.

I felt rather than heard him smile.

He whispered, "I can smell how wet you are, even through the water of the springs. You're lying, pet."

Abandoning my breasts, he turned me, one hand fisting my hair so he could look me in the eyes. I slapped my palms against his wet, smooth chest but he barely noticed.

"I told you what would happen if you push me, pet." Trystan's yellow gaze was intense. But there was a playful smile on his face.

I thought back to what Nerethus said. That Trystan enjoyed the fight.

He wants to play with me, I realized.

He pushed me so that I would push back.

So I rolled my eyes, testing his reaction. He smiled, gripping my hair until my neck strained as he pulled me closer. My nipples brushed against his wet chest, and I felt it all the way down to my core.

"Let me tell you what's about to happen," he purred, leaning down until our lips were nearly touching. "First, I'm going to splay you on the edge of the springs and eat your sweet little pussy until you can barely remember your own name."

I was surprised my skin wasn't on fire, because his words made me *burn*.

"Then," he whispered, "I'm going to fuck you with my fingers and stretch your cunt so that you're nice and ready for us later."

All of the blood rushed from my head and my skin began to tingle as I pictured his words. His free hand drew lines down my hip and across my ass cheek. Dragging his fingers around my waist, he dips down my front, tickling the thin patch of delicate black curls between my legs.

"Then," he whispered just as he dragged a finger through my soaking folds, "I'm going to spread your legs and fuck you until you can't even remember your own name, *Elsing.*"

"How the fuck do you know my na—" I gasped, cut off as he plunged a finger inside of me. My words turned into moans as Trystan chuckled in my ear.

"I hear everything, pet. Including the way all of the blood in your body is rushing towards your throbbing clit." His thumb brushed against me and my hips jerked.

"I especially like the sound of my finger fucking your pussy, Elsing," Trystan teased, plunging his finger in and out of me with slow, torturous strokes. He leaned forward, kissing his way across my jawline, licking and sucking and driving me *insane.*

My heart raced—not in fear but in lust. It had been so long since a man—or woman—touched me. It ate away at all logical thought in my head.

Trystan paused, and then his lips were on mine as he swallowed my moans of pleasure.

"I think," he whispered against my lips, in between kisses, "you want my brand of torture, Elsing. You want to be at my mercy. You ache for it—and that, Elsing, that is why you hate me."

My breasts heaved as I panted, unable to form coherent thought other than, "Fuck you."

Oh great, good job Elsing. That was the perfect response. But there was really no time to chide myself. In a single blink, we went from the middle of the hot spring to the lip of the edge as Trystan shoved me against it, boxing me in with his arms locked on either side of me. Then my hair was in his fist again as he tilted my neck back, baring me to him.

"I. Don't. Want. You," I panted, but even I could hear the blatant lie in my words.

Trystan chuckled. "Liar. Resist all you want, but your body tells the truth."

"As if you could handle me, Griffin," I retorted. The next second, I was airborne as he tossed me out of the water and onto the edge of the hot spring ledge. I landed hard, bruising my tailbone slightly, but then he was at my knees, pushing my legs open and exposing my wet pussy.

Trystan exhaled hard, his jaw slack as he looked at the very center of me.

Reaching forward with both hands, he carefully peeled the lips of my pussy open, exposing me entirely.

I squirmed under his gaze.

Trystan licked his lips and blurred. When he stopped, my legs were over his shoulders and he was leaning in, his yellow eyes locked on my cunt.

His head dipped and his tongue darted out a second later, licking me.

"Oh fuck," I gasped. He chuckled against me, repeating the action as he began devouring my pussy like it was his last meal.

I told myself I'd push him away, and yet there I was, grasping him to my pussy and grinding against his face with wanton abandon.

"Eyes on me, pet," Trystan demanded. He spanked my ass and I cried out.

"I want you to watch me. Watch as a God eats your delicious pussy."

Our eyes remained locked as he leaned down and sucked up my cream with an indecent slurping noise.

One of his hands disappeared as Trystan cupped himself, stroking his hard cock as he feasted on me.

The God moaned against my cunt. "You taste so fucking good. I could eat you for hours."

He dove back into my folds with a hungry growl. The pleasure within me spiraled higher and higher until my abdomen and legs began twitching.

"That's it," Trystan praised. "Give me every drop of cum, pet. Every. Fucking. Drop."

I moaned as his fingers suddenly joined his tongue, stretching me. A second later, he found that perfect spot deep inside me, and suddenly I was exploding.

"Trystan!" I screamed, my hips moving of their own volition as the orgasm overwhelmed me. Wave after wave of pleasure hit but I never looked away. He became a lifeline as his eyes held me steady while his mouth and hands drove me insane.

Then Trystan flicked his fingers, hitting that sensitive spot deep inside me. A warm, buzzing feeling spread across my stomach. Not an orgasm, but different.

"Come for me again," he growled, moving his mouth to my throbbing clit as his fingers plunged in and out—the lewd, wet noises it made echoed through the cave.

That warm feeling grew and suddenly I felt a gush of liquid leaving me.

Trystan let out a snarl as he attached his lips around my cunt, drinking down every single drop.

"You taste so fucking good," he murmured. "Such a good little fuck toy, aren't you?"

I panted, coming back to myself, my legs and arms tingling. I went to push up on my elbows and pull away, suddenly unsure.

"No, no," he said, his hands pushing my legs even farther apart. "We're not done, pet. This pussy is mine now." He pushed another finger inside of me, the mix of pain and pleasure otherworldly. "Mine to lick. Mine to fuck. Mine to do whatever the Hell I want." He plunged his fingers in and out with every word. "You. Are. Mine."

Then his mouth was around my bud again, sucking in time with the movement of his fingers. I cried out, "Oh!"

He chuckled. "Hold on tight, pet."

"What?" I asked, but I felt his claws grow, nearly breaking the skin on my thighs as he partially shifted.

Then he bit down. *Hard.* Right on my throbbing bundle of nerves. Before I could do anything other than shriek, Trystan *sucked*, and I lost myself completely.

There was no end and no beginning, just the feeling of his touch. His moans and growls as he drank my lifeblood sent me over the edge yet again. I cummed hard, my entire body twitching and out of control.

After my orgasm finished, he pulled back and splashed my pussy with water from the spring. A tingling feeling spread over my core for a moment before it stopped.

I glanced down, noticing the lack of puncture wounds.

Blood and shiny pleasure decorated his face. His golden eyes were wild, his feathered silver and brown hair unkempt from where my hands gripped him close.

"I want you like this every day, pet. Spread open for me, pussy pink and perfectly used. My bite marks all over." He traces a finger over my still throbbing pussy and I gasp. "Mmm, such a needy slut. You can take more, can't you, pet?"

I moaned, all reservations gone to the haze of pleasure that coursed through me.

"Say it," he growled, grasping my chin again as he pulled me towards him. I wrapped my legs around him automatically, his thick cock pushing up the seam of my ass.

"Never," I said, breathless. My hips began to circle as I rubbed my pussy up and down his manhood.

A sick, sick part of me was happy—*proud,* even—to see the shine of my cum on his chin and my blood at the corner of his lips.

"Then I'm going to fuck you, pet."

I lined up around his cock, the tip pushing in. But then I was dropped, my legs hitting the warm water. My balance was so thrown off that I almost fell in.

It was a monumental show of control on my part that my heart didn't skip a beat as I came face to face with the giant black Dragon.

Nerethus crawled down the cave walls, his ruby eyes pinned on me. The Dragon jumped, heading right towards me. I wanted to scream and faint but I did no such thing. I stood there, unwilling to shrink away in the face of this fanged monster.

There was a bright flash of light that made me wince. Nerethus changed into human form and stood before me, not a monster but a man.

A really large man.

He, at least, still wore pants, although they were soaking wet from the springs, causing the fabric to cling to his thickly muscled body.

"Are you alright?" Nerethus asked, his expression concerned. At the snap of his fingers, a large robe appeared in his hands.

"I'm fine."

The Dragon cocked his head, his black hair perfectly tousled. "You were screaming. I thought something was wrong."

Trystan's laughter echoed from above and I glanced up to see him sitting on the edge of one of the holes high up in the ceiling. His legs dangled from the edge as he watched us, a sly smile on his lips.

"Those were good screams, weren't they, pet?" Trystan winked at me.

Nerethus blinked. "Ah, I see. I apologize for interrupting then."

"You're not sorry," Trystan called. "I heard you watching." He lifted his hand, cleaning his fingers as Nerethus watched with hunger in his gaze.

Nerethus suddenly let out a roar that shook the walls. Trystan just laughed in return, disappearing into the ceiling tunnel.

"I thought you might have been hurt." Nerethus looked at me, his eyes roaming over every naked inch of me. "You're stunning, Elsing. Absolutely stunning."

I sucked in a small breath. "Thank you."

"You must be tired," he responded. "Come, get some sleep. We can discuss this all tomorrow."

I ignored the disappointed thump of my heart.

Nerethus was different. Trystan was easy to read. But the Dragon?

His true intentions remained hidden.

He held the robe open for me as I exited the water, goosebumps pebbling across my body at the cool breeze in the cave. Nerethus wrapped me in the dry fabric and I sighed happily.

He shocked me by picking me up and carrying me up into his room.

"I can walk just fine, Dragon," I protested, but he ignored me, all the while I was trying to ignore the way his hot hands felt against my bare legs where the robe peeked open, or how his arms brushed against my nipples through the thin fabric.

Nerethus made quick work of the walkway up to his room, depositing me on his bed moments later. A change of clothes waited for me.

I quickly slid on the cotton pants, tying the drawstring tight so they didn't fall down, since they were many sizes too big for me. Shrugging on the cotton top, I let it fall over my chest. It practically went to my knees.

Having the barrier of more fabric between us helped.

It had to.

"Do you want to keep your old clothes?" he asked.

"Burn them," I responded with a shake of my head.

He nodded. "As you wish. Now, get some sleep."

Then I was left alone again.

I crawled into his bed, sighing at the scent of sage on his sheets.

Sleep came quickly, but my dreams were filled with images of wings, claws, and two sets of hands all over me.

the clouds

chapter 7

*"***E***lsie, wake up!"*

It was rather disconcerting to wake up and only see the night sky above your head. I gasped, startled at the unexpected sight and the lack of any ceiling, and for a moment, I forgot where I was.

Uri's voice echoed in my ears, so close, I could have sworn they were right next to me.

But the bed was empty.

I was alone.

I shook off sleep as the memories slowly trickled back.

I'm in the Aive.

The home of the Mountain Gods.

My heart raced as I blinked, sloughing off the unsettling dreams that had plagued an already restless sleep.

My dreams repeated in my mind as I tried to remember them. Images of feathered wings darker than midnight gliding through a thick, tactile fog were still clear.

But there was something else.

The image of a beautiful person with black, shiny curls flashed in my thoughts for a brief moment, then it too faded away, replaced by another woman. One with glowing white hair and big blue eyes.

The images disappeared as the dreams faded into nothingness.

Dreams were never just dreams.

Witches knew better. But right now, I couldn't bring myself to care.

All I knew at that moment was how much I missed my Uri. The

mystery women would remain just that.

I must have seen them in passing, surely. I have lived a long life and I have seen many faces.

All I knew was that my heart ached for my feathery companion.

I have lived many lives, seen generations of humans rise and fall, and despite it all, Uri became my anchor, tethering me to sanity.

Not just my familiar.

My friend, when all others would look at me with disgust or fear.

My family, when all of my blood perished.

I did not fear death because I was crazy.

I did not fear death because I was tired of living life *alone*.

I've had dozens of lovers in my two centuries of life.

But never love.

Never anything real.

Uri was the closest companion I've had in the century since my parents were killed...

Except for *her*.

Daphne.

Even thinking her name was like a knife to my heart. Unconsciously, my hands reached up to press on top of my tunic-covered chest, as if to stem the blood flow from a wound that cannot be seen.

I couldn't even think of her name, let alone say it aloud. The wound was still too raw, open and infected with my pain. I felt it with every single breath I took as the realization hit me over and over again that she was gone.

She was gone. And I was still here.

A sudden tap at the window yanked me from my thoughts, and I jerked my head to the right, looking for Uri.

"Uri? Is that you?" My magic quietly unfurled.

But there was nothing.

I slid out of bed and padded over to the large window on silent feet, inspecting the moonlit clouds for any sign of them.

Nothing.

So in the quiet safety of the twilight hour, I finally allowed the tears to break free, giving in to my sadness.

They trailed paths down my cheeks, leaving heartbreak in their wake.

"I'm sorry," I whispered to the glass, my breath fogging it up.

A voice sounded in the distance. Not out in the sky but inside.

The Gods were awake.

Monsters, I reminded myself.

Gods, *yes.* But also *monsters.*

I stood up from the window and quietly walked over to the closed door.

"Freischalten," I commanded the magic within me, and it happily obeyed.

My magic felt better ever since leaving the hot springs and getting some sleep, even if it wasn't sound.

It's a relief to know that it was beginning to stabilize from the effects of the bracelet. Silently, I opened the door and peeked into the hallway, seeing nothing.

But light filtered through another door. It flickered, reflecting the movements of those within the room.

Trystan's room.

I needed more information on these Gods, and how exactly they came to be imprisoned here.

As quietly as possible, I made my way down the hallway and listened in on their conversation, hiding myself within the shadows.

"You need to take it easy on her, Ryst. It's too much too fast. Humans are fragile things, remember?" Nerethus murmured.

"Bullshit," Trystan objected. "I didn't hold back and yet she never even flinched. She's human, but I saw the coldness in her eyes. Elsing isn't fragile, that's for damn sure."

Nerethus was quiet for a moment before adding, "But she *is* human, and that means she's breakable."

There was a rustling and I peeked around the corner just barely, using the partially closed door to shield me.

Heilige scheiße.

It was a struggle to remind myself that the two males in front of me were monsters. Not when Trystan reclined on the bed, completely naked, cock erect, with Nerethus standing in front of him, equally naked.

I swallowed, forcing my heartbeat to steady despite the rushing of my blood, particularly in between my legs.

Gods, indeed.

Nerethus's body was sculpted to perfection. He was bulkier and larger than Trystan, but no less beautiful. A large black Dragon tattoo spanned his muscular back, both wings cresting near his shoulders.

A fire roared next to Trystan's bed, casting them both in a golden glow. For Trystan, it made his eyes and skin appear to be laced with gold.

Nerethus stood with his back to me, flexing his shoulders as he looked at Trystan.

"El-sing." Trystan tasted my name, reveling in every letter. "Such a pretty name. A powerful name. An *old* name." I tensed.

"I thought so too," Nerethus agreed, although the Dragon did not confirm which part he agreed with.

"Did you like watching us? Did your lips tremble with anticipation at the thought of tasting her cunt?" Trystan smirked.

I grabbed hold of the wall so my legs didn't give out beneath me. Blood rushed to my cheeks and warmed my skin.

I couldn't look away.

Nerethus blurred and the two Gods tumbled to the floor as the Dragon pinned the Griffin to the ground, holding his wrists above his head with one of his large hands. "You already know I liked it. My cock has been hard ever since."

Trystan struggled against him, but his eyes danced with mirth. "What are you going to do about it, Dragon?" Trystan rolled his hips and their cocks brushed, making both of them groan.

"Shall I tell you about how tight her cunt was too?" Trystan taunted the Dragon. "Or about how delicious her creamy pussy tastes?

A loud roar shook the windows as the two Gods blurred again, but this time, Trystan ended up on his front as Nerethus fisted his hair, trapping the Griffin.

"You've been a fucking brat ever since she got here. Mouthing off and pushing my buttons. Misbehaving every chance you get."

Trystan winked. "What are you going to do about it, scales?"

The Dragon yanked Trystan by the hair and dragged him to the edge of the bed as Nerethus sat down.

"I'm going to fuck the brat out of you, that's what." Nerethus growled and the sound set my hair on end as goosebumps rose along my arms. "But first, you're going to suck my cock until you choke on it."

Trystan smirked and opened his mouth, sticking out his tongue. Nerethus snarled and fisted Trystan's hair, thrusting his cock between the Griffin's lips. The Dragon's mouth fell open with a moan as he watched Trystan go to work, sucking and licking with a needy sound.

"Deeper," he ordered. Trystan gagged, taking the Dragon's entire cock down his throat.

Nerethus's head fell back with a satisfied sigh as he caressed Trystan's cheeks. "That's it. Just like that."

The Dragon thrust his hips in and out of Trystan's waiting mouth, making the Griffin's eyes water. I watched as one of Trystan's hands traveled down, wrapping around his own cock.

The two blurred again, moving too fast for my semi-mortal eyes to track, and suddenly Trystan was on his back, trapped beneath Nerethus in the middle of the bed.

Nerethus's ass muscles flexed as he lifted Trystan's legs. The Dragon snapped his fingers and a bottle of some unknown liquid appeared in his hands. Nerethus leaned down, squirting it somewhere based on the noise, but I'm unable to see.

Trystan suddenly let out a trembling moan as Nerethus thrusts forward.

"That's right. Take every inch like a good little cum slut," the Dragon taunted, thrusting again as Trystan let out another moan.

"Admit it." Trystan groaned. "You're thinking about Elsing being trapped between us, just like this. Elsing would sit on your face, trapping you with her sweet cunt as I fucked your ass. You'd be trapped, bird. Trapped and *ours.*" Nerethus picked up the pace, lifting Trystan's legs until they were over his shoulders. The Dragon bent down and pressed a hot kiss to Trystan's lips, swallowing his moans.

They groaned into each other, becoming one. I watched, unable to look away, as my own pleasure grew.

Something wet dripped down my leg as my core wept. I silently slid a hand into my cotton pants, my fingers brushing against my throbbing clit.

That image Nerethus described...

I wanted that too.

I shouldn't. I really shouldn't.

But I did.

"And then," Nerethus panted, his ass flexing with every thrust, "when you're ready to cum, I'll have Elsing sit on your cock so you can cum inside her before I make you lick her pussy clean, tasting both of you. Because you're mine, Griffin. Your body is mine."

Golden hands grasped Nerethus's shoulders as Trystan tossed his head back, cumming with a grating moan.

Nerethus shortly followed with a loud snarl.

They both fell to the bed, limp and sweaty, as their lips found each other again.

For a few moments, I watched them make out, their hands roving all over the other's body.

Suddenly, I felt like an intruder. I felt like I should turn away.

I went to leave but paused at Trystan's next words. "We can't trust her,

Nere."

My blood froze.

Nerethus sighed. "I know. But she's different. All of this is."

"She might be different, but we still can't trust her. At least not yet."

Nerethus went silent.

"We can still fuck her, though," Trystan added. There was a large *thump* as Nerethus shoved him to the floor.

The Griffin laughed but his words echoed in my head. The heat inside me died, and I knew in my heart that they were right.

They cannot trust me.

And I cannot trust them.

I silently made my way back to the Dragon's room and crawled into the now cold sheets, repeating the words over and over in my head as I prayed to Pertcha for strength.

I was going to need it.

the god of dragons

chapter 8

I've never been an early riser but the morning sun warming my face pulls me from slumber.

The bright light burned slightly, but it was so beautiful. I got up, stretching slowly. My body felt so much better. Which I'm sure was also to do with the Dragon's lush mattress. Aches that I'd long forgotten were suddenly gone.

But the air was chilly despite the warm sunlight on me. We were, after all, in wintar.

Padding over to the window, I pressed my hands to the cold glass and took in the sunrise as reds and oranges crested over the snow-covered tips of the Helvetas.

"It's beautiful, isn't it?"

I didn't even hear Nerethus enter the room, so I nearly jumped out of my own skin at his low voice right next to my ear. I willed my blood and my bones into stone, forcing myself not to move or react.

But he caught me off guard, and in that split second, in that brief, fleeting moment before I remembered reality, my mind went to last night.

To his naked body tangled with Trystan's.

Then I squashed the feelings of lust that followed like a bug in the dirt beneath my feet.

I couldn't fall for him. For either of them.

It could only be sex and nothing more. No feelings, no ties.

There was no other choice, and at the end of the day, they were monsters—and that meant *everything*.

"The view is lovely." My morning voice was hoarse as my breath instantly fogged up the glass. I wiped it off with my tunic sleeve.

"You're angry."

I turned around and looked him in the eyes, although I had to crane my neck back just to meet them.

"I am not angry, Dragon. I simply do not *know* you. You say you're not a man, and yet, what you are is actually far worse. I do not typically enjoy the company of men, and I enjoy the company of monsters even less. Regardless, I do not trust those I do not know. And even if you are miraculously different, I do not *know you.* Either of you," I amended, mentioning Trystan. "Quite simply, I don't trust you."

He didn't catch the double meaning in my words. He just nodded, looking away from me to gaze out on the slowly rising sun. Then he sighed, sliding one hand into his pants pocket. "In the 400 years we've been stuck here, it seems the Republic has done their fair job at ensuring we're hated."

I scoffed. "You've done plenty to contribute to that hate, Dragon."

Nerethus shrugged. "I am not a man. Do not look for his faults within me, nor anyone who calls the Aive home. We do not live by mortal rules or moral guides. We are beasts, Elsing."

"You kill," I spit out between clenched teeth.

"Yes." He looked me in the eyes. "We do. But the Republic kills too. Everyone kills. There is no such thing as bad or good, not truly. We all fall somewhere in the middle."

Then his large hands landed on my waist as he gently pushed me against the window. The cold glass seeped into my skin, making me shiver.

I forced my gaze to stay forward instead of checking to make sure I wasn't going to fall to my death, but the window overlooking the mountaintops loomed, and my heart raced.

Do not fear.

Do not fear.

I forced my breathing to calm, exhaling slowly, but that only brought more attention to the heat of Nerethus's hands. Raising one hand, he caressed my cheek, a look of curiosity in his ruby gaze.

"You forget, Elsing," he started, his voice low and rumbling, "we are also *Gods.* The very same type of being that your Republic devotes it's every move to. Have you considered that, yet?"

My heart thudded to a stop as I took in his words.

"How do I know you're not lying?" I asked.

Nerethus chuckled.

I hate to admit it, but for most of my life, I thought the Mountain Gods was simply a name made-up by humans. I did not think the monsters roaming the Helvetas were real Gods, just that humans couldn't think of anything else to call beings so magical.

It wouldn't be the first time humans mislabeled a magical being.

But reality sunk in as the Dragon watched me, his ruby eyes so inhuman with those vertical slit pupils.

But still, a God? A real God?

"Prove it," I breathed. "You say you're a God and not a monster, then *prove. It.*"

Then Nerethus smiled and *Heilige scheiße,* it was brighter and warmer than the sun rising behind me. His skin started to glow as if lit from within, and the midnight hues of his hair turned molten, lifting slightly as if in a phantom breeze.

Shadows of scales suddenly glowed red beneath the surface of his skin. His fangs sharpened and his eyes grew brighter, the dark red turning luminous as if lit from within.

The bastard even grew a few inches taller.

Or so I thought. It took a moment to realize he was levitating.

I sniffed, pretending not to be impressed. "It could be a glamor. Any magical creature with a lick of power can make a glamor. All this tells me is you're powerful, not that you're a God. I'm not convinced, Dragon."

Nerethus fought a small smile as his feet hit the floor and he went back to his normal, un-glowing self.

"I see. Would you like a demonstration, then?" he asked.

I nodded. "If you want me to believe you're a God, yes."

"As you wish," he murmured, pivoting and padding out of the room on silent feet. "Though, I cannot guarantee you will like it."

I scrambled to keep up, following him into the hallway, all the way to the living and kitchen quarters.

Trystan was drinking a glass of water near the sink. I struggled not to marvel at the fact that they have an inside water spout.

"Good morning, pet. Sleep well?" Trystan winked at me and my heart nearly thudded to a stop. I forced my face to be emotionless, betraying nothing.

Does he know I watched?

"I slept fine until I woke up and realized I had to see your face again, Griffin," I replied tightly.

The God of the Sky flashed me a wicked smile.

"You know I love when you're mean, pet."

"Our new guest requires a demonstration," Nerethus said, walking past Trystan to the other wing of the house. The one with the library where I arrived.

"Oh? A demonstration of what, virility?" Trystan chuckled, his eyes still on me. There's a blur as Nerethus suddenly punched Trystan so hard, the Griffin flew across the floor, hitting it with a hard *thump*.

I gasped, unsure what was happening.

"Oh, come on, really? You don't think we're Gods, Elsing?" Trystan laughed as he stood up.

Something occurred to me then.

Something that chilled me to the bone.

"You can talk to each other telepathically, can't you?" I asked, my voice frostier than the mountain air.

Trystan rolled his eyes at me. "Of course. Fuck, you *really* don't think we're Gods, do you?" He shot Nerethus an incredulous look. Nerethus just nodded and crossed his arms.

"I see. A demonstration it is, then." Trystan smiled at me with a wink. "I can help with that.

The next thing I knew, the world disappeared. I swallowed my scream as we appeared in a large glass room.

Trystan dropped me on my feet and I had to grit my teeth to keep from screaming as I looked down.

The floor was glass. I stared into the open air beneath me, my heart racing.

"So you do have a little fear in you, pet. That's good. Fear keeps you alive," Trystan remarked, circling me. On trembling arms, I pushed up to stand, refusing to look down.

I wasn't scared of heights.

But *mein Gott*, anyone would be scared of a glass floor when you're on the tallest mountain in the known world.

"You mistake me, Griffin. I do not fear falling to my death, nor do I fear you." I raised my chin, steadying myself. "I simply did not anticipate this."

Nerethus smiled lightly, hiding it behind his hand. But I saw.

"Do you have something to add, Dragon?" I asked, suddenly furious. "I believe I asked for a demonstration. Are you just going to stand here and laugh at me like an Arschloch? Or, are you going to prove to me that you're actually a God?"

Trystan chuckled, but Nerethus just watched me, his ruby eyes betraying nothing.

"Well? I'm waiting," I said, tapping my foot against the glass floor.

Trystan walked to the far wall and opened what I realized was a door in the glass. The cut was so fine, it was nearly imperceptible from the wall itself.

Freezing wind assaulted me and I gasped. Trystan blurred, grabbing me around the waist. I tried to pry his hands off, but it was no use.

"I believe you wanted a demonstration," he whispered in my ear. "I'm happy to oblige, pet."

Then he tossed me out of the window.

It only took seconds, but it felt like a lifetime passed as I plunged through damp clouds that tickled my frostbitten cheeks.

Time sped back up again, and with it brought the realization that I was falling to my death.

I opened my mouth, ready to scream when a huge shadow suddenly darted in from behind me. I slammed face-first into something hard.

Something warm.

Something that moved.

I hit a fucking Dragon, I realized, blinking. I scrambled to hold on, but Nerethus turned and I slid right off, tumbling back into the open air.

I flailed wildly as I fell towards the earth.

Then I hit something else. Something... soft.

I grabbed onto the feathers and yanked *hard.* The Griffin shrieked, hurting my ears. But I held on tight, putting my legs on either side of his back. Trystan flapped his wings.

I'm flying.

I'm really flying.

A giant black Dragon, nearly as big as the mountain itself, suddenly dove in front of us and the Griffin followed, plunging nose first down towards the ground.

Trystan really was a bastard because the second I thought I was secure, he twisted in a tight spiral, spinning upside down.

My grip slipped. His feathers were too soft to keep hold, and I'm shot into the air yet again. My hair whipped around me like streams of ebony shadows as the wind battered me.

This time when I hit the Dragon, I was ready. I pushed to stand on trembling legs, walking up his back before sitting in between two of the large protruding spines along his back.

I wedged myself in between the two spikes and settled where his scales met, using the lip to sink further down.

The Dragon beneath me rumbled, the sound vibrating against my inner thighs.

"Oh fuck," I gasped as the vibration hit my clit, sending bolts of pleasure through my body. There was a large gust of wind and Trystan hovered next to us.

In a flash, he shifted, becoming a man yet again.

But this time, he had wings. Giant brown and silver wings just like his Griffin.

Trystan only wore his feathers, so I got an eyeful of his naked body.

He landed on the Dragon's outstretched wing, walking up the bone of Nerethus's arm.

"Hello, pet."

"You... threw me off a mountain."

I imagined smashing my fear into dust and blowing it into oblivion. On shaky legs, I stood up and slowly stepped closer to Trystan, willing my eyes into wide innocence.

He didn't see my fist flying towards his nose until it was too late.

His nose *crunched* beneath my fingers, sending searing pain through my hand and up my arm.

The pain was worth it.

"YOU THREW ME OFF A FUCKING MOUNTAIN!" I screamed against the wind. "I'M GOING TO KILL YOU AND DANCE ON YOUR GRAVE!" Jerking my leg up, I kneed him in the balls. He groaned and fell to his knees. Nerethus flapped his wings hard, dropping Trystan into the sky. I managed to hang on by sheer will alone, but I quickly returned to a seated position.

Trystan appeared next to us again a moment later, floating on the wind with a wicked smile on his face.

"I wouldn't have let you fall, pet. Don't be mad. Plus, you can't kill me." He pointed to himself. "The whole God thing."

"YOU THREW ME OFF A MOUNTAIN!" At that moment, as if

we'd coordinated it, Nerethus flicked his giant tail and hit Trystan in the back, punting him into the clouds.

An eagle's startled shriek followed before he flapped his wings, righting himself.

His next shriek was far, far angrier.

All of a sudden, a sharp burst of magic from Trystan and a huge gust of wind hit us from behind. Nerethus rolled so fast I almost threw up.

There was another eagle cry again, calling another gust of wind to hit us.

Except this time, we're shot towards a mountain top. I thought it was far away, but Nerethus moved so fast.

Scheiße.

The Dragon banked just before we careened into the mountain, but he still slammed into the snow-covered rocks. He curled his body away from it and I slid off.

I'm not sure why, but this time when I fell, I closed my eyes.

Something smooth catches me, stopping my descent. I gingerly opened my eyes to see small black scales all around me.

Nerethus caught me.

His Dragon paw completely encased me.

Nerethus separated his claw-tipped fingers, allowing me to peek through. He gently raised me past his head and onto his shoulder, where he allowed me to find my seat again. He held onto the side of the mountain with his back two legs, holding himself completely, perfectly still.

Trystan appeared in the distance, flying straight towards us, claws extended. Nerethus growled, diving down just in time to avoid having his scales ripped open. The wind bent me backwards, the force pushing me against the Dragon's hard scales.

"Stärke." It's a risk to cast near them, but the relief in my back was palpable. That angle was miserable. Still, the wind batters my eyes as I tuck myself against Nerethus.

The Griffin dives at us again and Nerethus rolls, darting left and then straight up, making my legs dangle in the air.

Nerethus lets out a loud snarl and Trystan backs off. The Griffin followed as Nerethus began to ascend up into the clouds.

Oh thank you, Pertcha.

Vielen Dank, Mutter.

We flew back to the Aive in silence. It was surprisingly peaceful. As the glass castle that was apparently my new home came into view, I couldn't help but marvel.

The view from outside was so much better.

It occurred to me, then, why they call it the Aive. It's because it looked like a cross between a castle and a large aviary. It was seamlessly built into the mountainside, becoming part of it.

Nerethus slowly reached a claw back, looking at me with his ruby red eyes.

"You want me to get in there?" I asked, my voice hoarse.

The Dragon confirmed with a nod. It was still so bizarre to be talking to a giant Dragon.

"Fine." I huffed a sigh, pushing my tangled, wind-swept hair out of my face. It would be impossible to brush now.

I carefully sat down within Nerethus's claw. He waited until I was fully seated to move his arm and gently place me at the edge of the doorway.

The same doorway I was, just earlier, thrown out of.

As I glanced back at the Dragon, he started to change.

Red light began to glow from between his scales. It traveled along his body until his eyes were gleaming like newborn stars, that molten ruby alive with rage.

He flashed his fangs and I watched, in rapt awe, as the Dragon God opened his jaws, turned towards Trystan, and unleashed his flame.

Even from a distance, the air instantly warms from the Dragonflame. The Griffin shrieked and flew away, but Nerethus was fast, remaining on his tail. He released another stream of Dragonflame and the air turned so hot that sweat began to drip down my back and bead along my forehead.

I eyed the edge warily and took a seat on the glass floor, watching them and getting myself together.

Flying was amazing.

The second Nerethus put me down, my instinct was to ask to do it again.

But they cannot trust me. And they're right.

I can't trust them either.

I cannot fall for their magic and their tricks. My feelings needed to stay out of it.

Still.

Suddenly the scent of... roast game meat assaulted me before Trystan was shot through the glass door, skidding as he slapped out the flames burning his ass.

"Not the feathers! Don't ruin the feathers!"

"You could have killed her!" Nerethus was rage and ruin as he stepped through the doorway. I didn't even see him transform, but his red eyes were furious as he stalked Trystan, fangs bared. "What the fuck were you thinking? She's a human, for fuck's sake!"

Trystan smiled, looking up at Nerethus. "Our new pet wanted a demonstration. So I gave her one."

The Griffin went to stand, but Nerethus placed a hand on Trystan's shoulders, pushing him back down.

"No. Stay on your fucking knees. You almost hurt her. Our *guest*. The very same guest who was almost poisoned and beaten to death just a day earlier."

Trystan arched his brow, a wicked smirk on his face. "Come on, Nere. It was just a little near-death experience among friends." The Griffin winked at me.

I scoffed. "I did not enjoy getting tossed out of a window, you *verdammter idiot*."

"Since you decided to act like a feral pigeon," Nerethus said coldly, and Trystan sputtered at the comparison, "*Elsing* gets to pick your punishment."

Everything thudded to a screeching halt as I realized exactly what kind of punishment the God of Dragons was talking about.

Scheiße.

the punishment

chapter 9

*I*t's just sex.

The phrase repeated over and over again in my head as Nerethus looked at me, the picture of *hunger*.

It's just sex.

"Punishment?" I asked him, though I already knew the answer.

"Even Gods get punished, Elsing."

This wasn't the man.

This was the Dragon.

A million different ways to interpret this "punishment" ran through my head, each one making my blood burn. I was on fire by the time I realized I actually had to respond.

I don't know why I hesitated.

But something stopped me.

I don't need to know them in order to fuck them. My time in the hot springs with Trystan proved that. I understood him. We both enjoyed causing a little chaos. That's why I fucked him first. Even I could see the similarities, as much as that made me want to punch something.

The Dragon though, remained a mystery.

And he just saved my life for the second time. Nerethus held out his hand, waiting for my response.

"His punishment," I met his ruby gaze, placing my hand on his, "is your lack of company the rest of the day. I'm stealing you to spend it with me instead, and Trystan isn't invited."

Nerethus's mouth twitched and I knew he was fighting a surprised smile.

"Oh, come *on*. You can't be seri—" Nerethus wrapped his other hand around Trystan's neck and squeezed, silencing his protest.

Not enough that it would hurt the other, but enough that it shut Trystan up.

It didn't help that both Gods were naked. I watched as Trystan's cock twitched, growing hard.

"You heard her," Nerethus said to him. "You're on your own tonight. You watch and listen. Nothing else. This is what you get for almost killing our guest."

Trystan rolled his eyes as Nerethus released him. With a wink at me, Trystan walked out of the room. I couldn't peel my eyes away from his muscular backside, and based on the smirk he flashed over his shoulder, the bastard knew it.

All of a sudden I was alone with the Dragon. The room shrunk as I became hyper aware of his presence.

He watched me, those serpentine eyes curious.

"So, you got me alone." His voice was low and playful. Nerethus took a step closer, lifting a hand to brush it through my hair. He twirled the black strands around his fingers. "What ever will you do with me?" He leaned forward until our lips were so close I could feel his breath and taste his magic on my tongue. "Your wish is my command."

My heart stopped beating and I took a step back, needing the space to breathe.

I wanted him with every fiber of my being.

"I'm hungry," is what I said instead. "I want real food."

Nerethus smiled. "I would be honored to make you something to eat, Elsing."

No feelings.

Just sex.

Nerethus turned away from me and slid on a pair of leather pants, giving me a healthy look at his perfect ass. I had to bite my tongue to keep from rubbing my thighs together, desperate for his touch.

"Follow me." He walked out of the room and back towards the main living area.

I followed, reveling in the soft carpet beneath my feet. I didn't realize how cold they were until now.

"I need socks or my feet are going to freeze off."

Nerethus paused.

"Of course." With a snap of his fingers, socks appeared in my hands.

I fought my own smile as I happily put on the thick wool, sighing at the blessed warmth.

"You will have to remind me of these human things. We do not feel temperature. I find lava quite comfortable, actually. It soothes my scales." Nerethus nodded at my newly covered feet. "If you need something, all you need to do is say so."

"Thanks." I tried to be nice. I was grateful, truly. But that voice in the back of my head was screaming, *MONSTER! MONSTER!*

I shoved my feelings away again as we walked into the kitchen. Nerethus pulled out some wooden bowls and metal utensils from sleek stone cabinets above the counter area.

"Sit." He pointed to a chair at the countertop. I practically had to jump into the tall seat that was clearly built for a Dragon, but I managed to climb on.

As I got comfortable, Nerethus disappeared into a small side room. He emerged after a few minutes with a handful of fresh fruits and vegetables, and a little basket stuffed with a few things I didn't recognize.

The room must've had a preservation spell on it because most of the food wasn't in season.

He rinsed the fruit under the water spout before patting them dry with a small towel. Nerethus handed over a bowl of ripe blackberries and I dug in happily.

The tart berries burst on my tongue, both sweet and sour. I hummed happily.

Chopping sounds distracted me, and I watched as Nerethus got to work slicing and dicing my dinner.

He handed me a plate with some warm sliced bread, cheese, and fermented vegetables.

I tried not to rush, but it was hard to fight the huge wave of hunger that suddenly hit. I shoved a piece of bread in my face and moaned at the taste.

Nerethus smiled. "I'm glad you like it. We catch most of our food in our true forms, but occasionally try to cook something. Especially because Aleksander doesn't like raw meat."

"You've mentioned this Aleksander before. There's another one of you?" I asked between bites. "Another God who lives here?"

"Mhm," Nerethus confirmed with a nod, tossing some chopped vegetables into a large pot of boiling stock. The aromatic smell of the spices made my mouth water, so I busied myself with another piece of bread.

"Where is he, then? Is he not cursed like you?"

The Dragon looked at me, his eyes thoughtful. "Yes, he is cursed too. He is... here but not."

I paused. "Here but not? What does that mean?"

Nerethus paused for a moment, as if hesitant. "Aleksander... He's an Original."

"What's an Original?" I asked.

"There are different types of Gods."

"I know this already," I interrupted. He simply raised a brow, making it clear that I should let him continue. "Fine, sorry. Go on."

"Thank you. What I meant was that there are actually two different types of Gods. There are those like myself and Trystan. Lesser Gods. Then, there are the Originals. There are only five Higher Gods in existence, and Aleksander is one of them."

My blood froze over.

"What does that mean?" I asked.

Nerethus contemplated my question. "Again, it's hard to describe in mortal terms. A lot of this is just... known. But Magically, the Originals are far more powerful than Lesser Gods. Aleksander can astral project outside of the confines of the curse that keeps us here in the Helvetas, something which Trystan and I do not have the power to do. Aleksander's body can't physically leave, but his spirit can. The curse didn't stipulate astral travel."

"Right," I nodded, trying to follow.

"Higher Gods also have more responsibilities," Nerethus continued. "Trystan and I are Alphas and Firsts. Most of our power centers around our beasts and keeping the peace within our own kind. We have other powers, but they only relate to our beast shape. But the Originals... their powers are almost limitless."

I almost choked on my piece of bread. "No limit? None?"

Nerethus shook his head. "None. That's what makes them so powerful and gives them the ability to create. Aleksander created the underworld. He often disappears for days at a time. Sometimes weeks, depending on how many souls are facing judgment or if a spirit escapes the Beneath."

I had no idea what these places were, but what I did understand with perfect clarity, was the fact that I needed to stay as far away from this Aleksander character as possible.

An Original would complicate things.

"Great, can't wait," I muttered sarcastically.

Nerethus didn't react to my tone. He just finished up with whatever he was tossing in the soup.

He came around the counter and put his arms on either side of me, locking me in place.

My heart skipped a beat.

"What are you doing?" My voice was breathless. He reached one hand up to cup my cheek, brushing his thumb across my lower lip.

"Have I not made my desires clear?" he asked.

I stopped breathing at his words. "No, you have not."

"Then let me remedy that," Nerethus murmured. His hand landed beneath my chin as he tilted my head up so he could look me in the eyes as he said, "I want you, Elsing. I've wanted you since the moment I saw you bruised, battered, and left for dead in the forest. Even covered in dirt and blood, you were the most beautiful thing I've ever seen."

All thoughts emptied from my head.

Then I remembered who the Hell I was.

"You couldn't handle me if you tried," I met his gaze with a challenge.

The Dragon smirked. "Why don't you let me be the judge of that. After all," Nerethus leaned in, brushing his cheek against mine and pressing a soft kiss to the edge of my mouth, "you've never fucked a God before. And I'm not just a God, Elsing. I'm a Dragon."

Oh my Gods.

He chuckled as I trembled from his words. "Say yes, Elsing. Tell me to kiss you. Tell me you want this."

Nerethus pressed another kiss to the edge of my mouth, torturing me slowly. "Let me show you exactly how much I can handle."

Every thought emptied from my head as my body turned hot, even against the cold of the stone counter. Nerethus grasped the hair at the back of my neck, pulling lightly as he angled my head up towards him.

"I permit." I had barely said the word before his lips were on mine, slowly and precisely fucking me with his mouth. There was no other word for it. The way he coaxed mine open with his tongue as he sucked on my lower lip was masterful.

My bones turned liquid and I leaned into him completely, my hands coming to rest on his hard chest. The scent of his sage magic was everywhere, the herby smell mixing with the sweet taste of his tongue.

He tasted like sin and magic. And I needed more.

"Lift your arms." The Dragon's voice was pure sex and I complied without any further thought. He gently peeled my top—*his* top—off, carefully making sure my hair didn't get snagged. The cold air of the room hit my nipples, turning them even harder so they stand at attention.

Nerethus's jaw went slack and his pupils dilated as he looked over my naked breasts. His hands lifted, cupping them, and I wanted to melt at his touch.

"Gods, you're so fucking beautiful. Look at these. Look at how perfectly they fit in my hand. And these—" His fingers brushed over my hard nipples and my back arched on a gasp. "These are just *aching* for my touch, aren't they?"

Nerethus bent down, sucking my cold nipple into his hot mouth. The feeling of his lips and tongue lapping at my chest flooded my core as my clit began to throb and that aching need grew stronger.

Nerethus switched, letting my nipple escape his mouth with an obscenely wet *pop* sound that made me moan.

The Dragon stepped back, surveying the way I'm splayed out on his kitchen counter, topless and panting.

"See something you like?" I teased.

"Stay there and don't move while I finish making your food." There was no room for question in his order. "I want to cook with a view."

He... put me on display for him...

And I liked it.

"What if Trystan interrupts or the other God, Aleks, wakes up?" I asked, not because the idea bothered me, but because the idea made my blood *burn.*

"They'd enjoy the view as well," Nerethus said, his eyes roving over my naked body. "Then," Nerethus continued, "if they were hungry, I'd let them feast on you while you sat there and watched me cook."

Heilige scheiße.

"Mm," he hummed. "I can smell your wet cunt, Elsing. You like that idea, don't you? You like the idea of being displayed and pleasured, like our precious little fuck toy."

He pulled the soup off the fire, placing it safely on the counter to cool.

"You'd like that too," I retorted, my voice breathless.

Later, I would think back to this moment and realize that he never used any protection. Nerethus just grabbed the boiling hot metal barehanded.

The Dragon walked around the kitchen counter now that the food was finished.

No, walked wasn't the right word.

He *stalked.* Every movement was precise and calculated.

"Yes," he admitted plainly. "I would. I like being in control. I love the thought of placing you on the counter and letting everyone look at what is *mine.* Based on the sound of your blood quickening, you enjoy being *watched.*" Then his hands were on my breasts and his mouth was on my neck. "Maybe I'll blindfold you so you wouldn't even know who was pleasuring you."

My jaw dropped and I gasped as Nerethus pinched my cold nipple.

"Answer my question, Elsing."

"Yes," I moaned. "I want that. All of that. I shouldn't but I do." I writhed against him, unable to help it, but he continued to hold me in place, unmoving.

Nerethus inhaled slowly, running his nose up and down my neck. Scenting me.

"Your scent is driving me insane. You smell like blackberry wine." He paused and I felt his smirk against my neck. "Do you taste the way you smell, I wonder?"

I almost exploded then and there but Nerethus released my breasts, making me nearly cry out, missing his touch.

"Your dinner is ready and you need your strength."

"What do I need my strength for, Dragon?"

He didn't smile, but his eyes blazed with raw hunger. "I told you. I want to find out if you taste the way you smell. Eat your dinner so that I can eat mine."

Oh my Gods.

I said nothing as he placed a bowl of steaming soup in front of me. I didn't even question what was in it.

The first spoonful was so good I couldn't help but moan. A loud *crack* echoed through the kitchen as Nerethus gripped the counter so hard the stone split.

"Trouble, Dragon?" I asked around my next spoonful. The soup was incredible and after the trials of the past few days, it instantly put me at ease.

The Dragon growled but quieted down, waiting patiently for me to finish. My spoon clanged against the empty bowl as I sighed happily, my belly full and warmth coursing through me.

Looking to the side, I met Nerethus's red gaze.

Time stopped as we stared into each other's eyes.

Nothing else existed but us.

"Are you finished?" he asked carefully.

I shivered. It wasn't from fear, but from the barely held back need in his voice.

I pushed my empty bowl towards him, licking my lips. "I am."

That ended up being too much for the Dragon. He was up in an instant, swiping the bowl clean off the table, causing it to shatter on the floor. A second later, I was in his arms and the world *shifted* as we reappeared in his bedroom.

"Trystan got his chance to taste you," the Dragon growled, his red eyes flicking up towards me as he moved down my body. He ran his fingers along my stomach, sliding them just inside the waist of my pants.

I gasped, my breath hitching as I swayed on my feet. Nerethus kneeled and pulled my pants off, sliding them off my ass until I stood bare before him.

He rocked back on his heels, face slack as he took me in. His eyes sharpened and his fangs lengthened instantly.

"The heavens look dim in comparison to your beauty."

The air in his bedroom warmed and red, glowing veins appeared on Nerethus as his beast joined us. Nerethus stood, his body seeming even taller than it was before.

"Do you see what you do to me, Elsing? A Dragon's control is infinite; and yet you have mine in shreds," he snarled, looking away as if frustrated with himself.

"Then stop holding back," I taunted, walking backwards until the backs of my knees hit his bed. I sat down, leaning back as my legs opened.

Nerethus watched, jaw dropped, as I reached a hand down and trailed my pointer finger up and down my wet pussy lips. I followed the same path upward, dragging my wetness up and rubbing it against my clit.

"You don't know what you're asking for," his voice trembled. He prowled towards me, stopping at the end of the bed. I scooted back and he followed, getting on his hands and knees to *crawl* up the bed towards me.

It was a heady feeling, having a God want you so badly they would *crawl* for you.

I loved it. I wanted more.

I sucked in a sharp breath, reveling in the feeling. "I do know what I ask, Dragon. I know *exactly* what I want."

Nerethus's eyes fall shut again as he shudders. "And what is that, Elsing? What do you want?"

I smirked. "You, Dragon. I want you to fuck and use me until neither of us can move."

"I see," he purred, pulling my legs even wider apart, his eyes locked on my core. Slowly, so achingly slowly, he reached forward and grabbed my hand, bringing my fingers to his lips. His eyes flicked to mine and he flashed me a wicked smile. "Your wish is my command."

Nerethus sucked my fingers into his mouth with a snarl. My jaw dropped and my heart stuttered to a halt as he licked the pleasure off of my fingers.

A low, vibrating groan that shook the glass began to emanate from him, but I couldn't bring myself to worry.

It sounded like the Dragon was purring.

It was the same noise he made earlier when I was on his back.

Nerethus released my fingers and I let my hand fall to the bed.

He looked at me for a few seconds and then the world blurred. I kneeled on top of him, his hands on my thighs the only thing keeping me from face-planting into the covers.

My pussy hovered right over his mouth as he gripped my ass cheeks, one for each of his large hands. Nerethus's eyes watched me the entire time.

He smiled before giving me a single warning. "Grab onto the headboard."

That's all he said before he slammed me onto his mouth at the exact same time as he shifted his tongue. Forked and extra long, he sank into me.

Screams exploded out of me as the Dragon *devoured,* ripping the pleasure out of my body with a reckless determination that sent bolts of fire to my core.

Without looking, I reached for the headboard, grasping for something to hold on to as my legs struggled to work.

"Good girl," Nerethus purred. "Eyes on me. Don't look away." His words were muffled by my cunt. I looked down, watching as he parted my pussy lips and used his elongated, forked tongue to lap me up like a hungry kitten. Then he speared me with his tongue again and I nearly blacked out.

"Fuck!" My scream was guttural but I didn't look away. My eyes stayed locked on the Dragon's. Self-control became a losing battle as he fucked me with that serpentine tongue.

"Stop worrying about crushing me and sit on my fucking face. I'm a God. I don't need to breathe."

"Oh fuck," I moaned, putting my full weight on his face. He let out a pleased groan that made me even wetter than before. Nerethus pulled his tongue out of me and moved up, attaching his lips around my clit and *sucking.* The wet sound combined with the suction sent me hurtling head first towards that cliff. I gripped his hair tightly, riding his face as my orgasm neared. Nerethus groaned in pleasure, lapping at my clit as he plunged two fingers inside me.

I fell through space and time as my vision went black and stars burst behind my eyes. The pleasure was so immense, it felt like my soul left my body.

"Yes! Just like that," Nerethus moaned happily as I cummed all over his face.

My cunt twitched, squeezing his fingers. Nerethus inserted another, stretching me even further. It was painful in the best way possible. The feeling of being full of him made me frantic and needy, shredding the remnants of the control I attempted to maintain.

"More," I whined. "I need *more.*"

Nerethus' responding grin was pure sin. "Did you think I was done? I asked for every last drop and I'm not going to stop until that's exactly what I get. Now," he curled his fingers inside me and then suddenly his entire arm vibrated, heating slightly, *"come for me again."*

"Oh my Gods," I cried out at the combination of his fingers plunging in and out of me, stretching and pressing and kneading in tune with the lick of his tongue—it was too much.

"Don't stop," I ordered him. "Don't stop, don't stop."

"Never," he growled. I was shot towards that cliff once more as I orgasmed again, my legs twitching as I held onto him for dear life.

"Mhm, that's it," he praised, though his words were muffled by my body. "Just like that, Elsing. Give me everything."

Gripping his hair tightly, I ground against his mouth, covering his face in my pleasure. He didn't seem to mind. If anything, it seemed to drive the Dragon absolutely *mad.*

It only made him want *more.*

"Again!" he demanded. I whined in protest, unsure if I could, but he simply shook his head against me and added a fourth finger. My body obeyed his every command. I was caught in the whirlwind of pleasure.

His fingers and mouth were a drug and I chased the high of it all, over and over again.

"Oh fuck, it's so tight." My voice trembled with need as he rubbed his fingers inside me, moving them in and out.

The Dragon chuckled. "Yes it is. You're taking my cock next and this tight pussy needs to be stretched out so that I can fit." Then he shocked the Hell out of me by taking his tongue and…

"Nerethus!" I gasped as he licked my other hole, the one between my cheeks. I had never been touched there before but *scheiße,* it felt so good.

His thumb moved in lazy circles on my clit, putting pressure in the exact right spot.

I gave in to the feeling, my back arching as he wrung yet another orgasm out of me. My cries became whines and desperate pleas. A warm, rushing sensation between my legs began to spread across my abdomen.

"I don't, I don't know what—" I couldn't even form true words, but somehow the Dragon understood.

"Don't resist it, treasure. Let it happen."

A rushing feeling takes over and suddenly liquid bursts from me, spraying the God of Dragons in the face.

"Fuck yes." He laughed, eyes unhinged. "Give me every fucking drop." Nerethus attached his mouth over my pussy, swallowing every drop with a greedy moan, just like he said he would.

I had never seen anything so hot in my entire life.

"Doesn't she taste amazing?" a voice called. I froze, startled.

We were being *watched.*

"You just got wetter, Elsing." Nerethus chuckled. "Do you like having an audience?" His fingers curled and I saw stars.

"Yes," I admitted.

"Would you like him to join us, or shall I send the bird away?" Nerethus's question was serious.

If I asked, he would send Trystan away.

I almost said yes. Until I remembered what I saw last night.

Flashes of their naked bodies twined together ran through my mind, along with the hot look in their eyes as Nerethus fucked Trystan in the ass.

If this was a game, then I was going to win it.

"Let him watch." I turned to look at Trystan over my shoulder.

"Good choice, pet," Trystan winked. He leaned against the bedroom door frame, arms crossed and shirtless. The pose emphasized his muscular biceps, but it was his eyes I couldn't look away from. They were full of lust and barely restrained aggression. Like he was one second away from pouncing.

"Remember your punishment. You can look, but not join," Nerethus reminded him, sounding barely restrained himself.

Seeing these two Gods come unglued turned me on more than I'll ever admit.

Trystan scoffed. "Rude." But his eyes remained on me, unable to look away from my naked body.

Nerethus carefully sat me down, rolling out from underneath me. I hit the covers as he stood, now fully naked. Wait—

"When did you get naked?" I asked, mumbling.

Nerethus winked at me. "You were distracted."

Nerethus snapped his fingers and a chair appeared next to him. There was a crash as some of his treasure hoard clattered to the floor on the other side of the room where the chair *used* to be.

Nerethus pointed to the chair.

"Sit," he ordered Trystan.

I half expected Trystan to snark back at him and put up a fight. But the God of the Sky was quiet as he prowled forward, his gait confident, and his hard cock already evident through his gray cotton pants.

Trystan sat, and Nerethus ran his hand through the Griffin's hair. Trystan's eyes shuttered closed at the Dragon's touch.

"Say it." Nerethus smiled.

Trystan chuckled and Nerethus's hand tightened, pulling on Trystan's hair and baring his neck.

"Say it," the Dragon growled.

Trystan smiled but his eyes were hazy with pleasure. "Please, Nere. Kiss me."

"That's better."

I managed to sit up on trembling elbows, watching them carefully. Nerethus met my gaze and flashed me a wicked smile as he fisted Trystan's hair, pulling his head back even farther so that the Dragon could press a hot kiss against his lips.

Trystan moaned and Nererthus swallowed the sound.

"Mmm, you taste like her." Trystan smiled, sucking my cum off of Nerethus's lips.

"Like blackberry wine," Nerethus whispered back. The Griffin groaned in assent.

"Fuck yes."

Their mouths battled for dominance as Trystan savored my taste. Nerethus broke off and the Griffin hissed, missing his touch.

Nerethus blurred, moving too fast for me to see, but suddenly he bit Trystan's neck, tearing the skin with a wet noise. The Griffin jerked before his head fell back with a loud moan.

"Oh fuck, you're such a bastard," Trystan moaned, his hand going to his hard cock. The next second, his pants were gone. Trystan palmed his length, stroking himself as Nerethus drank deeply.

I couldn't look away as Nerethus slowly reached a hand down and brushed a thumb over the precum gathered at Trystan's tip. The Griffin shuddered. "Please."

Nerethus pulled back, not bothering to close the wounds. Blood dripped down Trystan's chest and for some reason... I wanted to taste it.

I had never craved blood. But right now, I needed it.

"Do you want a taste, Elsing?" Nerethus asked calmly.

Wait. What happens if I drink the blood of a God?

Trystan's eyes shot to me and he smirked, challenging me to say no. Seeing that on his face erased all of my concerns.

"I do," I answered the Dragon finally, and Trystan's eyes nearly fell out of his head. The Gods watched as I scooted off the bed and approached them, naked as the day I was born.

"Hello, pet," Trystan purred, but Nerethus yanked his hair back, baring Trystan's neck to me.

The blood of the Gods is said to be sacred. I watched as a bead of blood dripped down Trystan's abdomen, my mouth filling with saliva as hunger suddenly turned my belly into knots.

I needed to taste him.

I needed it more than I needed my next breath.

Reaching forward, I brushed a hand against his hard cock, making him jerk as I stuck my tongue out and licked the blood trailing along his ripped abdomen.

"FUCK," Trystan moaned at the sight.

I couldn't respond as his blood hit my system. My magic wanted to explode and I trembled, not because of Trystan's blood but because of the effort it was taking to keep my magic under control. My veins filled with fire, but it didn't hurt.

No. It felt good.

So fucking good. My mind emptied of all thought and there was just *need, need, need.*

"What's happening?" I moaned, rubbing my legs together, desperate for some friction. "What the fuck did your blood do to me?"

"Our blood has certain… aphrodisiac qualities," Nerethus explained.

"Surprise." Trystan's laugh told me he was immensely enjoying the way I squirmed against him.

I licked up every drop of blood and made my way up Trystan's chest until I was at his neck. Nerethus caressed my hair and murmured quiet praise as I fit my teeth into the fang marks and bit down hard.

"Ohhh, yes." Trystan's moan was so guttural, it made my core flood with moisture.

I didn't have sharp fangs but the wound had already been made. Simply squeezing it made the blood flow in earnest again. I swallowed him down with a greedy moan. He tasted like the sky. So much, I wondered if we were no longer in the confines of the Aive, but on a cloud.

Then Trystan began to move, thrusting his hips into the air as he moaned in pleasure. I pulled back, blood covering my body. Ropes now held Trystan to the chair as he strained, stroking his cock even harder as more precum began to drip down the side.

"He's feeling the effects of my bite too," Nerethus commented, leaning down to take another short drink from the wound on Trystan's neck.

I was transfixed at the sight of the blood covering his face.

It only enhanced the Dragon's beauty.

Leaning forward, I gently grabbed Nerethus's chin and tilted his face towards me.

I met his ruby gaze. "Kiss me."

His answering smile made my heart stutter. "Do you think you're in charge here, Elsing?"

Begging it was, then.

"Please. I-I need more. Kiss me. Touch me. Just fucking do something, *please.*" My voice cracked as the pleasure made me tremble. "I *burn.*"

Trystan moaned again. "God fucking damnit, Dragon. Don't just sit there. Give our pet what she needs."

Ours.

Ours. Ours. Ours. Ours.

The word repeated over and over in my head, driving me into a lust-filled frenzy.

Nerethus licked at my lips, working my mouth open with his tongue until I opened. He fucked me with his mouth, swallowing my moans of pleasure as I wrapped my arms around his huge body.

His hands landed on my waist as he easily lifted me into his arms, not even straining. I wrapped my legs around him, never breaking the kiss.

We were a blur as he transported us back to his bed. I hit the covers hard, bouncing twice, but Nerethus was already on me, pressing our bodies together.

"Watch, Trystan," Nerethus ordered the bound God. "Watch as I fuck Elsing. As you sit there unable to move or do a damn thing about it." Nerethus's eyes burned with lust as he pulled my legs apart.

"Fucking bastard," Trystan snarled, but his eyes were still filled with need. "Show me her cunt. I want to see what I'm missing."

Nerethus spun me on the bed so my open legs faced Trystan.

"Show him," the Dragon whispered in my ear, his breath on my cheek. "Show him that pretty pussy, Elsing."

I trembled under the weight of Trystan's gaze.

It made me feel like my skin was on fire. There was power in knowing that merely seeing my body did this to him.

A *God*. I did this to a *God*.

Trystan moaned at the sight of my wet, used pussy and I opened my legs farther, the action spreading my lips open for him.

Nerethus chuckled in my ear. "It feels good, doesn't it? Seeing how much he wants you. Look at how hard his cock is, all shiny and covered in precum. That's all for you, Elsing."

Trystan growled, fighting against his bonds, his yellow eyes blazing. "Fuck yes it is. Now take care of her before I shred these fucking ropes and break every single one of your precious rules and do it my damn self!"

"Do it and I'll slit your throat," I hissed, and the Gods chuckled. I blinked in confusion.

"We are immortal," Trystan smirked, "and we heal fast."

"Most of us enjoy a little violence," Nerethus chuckled.

Then he was spinning me back to the side so that Trystan could watch as Nerethus dragged his hard length through my wet folds, coating himself in my pleasure as his cock turned shiny. The Dragon let out a pleased groan. "You're so wet."

There was a moment when he paused, and I realized Nerethus was debating how much to hold back, not wanting to hurt me. His cock was huge. The biggest I have ever taken. There was a worried look on his face.

"Don't hold back," I ordered. "Don't you fucking dare."

Nerethus's eyes shuttered. When they opened, the red of his irises glowed as if lit from within.

"It's going to be a tight fit."

I reached down and wrapped my hand around his cock, squeezing. His entire body jerked and his eyes shut as a moan fell from Nerethus's lips.

"Good," I snapped, baring my teeth at him in an open challenge. "Now show me what it's like to be fucked by a *God.*"

The answering snarl shook the entire castle. In a single breath, he pushed inside of me. I gasped in equal parts pain and pleasure at the feeling of his hard length.

I hadn't had sex with a man in many years, and my muscles aren't used to it. But I relished the burn.

He pushed in farther, and I moaned at how delicious it felt.

But it wasn't enough. He was still holding back and treating me like some fragile human.

I didn't want the man.

I wanted the *Dragon.*

"You're holding back." My voice was raspy as I threw the Dragon's own words back in his face.

Nerethus met my gaze, the beast hovering beneath his skin.

"Humans are so fragile." Another five centimeters. "I don't want to hurt you."

I wasn't about to give him a choice in the matter.

I shoved him back and he fell against the bed, his red eyes alight with lust. The Dragon watched in rapt silence as I crawled into his lap and lined up my core just above his hard cock.

With a deep breath, and in a single move, I spear myself on him, taking his entire length.

"Gods!" My cries mixed with Nerethus's moans.

"Ride him," Trystan encouraged. "Ride his giant cock, pet. Suck him dry."

I lifted and sat down again, my hips beginning to circle as I rode him hard.

Stars burst behind my eyes and every nerve ending in my body lit on fire as the pleasure became too much.

With a snarl so loud it shook the glass, Nerethus flipped us so my face was pushed into the covers, and my ass faced Trystan.

The Griffin groaned. "Fucking Hell. Now that's a sight."

Large hands palmed my cheeks and Nerethus made a low, pleased sound. Then a sharp, snapping sound followed by the sharp sting of pain as he spanked me. It's followed by massaging, and then another slap as his palm smacked against my cheeks.

I moaned at the hot sting of pain, my core growing wetter. Another slap, but this time I jerked as his palm slapped my clit. My mouth opened on a scream but at that very second, Nerethus thrust inside me. I cried out, stretched and deliciously filled.

Nerethus picked a demanding, harsh rhythm, fucking me with reckless abandon. All I could do was hold on. Nothing else existed except the feeling of him.

"You feel so good," I groaned into the sheets. "Don't stop. Don't ever stop."

"That's it, take it all. Take every fucking inch," he growled, thrusting harder and harder until I swear I could feel him touching my organs.

Maybe the afterlife was a myth, because it felt like paradise.

Then another feeling rose within me.

One infinitely more dangerous.

Hunger.

"Harder!" I ordered, needing more.

"Fucking perfect," Trystan groaned in the background. "She's perfect."

Nerethus yanked me up, turning us so I faced Trystan. He fisted my hair, bending my head back so that I was pressed against his chest. His other arm wrapped around my waist, holding me up easily.

Nerethus began thrusting again in earnest and my eyes fell closed.

I ceased to exist, merely a conduit for pleasure as the Dragon drew another orgasm from me.

"Come again with me, Elsing. Give me one more," Nerethus murmured, panting. "You've been so fucking good for us."

"I don't think I can," I whined, my voice hoarse.

Nerethus chuckled. "I can smell that you're lying, Elsing."

He was right. It might kill me but Gods, what a way to go.

All I could think of was *more, more, more.*

The world disappeared and my screams filled the room as I exploded in an orgasm so powerful, I almost passed out.

With a raging snarl, Nerethus emptied himself inside of me, his entire body trembling.

I was a mewling, shuddering mess as Nerethus slowed. My entire weight was in his arms as we sat in silence, trembling in the aftershock.

Slowly, he pulled out. I whined in protest, missing him instantly.

"I'm not going anywhere," he murmured, lowering me lightly to the bed, brushing my damp hair out of my sweaty face. He wrapped me in his arms, rocking us gently as his hands rubbed my back and arms.

Who was I, anymore? Whining and begging for a man.

Though they donned the shapes of men, they were not.

These were Gods, and I finally believed them. I've had many lovers before, but nothing, *nothing* came even close to this.

"Such a good girl," he purred in my ear. His praise felt like standing in the warm sun.

"What about me?" Trystan's eyes were feral as he struggled, mad at being held captive for so long. Thick ropes of white liquid coated his stomach.

Nerethusmade a *hmm* noise and released me from his hold, his elbows to prop himself up on the mattress so he could look at Trystan.

There was a look of decadent relaxation on the Dragon's face. The type of look that was only brought on by intense lovemaking. He seemed lighter. Happier.

In his relaxation, he was even more divine. I drank him in. All that deep umber skin glowing, accented by the slight red outline of scales.

He glanced to the side, looking at me with a lazy smile and oh—to be looked at that way. His ruby eyes were full of pride and contentment.

I couldn't look away.

"What do you think, Elsing? Was Trystan a good boy for us?" he asked, glancing at Trystan and then back to me. "It is, after all, *your* punishment."

Trystan smiled wickedly as I pushed myself up to a sitting position on shaky arms. A warm hand landed on my lower back as Nerethus helped me up.

Trystan made a low noise as I widened my legs, watching Nerethus's pleasure drip out of me. The Griffin's yellow eyes were locked on my core. He licked his lips, trembling with need at the sight of it.

Then I remembered how he pushed me off a mountain.

This mountain.

And for that, I was still *furious*.

"No."

My voice echoed through the room and Trystan blinked in surprise. Nerethus simply watched me, his head cocked.

"No, he wasn't good at all. So I want you," I reached a hand down and swirl it through the trail of cum dripping out of me, "to lick me clean, but don't swallow it. I want you to hold onto it and then go over there and spit it in Trystan's mouth."

Trystan's jaw dropped. "Holy *fuck.*"

Nerethus went stiff, his eyes almost rolling back in his head. "It would be my *pleasure.*"

One second later and I had a Dragon's head between my legs.

He angled us so my legs were spread as wide as possible, allowing Trystan to see right inside of me—and see everything Nerethus does.

I nearly exploded as the Dragon lifted a finger, gathered our combined cum, and pushed it back inside of me.

"Oh my *God*." My moan is high-pitched as he fucks me slowly with his long, thick fingers, using our pleasure as lube.

"You look so pretty in my cum," he commented. The wet squelching noise he made with every thrust of his fingers bounded through the room and Trystan groaned.

"I want to taste her, lizard. Hurry the fuck up."

Nerethus glanced back at the Griffin with a smirk. "No."

Then slowly and methodically he added another finger, stretching my sore inner walls.

That soreness quickly turned to burning need as his hands heated up, relaxing my muscles further.

"So tight," he muttered. "Still so tight. Someday soon, you'll fit us both at the same time." I nearly *exploded* then and there.

Then the Dragon's fingers were gone. I whined, feeling empty, but his mouth replaced his hand and he shifted his tongue, sliding it all the way inside of me like a hot, wet cock. My hands slid into his hair to hold on.

With his long tongue, Nerethus licked away every drop of pleasure. It was slow and methodical. He took his time with it, turning me into a puddle.

I moaned, riding his face lazily, as my soft cries turned to pants.

Nerethus pulled back after a while. My vision had gone hazy but I watched as the Dragon stood, mouth full, and padded naked over to Trystan. The Griffin's eyes were unhinged and he licked his lips, struggling against the ropes.

Not to escape, but to pull Nerethus closer.

The Dragon ran his wet fingers up the Griffin's neck, clasping him beneath the chin and tilting his head back.

Trystan opened his mouth and stuck his tongue out with a wild smile on his face. The sight sent shivers down my spine and I *hungered* again.

I sat up more and watched with wide eyes as Nerethus leaned down and spit our creamy pleasure on the Griffin's waiting tongue.

Trystan moaned and his eyes fell shut as he swallowed it all with glee.

"Such a greedy slut," Nerethus purred to Trystan, and my jaw nearly fell off my face. The Dragon pressed a hot kiss against Trystan's lips and they moaned, both caught up in the moment. Trystan's bonds disappeared, and then the Dragon was in front of me as he pulled me into his arms and scooted us up onto the bed.

I meant to say something to Trystan. Something snarky.

But exhaustion hit me and suddenly I was unable to keep my eyes open. Everything faded and I listened, as if from far away, as Nerethus and Trystan spoke in a different language. They went back and forth for a while as Nerethus wrapped me in his arms, caressing and petting my hair.

"Fine. Fucking FINE." Trystan's footsteps leaving the room followed his outburst.

A part of me felt bad. But that part was so far away.

A bigger part of me didn't give a fuck.

"Get some sleep," Nerethus whispered, pressing a kiss to my temple and inhaling my scent. Within seconds, I was drifting to sleep without a care in the world, tucked in the arms of the monster who devoured me.

the god of death

chapter 10

I woke up the next morning sweaty and overheated. Likely because a fire-breathing Dragon in the shape of a man was wrapped around me like a lichen against a sea rock.

As carefully as I could, I eased out of the Dragon's hold, desperate for the cool morning air.

I glanced back, looking him over.

He was so serene like this. His black hair mussed and a sleepy smile on his face.

I forced myself to turn away.

It was so much easier to hate the Mountain Gods when they were awake.

I thought this situation would be black and white. Instead, it's an amalgamation of gray.

I exhaled and imagined my strained emotions leaving my body. Once. Twice. Three times.

Numbness descended and I welcomed it, but it was thinner than it was before—and more easily broken.

I quietly walked over to the large dresser near one of Nerethus's piles of treasure. It seemed the legends of Dragons hoarding riches were right.

Ornate chests filled to the brim with gold coins, jewels, and encrusted crowns decorated the far wall.

Gott Verdammt!

The Dragon had enough money in his bedroom to support a small nation for a hundred years!

With a sigh, I quietly opened the dresser drawers and found another one of his shirts. Sliding my arms through the holes, I let it fall over my body. This one came nearly to my knees, so I didn't bother with pants.

The soft cotton fabric smelled like him: fresh sage and the warm heat of Dragonflame.

I padded out of the room and headed to the living area. My throat felt like shit after all of the screaming last night, and I desperately needed water.

The Aive was silent.

Trystan must still be asleep as well.

Which meant that for the moment, I was alone.

I walked slowly, stopping periodically to examine the hallway more closely in the morning sunlight.

The paintings that lined the wall seemed innocent enough, but something caught my eye.

A scene of men and women enjoying tea.

It seemed innocuous enough.

But something about it was... *wrong.*

I leaned in closer and realized their faces all had faint skeletons visible on their skin. I could almost hear their screams echoing in my ears, as if from a distance.

Their tea cups were not filled with tea, but blood. I blinked, and the scene animated, blood overflowing and dripping down their cups, covering their hands in red.

Their screams grew louder and for the briefest moment, it was so loud I wondered if they were standing next to me.

Another blink and they went back to normal as silence descended once more.

I continued walking and a dark feeling settled deep in my stomach as I realized that every single portrait on the wall was the same.

I will not be afraid, I told myself. *No matter what dark secrets the Mountain Gods held here.*

But the portraits seemed to watch me as I passed them, causing the hair on my arms to stand on end.

I almost passed the last painting when something stopped me.

It was a portrait of a man and his hound.

Simple enough.

And yet.

And yet, something about it disturbed me.

Perhaps it was how the dog seemed to be drooling blood. Perhaps it was how the collar around its neck looked to be made of ivory finger bones that stood out starkly against its black fur, attaching to a leash that appeared to be made of... *stomach lining.*

I felt bad for the dead dog, but it was the hateful, dead look in the man's flat eyes that bothered me the most.

One blink and the man was screaming at me as the dog barks.

I leaned forward and pinned the man with my glare. "Scream at me again and see what happens."

I allowed a small amount of my magic to rise to the surface. Whatever the portrait saw within my face, shut him up.

"I thought as much."

The answering silence was bliss, even though my unease lingered.

I shook it off and walked the rest of the way into the living room, the stone floor cold beneath my feet.

Unsure how to use it, I grabbed a cup off the shelves near the counter and put it under the water spout, turning it all the way to the left.

Water shot out of the spout so hard it sprayed me, soaking through the white shirt I threw on minutes earlier.

"Scheiße," I hissed, turning the water spout off. My cup was full but the counter was soaked—as was I.

Annoyed, I turned around, only to run into a wall.

Déjà vu made my mind whirl as I backed up, realizing I didn't run into a wall, but a person.

"Nerethus—" I broke off as I looked up and met the pale green eyes of a complete stranger.

I tried to say something else, tried to will my mouth to move.

But I couldn't speak. I couldn't move. I couldn't do anything at all as I gazed into the eyes of one of the oldest beings to exist.

The being in front of me looked like a man for all intents and purposes. A very normal man with tousled dark blond hair and the shadow of a blond beard on his face. He wasn't quite as tall as Trystan and Nerethus, or as wide and bulked with muscle, but that did nothing to detract from his power. His coloring and his features were plain in comparison to the beast Gods, but somehow he was even more striking.

One look and I knew this man was infinitely more powerful than the others.

But this wasn't not a man.

This wasn't even a God.

Shadows swirled around the edge of his image, trailing around his arms and lifting his hair as if on a phantom breeze.

The look in his eyes though. The way black and silver lightning flashed within his green irises.

One blink and he was all shadows, a black cowl over his head as eyes of pure onyx watched me. A giant scythe was held in his right hand, with the staff end touching the floor. Screams of the dying sounded in the distance.

One blink and it was gone.

This was not a man.

This was *Death*.

"What," his voice was rich and calculated, with an accent not of this world, "are you doing in my house?"

I will not be afraid. I refuse.

I took a deep breath and shielded myself, infusing my body with strength.

"I am not here willingly," I responded, my voice trembling.

"And yet, you are still in my house."

I shrugged. "Ask the Dragon. He's the one who brought me here."

"How?" he demanded, and took a step closer to me.

I gasped and stepped back until the cold counter met my skin, but he followed, crowding me, so close I could smell his spicy cologne in the air and feel his breath on my face with every exhale.

He was dressed casually, in simple black cotton pants with a white short sleeved tunic that was practically painted on judging from the way it hugged every curve of his bicep and the planes of his muscular abdomen. Death looked normal—except for the black tattoos covering his bare arms.

The tattoos twitched and moved, winding around his forearms and fingers like live snakes made of inky shadow sitting just underneath his skin.

I snapped out of it and realized I was staring.

Meeting his gaze, I refused to back down or show him an ounce of fear. "I was poisoned and left to die just within the border of the Mountain Gods' realm, and I woke up here. So tell me, Death..." The God of Death blinked in mild surprise. "Are you always such a shitty host?"

The God's eyes closed and he took a deep breath, the shadows around him pulsing and writhing in anger. When he opened them though, there was no anger.

Just interest.

Far too *much* interest for my liking.

"It seems much has happened while I was asleep. My friends have much to explain," he said, but he didn't back away. He continued inspecting me, searching for any weakness.

"It's rude to stare," I said, and the God of Death smiled again.

But that smile sent chills up my arms.

"Is it?" he asked, a pleasant smile on his face. "You forget yourself, little human. You stand in my kitchen." Death looked me up and down, goosebumps following on my skin. "You stand nearly *naked* in my kitchen, in a wet T-shirt, no less." I sputtered, trying to come up with a rude response. But words died on my tongue as his green eyes met mine. "I will stare at whatever I please. That includes you."

I understood now what Nerethus and Trystan meant. How they're Lesser Gods, and Death was Higher.

An Original, they called it. One of the first Gods. One of Five.

I didn't fully understand then, but as I looked Death in the face, the difference was plain to see.

"Aleks!" Trystan called as he and Nerethus walked into the living area, right on time. The Griffin walked over to the God of Death and slapped him on the shoulder. But Death didn't move a muscle, unaffected by the Griffin's immense strength. "I see you've met our new roommate."

"Yes, care to explain? I did not authorize an uninvited guest."

Trystan rolled his eyes but I noted the flash of fear in his yellow eyes.

The Dragon followed into the room, approaching us and tucking me against his side. I allowed him to put an arm around me, relishing in his warmth. I didn't realize how cold the room had become until just now. My breath created a cloud of fog with each exhale.

"I found her half-dead and felt it prudent to bring her here," Nerethus explained calmly. "I would have asked, but you were away."

Aleks crossed his arms. "You see wounded animals all the time. What made you adopt this one?"

Anger quickly replaced my fear. "I am no animal and you will not address me as such."

Trystan choked and Nerethus went so still he might as well have turned to stone.

But Aleks just smiled lightly. "That remains to be seen. This is my home, human. I will address you however I please."

I sniffed, unafraid and unamused. "How comforting to know that even the great God of Death is still just another *Kotzbrocken* male. It's a relief, really." Trystan made another choking noise and I turned to him. "Something wrong, Griffin?"

"Nope," he replied with a cough, busying himself and looking away.

Nerethus tightened his arm around me and Aleks blinked in surprise. Then the God of Death switched languages. Death and the Dragon go back and forth, and whatever was being said seemed to piss the latter off, because a low growl quickly echoed through the room. Death didn't seem worried, but Trystan pulled me out of Nerethus's arms so we could watch from a distance.

"You've done it now. I haven't seen Nerethus this pissed off in centuries," he said quietly.

I cleared my throat and looked at the Griffin, announcing loudly, "So you mean I *shouldn't* mention how you fucked me with your tongue in the hot springs two days ago?"

Trystan's eyes went wide and he looked at the God of Death, who's full attention he had. Nerethus looked at me with a small smile on his face, fully aware of what I was doing.

Was I being protective over the Dragon?

"It seems we have *much* to discuss. You will update me on everything that's happened while I was Below. Now," Aleksander said, walking out of the room.

The three of us didn't move for a moment, unsure what to do. But then Nerethus sighed. "Come on, Elsing. We must follow Death to the library. I convinced him to go easy on you, but... he is owed some answers and it cannot be avoided. Even by me."

So.

Death was in charge here.

That was a problem.

"Fine," I bit out, and we followed Death to the other wing of the Aive.

The paintings didn't scream at me this time.

"We're in trouble," Trystan sang. There was a low grunt as Nerethus elbowed him in the stomach. "Rude," he complained.

"Get over it," Nerethus growled in response.

The fire was lit and roaring when we entered the library. This time, I actually looked around, admiring the floor to ceiling rows of books.

Thousands of tomes bound in various shades of leather climbed towards the never ending ceiling.

I carefully, *so carefully*, reached out with my magic and tasted the spell. Spicy black pepper coated my tongue and I had to swallow the sneeze that built in response.

Death built this.

I didn't understand how I knew, but of this, I was sure. I took a seat on the chaise lounge I woke up on just a few days prior.

Trystan took a seat on the floor, his wings manifesting as he spread them out, allowing the fire to warm his feathery appendages. One of his wings rested delicately on my knees and I absentmindedly reached out to caress the soft feathers.

Death watched, a cold look in his green eyes.

"Let's start from the beginning." The gorgeous man pinned me with a dark stare. "I am Aleksander, God of Death, Original, Soul Eater, Reapyr of the Damned, and Lord of the Below. All know and fear me. Now, who the fuck are you and why are you in my house?"

One blink and his black cowl returned, the shadows curling around him. Another blink and he was back to normal.

I waved him off with my hand. "Do stop the shadow show. If you're trying to scare me, it won't work."

Aleks blinked, and for a moment I swore he fought a smile.

"Tell me who you are, or I'll eat your soul." The air went cold and Nerethus growled again but suddenly the sound stopped.

I glanced to see ropes of shadows holding Trystan and Nerethus down, making it very clear he would stop them from catching me.

Death could stop them.

Fuck.

"My name is Elsing Wylder," I begrudgingly answered.

"Elsing Wylder." Death removed the shadows from the other Mountain Gods and Nerethus wrapped an arm around me, his warm thumb rubbing a slow circle on my abdomen. "Why were you left for dead in the Helvetas? Within our territory, no less?"

I needed to be careful with this. Careful and honest, which was a delicate rope to walk.

I didn't look away from Death as I responded, "I was taken to Schollen Gorge, beaten, poisoned, strung up, and left to die at the hands of the Mountain Gods."

"Clearly. But you did not answer my question." Death narrowed his eyes. "*Why* were you in that position in the first place, Elsing Wylder?"

I don't think any of them were prepared when I shrugged and answered honestly. "Because I murdered someone."

the murder

chapter 11

"How interesting." Death watched me with a new gleam of interest. It was his area of expertise, after all. "That explains your aura."

"Excuse me?"

One corner of his mouth twitched in a phantom smirk. "I'm the God of Death, Elsing Wylder. Do you think I do not see the black abyss of your soul? It's a color that only appears on souls who have taken a life. I was confused as to why it was on yours."

The truth about my murderous past sat heavy in the air. Nerethus and Trystan looked at me with equal parts curiosity, concern, and lust, which was both concerning and a turn on.

"And why did you kill someone?" Death prodded me for more answers.

They would get the truth, but only a piece of it.

"I killed the man responsible for the death of my best friend. Her name is—*was*—Daphne. Her name was Daphne."

Saying her name hurt, but Aleksander must have sensed the honesty within my pain because he nodded, going quiet. Nerethus pressed a soft kiss to the side of my head and my heart warmed.

Even if I didn't want it to.

"Revenge," Aleksander murmured. "An admirable notion. Stupid, but admirable. Tell me about this murder of vengeance, Elsing Wylder. Let me taste your rage."

His shadows seemed to hiss in anger, as if ready to strike.

I imagined hissing at them right back.

"One week ago, I began the process of poisoning a man named Albrecht Bucher. He was Interlaken's butcher." I had to pause my story to glance at Trystan as he burst out laughing.

"Wait, wait. You're saying the butcher was named Bucher? That's *dumb.*"

Aleks shook his head in annoyance. "Continue, Elsing. Ignore the wayward bird."

Trystan scoffs but I continued. "Daphne is... *was* my best friend. She died six moon cycles ago because her husband accused her of adultery."

The fire crackled in the corner and suddenly I was too warm.

Suddenly I was watching her demise again as I recounted the tale. "The Republic lists adultery as one of the major sins, and the Interlaken Shauptmann deemed it evil enough to deserve death. There was a trial, but it was useless."

Nerethus continued rubbing my side with his thumb, drawing slow circles on top of the thin tunic fabric.

It grounded me, and I hated him for it.

"Nothing could have been said or done to change his or Albrecht's mind." I paused, thinking over my next words carefully. "After Daphne was killed, I turned my focus to Albrecht. I knew I'd get caught but I didn't care. I wanted him to die a painful death. I wanted him to *suffer* just as she suffered."

I met Death's gaze again and *smiled.* "So I stole some hemlock and deadly nightshade from the Apothe." I left out that nothing had to be stolen, because I was the Apothe in question. "I mixed the poison and went to Albrecht's house, claiming I wanted to atone for Daphne's sins. It's pathetic, really. How easily men are swayed by wide eyes, red lips, and a hint of cleavage. He never questioned why I was seducing him, the daft idiot."

Trystan snorted, a look of predatory pleasure on his face.

"We drank wine and I pretended to laugh at all of his sexist, horrible jokes. He never tasted the hemlock in the wine or the nightshade I had rubbed on my lips. Just as he was about to slide his fat, ugly cock inside of me, the poison hit his heart and I laughed as Albrecht Bucher took his final breath. His body was discovered the next day in a rather... compromising position in the town square. Someone had dragged his corpse into the stables and positioned him like a little piglet, mouth pursed to suckle on a milky teet."

Death didn't react, but the corners of his lips twitched as if he fought a smirk.

"I was blamed, of course. They all expected me to deny it, to fight the charge. But I regret nothing. He deserved the suffering and humiliation. I told the Shautpmann as much and I was tossed into a prison cell to await trial, despite the fact that I knew what fate would befell me, regardless of any court proceedings."

I considered my next words. "It was decided that I didn't deserve a swift death. I was to suffer. So, after a night of being tormented in the stocks and pelted with rotten food, I was taken to Schollen Gorge, poisoned, beaten, and strung up. I thought the Mountain Gods would kill me and I'd be eaten alive. I never expected to wake up in their *gottverdammt home.*"

"Wait, you thought we were going to... *eat you?*" Nerethus said, shock in his voice. "We do not *eat* humans. Why would they think that?"

"Well..." Trystan coughed and sent Nerethus a look. "We don't *usually* eat humans. But sometimes we get a bit peckish. Humans don't taste good but beggars can't be choosers. The mountain goats around here are fucking *fast.*"

I blinked. "You were outsmarted by a goat?"

His face went stone cold and Trystan looked away with a tight sniff. "I don't want to talk about it."

"How embarrassing for you. The Great God of the Sky, a Griffin, outsmarted by a pea-brained mountain goat the size of a fat cat."

Trystan's eyes went from normal to glowing in an instant and suddenly he was on his feet, looming above me.

"Sit. Down." Death didn't yell, but his voice bounced off the walls of the library, a layered sound filled with the screams of the damned.

The fire banked as the air turned so cold my ears hurt. Death's shadows whirled, angry and very much alive.

The Griffin bared his fangs but sat back down, his eyes lit from within. "I'm going to fuck you until you scream, pet. You know what happens when you push me."

Despite the cold air of the library, I'm suddenly burning for his touch. Our eyes remained locked as my breath came fast and hard. I pressed my thighs together, desperate for the friction.

"The Griffin is right. Neither of us eat humans. Well, uh, not *anymore* at least," Nerethus commented, looking chagrined. "And the poison in your system would have poisoned *us* if we had eaten you. I do not like the taste of hemlock and nightshade. It hurts my stomach."

I glanced at the Dragon. "Oh poor you, you might get a tummy ache. How fucking miserable. Meanwhile I was hallucinating and shitting myself."

Trystan snorted.

I looked back at the God of Death. "That's how I ended up here. I killed a bad person who deserved to die, and I don't regret a single moment. In fact, I'd kill him again if I could, that fucker."

Aleks was silent for a moment before he stood with a nod. "Well, you're stuck here for now until we figure out another arrangement. A house of your own somewhere within our territory, perhaps."

"Right. You're all cursed."

Aleks pinned his friends with a heated glare. "Just how much have you told our guest?"

Nerethus met his gaze but Trystan looked away.

"They told me enough to explain why I cannot leave, as that was the first thing on my mind when I woke up with two strange men staring at me." I waved my hand towards the beast Gods.

"We're not creeps, Elsing." Trystan sounded so affronted, but Nerethus blushed slightly.

"That remains to be seen." I repeated Aleks's earlier words and the God of Death looked mildly amused.

"You can stay here for now. I will create a new wing for you—"

Nerethus interrupted him. "No. She will stay in my room. I can stay with Trystan."

I turned to the Dragon. "Who said I want to stay with you?"

Nerethus's brows furrowed and hurt flashed through his ruby eyes.

Aleks added, "You want her in your space? Is she the newest treasure in your trove, Dragon?"

I went still, looking at the Dragon and expecting his denial.

But he said nothing. Instead he looked... *sheepish.*

Oh my Gods.

I'm his treasure.

"Elsing will stay in my room, for now," the Dragon growled, flashing his white fangs.

"No," Aleks said. Nerethus stood an instant later, smoke streaming from his nostrils. Aleks rolled his eyes. "Calm down. She will stay in my room and the three of us will stay in your wing."

"Why?" Nerethus snarled, sounding unhinged. Even Trystan looked at Aleks with confusion in his golden eagle eyes.

"Because, I don't trust her, and you're getting dangerously attached for having only known her for what, two days? Use your fucking brain, Nerethus. We do not know this woman."

"Fine," the Dragon bit out, but I'm surprised the library wasn't on fire. He sounded furious. "But she *can* be trusted, Death. This I know."

"Hm." Death leaned back in his chair, the tattoos on his arms writhing and twirling beneath his skin. There was a flash and I realized he was wearing thick silver rings on a few of his fingers.

His *very large* fingers.

Don't think about that. Don't think about that. Don't think about that.

Two Gods was plenty. Too much, even. I don't need to fuck with Death too.

Even if he was the most beautiful person I've ever seen in my entire life.

Aleksander glanced at Trystan. "The Dragon says she can be trusted. What say you, God of the Sky?"

Trystan's body was still, but his neck twisted like an owl as he looked towards me.

Goosebumps break out over my body and Nerethus growled. Aleks snapped his fingers and the room went black. Before I could scream, the light of the fire illuminated the library once more.

Nerethus was no longer beside me. He was pinned against the bookshelves near the fire underneath rope made of shadow. The Dragon struggled against the shadow bonds, his eyes glowing red and his fangs fully extended.

"Answer me, Griffin," Aleks asked, his voice like velvet night.

Trystan stood slowly, prowling towards me with a hot look in his eyes.

My breath came faster and I rubbed my thighs together again.

The God of the Sky looked at me like I was his next meal.

He placed both of his hands on either side of me, leaning forward and trapping me within his arms.

"I'd like to propose a bet," he said with a wicked smile, not to me but to the God in the chair behind him. Aleks examined one of the ropes of shadow as it winded between his fingers.

"What's your bet, Trystan?" A curious glint flashes through the God of Death's cool green eyes.

For a moment, fear rose within me.

Then I squashed it.

I will not fear him.

The God of the Sky leaned down and nuzzled my jaw, pressing kisses up the side of it until he reached my ear. Then he sucked my earlobe into his mouth.

My lips parted on a sigh and I tried to keep my eyes open, but it was so hard.

And what he was doing felt so good.

Trystan pulled back and smiled at me, the picture of dark delight. "Our new pet is a bit of a sadist. I was forced to watch as Nerethus fucked her and licked her clean. So, Death, I'll bet 100,000 gold coins that when I tell Elsing to spread her legs, right here, right now, so I can lick her tight cunt, she'll do it."

My jaw hit the floor and I sputtered, shocked beyond belief. Trystan lifted a hand and stroked my collarbone, sending bolts of pleasure bursting through me at his touch. The fight slowly bled out of me with every stroke of his fingers. "If I win, then I say she *can* be trusted."

"And if she tells you to fuck off?" Aleks asked, watching the emotions warring across my face.

Trystan's answering smile was bloodthirsty.

"Then she can't be trusted and you win. *Again.*"

Fury made me forget the fragility of this situation. "Fuck you. What makes you think I'd *ever* listen to your orders? What makes you think you *deserve that?*" I was seething and nearly seeing red. "I'll give you the answer and save you the time, you fucking asshole. You don't deserve that. You don't deserve *me*. Fuck off, Griffin. "

Nerethus growled, looking ready to commit a murder himself. Aleks merely watched, looking amused, curious, and completely untrusting of anything I had to say.

Trystan, on the other hand, didn't react.

His gold eyes gleamed and a predatory smile appeared on his face.

That didn't bode well.

"Humans are so... prude. I doubt she will do it," Aleksander said.

My fury shifted into rampant indignation at his words.

He thought I was weak—so I willed myself to stone.

"And Gods are such assholes," I add, lifting my chin.

Hands gripped my wrists and yanked my arms into the air. I looked around, frantic, and realized no hands were holding me.

No physical ones, at least.

My feet dangled a few inches off the ground as Trystan controlled the air in the library, using it to hold me aloft with invisible hands.

Trystan leaned back, watching me struggle with pleasure in his yellow eyes. "Did you forget? I am God of the Sky, pet. I control the very *air you breathe.*"

My lungs suddenly ached as a heavy weight settled on my chest. I gasped, trying to breathe, but it was no use.

Trystan stood, coming to my side as he flicked his fingers and the air flooded back into my lungs.

I struggled against the invisible bindings that held me, but it was no use.

"Put me down," I demanded.

Trystan shook his head. "Nope. Now, be a good little pet and spread your fucking legs."

Aleksander inhales. "I can smell how wet her cunt is." I must have hallucinated it, but for a moment, I could have sworn hunger flashed through Death's eyes.

A full-body shiver worked its way from my toes to my nose at his words.

Scheiße.

I shouldn't want this.

And I... I didn't. Not like this. Not for the reason Aleksander might think as he watched me struggle in the invisible bands holding me aloft.

Trystan nodded back to him. "She's quite the little slut, our pet. Always wet and ready to be filled with cock, like a good little fuck toy." The Griffin looked back at me with a wicked smirk. "Now, I said *spread your fucking legs.*"

the small death

chapter 12

"Say no and he stops." Nerethus's voice cut through the haze of lust.

I met his gaze.

"Repeat my words, Elsing. This is a lot for a human, and you need a safe word."

I nodded, trembling. "Fine. How about *hemlock?*"

Nerethus nodded. "*Hemlock.* Remember it. You say *hemlock* and everything stops. "

"Good girl," Trystan purred, then he did something I really should have seen coming. "Now let's show Aleksander what he's missed."

Invisible ropes hooked into my still damp shirt and rolled it up, baring my core and my breasts to the Gods in front of me.

Hands made of air gripped my ankles, spreading my legs open.

I growled, struggling to escape and shut my legs against the power that pulled on me, but it was no use.

I was completely exposed. There wasn't a single part of my body they couldn't see.

I quivered under the weight of their gaze.

Aleksander's eyes remained on mine. I watched, breathless as his eyes began to travel down my body so very slowly.

He stopped at my breasts, staring for so long it made me restless. Then his eyes continued their path south.

So wet it was dripping out of me, Aleksander stopped, staring at where I ached most.

Trystan lifted a hand, running the tips of his fingers through my wetness, swirling it around. "You're such a fucking slut, pet. Look at you. Your cunt is crying to be touched."

My heart raced.

"Is she this wet every time?" Aleksander asked, his voice neutral and unaffected. I didn't imagine the way his eyes turned pure black and the shadows around him darkened, shrouding him in midnight.

He might pretend to be unaffected, but I could see his control wavering.

Nerethus fumed in silence. His red eyes burned with fury and need. A glance down between his legs confirmed the latter. The Dragon's huge cock was straining against his pants. Drool floods my mouth at the sight.

He liked watching too, then.

I met Trystan's yellow gaze and bared my teeth. "Are you going to just stand there or eat me out—" My words ended in a strangled moan as the God of the Sky dove between my legs, his tongue lapping at my core.

His hands reached back to grip my generous ass, each palm on my cheeks as he pulled me tight against his lips.

"Oh my God, that feels so fucking good," I whined. Already, my body was on the verge of explosion.

Simply being watched by the Gods at the edge of the room was enough to get me there. The feeling of their eyes on me, their lewd comments about my body and what Trystan should do to me—it was enough.

The rough feel of Trystan's hot tongue sent twitches through my core.

"Are you sore from last night?" he whispered against my wet cunt, lapping up every bit of my arousal.

"A little," I admit.

"I'll play nice this time, pet," Trystan purred. "But next time, it'll be both of our cocks inside of you. Mine and the Dragon's."

My walls clenched around his fingers as I imagined being filled to the brim by both of them at one.

Death didn't move. Didn't get up to join. But he never looked away.

Not once.

The shadows around him grew darker as he focused on my nipples. His tongue darted out as if he was physically craving me.

Was this divinity?

The sensation of three, all-powerful Gods wanting me, wanting to be the ones wringing pleasure from my body, their names a moan on my lips—it was divine, and I wondered if maybe this is what it meant to be Godly, to be *more*. Maybe it felt like this. I am not one, but at that moment, I *was* a God.

They worshiped the temple of my body and prayed at the altar of my pleasure.

Trystan, true to his word, remained gentle, even as his fingers picked up the pace. His fingers curved, tapping against where I'm most sensitive, and his other thumb drew slow circles around my throbbing clit.

"Why don't we show Aleksander just how talented you are, pet."

I was suddenly overtaken with the sensation of being touched by dozens of invisible hands. They pinched my nipples and caressed my breasts, swirling around my core and pressing against the hole between my cheeks.

His fingers pumped in and out of me. I whimpered as a warm sensation washed over my lower stomach. My back arched and with a ragged moan, the climax hit me.

Liquid gushed from me and Trystan let out a happy moan, bending down to lick me from asshole to clit and back again as he swallowed every drop.

"Such a good little pet," he purrs against my lips. "How does it feel? Knowing they're barely a meter away, watching as I play with your needy cunt." Trystan emphasized his words with a pump of his fingers. I moaned.

The invisible hands lowered me until I was laying back on the daybed, with Trystan standing over me. He cupped my sex, his fingers brushing the short black curls on my mound.

Trystan leaned down and brushed his lips against mine. "This is mine now, Elsing Wylder. This pussy is *mine.*"

I gasped but Trystan pressed his lips against mine, swallowing the noises I made as shock turned to need.

"I can't wait to fuck you until you scream," Trystan whispered, turning to walk over to Aleksander. I panted, struggling against the invisible hands that pressed me into the lounge.

Everything went hazy as I watched as Trystan dropped to his knees in front of Death.

Aleksander didn't rush. He watched Trystan for a moment before his arm darted out, his hand around the Griffin's neck.

"Have a little taste." Trystan's voice dripped with pride.

Death said nothing. He simply leaned forward and kissed him. Trystan let out a quiet moan as Death sucked on the Griffin's lips, tasting my pleasure.

The shadow of Death's hard cock slowly began straining through his tight pants. The veins of his arm bulged, like it was taking every ounce of control not to unleash himself on us.

On *me.*

Death made a low, pleased sound as he pulled away, sitting back in his chair. Trystan was unbothered. He stood and walked back over to me.

I felt the invisible bonds dissipate and suddenly I was able to move.

"Aleks, give me your shirt," the Griffin demanded. "Our pet worked up quite the sweat being a little cum slut for me."

Aleksander raised a brow, but to my shock, he nodded. With smooth, precise movements, he stood and stripped off the tight short-sleeved shirt he was wearing and—

Oh.

My.

Fucking Gods.

Every ounce of logic emptied from my head as I took in Death's tattooed torso. At the silver bars piercing his nipples, at the way some of his tattoos were *alive*, just like the shadows on his arms.

I couldn't look away. It was too much to take in.

A faint trail of darker blonde hair trailed down his stomach, disappearing into his pants. While he's the shortest of the three, he's pure muscle. It was like looking at a painting. He was too perfect to be real. They all were. And yet here they sat, watching me, needing me.

What the hell is happening to me?

"I need... some space." Suddenly, I was desperate for some air.

"Are you okay?" Nerethus asked with concern. He had gotten free from the shadows and crowded me from behind, his hand hot on my lower back.

His presence wasn't oppressive or overwhelming.

But it should be, and that was a problem.

"I'm fine. Almost dying just takes a lot out of a person. Getting tongue-fucked by a God in front of a complete stranger while being held in the air does too."

True. All true.

Trystan motioned for me to lift my arms and I did, allowing him to slide Aleksander's shirt over my head.

My eyes nearly rolled back into my head at the intoxicating scent of Death. Spice, like pepper and patchouli, mixed with the heady, smoky scent of incense.

"I'll show you to your room for the time being, then." Aleksander stood and light returned to the room as the firelight glowed.

Yet again, he looked normal. Unreasonably handsome and a little terrifying, but he looked like a man.

It was a facade. One meant to lull me into a false sense of security.

"Fine." I flashed him a tight smile. "Lead the way, Soul Eater."

I didn't miss the way Aleksander stilled at my use of his nickname. It seemed this was one he didn't like, based on the cold look in his eyes.

"Until next time, pet." Trystan winked. I rolled my eyes at his antics, though I appreciated his levity.

It was needed. Especially since I no longer have Uri.

On silent feet, I trailed after Death as he walked out of the library, turning right, and disappearing down the hallway. This is a part of the Aive I haven't been in yet. I followed tentatively, because with every step the air grew darker and darker, until I actually ran into Death's hard back, unable to see that he stopped.

His bare skin against my cheek was cold and refreshing. I wanted to wrap my arms around him and get lost in his spicy scent.

His muscles tightened and something in that movement shook me out of it. I stepped back quickly, pretending nothing was wrong.

Still, Death said nothing.

With a wave, the hallway behind us disappears, and the air lightens, exposing some sort of door.

An entire wall of shadow snakes guard a huge black iron door accented with a plain silver doorknob.

"This is my room. Touch anything and I'll—"

"Yeah, yeah," I breathed. "You'll eat my soul. I get it. You don't need to keep saying it."

Aleksander sighed and opened the door, stepping through the threshold. I eyed the shadow snakes warily. Small red eyes blinked where their heads were, like rubies within midnight fog.

One of the snakes reached out and I paused, seeing what it would do.

But it just sniffed me. If it even had a nose.

"They're memorizing your scent," Death called. "Ignore them."

I don't know what I expected from Death's room.

But wasn't this.

It's... *leather.*

Everything, aside from the silky black bed sheets, was leather.

The four poster bed frame was all black leather, stamped and attached with dark silver studs.

More macabre artwork lines the walls, along with various torture instruments and paintings of scaping, bloody battle scenes.

I slowly turned to Death.

"I prefer the Dragon's room."

Death eyed me with thinly veiled disdain. "Too bad."

"It resembles a dungeon," I attempted to reason with him, feeling uncomfortable.

Death shrugged. "Again, I really don't care. You can stay here until we sort this all out. The bathroom is through there." He nodded at the far wall where an open door lay next to a leather upholstered dresser and small black writing table.

"Your friends were better hosts." I picked an invisible piece of lint from the shirt he lent me, adjusting my demeanor to match his.

If he wanted to be mean, that's fine by me.

I could be mean too.

Death went still, his jaw locking in frustration. In a single second he was standing right in front of me, bearing down on me.

My breath caught in my chest at his proximity.

"Let's get one thing straight, Elsing Wylder." The air cooled to match Death's frosty tone. His shadow snakes appeared again as his eyes turned black. "You are in *my* house. Just because two Lesser Gods think your cunt is made of gold doesn't mean you get any leeway with me. You think yourself above fear, but you're just an ignorant little girl. You know nothing of true fear. Though," Death paused, leaning in close until we were almost nose to nose, "if you keep being a pushy little brat, I will show you, and I can promise, you won't like it."

"You don't have a fucking clue about me, Soul Eater."

It's so brief I almost don't catch it, but Death *inhaled* and for a moment, I felt a tug at my chest, beneath my breastbone.

Everything went blurry and then I snapped back to normal, my skin tingling.

"Fuck with me, Elsing Wylder, and I *will* eat your soul."

Oh *fuck.* That feeling of something being pulled from me was Death *inhaling* my soul.

Then he was gone. In a breath, Death disappeared, leaving me alone in his sparse bedroom.

I sighed and sat on the end of the bed, my head in my hands and my heart filled with discontent.

Where is Uri when I need them?

I miss my familiar.

I miss my friend.

the glade

chapter 13

With Death awake from his astral slumber, we adjusted to a new normal. I spent most of my days in the living room or Death's leather-covered dungeon reading books from the library.

I blazed through histories and tomes about the Helvetas. Most of these books I had never seen before, and some were so old I was scared to turn their pages, lest the pages fall out. But the interesting part was how they all contained sections and chapters I've never read.

The Republic was keeping more secrets—and I intended to find out why. I was reading an encyclopedia about the flora and fauna native to the Helvetas. Half of the herbs were unknown to me, and most of the animals listed are now extinct. Suddenly, the feeling of being watched rushed over me and I looked up from my book to see Death, leaning against the library door, his tattooed arms crossed.

Death glared.

I glared back.

He raised a perfect blond eyebrow and his snakes writhed in the shadows.

I looked unimpressed, because I *was*. He thought he could intimidate me?

Ha!

Somehow Nerethus always managed to sense when tensions were running high. Whenever Death and I began our glaring competition, the Dragon mysteriously appeared and got all growly, worried that I was upset or hurt.

All the while, Trystan would watch from the background, wicked amusement in his eerie yellow eyes.

I ignored the winks, even if it made my core throb.

This cycle repeated daily.

I avoided them, and they left me alone.

I could only guess that Aleksander ripped the two Lesser Gods a new asshole for so easily falling for my charms. He was right. They trusted too easily.

It had been two weeks since any of them last touched me. Nerethus treated me like I was practically made of glass, much to my annoyance.

But this was for the best.

It had to be.

My... *emotions* were getting the best of me. This much distance was helping me stay neutral. At night, when I was fast asleep, that neutrality dissipated as the three Gods took over my dreams.

Every single night over the past fourteen days I've dreamt of them.

Of their hands and mouths roaming my body.

Of the Dragon's low praise.

Of Trystan's pleased moans.

And worst of all?

I dreamt of Death kissing me with enough passion to burn the world to the ground.

The book in my hands slammed shut and I stood, suddenly overheated and in need of fresh air—and some goddamned space.

"I want to touch the ground," I announced to Death.

Nerethus was by my side a second later. "Are you alright? What do you mean by this?"

"Nerethus," I said, trying not to get annoyed. "You ask me that every day. I'm *fine.* But I am also not used to living amongst the clouds. I miss the ground, Dragon. I miss the real world. I want to feel the mud beneath my boots."

True.

All true.

And yet, it was also a *complete and total lie.*

Aleksander surprised me by nodding. "Why don't you take her to the glade?"

Nerethus blinked. "I... I should have thought of that."

"Mhm," Aleksander agreed. "You should have. Take that feral bird with you. He's annoying the shit out of me lately. Celibacy doesn't suit him."

So no one had been fucking, then.

Nerethus sighed and looked back towards his wing of the Aive, as if staring through the walls.

Seconds later, Trystan appeared next to Aleksander, wearing black leather pants and no top, the silver feathers in his brown hair askew. "What's up? You said we're going somewhere?"

I pressed my lips together so as to not allow a single drop of drool to escape, lest he realize just how horny I was.

But God, he was so beautiful. They all were. The longer I was around them, the more I was affected by it.

Maybe this was a bad idea.

"Let's take a flight and visit the glade. Elsing wants some fresh air."

"Fuck yes." Trystan nodded before looking at me with a smile. "I've missed you, pet. You're riding *me* today." Trystan winked and suddenly I was tossed over his shoulder, my ass in the air.

"Don't you dare throw me off of this mountain again you overgrown pigeon!" I screamed as he walked out to the living room. I pounded my fists against his back but it didn't slow or stop him. If anything, it seemed to amuse him.

"Hold on tight!" He laughed, using his magic to open a window. Still over his shoulder, he breaks into a run.

"You fucking BASTARRRRRD!" My scream turned manic as he jumped out of the window. The wind made my eyes water and sucked the breath right out of my lungs as we began plummeting towards the ground.

"I AM GOING TO KILL YOU!" I screamed into the clouds as I pushed off Trystan's back. He disappeared from sight and I'm *falling, falling, falling.*

Then I hit something.

It wasn't hard like Dragon scales.

It was as soft as a pillow.

I righted myself on Trystan's back, trying to grasp onto his soft feathers.

Trystan flapped his huge brown and silver wings, hovering as Nerethus caught up. The Griffin looked back at me, his neck twisting in that unnatural way.

Then the bastard *winked.*

That was the only warning I got before he tucked his wings against my legs and dove straight down towards the ground. I nearly tumbled from his back but gripped his feathers tightly, burrowing down into the thicker section of feathers around his neck.

"I'm flying with the Dragon next time," I hissed into the Griffin's ear.

I never thought birds could pout. But I swear the asshole pouted at me, his eyes wide and innocent.

I blamed my answering smile on the freezing wintar air that numbed my senses. Clearly my brain was numb too, or I was just permanently fucked from too much poison.

The sky went black as Nerethus approached, his giant black wings flapping slowly. Trystan flew in between the mountain peaks and I began to relax, enjoying the slower speed of things.

A hard, warm nose nudged my back and Trystan let out an affronted squawk. But I allowed the Dragon to nuzzle me from behind. The fact that such a large being was able to regulate their flight to such a minute detail was beyond me. The precision and skill it took to not just follow Trystan but to maintain his exact speed enough to nudge me was... well, impressive.

And a bit terrifying.

Nerethus removed his warm snout and overtook us, his great scaled body blocking out the sun and coating us in darkness for a moment.

Trystan let out another affronted shriek.

"There's nothing wrong with going slow, Griffin," I reminded him. "Be grateful he doesn't turn you into roast dinner."

I stroked one of his neck feathers, marveling at how silky they were. The Griffin shivered beneath my touch.

"Well, well, does someone have a feather fetish?" I teased him, petting his feathers slowly. Trystan squawked but it was hesitant.

So he did have a feather fetish then.

How interesting.

I tugged lightly on one of his neck feathers and the Griffin made a choking sound. My laughter echoed against the wind.

We coasted through the mountains, weaving in between the snowy peaks, and I found myself relaxing for the first time in weeks.

Wintar in the Helvetas was harsh, leaving most of the plants frozen beneath layers of ice and snow. The only sound to be heard was the light whistling of the wind and the flapping of wings. The snow absorbed all other noise, blanketing the world in blissful quiet.

The already harsh terrain was even harsher at this time of year. We passed another mountain, descending further. If I reached my hands out, I could touch the snow.

But without gloves, that sounded like a miserable idea and a quick way to get frostbite.

Trystan and Nerethus descended slowly and landed in a large, flat valley below the western Helvetas.

I went to slide off Trystan's back but he raised his wings, keeping me from dismounting. A second later and I understood why, as Nerethus suddenly blew a huge stream of fire on the glade floor, melting the snow.

The air grew hot and sweat dripped down my back, coating the black dress I put on this morning. It was tight but comfortable, with leather laces cinching in the waist and long, gauzy sleeves that fell off my shoulders.

Last week, when I went into Aleksander's room, clothing was waiting for me. Clothing that fit *perfectly*. Most of the items were black, but there were a few white tunics and dark blue gowns I was saving for later.

Black was useful after all. It was so good at hiding the color of freshly spilt blood.

A bright flash of light and the Dragon shifted, becoming a man once more.

A very *naked* man.

Nerethus walked barefoot over to me and put his hands around my waist, lifting me off the Griffin. I slowly slid down and we both inhaled sharply as his hardening cock brushed against my stomach.

The cold air made my nipples hard—noticeably so—and judging by the way his eyes widened, the Dragon noticed.

Another flash went off behind me as Trystan shifted, leaving him naked aside from the silver and brown feathered appendages tucked against his back.

So.

Very.

Naked.

And I was directly between them.

"Can't you just... magic some clothes on? I've seen you shift and you didn't lose your pants," I sputtered.

Trystan smirked and wrapped his arms around my waist. Nerethus watched, his ruby eyes missing nothing.

"Your cheeks look a little bit red, pet. Do you feel overwhelmed, being in between two naked Gods?"

I grit my teeth, angry at how right he is.

"Hear that?" Trystan asked Nerethus, "Her heartbeat sped up when I said that. I think our pet likes being trapped."

Do not fear.

The thought ran through my mind and injected steel into my bones. I met Nerethus's gaze without embarrassment. "And if I do? What the fuck are you going to do about it then, Dragon?"

Trystan chuckled in my ear as smoke trailed out of the Dragon's nostrils.

"Oh dear." Trystan laughed. "I think our Dragon likes when you challenge him."

Ours.

Ours. Ours. Ours.

"I do." Nerethus's voice was all beast when he answered. "But, I also know Aleksander will eat our damn souls if we fuck up this little 'trip.'" The Dragon stepped closer and his hard cock brushed against my abdomen.

With a single finger, he reached up and brushed my hair against my cheek, tucking it back behind my ear. "If we had all the time in the world, I would burn your clothes off and fuck you right here. I would give that greedy little cunt exactly what it wants: to be used and filled. Isn't that right?"

Oh *fuck.*

I couldn't even form words but I managed some semblance of a nod.

"Yes, I thought so." Nerethus learned forward and pressed a kiss against my lips. I moaned into him but he pulled back, making me pout.

I blinked and stepped to the side, needing space from the heat of their bodies. "Yes. Well, I'm going to look around and enjoy being on the ground again."

Trystan's brow furrowed. "Yeah, what exactly is it you want to do?"

I sent him an annoyed look. "I'm going to look at the fucking plants and walk around. I bet no one has been in these parts of the Helvetas for centuries, thanks to your little curse. That means new plants, new trees, and new flower species. What else do you think I'd do?"

"So you like plants." Trystan nodded. "That's, uh... That's cool. I like mountain goats—" Nerethus slapped the Griffin in the back of the head.

"What? It's true!"

"You like *killing* and *consuming* mountain goats. This is not the same."

"You know what? That's rude. At least my hobby isn't collecting useless *treasure.*"

The answering roar was all I needed. I walked away from their lovers' tiff, the black leather boots Aleksander gave me squishing sounds in newly melted mud with each step.

There was no noise but I paused, looking behind me.

Both Gods followed behind me, their eyes wide and curious.

"No. Absolutely not. This isn't how this is going to go. Are you planning on following me around all day like godsdamn wet nurses?" I glared at them, despite the fact that I actually didn't mind their company at all.

I should have minded. I really should have. The fact that I didn't was exactly why I had to be such a bitch.

It was for the best.

Nerethus looked hurt but nodded. "Fine, come on, Ryst. Let's hunt some mountain goats. I'm hungry."

The Griffin sighed before shocking me by leaning in to press a hot kiss to my forehead. His lips were so soft as he took his time, whispering, "Be safe, pet. Or I'll spank the shit out of you."

Another flash of light as they both shifted into their beastly forms and flew off, leaving me alone once again.

The forest was silent. The only sound was my heart *thud thud thud-ding* in my ears.

Okay.

Time to get to work.

I spent hours looking around the glade, inspecting the different plants and grasses left over from sommer. Most were dead, but some were surprisingly still alive, protected by the dead leaves that insulated the seedlings before the snowfall.

A few herbs caught my eye and I pinched them off at the base, tucking the stems in the waistband of my undergarments.

Potion making has never been my favorite activity, but I easily fell into the familiar habit of foraging. It was so relaxing.

No noise, no company. Just me and the forest.

I shoved my racing thoughts into a box and imagined chucking it off the mountaintops as I zoned out, thinking only about the plants in front of me.

Nerethus and Trystan returned a while later, both covered in blood and bits of white fur. They shifted and Nerethus shoved Trystan into the mud with a splash.

"The fat one was mine, you shit," the Dragon snarled, furious.

Trystan cackled maniacally as he got up and shook off the mud, causing it to hit the Dragon in the face.

"Back so soon?" I called pleasantly, walking over to them.

Nerethus looked taken aback. "The sun is almost setting, Elsing. We've been gone for hours."

I blinked, looking to the sky. It was covered in shades of red and purple as the sun began to disappear to the west.

"Oh. Right," I said, and at that moment the cold hit. My hands shivered and the wet mud began to soak into my boots.

"Fuck, we need to get you home. You're so cold," Nerethus grabbed my frozen hands. The Dragon shifted and Trystan helped me onto his back. The Griffin surprised me by remaining in his human form, choosing to sit behind me on Nerethus's back instead of shifting.

"You need my warmth, pet," he whispered in my ear as Nerethus took off. My shivers got worse and Trystan wrapped his arms around my waist, his large hands resting on my lower stomach. He pulled me back against him, his cock pressed into my ass.

The thin membrane in between the Dragon's black scales began to glow dark crimson. Seconds later and his scales heated as he channeled his fire.

I sighed happily.

As we flew home, the sun set fully and darkness blanketed the world.

Above the clouds, I could see so much more. Galaxies of every color swirled and glimmered between purple and silver stars. The moon was full tonight and I could faintly make out the dark craters etched on its surface.

It felt like a dream.

I lifted my hands, safe in Trystan's arms, as if to touch the glowing white moon above.

"Do the Gods know what it's like to wander amongst the stars?" I wondered, twining my fingers through the evening air. The thought was meant to stay in my head, but Trystan squeezed my sides as he pondered the question.

"Only the Originals. But sometimes I think we're not meant to go there. That it's... not for us to understand," Trystan said, shockingly thoughtful. "Aleksander has certain stars he frequents. It scares me."

Nerethus snorted in what I assumed was agreement.

"There are things even the Gods cannot know."

Another question plagued my mind. "Who made the Gods, then?"

Trystan was quiet for a moment.

"The Lesser Gods, like Nerethus and I, were all created by the Originals. Most of us were made by Pennios, the God of Light. But oftentimes one or two of the others would create in tandem."

"Well, someone made Pennios. Who, then?" I asked, my arms dropping to my sides.

"We do not know. They simply *are*. There are only five of them. First came Pennios, the Lord of Light. With the creation of the first star, eons and eons ago, *light* came into being, and with it, Pennios. Anemara was next. You know her as Love."

I listened as Trystan explained how the Gods came to be. "Pennios and Anemara are so strong, it created an imbalance in the universe. No matter what, there must *always* be balance. Good simply cannot exist without evil. One cannot go on without the other. It's the Great Conundrum. Out of this imbalance, a giant black hole the size of our world erupted, and out from it, Aleksander and Rhaeta emerged. Death and War."

"A black hole?" I gasped. I've only read vague theories written by psychotic, narcissistic old white men, but I knew enough to understand.

"And no," Trystan nuzzled my neck as he draped his soft wings on my shoulders, "before you scurry off and ask him about it, he doesn't remember anything before he emerged."

Hm. Interesting.

"Sometime later, Uriel was born. No one knows what from though."

"So the Lesser Gods are born from the Originals? Does that mean Death's your daddy then?"

I didn't know it was possible for Dragon's to forget how to *fly*, but one second everything was fine, and the next, we were plummeting towards the ground as Nerethus made some horrific choking sound.

Trystan sputtered as Nerethus righted himself, flapping his wings to stop our rapid descent.

I glanced over my shoulder at Trystan, who stared at me with wide eyes and pursed lips.

His body quivered lightly and I realized he was holding back a laugh.

"You—you think Aleksander is our father?" Trystan exploded with whooping laughter, nearly falling off Nerethus's back as the Dragon continued the journey back to the Aive. "Holy shit, I can't breathe. Oh Gods, I wish Uriel was here to see this."

Trystan was still snorting as I continued on, unable to let go of something that's been bothering me. "There *is* something beyond the Original Gods, then," I glanced back at him. "Something—or some-one—pulling the strings. Gods don't just randomly exist. Someone *made* Aleksander and the other four."

"Maybe." He shrugged. "Or maybe it's all just a game of chance. Dump all of the players on the table and see what happens. No purpose, no agenda. Just energy and nature," Trystan said quietly, his laughter finally finished.

"Hm."

I thought over our conversation as we approached the Aive. It looked so different from this angle. Thanks to the mostly calm journey, I can finally get a close look at everything. The light of the moon shone brightly upon the glass castle amongst the clouds.

It was so modern on the inside compared to Interlaken and anything I've ever seen, but the outside was traditional. Glasswork lattices framed giant windows covering nearly every surface. White and silver metal connected between the glass, winding around the mountain.

For the mountain to have curved around the Aive like this, it must have been built centuries ago, when the land was young and wild.

Long before the Republic became our reality.

Nerethus slowly descended and gripped onto a long silver bar attached to the mountainside. This allowed him to perch and pull up next to the open doorway connected to the living area.

I hadn't noticed the bar before.

Trystan held out a hand and helped me off, setting me within the doorway. He jumped after me, landing with a roguish grin.

A bright flash of light announced Nerethus as he shifted, swinging into the room.

Yet again, they were both completely naked.

"Thank you for the ride," I said quickly, giving them a nod before turning to head back to the library like a scared little puppy.

"Dine with us, Elsing." A hot hand on my waist stopped me. I glanced back at Nerethus, who now stood right behind me. "I... *We* miss your company."

Trystan smiled, coming up to stand next to Nerethus. "We also miss the taste of your pretty pink pussy."

I bit my lip and met the Dragon's ruby gaze. "And Aleksander? You expect me to believe he misses me?"

Trystan coughed. "Okay well. We as in... the two of us." He motions to himself and then the Dragon. "But Aleksander is... intrigued. I can tell."

I crossed my arms. "Oh really? I think that's a damn lie. The only thing Death wants from me is my ass *out* of his house. I am an unwanted guest to him, and nothing more."

"Regardless," the Dragon started, "we still would like it if you dined with us this evening. Nothing has to happen."

Trystan started to interject and voice his displeasure at the idea, but Nerethus snarled, shoving the Griffin away from us. The Dragon was so strong, Trystan nearly flew into the air as he tumbled to the ground.

But then Nerethus was right there, cupping my cheeks and tilting my face up towards his. "Nothing at all. This is whatever you want it to be, Elsing. But I... Dine with us tonight. *Please.* I want to fuck you until the only name you know is *mine,* but more than that... I just want *you.*"

Gottsverdammt!

I pulled away from him, ignoring the hurt in his eyes as I stomped out the room, pissed off.

This wasn't how this was supposed to go.

He was falling in love with me and I could see it so fucking plainly on his face that it *killed* me.

Before I could stop myself, I called back to them. "Fine. I will dine with you tonight, but one of you is cooking."

I turned away again before I could see the stupid smile I knew was on Nerethus's gorgeous face.

Mutter, gib mir Kraft.

Mother, give me strength.

the meal

chapter 14

The stone floor was cold beneath my feet as I walked silently down the hallway, ignoring the way the skeletal paintings glare.

I'm not scared. I'm *anxious*.

My heart beat faster than normal as I attempted to control the wild energy running through me. The slowness was difficult, but in the battle of wills against my body, my mind would always win. So I forced stillness and calm into every step, every breath, every *thought*.

Three male voices sounded from the distance as I approached the living area, my black dress trailing behind me.

This one was made of a silky material so thin it was nearly sheer. But on top was a delicate layer of red glitter so fine it was barely perceptible. The wet look of the silk and the shimmering detail on top of it gave the dress the appearance of being made out of fine Dragon scales.

Ones that matched a certain Dragon I know. The arms of the dress ended in bell sleeves, and the glittering mesh traveled all the way to the ground, dragging along with the train of the gown. It would be modest, with the long sleeves, if not for the low-cut neckline. I added a crimson red corset with black leather laces on top of the dress. My already large breasts were heaving with every step I took, nearly exploding out of the top.

My black hair hung loose behind me in bouncy waves, shining from the rose oil I had painstakingly brushed through it.

I dug through the cabinets in Aleksander's bathroom and found a bloodred lip rouge and some kohl. A few moments earlier, I had smudged a light line above my eyelids and painted my lips until I barely recognized the person reflected in the bathroom mirror.

It was all worth it as I turned the corner and entered the kitchen area.

A loud, shattering sound followed as Trystan dropped the bowl he was carrying. Ceramic shards scattered along the floor, but Trystan paid no mind. His yellow eyes were wide and his jaw was practically on the floor.

Nerethus, who was dressed in a fine white shirt and tight gray trousers, watched me with hungry eyes.

The air warmed and the fireplace behind me in the living area roared as it doubled in size.

"Don't you dare shift inside my castle, Nerethus." Aleksander's order cooled the air as the shadows bubbled. The Dragon growled in return and Death rolled his eyes. "Two words, beast. Self-control. Try it."

Nerethus flashed his fangs, but Death ignored him and looked directly at me. He met my eyes and time stopped. They lowered, slowly roving over every inch of me from head to toe, as if he was savoring the sight of me.

His gaze finally lifted, meeting mine again.

A blink, and pale green turned pure black as a gray cowl appeared over his head.

Another blink, and it was gone.

The other Gods froze as Aleksander walked towards me, resplendent in black leather pants and a plain black short-sleeved shirt.

He approached me, stopping so close we were nearly touching. His black pepper and patchouli scent rushed over me and made my insides turn molten.

Death raised a hand and gently ran a finger down the side of my face.

Then one of his snakes left him. It traveled down his finger and onto my face. It felt... not how I expected. The shadow snake was *warm* and soft, so soft it almost tickled me as it slid down and around my neck, settling around my clavicle like a necklace. The burning that followed was unexpected too, but it was brief, as the snake settled into my skin like a tattoo.

Or a *collar*.

"I don't recall giving you permission to collar me, Aleksander," I sneered, furious at the thought.

He watched me, arms crossed as the other snakes writhed on his arms, some still beneath his skin.

"I don't recall asking," he responded calmly.

"Am I your property now?" I lifted a hand to touch the shadow snake on my neck, but there's nothing. Merely a tingling warmth on my fingertips.

Aleksander crossed his arms, watching me with a suspicious glint in his eyes. "Yes. You are." He raised a hand and ran it over the snake. "Everything here is."

The shadow trembled under his touch, causing my skin to tingle. Goosebumps broke out on my arms as Death ran a finger along the snake's back, tracing around my collarbone. "Now I can keep an eye on you."

I went still. "First I'm your property, and now you want to spy on me? You've got some serious trust issues, Soul Eater."

"I don't trust anyone," he said, his voice hollow.

First, I pitied him.

Then I *understood* him.

"How sad," I taunted, and he stepped back, startled at my read. "Poor Death is *lonely*."

"It's not sad, it's life." he hissed. "I do not busy myself with such silly things as human emotions. I am the end of all things and when there is nothing left on this godforsaken earth, I will stand alone, watching over the souls of the damned for all eternity."

I crossed my arms. "*Scheiße*, you're so dramatic."

"I've been saying that for years actually. But can we pick this up a little? I'm *starving*," Trystan interrupted. His stomach growled loudly a moment later. "Finish whatever fucked up, weird foreplay this is later.

Preferably while I watch."

I looked at him fully and *my* jaw nearly detached.

Trystan wore a leather kilt, exposing every bit of his toned legs. That's not what made my heart stutter though.

It was the way Trystan's shirt was shimmering red and completely fucking sheer.

Just like the top layer of my dress, his shirt accented a bright red bite mark on his neck that I knew he could heal.

It was there because he *wanted* it to be visible.

My gaze snapped to Nerethus, but the Dragon merely flashed a pleased smirk.

So.

Dragon staked his claim, each of us dressed in clothing resembling the Dragon's scales.

Except for Aleksander.

No one can claim Death.

Nerethus approached, pulling me away from Aleksander and bending down to press a soft kiss to my temple.

"You look good enough to eat." The Dragon's voice in my ear made my knees weak enough that I had to grab onto him just in case they gave out. "I *particularly* like the way you and Trystan wear my colors. It makes me *ravenous*, Elsing. Absolutely. Fucking. Ravenous."

My exhale was shaky as Nerethus gently pulled back and wrapped an arm around my back, his hot hand perched just above my ass. The Dragon escorted me over to the big wooden table next to the glass window.

The moon was still full from earlier, but now there wasn't a single cloud in the sky.

And tonight, we dine amongst the stars.

Nerethus, ever the gentleman, pulled out the chair for me. I bit my lip, hating myself for how much it made my heart burst.

He leaned down, whispering in my ear as he pushed my chair in. "If you want the shadow gone, all you need to do is say so."

"You could do something about it?" I asked casually.

But he had gotten my attention.

Nerethus's breath tickled my cheek. "For you? I would bring the entire Helvetas down upon him."

The Mountain shook, the floor beneath my feet tilting slightly. It was so subtle, I would have missed it if not for the tinkling noise of the silverware and plates knocking together.

"It won't kill him, but it will delay him significantly. Long enough for us to hide our tracks."

"What about your treasure hoard?" I asked.

Nerethus pressed a soft kiss to my cheek and I wanted to melt into his touch. Staying upright was a struggle.

"You're the only treasure that matters, Elsing. I have everything I need right here."

The Mountain rumbled more and dust fell from the ceiling. Trystan blinked, his brows furrowed in confusion.

Death watched us carefully and I couldn't look away from his green gaze.

A low growl sounds in my ear. "Give me the signal and I'll do it, Elsing."

I stilled.

Death was to my left, sitting at the head of the table, which put Trystan across from me and Nerethus on my right.

"It's fine," I told Nerethus, but the Dragon didn't look convinced. "For now," I added.

Breaking out of the trance of Death's gaze, I turned my head and looked into Nerethus's ruby eyes.

I allowed a small smile to form on my face, reflecting the warmth Nerethus's words made me feel.

Thank you. I tried to convey the words and the Dragon settled, mollified for the time being.

The snake around my neck was unexpected, but not a problem.

If I was a human, it might have been. But I'm not.

I was shocked, though. Nerethus and Trystan would... help me *escape*.

They would leave the Aive—leave *Aleksander.*

For... *me.*

They would do that for me.

Why?

They barely knew me.

I didn't even notice when food was set in front of me. Trystan made a happy noise, but I couldn't make myself react. The others dug in, oblivious to the war inside of me.

Remember what they did.

Remember her.

As if I could forget. And yet—here we were.

My brain and my heart waged war as I speared a potato. I'm sure it was well-seasoned, but I tasted nothing.

I cannot fear. *I will not.* Nor will I doubt.

"Cat got your tongue, pet?" Trystan teased, a playful smirk on this face. "You're unusually quiet. By now, you're usually telling me to 'go fuck myself' but you haven't said a damn word."

I fought my way out of the daze of my mind. "Perhaps I have nothing to say," I replied, taking a bite of some mystery meat that I really do not want any information about. I bit down and cringed at the texture.

"Oh. Do you... not like meat?" Nerethus asked, sounding concerned and confused.

Trystan went still but Aleksander continued eating, content to watch our verbal volleys.

I sighed and grabbed the cloth napkin next to the plate setting, dabbing my lips. Behind the napkin I spit out the meat, too disgusted at the fatty, chewy texture.

"No," I said, lifting my chin. "I don't. I will eat it if I have to. However, this," I stuck a fork in the mystery meat and lifted it in the air, "is disgusting and pure grizzle. The chewiness is going to make me *hurl!*"

"What? The fat is the best part!" Trystan cried out around his own mouthful of meat. Red blood from the uncooked center dripped down his chin.

My appetite returned, not for the meat on my plate but for the God across from me.

The God of the Sky winked at me, ever the flirt.

"Freak," I muttered.

"I'm sorry, Elsing. I didn't realize," Nerethus placed a warm hand on my right thigh and I nearly sighed. His warmth always felt so nice.

"You didn't ask, either," Aleksander added.

He was pissing me off tonight.

"Neither did you," I lifted my glass and took a sip of the liquid inside it. Spiced wine and the flavors of cinnamon and citrus danced on my tongue as the alcohol hit my system. I turned to Nerethus and placed my hand on his cheek for a moment, brushing his cheekbone with my thumb. My hand looked tiny against his large face. Everything about him was large.

"It's okay. You didn't know. But do pass me more of those sweet-tasting carrots and some extra potatoes."

"Of course." The Dragon smiled and grabbed the bowls with the extra vegetables, taking his time to spoon them on my plate.

I turned to Aleksander and flashed him a cold, tight-lipped smile. "See, now that is how to have a normal, adult conversation. Something which you seem to have never learned, which I find rather concerning considering how you've been alive since the dawn of time."

Trystan choked on his meat and Nerethus sighed before blurring. He appeared behind Trystan, hitting him hard on the back.

Since the Griffin was across from me, that meant the wad of half-chewed meat landed on my cheek. Nerethus and Trystan watched in horror, the latter cough-laughing, as the mystery meat fell slowly from my cheek, landing in my lap.

"Sorry, sorry. I—uh, took too big of a bite." Trystan cleared his throat as Nerethus returned to my side of the table, taking a seat next to me once again.

"Fate is a bitch." Aleks tipped his glass at me in a mock salute.

"You would know, wouldn't you?" I gave him my most vicious smile, taking a large sip of my wine.

"You know much. Too much." Death nodded to the Dragon and the Griffin. "I take it these two told you about me? About what I am?"

"They did." My voice was cold enough to turn water into ice.

"Then you know that fucking with me is a bad idea. Because Elsing," Aleksander leaned forward, his voice everywhere, echoing around the room in dozens of layers of whispers. *No one is more powerful than Death. Not even a God. Definitely not a wayward human girl.*"

"Oh good, things are getting interesting." Trystan hummed as dust fell from the ceiling and the glass vibrated.

I lowered my voice to a whisper and leaned forward, my eyes wide. "And I still think you're full of horseshit."

Aleksander ground his teeth together so hard I was surprised they didn't break off. He flashed the other Gods a glance. "She's got a fucking death wish, doesn't she?"

"Exactly!" Trystan pounded his fist on the table, a manic smile on his face. "She's insane, just like us. And more importantly, she's not afraid of us. Come on, Aleks! You have to see the appeal. The chances of this happening are zero to none. Stop being such a prickly bastard about it because I know for a fact that you've had a hard-on for her ever since you caught her scent."

My heart thudded and I turned in slow motion, looking at Aleksander in shock. Nerethus tightened his hand on my leg—not in warning, in comfort.

As if to remind me he's there.

Aleksander watched me, frustrated.

I took a sip of my wine, savoring the rich flavor. It was divine. Not that I would ever admit that aloud. Their egos were big enough as it is.

"How interesting." I swirled the wine in my glass. Aleksander gripped the sides of his chair, his rings glinting in the light against the stark black shadow tattoos that moved about his arms. "You don't hate me at all. Here I was, thinking you wanted me out of your house." I huffed a laugh. "But you don't hate me, you hate how much you *want me*. A poor, lowly human." I threw his words back in his face and slammed my empty cup down on the table hard enough to vibrate the plates. "What is it you said, again? Oh, yes. Fate *is* a bitch."

Aleksander went still for a moment and nobody said anything. It felt like the fates themselves were holding their breath, waiting for Death to react.

Nerethus massaged my leg, subtly pushing open the slit of my dress so my thigh was bare to him all the way up to my hip bone.

Trystan shoved his chair back and stood, the sound unnaturally loud against the grating silence. The Griffin stalked around the wooden table until he stood behind me. He reached a large hand into my hair, gripping tightly as he tilted my head back to meet his gaze.

"How about we all play nice for a change?" Trystan's voice was low. Nerethus's hand on my leg tightened as he began running his hand up and down between my knee and my upper thigh.

His fingers bruised higher and higher with each pass.

"Hmm, we could." My voice trembled with need already. "But I don't want *nice.*"

I leaned back in my chair and reached a hand up to grab Trystan's shirt, pulling him down towards me. He happily obliged and slammed his lips against mine. He licked against the seam of my lips, coaxing my mouth open. I acquiesced with a moan.

But this position also gave me the perfect leverage to reach my hand across his shoulders and *scratch.*

His skin broke beneath my nails and Trystan hissed in pain against my lips. Then he kissed me harder.

"I don't want *nice.* I want your *worst.* Show me why everyone fears the Mountain Gods," I whispered against his mouth, our eyes still locked on one another. "Unless you're too much of a fucking *pussy.*"

The Gods went still, the Dragon and the Griffin looking to Death as if waiting for the explosion to come.

I need to make this work.

This needs to work.

My eyes met each God for a few seconds as I leaned back in my chair and let my legs fall open. My knees brushed against Nerethus and Trystan as I reached down and pulled my dress apart, baring myself to them.

"So, what will it be?" I ask them.

Please work.

My worries are quickly assuaged as Nerethus let out a low noise and trailed his fingers up my legs, cupping my cunt and feeling exactly how turned on I was.

I jerked in the chair, hitting my knees against the table, but I was so overwhelmed, I couldn't even feel the pain.

"Oh my fucking *God,* you're so wet," Nerethus murmured, tracing a finger up my throbbing pussy.

He inserted a single finger, curving it up to hit my most sensitive inner walls.

"Oh fuck," I gasped, arching against his hand as my arms flailed for something to hold onto. Trystan grabbed my wrists, pinning them behind my back so I was unable to move.

The Griffin leaned down and ran his nose along my neck, licking and tasting the sweat building on my skin as pleasure built within me. "Look at you, pet. Look at how fucking drenched our Dragon's hand is. He's barely touched you and you're already dripping down his arm, ruining the chair with your cum," Trystan whispered in my ear before pressing a hot kiss to my mouth as he swallowed my moan.

My chair was suddenly gone and I lost my balance, but by the time I could react, I was already in the air as Nerethus slammed me into the dining room table, sending plates and cups flying as they shattered on the stone floor.

He was barely in control as his scales began to shimmer red beneath his skin.

I faced Aleksander, who played absentmindedly with the silver rings that decorated his tattooed fingers. He watched me the way a wolf watched a bunny. Then Trystan was hovering over me, grasping my wrists in one hand as he pulled me flat against the table while Nerethus pushed my legs open, hiking my dress up to my waist. He pressed a hot kiss to my neck as Trystan and Nerethus, in tandem, began to slide down the sleeves of my dress, which pulled my corset just enough to expose my pink nipples to the cold air. The position of the tight garment shoved them up, presenting them to the Mountain Gods.

The Dragon pulled my skirt apart through the new slit he tore in it until there was no hiding anymore. I was completely and utterly exposed to them.

There was a moment of stillness.

No sound. No reaction. Just shock.

Spread across the table like I was Death's dessert.

Aleksander looked me up and down with unabashed slowness. Death took his time.

"You want this?" he asked and I blinked, surprised. Monsters shouldn't care about honor.

So why do they care about mine?

"I know you think I'm just some weak, lowly human. Unable to defend herself against the big scary Gods. But trust me, if I don't want something, you will know. I am not one to suffer in silence."

One corner of Death's perfectly lush lips tilted in a half-smile. "Be careful what you wish for, Elsing Wylder. Be careful what you *unleash.*"

Pissed off, I ripped my hands out of Trystan's grasp and sat up, pushing past Nerethus so that I was on my hands and knees.

"I think," I licked my lips, "the only one you should be afraid of unleashing, Death, is *me.*"

The beast Gods groaned in unison as I slowly and methodically *crawled* towards Death. "Holy fuck," Nerethus moaned.

"Gods yes. Slower, pet. Crawl slower." Trystan's voice trembled with need, but his order sent heat searing through my bones.

My hips swayed back and forth with every movement until I hovered over Aleksander's plate.

Face to face with Death; *Devourer of Souls.*

I sat back on my ankles so I kneeled on the table in front of him.

He never expected the way my hand darted out as I grabbed hold of his hair and leaned in close until our lips nearly touched.

I stopped there and waited, letting him suffer.

"For once in your eternal life," I whispered, "stop worrying about being stabbed in the back. You're an Original. You're a God. So *fucking* act like it and *take what you want.*"

I brushed my lips against his, surprised at how warm they were despite his chilly presence.

Still, Death didn't move.

His eyes were fully black now.

Shadows undulated behind him like he wore a cape made of midnight waves.

"Remember that you wanted this." His voice shook, as if it took all of his energy to keep it together.

But I didn't want him to keep it together.

I was not the one who needed to be unleashed.

It was *him.*

"I *choose* this, Aleksander." He blinked. I realized that was the first time I've ever called him by his real name. I placed my hand on his cold chest. "I choose *you.*"

There was a dark growl followed by a shout behind us as the world disappeared into a haze of black shadow as finally, *finally* Aleksander pressed his lips against mine.

Death felt... perfect.

The feeling of Aleksander teasing my lips with his tongue was like the answer to a question I've never known how to ask.

Our lips fit together so perfectly it made me want to cry. He kissed me with the slow confidence of a male who knew exactly what he was doing.

"You taste like blackberry wine," he murmured against my lips. Aleksander took my lower lip between his and *sucked,* destroying my ability to form a coherent enough thought to respond.

I braced myself, unable to help the way I leaned forward against him. My hard nipples brushed against his chest and he groaned.

"Are you going to steal me away, Death?" I whispered between kisses. "Are you going to hoard me all for yourself in your leather dungeon, the way the Dragon hoards his treasure?" He made an annoyed noise.

"No." He didn't sound happy about it though. He sounded like he wanted me all to himself.

Aleksander pulled away to stare into my eyes and it was an effort not to pout.

I missed his touch already.

Aleksander pressed one last kiss against my lips and whispered against my mouth, "I don't mind sharing."

There was a snapping sound and the shadows disappeared, sucked back into his body, revealing Nerethus and Trystan waiting for us.

"Fucking finally," Trystan asked, his arms crossed. He and Nerethus blurred, launching into action, and suddenly I was splayed out against the table again. Nerethus held my legs open while Trystan held my wrists above my arms, which caused my back to arch.

"Now, let's try this again, shall we?" Aleksander leaned back in his chair and took another sip of wine. He wiped the ruby liquid off of his lips with the back of his hand and I followed the movement, wanting to taste him again.

I glanced at Nerethus but Aleksander's shadows were there, holding my neck in place. Death *tsked.* "No, no, none of that. Eyes on me."

I fought against his hold to no avail. His shadows crawled over my body, making their way to my ankles and my wrists. Somehow he used them to secure my limbs to the wooden table, locking me there. Nerethus and Trystan released their grip and stood back, walking around the table, surveying my body with glowing, heated gazes.

"You all seem to have forgotten who's in charge around here." Death's voice echoed throughout the room, layered upon itself in a way that could be nothing else but divine.

Nerethus and Trystan dropped to their knees as Death's shadows pushed them down. But I never once looked away from Death. Our eyes remained locked; the bunny and the wolf.

"Let me describe what's going to happen." Aleksander took another sip of wine from his glass. "You're going to lay there, open and exposed, unable to move while I wring every ounce of pleasure from your body."

I trembled at his words.

"Right now, my shadows are around Nerethus and Trystan's cocks, jerking them off."

Aleksander smiled as my breath became shallow. "The Dragon thinks you're all dressed in his colors, but he forgot something very important. Black is *my* shade. My color. My *domain*. Which means you're all marked by me. You all *belong* to me. And I can do whatever the fuck I want."

Oh *scheiße*.

Death leaned forward, abandoning his wine glass as he rested his chin on his palms.

"And right now? Right now I want your fucking *pleasure.*"

Aleksander's head snapped to the side as the shadows holding the beast Gods dissipated, leaving them gasping.

"Nerethus," Aleksander ordered casually, "fuck Trystan's bratty mouth, will you? He's been annoying these past two weeks, mouthing off constantly. Fuck the brat right out of him while I make our vicious little guest cum."

Scheiße.

He had barely even touched me and already I was dripping.

Trystan cursed and out of the corner of my eye, I watched as shadows pulled the two beast Gods into my eyesight, so they're standing next to Aleksander.

"There, that's better." Death glanced at Trystan. "Now, get on your fucking knees."

The Griffin fought it, but I saw the maniacal glint in his eye.

He loved this.

Nerethus did too. His eyes might have been more guarded than the rest but as Trystan unbuttoned the Dragon's pants and his giant cock sprang loose, the tip already glistening with precum, it became evident that the excitement was mutual.

"Be a good little God and suck his cock. Dragon, don't stop, even if he chokes on it. I want you to feel the back of his throat. But neither of you can cum without my permission, is that understood?"

Both gave shallow nods.

"Don't hold back," Trystan said to Nerethus. I nearly melted into a puddle on the table as he fisted Trystan's hair and pushed his hard cock into the Griffin's open mouth.

Trystan moaned and sucked and I lost myself at the sight of it, at those two beautiful Gods.

"Oh my Gods, yes. Just like that. Take every fucking inch," the Dragon cried out as his head fell back.

The world turned hazy as I watched them duel for control and pleasure.

They were so beautiful, and the sight of Trystan on his knees before Nerethus was enough to make my legs tremble. I tried to close them, needing the friction, but the shadows held firm. My core throbbed, aching for touch. I felt so empty.

I wanted to be *filled* with *divinity*.

"Didn't I tell you to keep your eyes on me?" Aleksander snapped. His cold hand replaced the shadow on my left ankle. I jumped as he ran his hand up my calf, teasing me.

His eyes were as black as the midnight sky above us, and for a moment...

"That's better," he murmured. "Now, what to do with you?"

Lazily, he dragged his fingers up the inside of my legs, brushing my sensitive skin. The sound of Nerethus groaning as Trystan gagged around his cock in the background set me on edge.

I craned my gaze, watching them.

Trystan was hard too, the tip of his cock poking out from the folds of his kilt, where it glistened.

Suddenly two fingers were pinching my clit. My brain went blank and I shouted an incomprehensible curse at the zing of pleasure it caused.

"I told you not to look away from me. You don't do well with rules, do you?" Aleksander rubbed his pinched fingers down my outer lips pinching my clit in between them and massaging lightly. The sensation was strange, both pain and pleasure pulling from somewhere inside of me.

"Are you going to toy with me or fuck me?" I meant to sound sexy, but it came out as a whine.

"You, Elsing Wylder, are not in charge here. I am. You're at my mercy, and of that, I have little," Aleksander murmured. One thumb stroked down my center, spreading me open to reveal the wetness that awaited.

"Soaking wet." He smirked. "Perfect."

"Fuck yo—" My words ended in a moan as his thumb rubbed my clit.

"Your pleasure is mine, Elsing Wylder. Mine to give and mine to take."

I let out a grating moan and laughed. "Fuck you. I belong to *myself* and no one else."

He slid a finger inside of me and vibrated it back and forth. My hips followed him, twitching and writhing under his touch. I couldn't help the needy moans that followed suit.

"The moment I tasted you, I felt fate's conniving hand. You are meant for us. The others were right, though I greatly dislike admitting that."

He pulled his fingers out and thrust inside me again, stretching my pussy and making my legs quiver. His cold fingers against the burning inferno of my body felt like a shock to the system. It also heightened the pleasure.

Then Aleksander's fingers disappeared and something *else* pushed into me.

Something cold and tingly.

"What is tha—" I broke off as I looked down and watched, both in awe and in horror, as one of Death's shadows slid inside of me, thrusting in and out. It was thicker than his fingers and the way it filled and stretched me was so good, I nearly saw stars.

"Oh fuck," I cried out.

"Ride my shadows, Elsing. Ride them like you'll ride me," Aleksander ordered.

My hips moved of their own accord as I began fucking the shadow.

"That's it. Give in to it." There was a blur and Aleksander was at my side, leaning over the table with a dark smile, his eyes pure black as he looked at my pert nipples.

"I've wanted to taste these since the morning we met. That shirt you wore was completely sheer. One look and I was ready to bend you over and fuck you right against the counter. But these?" Aleksander brushed my nipples with his fingers lightly and I jolted, gasping. "These are mine too."

Then Death leaned forward and sucked my left nipple into his mouth, using his other hand to pinch my right one.

I moaned. "You should've done something about it instead of being a bastard and waiting."

Death chuckled against my breasts, biting down lightly on my nipple and then pulling back to blow on it. The mix of cold air against the hot burn of pain was enough to drive me insane.

The shadow inside me increased its speed and something else pressed against my tight asshole, pushing in gently.

"Later," Aleksander mumured around my nipple, "Trystan is going to fuck your ass while the Dragon fucks your pussy."

"What about you?" I moaned, barely able to form words but doing so out of sheer will.

"Me?" Death chuckled. "I'm going to fuck the brat right out of your pretty red mouth and I'm only going to stop once you've swallowed every single drop of my cum."

The pleasure within me built as the shadow at my ass began to pump in and out in time with the one fucking my cunt. It's too much.

It felt too good.

The orgasm came so hard and fast, I lost my vision and all sense of time.

"Good girl," Aleksander whispered against my breast. The orgasm left me breathless and panting, my body covered in sweat.

Nerethus growled so loudly I was shocked I didn't notice it earlier.

"Let. Me. Cum!" he snarled at Aleksander.

"Hm." Death shrugged. "Did I not hear you planning to take Elsing and escape earlier? That's not very nice, Nerethus. Not nice at all. Bad boys don't *get* to cum, do they?" Aleksander purred, pulling back to look at them.

Nerethus's eyes were wild as Trystan gagged on his cock.

"He meant well," I gasped as the shadows slid out of me. Aleksander scooped me up, his arms under my knees, as he nodded to the table.

"Trystan, stop."

Nerethus's huge cock slid out of Trystan's mouth with a *pop*. The God of the Sky was breathing hard, his pupils blown out.

"Clean up the table," Aleksander ordered casually.

I watch as the two men, both manic and breathless, blurred over to the table and leaned over the spot where the shadows fucked me.

Nerethus shifted his tongue and it darted out, forked and long, as he sucked up the puddle of my cum. Trystan joined him, moaning as he lapped up every drop.

They met in the middle and their tongues clashed, dueling like soldiers on a battlefield. The duel turned hotter and soon, Nerethus was crawling on top of the table, his lips locked with Trystan.

I couldn't move.

I couldn't breathe.

I couldn't do anything except watch as my cunt throbbed at the sight of them.

"Aleksander?" I asked, breathless.

"Yes, Elsing?" Death replied.

I let out a shaky exhale and looked back at him slowly. "I need your cock inside of me. *Now.*"

Trystan and Nerethus jerked their heads up, looking at me. Death's eyes went completely black until there was no color left in sight. His body trembled slightly.

Then a wicked, evil smile appeared on his face, his white teeth gleaming from the moonlight overhead. He leaned down and brushed his lips against mine.

"No."

There was no time to process his response as he snapped his fingers and the room went dark.

Shadows blackened the air until I couldn't see anything. The wind suddenly whipped my hair as the world turned upside down.

I heard the clicking sound of metal as something attached to my legs and hands.

Something *cold* in a way that only metal could be.

I fought against it, confused and disoriented, but the shadows quickly faded away.

We weren't in the dining area anymore.

We were in Aleksander's bedroom.

Well, he and the other Mountain Gods were.

I, on the other hand, was strung up on a sideways cross, my hands and ankles both cuffed to the wood, leaving me unable to move.

This wasn't here before.

He must have spelled the cross to stay hidden.

Before I could say anything, there was red silk against my mouth as I was gagged. It didn't fully block me from talking, but it muffled my words.

"That's better," Aleksander murmured as he tied the fabric behind my head. "Blink three times if you need to stop."

His words were kind and honest. It was enough to surprise the Hell out of me, so I blinked and nodded.

"Do it," Aleksander ordered.

I blinked once.

Twice.

Three times.

"Good."

Aleksander pinched both of my nipples and pressed a kiss against the silk fabric, and I couldn't help but moan.

I wanted the fabric between us gone.

I needed his lips. I needed his skin on mine.

I needed *him.*

Aleksander chuckled, pulling back.

He retreated to speak with Nerethus and Trystan. The Dragon's cock was still hard. It poked out from his pants. Trystan's eyes were still wide and his chest was covered in sweat.

But I couldn't do anything. I could only wait and watch as the three Mountain Gods turned and looked at me, their eyes roving over my naked body as they decided what to do with me.

Their *prize.*

the cross
to bear

chapter 15

I wondered when Death would snap.

When his perfectly crafted facade of politeness and humanity would fall.

He could put on the image of a human, but I knew the truth. I knew the beast hidden within.

He was a monster.

They all were.

And I was going to force the monsters out of them.

Aleksander snapped his fingers again and three chairs appeared. The Gods sat down and Death snapped his fingers once more. A table appeared, a glass jug of wine with three glasses on top of it.

With a swish of his hand, Death released the shadow snakes that sat beneath his skin. I watched as they lifted the jug, pouring three glasses of wine. The Gods all grabbed a glass, though Nerethus and Trystan were more hesitant. Not at the alcohol but at the snakes nearby.

Just as Nerethus lifted his glass to his mouth, Aleksander raised a hand.

Nothing was said. Not a single word. With nothing more than a thought, Death stopped Nerethus in his tracks. His glass was tilted, forcing the Dragon to fill his mouth with the liquid. But he couldn't pull the glass away. Couldn't swallow, couldn't even breathe.

"Don't swallow," Aleksander commanded, motioning instead to me. "Spit the wine in her mouth."

Nerethus's eyes took on a feral glint as motion returned to his limbs and he set the glass down, his mouth still full of spiced wine. His head swiveled towards me, his red eyes full of fire, as he slowly walked across the room.

The Dragon arrived at my side and took my face within his large hands. He tilted my head back and moved the red silk gag from my mouth to instead cover my eyes.

Everything went dark.

I managed a quick gasp before my mouth was full of wine, the taste spicy and warm as Nerethus pressed his lips against mine. I swallowed, taking every drop.

"I prefer the taste of you," he murmured. I sighed into his mouth as he slid his tongue in between my lips, flicking lightly and driving me insane. I sucked on it the way I'd imagined sucking on his huge cock and the Dragon moaned in response.

"Enough," Aleksander ordered, and if I wasn't so horny, I'd be embarrassed at the whine I made when Nerethus pulled away.

He moved the silk gag back over my mouth, pressing a kiss to the slightly dampened fabric.

It was alarming how much it relaxed me to look into the Dragon's eyes. His chest heaved as he brushed a piece of my stray hair behind my ear.

"Trystan," Aleksander said, and suddenly I could hear their conversation.

"Hm?" the Griffin asked, sipping wine from his glass.

"Go over there and fuck Elsing for me."

My jaw would have dropped, but the gag prevented it.

"Get her pussy nice and ready so she can take Nerethus's cock while you fuck her ass."

Trystan's eyes closed and his head fell back against the chair with a groan.

"Fucking *finally.*"

Aleksander pinned Nerethus with his gaze. "You. You, I have plans for. Come over here, Dragon."

Nerethus and Trystan traded places, pausing momentarily to exchange a searingly hot kiss. Then Trystan was looming over me with a maniacal grin on his beautiful face.

"It's time to play, pet." Trystan stepped next to me and pinched one of my nipples before slapping my ass. The sharp noise echoed through Aleksander's bedroom and I gasped at the leftover sting.

Trystan did it again, grabbing my ass cheeks and massaging where he just spanked.

"I'm going to fuck your ass tonight, pet. Have you ever done that?"

I nodded, unable to answer him verbally.

Trystan's answering snarl was furious. "And did you enjoy it? Their cock in your ass?"

I rolled my eyes and shook my head, because no, I didn't.

Trystan smiled and grabbed one post of the cross. Suddenly I was moving.

"Then clearly they didn't do it right. Let's make sure you enjoy every *inch.*"Trystan turned me upside down so my hair hung, brushing against the floor.

It also meant my pussy was just in front of his face. I was spread open completely.

The God of the Sky reached forward and parted my lips until I was gaping just enough to feel the cold breeze on my inner walls. I watched in a daze as Trystan leaned forward and spit on my pussy. The hot liquid landed on me like a burn. I felt it drip inside of me.

Then his mouth was on my cunt.

Trystan devoured me with a rabid fervor. He ate me like a man *starved.*

"It's been too fucking long since I've tasted you, pet." He snarled. "I want to eat your cunt every single day of my goddamn life, do you hear me? Every fucking day, pet. I *crave* you."

Then he sucked on my clit—*hard.*

The explosive orgasm that followed had me thrashing against my restraints as I screamed muffled expletives into the gag.

"Yes, yes, yes," he goaded, two of his fingers plunging inside of me, the sound so indecently wet it made us both moan.

"Fuck yes, you're so fucking wet. You want this just as bad as we do, don't you, pet? Mmm." He moaned and it vibrated against my clit, sending me into another orgasm. "That's right, come again, pet. I want your cream all over my face."

Trystan added a third finger and made a "come here" motion with them, hitting a spot inside as he took his other hand and pushed it on my pelvic mound. The wet sound of him fucking me with his hand and mouth became louder and louder. Finally, a warm tingling sensation took over my lower half as I lost control.

Liquid sprayed all over his face as my muffled screams turned into whines.

"Yes! More!" Trystan demanded, not stopping the onslaught. "Give me one more, pet."

"I can't," I cried, the words muffled against the gag.

"Yes, you fucking can." He attached his mouth to my clit and sucked hard once again, inserting a fourth finger inside of me. It stretched me to the point of near pain and the warm tingling sensation increased again until I saw stars.

I exploded once more, and without hesitation, he swallowed every single drop.

I was a screaming, quivering, sweaty mess. Even with the gag in place, I couldn't help but cry into the fabric. Sweat dripped down my back and tears fell from my eyes as Trystan pulled back, breathing heavily.

His face was covered in my wetness but he looked so pleased with himself as he reached the post of the cross and turned me again, putting me right side up. The blood rushed from my head and the world spun.

Trystan pressed a kiss against my lips and I moaned, tasting myself.

"You need a reminder of who is in charge here, Dragon." Aleksander's voice was so dark I was surprised it didn't suck up all the remaining light in the room.

Trystan and I both went still, turning in unison at the sound. We watched in awe as Aleksander walked behind a now seated Nerethus, fisted the Dragon's short black hair, and pressed a hot kiss against his open lips.

"Oh fuck," Trystan whispered, and I didn't imagine the way he leaned against me as if it were *his* knees threatening to give out at the sight. "It's been centuries since they were last together."

Curious. There had been a rift, then.

Thoughts dissipated as I watched Death devour the Dragon.

They were so beautiful together it didn't seem real.

Suddenly those invisible hands made of air unlocked the cuffs that attached me to the cross. I fell, unprepared, but Trystan's arms were there. Warm and sure.

"Shh," he whispered, his breath hot against my ear as he cradled my naked body against his. The gag released too, the red ribbon silently falling to the floor.

I was struck silent as Trystan carried me over to Death's bed, not letting go until we were both seated on the plush mattress and silken sheets.

"Watching them turns you on too, doesn't it? They're so hot together." Pausing, we both looked to the Gods in front of us and sighed.

Trystan kissed my cheek, whispering against my skin, "Ride my cock while we watch them, pet."

I nodded and he pulled me onto his lap so my back was to his front, with his arms around my stomach. He spread my legs and I moaned as he lowered me onto his hard cock, spearing through my wetness. He felt thick and warm and it was fucking *perfect.*

He groaned into my hair, pressing kisses to my neck and shoulders as his hands began to knead my breasts.

My vision blurred, but I refused to look away as Death pulled back from Nerethus and walked around him to take a seat in one of the empty chairs.

"It seems," Aleksander noted wryly, "we have an audience."

Then the Soul Eater *smiled*.

"Let's give them a show, Dragon. Come over here, get on your knees, and suck my cock."

I clenched around Trystan, who fucked me at a leisurely pace, the feeling of him stretching me too good to be true.

"Oh my God. Do that again, pet." Trystan cursed as I tightened my inner stomach muscles again, bearing down on him. He stiffened against me with a moan. "Fuck, FUCK!"

"Don't come." My snarl rivaled the Dragon's. "Don't you dare come yet."

Trystan laughed against my back as he fisted my hair to tilt my neck back.

"Bratty *and* bossy, hmm? Too bad for you, I fucking *love* it." He pressed a hot kiss against my lips and for a moment, we forgot about Nerethus and Aleksander.

We forgot about anything else.

It was just us—our lips dueling for control, our bodies intertwined.

I pulled away from Trystan at the sound of a zipper, and together we turned and watched as the Dragon kneeled before Death himself.

Nerethus pulled Aleksander's hard member out of his pants, and Death let out a shaky exhale.

Every bone in my body went limp as I took in Death's tattooed cock. He wasn't as thick or as long as the Dragon or the Griffin, but the tip was pierced with a black barbell that made me shiver with need and anticipation. Midnight black tattoos twisted around down his length and for a moment, I imagined what it would feel like to have him inside of me. To feel that metal bar for myself. To see those tattoos entering me, glistening in my pleasure.

As Nerethus leaned down and licked the tip of Aleksander's cock, Trystan thrusted. I sighed as the Griffin started to fuck me in unison with Nerethus's movements. Every time the Dragon took Aleksander's cock in mouth, Trystan thrust into me. We fell into a new rhythm and I lost myself to it. The sensation of watching them mixed with the feeling of being fucked by a God was all too much to handle.

My orgasm crested and just as I was about to fall off that cliff again, Trystan pulled out.

I squeaked in shock.

"Don't you dare cum yet, pet." He threw my earlier words back in my face as he leaned down and took one of my nipples in his mouth, sucking and biting.

Shock turned to anger.

"I'm going to fucking kill you. Get back inside of me and finish the goddamn job." I sounded like a wild animal.

Not all that different from the Mountain Gods.

Not any less monstrous.

Trystan laughed against my breast and bit harder. Not enough to break the skin but enough to make me writhe against him.

"What do you think, boys? Should our little pet be allowed to cum yet?" It took a moment to realize he wasn't speaking to me. I pulled back, ready to unleash another hurricane of insults, when a hot mouth landed on my core.

I moaned but Trystan caught the sound with his mouth, swallowing my gasps and groans. I tried to pull away and look down, curious which God was eating me out. But Trystan grasped my hair again, forcing my head forward. A warm vibration told me all I needed to know.

"Nerethus," I whined. "Make me cum, Dragon. Please."

How did I get here?

How was I in Death's bed, alongside two Gods who were devouring me like I was their final meal?

And yet, here I am *begging* for more.

Pertcha save me.

Trystan pulled away and I let out a mewling, needy sound as I reached for him, but two ice-cold hands grabbed my wrists and pulled my arms above my head, locking me in place.

Aleksander's face appeared above mine, his eyes pure black.

"Not yet."

Nerethus pulled his mouth away and everything blurred as my sense of gravity disappeared. I returned to reality with the Dragon naked beneath me on the bed.

Hands pushed on my lower back until my face brushed against the Dragon's, our hot breath mingling.

"Fuck her, Nere. Get her relaxed," Aleksander ordered, laying back on the bed as he stroked himself, watching us.

I didn't know where to look as Nerethus gently lowered me onto his huge cock. I moaned at the feeling of him slowly entering me, stretching me to the point of near pain.

"I missed this so much," Nerethus groaned. "Missed *you* so much."

I didn't even have to move. The Dragon held my hips in place as he thrusted into me from below, his movements frenzied.

I needed to jump off that cliff into the unknown. The pleasure was too much. My nerve endings were fried.

"Please," I begged. "*Please.*"

Aleksander considered my plea. "You're so pretty when you beg."

Then he was there. Death loomed over us. He grabbed my face, forcing me to look into his onyx eyes. "Be a good girl and cum on the Dragon's cock."

The orgasm was *there* and I began quivering, crying out for them as pleasure assaulted me. I went to close my eyes but Aleksander gripped my face harder.

"No," he snarled. "Don't look away. Your pleasure is *mine.*"

Nerethus groaned beneath me and wet, slapping sounds echoed through the room. My gaze locked with Death's, I exploded as the pleasure became too much.

"Good girl," Aleksander murmured as I fell apart in his arms. Then his mouth was on mine and he was swallowing my moans.

Feeling returned to my body as the orgasm abated. I leaned forward, but he was already gone as hands pressed against my back, pushing my front down to brush against Nerethus's bare chest. Behind me, Trystan pulled my ass cheeks apart and cold liquid slid down my crack.

"Relax, treasure," Nerethus whispered in my ear, fucking me slower now. "Focus on me. Focus on my voice."

"It's so much."

Nerethus pressed kisses against my cheek and caressed my hair. "I know. Just relax into it. Trust us, treasure. Trust that you're safe here."

My logical brain was screaming at me that he was wrong. He was wrong, wrong, *wrong,* but fuck, I could pretend otherwise.

For now, I could pretend.

"Okay," I told him and he made a pleased sound, swirling his hips. Slow and seductive, his warm lips met mine. I lost myself, fully under the Dragon's spell.

Suddenly a thumb pushed slowly inside. It was different, but I liked it.

"Relax," Nerethus whispered against my lips. Then his serpentine tongue was flicking against the seam of my mouth as he teased me, inviting me to play.

Trystan pushed his finger in further until it was all the way inside of me. Then another, until I was a moaning, whimpering mess in their arms. His fingers disappeared and I whimpered, missing the fullness, but something bigger replaced it. The Griffin pushed inside of me slowly as Nerethus stilled as to not jostle him.

"Oh my Gods." I cry out at the feeling of being so full, so stretched.

"Yes, we are your *Gods,*" Aleksander murmured. "Now consecrate this holy bed as your Gods see fit."

Nerethus reached down and rubbed a circle around my clit with his thumb, and the action distracted me enough that my muscles relaxed and Trystan was able to slide all the way in.

"Oh fuck."

"Holy shit, I feel your cock inside her," Trystan cursed.

Nerethus quivered below me. "She got so much tighter. I don't know how long I can last."

"None of you will cum until I say so."

Aleksander's order was unyielding.

The Dragon and the Griffin began thrusting in unison and my bones turned to ash as I melted into them, unable to move or produce coherent thought.

I was filled and used but at the same time, I had never felt so purely *connected* to another being. They were in me and I was in them. We were one and the same and with every movement, our bodies merged until there was no end and no beginning.

Just us.

Just them.

Just *me.*

The pleasure quickly built as they fucked me. Everything was more sensitive, more full, just *more more more.*

"Aleks," Nerethus groaned. "Please. I can't last much longer. She's so fucking tight like this."

"I can feel you through her walls. I'm close too," Trystan moaned, pressing a kiss to my back as we all clung to each other.

"Eyes on me, Elsing," Aleksander ordered. Through the blurred haze of pleasure, I watched as he stroked himself.

"Fuck my mouth."

The demand left me before I could overthink it.

Aleksander stilled and I could have sworn his shadows grew darker.

"Fuck yes," Trystan snarled. "Do it, Aleks. Give our girl what she wants."

Death's eyes landed on my mouth, focusing on how my tongue darted out to lick my lips. He crawled towards me and I slid halfway off Nerethus's chest, facing sideways, as I opened my lips and stuck my tongue out.

Aleksander muttered a whispered curse as he brushed the tip of his cock against my lips. My tongue darted out and I tasted the glistening precum on his tip. The metal piercing was cold against my tongue. I explored it, licking and sucking. An explosion of mint and spice burst in my mouth as I finally got a taste of him.

He tasted like everything and nothing.

The end and the beginning.

He was all of it and more.

Aleksander slid between my lips as he grasped my hair, fucking my mouth in earnest.

Nerethus and Trystan were a cacophony of feral snarls as they fucked me harder.

Time and truth disappeared.

I knew nothing.

Just pleasure.

Just the Gods of the Mountain as they revealed the monsters within, monsters that devoured me body and soul.

"Beg for it," Aleksander ordered.

"Please," I whined around his cock before he thrust so hard he hit the back of my throat. I gagged around him but he didn't stop.

"Much better." Death smiled. "Come with me. *All of you.*"

Everyone's movements became frenzied and all I could do was lay there as stars burst behind my eyes.

A stream of hot liquid shot down the back of my throat and I swallowed every drop, unable to get enough of his taste.

Trystan groaned at my back as hot liquid filled my ass, while Nerethus cummed with a hard thrust, emptying himself inside of me.

I blacked out as they pulled out of me.

Hands gently laid me against the bed and a hot towel cleaned between my legs.

I didn't know which hands belonged to which God, and I didn't care.

They curled around me, petting my hair and rubbing my arms, whispering praise and affection.

I had never felt so dirty and so special.

It was addictive.

But I couldn't lose myself.

Not truly.

I forced my lids open to discover I was in Trystan's arms while Nerethus rubbed my back. Aleksander lounged beside the Griffin, watching me. His eyes were back to their normal pale green. Death looked... relaxed.

Perfect.

I sighed and pulled away. The Gods went still, sad at the loss of contact.

I huffed a laugh. "Don't pout. I'm going to get more wine."

Aleksander raised a brow. "You do know that I can bring some with the snap of my fingers?"

"Some of us prefer doing things the old-fashioned way. Besides, I need to use the bathroom, unless you want me to piss all over your bed. I have many kinks but that isn't one of them... although I could be persuaded. It's *your* bed, after all."

Aleksander rolled his eyes and Trystan laughed.

"And maybe I would... like to do something. For all of you. Let me bring some wine and some food before I pass the fuck out," I admitted, biting my lip.

Aleksander sighed but nodded. "Be quick, or they'll start whining and bickering."

"Uh, rude." Trystan looked offended.

"We do not bicker." Nerethus sniffed, but my heart melted a little as the Dragon pulled the Griffin into his arms and whispered something into his ear.

Trystan laughed. "We bicker a lot, actually."

"Like an old married couple." Aleksander nodded.

I walked into the bathroom and relieved myself before sliding on one of Aleksander's spare shirts and padding out to the kitchen area.

It took a few moments to get everything perfect and locate what I had in mind, but I returned to the bedroom a few minutes later carrying a tray of cheese and meats in one hand, and a full jug of fragrant wine in the other.

My hands trembled under the weight.

At least, that's what I told myself.

It was the weight and not my nerves.

It had to be.

Placing the tray on the bed, Aleksander snapped his fingers and four empty glasses appeared. Trystan poured us all a glass of the ruby liquid, and then the God of the Sky set about entertaining us with a story about a mountain goat, and his elaborate plans to infiltrate their nest.

Nerethus's echoing laughter was sweeter than any wine.

The Gods did not notice how the wine in my glass didn't get lower. How I seemed to sip at it, but I never actually swallowed.

Soon, their eyes fell closed and conversation faded into the background. Nerethus pulled me tight against his chest in between him and Trystan. Aleksander laid on Trystan's left, his arm above his head, the picture of relaxation.

They went quiet and in moments, soft snores filled the air.

I sighed into Nerethus's chest and opened my eyes, looking my fill. I had to look while I could.

He was so beautiful.

They all were.

I reached out and brushed a hand against his cheek and even in his sleep, the Dragon nuzzled closer to me.

It was such a shame.

They were never supposed to be like this, you know.

Never supposed to be beautiful or kind of any sort.

It's made everything more difficult than I ever planned.

But regardless of their beauty, or how much my heart yearns for them, I came here for a reason.

Her.

Daphne.

In every moment of doubt I've had over the past few weeks, I whispered her name.

Daphne.

Daphne.

For her, I would do this.

For her, I would fulfill my true mission.

Because the Mountain Gods had to die.

And I'm going to kill them.

not all
monsters have
sharp teeth
& claws

now

the revelation

chapter 16

I t was a fluke, really.

I thought they'd eat me, I thought I'd die.

But I *hoped* for this.

Had planned for it, even. Just in case.

Uri is the only being alive who knows my true identity, my true purpose.

Too bad for the Mountain Gods, they didn't realize the truth. They looked at me and saw a pretty face and big tits. They never saw the monster sleeping beneath my flesh. Not until it was too late.

It's why I left my family and went out into the world on my own. I was never much for monster-hunting. When I looked into the eyes of the very beasts I was born to kill, I saw myself reflected back.

I'm the monster, not them.

My parents refused to accept that truth.

"We're not monsters!" they would scream at me, drunk on righteous power. But I saw the truth. I saw right through them, and so after they died, I left. All of my cousins did the same. Our generation was sick and tired of the centuries of bloodshed, all for what? For good?

No. At some point, our hunting became self-serving, and we saw that. So I started over.

Started anew. I renounced my old life and my old ways, content to study plants and flowers.

Then the Mountain Gods began attacking more villagers.

Then the sacrifices started.

I went out there, you know. After Daphne died.

I found her remains—a puddle of mutilated flesh and gnawed-on bones.

So I would do this.

This last job.

For her.

For Daphne.

For the love I never had, for the best friend I lost—even if it kills me in the process.

It's easy to risk it all when you have nothing left to lose. I just... I never expected *them.*

"They killed her. They killed Daphne." The constant reminder runs through my thoughts. In every moment of doubt, I repeated those words.

I would do this for her.

For my sweet girl. For the human who became my lifeline.

With a sigh, I reach beneath Nerethus's pillow and grab the dagger I hid there earlier, the silver blade cold and heavy in my sweaty palms.

"I'm sorry, I'm so sorry," I want to scream. But I say nothing.

Turning, I face Trystan, his face relaxed from the paralytic effects of the poison.

My hand shakes but I will stillness into my bones, holding the picture of Daphne's bloody remains close in my head until there's nothing left inside of me except anger.

So much anger.

I lean forward and press a kiss against Trystan's cheek, driving the dagger into his throat.

Unfortunately for me, he wakes partially, fighting through the poison.

It must be the pain.

Oh, well.

His yellow eyes open and he looks at me with confusion as he chokes up blood, the red liquid dripping down to the bedsheets, coating his face.

I cup his cheek and gaze into his eyes. "I am no one's *pet.*"

I twist my dagger, opening the hole in his throat as blood quickly coats my hands. The wound heals so fast, it's already sealing shut when I withdraw the blade, so I bring it down on his heart too.

He writhes and coughs, jostling the others.

I need to move fast.

This will only slow them down. It won't kill them. My magic has to finish the job. Magic I've fought tooth and nail to keep locked up. Already I feel it rising to the surface, begging to be used after weeks of playing pretend.

The flesh wounds will heal, but their magic is greater than mine. I need them wounded and slow if I'm going to finish the job.

And I *will* finish the job.

Nerethus twitches in his poison-induced sleep. I crawl on top of him and straddle his wide body. Even paralyzed, his cock hardens beneath me.

Ignore it. Don't be weak, Elsing! I berate myself and snarl, angry at the lust for them that just won't go away, no matter how hard I try.

Nerethus's red eyes open, blurry and hazy. He blinks, confused, and I learn forward, caressing his cheek.

"For what it's worth, I didn't want it to be this way," I whisper. "You were never supposed to be so kind and charming. It would have been so much easier to hate you if you were an asshole." I slide my dagger across his throat, slicing through his carotid artery. Blood sprays me in the face. Nerethus chokes on it, sputtering.

He's stronger than Trystan. The sage flavor of his magic is more intense as his body resists the wound. Which means I need to cut deep enough so that it can't heal quickly.

I'm powerful, but even I can't take a Dragon.

"I'm sorry," I whisper, and press a kiss to his lips too. He's jerking so hard beneath me that my lips land on the side of his mouth, but I'm already rolling off him.

I saved the most difficult monster for last.

Aleksander's appearance really fucked things up. His presence forced me to change my entire plan. Because how the Hell am I supposed to kill *Death?*

Luckily none of them seemed to notice the nature of the books I've been reading the past few weeks. The encyclopedias on different poisons, the tomes on Death himself.

I've been reading about him this entire time and the idiots never noticed.

They were too busy, enamored by my beauty.

It's always been that way with males.

Death is still, the poison working its way through his system, paralyzing every muscle so he's unable to move.

The herbs I collected at the glade worked nicely. I tripled the dosage, assuming their metabolisms work faster than a human's. It was the same poison I gave Albrecht Bucher.

Uri would cackle with glee if they were here.

I miss my friend.

Shaking off the melancholy, I climb on top of Death, ignoring the way the other two Gods twitch and choke, trying to heal despite their horrible injuries. It will take them a while.

But Death.

"You are a problem, you know that? You weren't supposed to be here," I soliloquize to myself as I contemplate where to stab him. "You were right not to trust me. I almost laughed the first time you admitted it. Don't tell the other two, but you're the smart one. You saw right through me, didn't you? Can you see the blackness of my soul, I wonder? When you look at me, do you see the monster hiding in my bones?"

I glance at my bloody dagger.

Uri did love the eyes. An injury to the brain might be the only solution to slow him. At least until I can use my magic to decapitate him.

I crawl up his chest and raise my dagger, positioning it above his eye.

"I do not fear *Death*," I swear, bringing the dagger down with all of my strength.

An arm catches me, squeezing my wrist so hard it hurts, my blade hovering in the air.

In the millisecond it takes for me to glance up and see that it's Aleksander's hand that stopped me, Death wakes up. I meet his furious onyx gaze, the blackness swallowing all color in his eyes. The veins of his face turn black and his shadows writhe in anger as he glances at the dagger, and then back to me.

"I *knew* you were lying. That's all humans are good for."

Ah.

Perfect.

I smile, tasting blood. "Surprise."

Death shoves me off him and I tumble to the floor, rolling to absorb the shock and quickly getting to my feet. Aleksander stands, naked save his shadows and his tattoos. He raises a hand and a giant scythe appears as a black cowl covers him.

"I am Death, Elsing Wylder, and your soul is *mine.*"

He swings his scythe so fast I nearly get cut in two. I veer out of the way and can't help but laugh.

"You know, for an Original, you're easy to manipulate." I crack my neck and take a deep breath, letting the magic that's been begging to be released deep within me free, after weeks of confining it. "Human this, human that, yet you never looked beneath the surface. You never once *asked* if I was human. Instead, you did what all males do: you *assumed,* and that assumption will be your downfall."

The Aive shakes and the air turns electric. For some odd reason, I don't feel the need to cast, not even in my own mind.

The magic within me is stronger than ever before. I picture lightning traveling along my hands and the glass ceiling above us shatters. Shards of sharp glass rain down on us as I slap my hands together and blast Death with bolts of lightning.

The lightning sears Death, leaving holes in his skin that the shadows quickly cover as the skin begins to seal up again. Aleksander snarls, "You're not human."

I clap my blood-covered hands. "Took you long enough. Shall I give you a prize, I wonder?"

"You're a fucking *Witch*." His shadows darken in response.

"Correct! And now, you're going to die."

I slap my palms together and close the gap between us, summoning more lightning from the heavens. There's a loud boom, but this time Aleksander disappears, and the lightning hits the floor, leaving a large hole.

"You can try." The fury in Aleksander's voice makes me shiver. He appears behind me and swings his scythe down against my side. I turn away but not fast enough. Pain sears through me as the blade slices into my muscles. Burning pain follows, threatening to send me to my knees. I clutch the bloody wound, holding my flesh together.

"Heilen," I hurry to release the cast, repeating the word again as my magic burrows into the wounded flesh, knitting it back together again. It burns like the devil but I can't spare a moment of hesitation.

Not as Aleksander stalks towards me. I back up quickly, gathering my magic to summon more lightning.

"There are no other Wylder's in the Under Realm. I looked. That's not even your real name, is it?" His voice is so dark it raises the hair on my arms. "Was any of it true?"

But I give him my best smile and curtsy as best I can. "Elsing Jäger, at your service."

Aleksander goes still. "You're a *Jäger*?"

I smile. "So you know my family, then?"

Aleksander scoffs. "You're a bunch of monster-hunting, power-hungry megalomaniacs."

"That's a bit hypocritical to say, don't you think? The first part is correct, and arguably so is the latter. I do not agree with what my family has done, but I do agree with their mission. To rid the world of the monsters who prey on innocent humans. That's what you all are—monsters. Your reign of terror ends here, with me."

"I'm going to kill you," he promises.

"I know."

I slap my hands together and lightning shoots down from the sky, hitting Death right on his stubborn skull.

The smell of burnt hair and flesh makes me want to gag but I don't. I fight my disgust and scream, forcing more magic into the blast, trying to burn right into his brain.

The lightning explodes fully and everything turns white as my ears ring. The Aive shakes and when I take a step back, my bare feet are sliced up by the glass shards on the ground.

I breathe heavily, waiting to get my vision back, hoping Death is lying prone on the floor.

But Aleksander stands, only partially harmed. His face is half burnt, but he watches me with calm fury.

Fuck.

FUCK.

I can't believe that didn't kill him.

"You will regret this," he swears. The shadows on his skin detach, swirling around him. For the first time, I notice bright red eyes on each of the shadow snakes.

Dozens of eyes now watch me as they writhe faster.

Aleksander lifts his arms and suddenly the shadows are shooting towards me.

Moment of truth.

I take a deep breath and try not to panic as I let them swarm me, not fighting back like the God of Death expects.

Freund, ich bin ein Freund.

Friend, I am a friend.

I frantically cast as the shadows tighten around me, their bodies covering every inch of my skin, leaving a tingling warmth in their wake.

But then they just stop.

I feel more than hear a sigh of pleasure as they settle into my skin, ingratiating themselves on my bones.

"Freund, Freund, Freund," they whisper happily.

Heilige scheiße. They ARE sentient.

"What the fuck?" Aleksander's eyes go wide in shock. The room comes back into view as the shadows settle, allowing me to see once again.

Death looks furious.

I chuckle, tracing a line up my arm, tickling the shadow snakes. "You paid me no mind these past few weeks, locking me away in your bedroom with your minions guarding the door." I glance up at him with a smile. "It was a test, giving them my blood. How I do love to be proven right. The shadows answer to a master, but regardless of their make, we all answer to the hand that feeds us. So day after day, I pricked my hand and fed them drops of my blood."

Aleksander curses.

"Now they're mine, and you, Lord Death, are well and truly fucked."

My magic explodes from me with a thought as I yank lightning down from the heavens, burning the God of Death.

This time, it works.

The shadows are boosting my power.

Perfect.

Aleksander groans, going down on one knee as I burn his skin too fast for him to heal.

With careful steps, I approach, raising the bloody dagger that dangled at my side.

Aleksander can't fight back as I crouch and lift the blade.

I'll stab him in the head.

He can't possibly heal from that, can he?

"I do not fear Death," I breathe, swinging my arm down with all my might, my blade pointed at the top of his skull.

Right before my blade touches his scalp, something huge and black explodes through the window, spraying more glass around the room. I raise my arm to shield my eyes but something hits me, knocking me back to the floor. The air is knocked out of my lungs and stars burst behind my eyelids as pain explodes in my head.

Everything goes quiet for a moment.

Did the mountain come down on top of me?

It feels as if I'm pinned under fallen rocks.

Then the rocks *move.*

I'm not pinned by rocks.

I'm pinned by a... body?

I wince, opening my eyes despite the pain in my head.

Everything is blurry and my ears are ringing, but big black eyes hover above me. Soft black curls brush my cheek as a warm, delicate hand clasps my face, caressing lightly.

"There you are," a lilting voice says. "I've been looking for you everywhere, Witch."

the god of tricks

chapter 17

I blink, confused as the face above me becomes clear "Who the fuck are you?"

The beautiful person sighs, rolling their gleaming black eyes. "Good Gods, did they fuck your brain away? It's me. Uri. Your familiar."

Everything comes crashing to a halt as my heart crumbles into my stomach.

This... This is Uri?

My Uri?

"Uri?" I croak. "But Uri is a raven. You clearly aren't. You're not my Uri."

They snort, and their voice drops, becoming scratchier. "I *am* a raven, actually. It's my first form. But I'm also *this.* "They motion to themself, pulling away from me slightly. I can't make my body move. It's frozen in shock as I stare at the beautiful being above me. "Or I used to be. I haven't been able to take this form in over 500 years."

"Uriel?" a scratchy voice calls. "Is that you? We thought you were dead!"

Uri... Uri*el.*

The God of Tricks.

No.

No, no, no, no, NO.

"You're no raven," I hiss. "You're an *Original.* Ten years, Uri. You've lied to me for TEN FUCKING YEARS!" I didn't set out to end up shouting in their face but my anger streams through the gaping wounds of my aching heart.

"I wanted to tell you so bad, Elsie. But I couldn't—"

I cut them off, leaning forward and baring my teeth in their face. "I don't want to hear it. I don't give a fuck if you couldn't tell me, you should have found a way instead of pretending to be a bird for ten fucking years. Instead of pretending to be my *friend*."

"I'm not lying. I really couldn't tell you. I've spent every second of the past month looking for a way to get to you, to break my curse just enough to be with you," Uri pleads. "Don't be mad, Elsie. Please," they say, voice wavering. Uri blurs, grabbing my dagger, moving faster than I can track. "No more stabbing though."

Their eyes are waiting, ready for me to go back to my normal self which would involve joking back.

That life, that version of me?

They're dead.

I crawl out from under them, needing some space, all the while ignoring the hurt reflected on their beautiful face.

"You're not my familiar." I cough. "My familiar is a raven, not a meddling *God*."

The lying God reaches for me but I stumble back. "Don't fucking touch me. You lied to me."

"I'm not the only one who lied, little Witch," they say gently, as if I'm some fragile flower ready to break. I close my eyes and bite my tongue, the hot, metallic flavor of blood flooding my mouth.

I know.

I *know* they're right, and yet it doesn't stop the hurt of betrayal.

I feel like I'm breaking, shattered on the ground of Death's bedroom alongside the pieces of glass that were once windows.

A harsh wind hits me in the face and for a second, I can breathe again as the freezing temperature brings me back to myself.

"Uriel!" Aleksander calls. He jogs over and grabs the person in a tight hug, swinging them around as they giggle affectionately. There are a few following groans as the other two Gods roll out of bed, both of their wounds now healed.

They all ignore me, too in shock at the sight of the new person to pay me any mind. Aleksander sets the person down and Nerethus swoops in, giving them a gentle hug. Trystan comes to their back and wraps his arms around the both of them as they all whisper and laugh. Aleksander even cracks a rare smile, his eyes back to their normal pale green.

Happiness and relief are evident on all of their faces.

I watch the reunion with a hollow heart, feeling like an intruder.

"We thought you were dead!" Nerethus says.

"Nope," the person claiming to be Uri responds, "not dead. Just cursed. I haven't been able to shift in centuries."

I scoff, sure that's another one of their lies.

This cannot be my familiar.

They cannot be my raven. My friend. I don't want it to be true.

I don't know whether they can mindspeak, but the Mountain Gods go still as they look towards me in unison.

"You tried to kill us," Aleksander snarls. "The only liar here is you, Elsing *Jäger.*"

"Elsing... Why?" Oh *Gods,* the pain in Nerethus's voice cuts me deeper than any dagger ever could.

"Damn, I owe you a pile of gold then, you fucker," Trystan mutters to Aleksander and I frown.

The person sighs, looking embarrassed. "Really, Trystan?"

The God of the Sky shrugs innocently.

"You... took bets on whether or not I would try to kill you?" I ask in disbelief.

The person gives me a knowing glance. "Men. Doesn't matter if they're God or human, they're all small-brained idiots."

Trystan frowns, hurt. "Hey. Not cool."

"I would say I'm sorry, but I'm not." Uri shrugs.

Something inside me snaps. "Oh, you want to say you're sorry? You want to apologize? Great, you should have done so TEN YEARS AGO, URI!"

The person blinks, hurt and relief playing across their face in equal measure at my words. It's the first time I called them by my familiar's name. I don't want to believe it.

But... I think it's true. And it makes me want to stab something again.

"Where the fuck is my dagger?" I snarl, feeling violent. Trystan gives me a thumbs-up which is frankly, very concerning. Nerethus slaps him on the back of his head, making the Griffin wince.

"Idiots," Uri mutters while I try to find the dagger they took.

"ENOUGH!" Aleksander bursts and I'm suddenly unable to move. I glance down as something cold wraps around my wrists and ankles. Black shackles now weigh me down, keeping me in place so I cannot run away.

"Freigeben," I whisper, but the cast doesn't work. The shackles do not move.

"Your magic will not work, Witch," Aleksander snarls.

I sigh and fall to my knees, looking up at the four of them. "Fine. Just get it over with then."

"Oh, Elsie," Uri says, sounding disappointed and sad.

"Uh, Elsing?" The Dragon clears his throat. "What are you doing?" he asks, as if I hadn't just slit his throat, despite the blood still drying on his neck.

I shrug, feeling defeated. "Get it over with. Kill me. Cut my head off and toss my body into the wind. Don't just stand there and look confused," I order. "If you're going to do it, do it!"

Nobody moves.

Trystan looks confused and scratches his head.

Nerethus watches me with concern. Again, how can they not be angry? I just tried to kill them.

Aleksander, however, looks slightly agreeable to the idea. A set of giant black wings springs into existence behind Uri's back and the left one extends, slapping Aleksander in the face so hard it makes Death stumble.

"Okay, nobody is killing *anyone,*" Uri says, chiding us. "Well, unless they deserved it. But Elsie doesn't deserve to die."

"She poisoned us and tried to kill us," Aleksander says in disbelief. Uri's neck twists but their body doesn't move. Their head swivels towards him and they bear a full mouth of black, pointy fangs.

Goosebumps break out on my arms at the sight.

Damn.

Uriel is *scary.*

The other Gods all freeze, varying terrified looks upon their faces.

Aleksander holds their gaze for a moment before cursing and looking away, mumbling under his breath about "fucking birds."

Uri clears their throat, black fangs going back to normal. But their wings stay. They look exactly like the raven's wings, just much larger. They're feathered and pure black, but with a sheen of midnight blue and purple.

I blink and look at Nerethus, examining his hair.

"Are you two related?" I ask, motioning to the two of them. Nerethus's red eyes go wide and Trystan lets out a noise like a dying donkey. "Is Uriel your sibling? Or, uh, parent?"

Trystan sputters as Nerethus blinks in shock.

"I helped create him." Uri nods. "So, yes? But at the same time, no. Divine creation is..." Uri struggles to find the right word. "It's not like human biology. There are rules with you lot. But there are no rules for Originals."

"So you're related," I repeat. "Does that make this incest?"

Nerethus looks around awkwardly and Aleksander sighs, taking over. "Pennios, Uri, and Rhaeta created Nerethus together. Many of the Lesser Gods were created by a single Original. But the more powerful ones were made by multiple Originals. Nerethus is one of those Gods. Trystan was created by Pennios and Rhaeta. But that doesn't make the two of them related."

I furrow a brow. "That makes no sense."

"It's not meant to." Uri smiles. "But no, we are not related in the way you're referring to."

"How come you look alike?" I ask.

Uri and Nerethus both share similarly deep complexions, their skin a beautiful dark umber shade. And both have midnight black hair that reflects multiple colors.

Nerethus takes a deep breath. "We look alike because Uriel tricked Pennios, which did not go over well."

Uri snickers and Trystan gives her a high five.

"How?" I ask, needing clarification.

"We all agreed that our creations could be made in Pennios image, but Pennios, as lovely as they are, well..." Uri breaks off, sighing. "Well, they can be really fucking annoying, if you must know. I was also so hungry that day. There weren't enough humans or animals around back in those days and I'd just tried my first eyeball. Oh—" Uri gasps, their eyes alight. "—it was so delicious. And I wanted more. But Pennios wouldn't create me a pile of neverending eyeballs, so I was... Well, a little mad about that."

Aleksander sighs. "Uriel got hungry and made all of her creations in her image, going against Pennios."

"You fucked over the God of Light... because you were hungry?" I ask slowly.

Uri brushes a stray curl behind their ear with a warm smile. "Yep."

"Right," I nod. "I see how you ended up cursed."

"Pennios didn't curse me," Uri defends, before admitting quietly, "but I might have been exiled from the Divine Realm after that. Nerethus is, uh, the only creation of mine that still lives. Pennios and Rhaeta killed the others. Jealous bitches."

"How long is your exile again?" Trystan asks and Uri hisses at him.

"You know damn well how long it is!"

I wait for the answer, but I'm surprised when it comes from Nerethus. "I'm exiled for 50,000 years. It's part of why we made the Aive. Long ago,

Uriel lived here with us."

"Hm," is all I have to say in response. My mind is a whirlpool of information.

But the weight of my actions is heavy on my shoulders.

"Now that introductions are over," Aleksander says darkly, "let's get to why I shouldn't eat your soul and toss your rotting corpse off the mountain?"

Uri smacks him with their wing again. "Touch my familiar and I'll tell Rhaeta about the time you 'accidentally' ate the souls of her Temple Priestesses just because you were hungover and cranky."

Aleksander's eyes narrow and he spits out, "I *thought* the priestesses were marked for death, and I was only hungover because *you* spiked the damn ambrosia, Uriel."

"Not my fault you can't handle your liquor," Uri says before looking towards me. They take a step forward until they stand before me, kneeling down so that we're face to face.

"Now, I think it's time we *all* tell the truth, don't you?" I hate the knowing look on their face. That knowing, gentle smile.

"Nope, I don't actually," I snarl and Uri smiles wider, but gives no quarter.

"You know I'm right, Witch. Tell them the truth." I look away, and a soft hand lands under my chin, pulling my face back towards them.

My eyes meet Uriel's as they raise a brow. "*All* of it." I so badly want to tell Uri to be quiet as they open their mouth again. "Tell them why you *really* murdered Albrecht and ended up as a sacrifice. Tell them about Daphne, Witch."

Daphne.

Oh God.

I'm so, so sorry.

the truth

chapter 18

"Daphne?" Trystan asks. "That was the girl you were friends with who was murdered, and then you seduced and killed her husband?"

I blink, but Uri nods.

"What about her?" Trystan's question is innocent enough but I stiffen and look down.

"That is... true. You told them part of the truth, at least. But Elsie..." Uri pauses. "You know that isn't even close to the whole story."

"Why does this matter?" Aleksander says, sounding bored and frustrated.

Uri grinds their teeth, looking back at him. "Because, you lumbering *oaf*, she thinks you *ate* Daphne."

Nerethus makes a choking sound and Trystan's jaw drops.

Aleksander however, takes a step back, confused and alarmed.

"I'm sorry, what?" Death looks at me. "You think we *ate* your friend? Why the fuck would you think that, Elsing?"

Now it's my turn to be confused.

"Mhm, see? This is exactly why we need to talk," Uri says.

"You killed her," I tell them, my anger and pain bubbling over. "I found her remains afterwards too. Piles of skin and chewed on bones. That's all that was left. And for that, you all deserve to die."

Aleksander cocks his head, his brow furrowing. But it's Nerethus who steps forward, joining Uriel on the floor in front of me. He kneels and I struggle against the chains holding me down, unable to handle his close proximity and the comfort it brings.

"Elsing," the Dragon says slowly. I already hate where this is going. "We didn't kill her. You're the first woman—*Hell*, the first *person* that we've seen in centuries."

The world stops turning and time halts.

Something new and *cold* invades my body, freezing my blood and turning my bones to ice.

Fear.

Fear because even though I don't want to believe him, I can *feel* the truth within his magic.

And that—fuck.

I don't like what that means. If that's true... then I do deserve to die.

"But you... You demanded sacrifices," I breathe. "To keep you out of our towns, the Mountain Gods demanded we sacrifice someone every solstice, letting you eat them alive in exchange for not attacking us."

Trystan's eyes go wide as he stands behind Uri and Nerethus. Aleksander sits down, the anger draining away from him and sadness taking its place.

"Fuck," Death runs his hand through his hair, looking equal parts frustrated and defeated.

Dread and fear begin to drown me. I choke on it, because I'm afraid. I'm so, so afraid that I know what they're about to say.

"Sweetheart," Trystan says and I flinch at such a kind nickname. So different from his usual brazen flirting. "We've never demanded a sacrifice."

"*Ever*," Nerethus agrees, his ruby eyes pleading with me to understand. "Human meat doesn't even taste good. It's all stringy and flavorless."

The other Gods nod in agreement.

"You—" I choke off, the lump in my throat too big to speak.

"Elsie, the sacrifices were never meant for them," Uriel says carefully. "They didn't kill Daphne."

"Then who did?" I ask, my voice trembling, and a single tear falls down my cheek. Nerethus reaches forward and brushes it away, his own eyes full of pain.

Uriel takes a deep breath. "The Basilisks did."

Aleksander is beside Uri instantly, his eyes furious. "Tell me everything."

"Later," Uri mutters, turning her attention back to me. "Now it's my turn to tell some truths, I think. I owe it to you, Elsing. I owe it to you… because you are the one I love the most."

"Don't," I breathe. "Please, don't."

Uri smiles sadly, their black eyes shining with unshed tears. "But it's true. I will always be your familiar, Witch. But you? You will always hold my heart within your hands, no matter how much you hate me."

"That's the second time you have called her that." Aleksander asks. "What do you mean, *familiar?*"

"Yes," Uri says with a smile. "Familiar. Elsing can use my magic, and I hers. Our souls were meant for each other."

I scoff, although their words make me want to sob and crawl into a ball. "But you lied."

Uri takes another deep breath, nodding. They sit back on their ass, bringing their knees to their chest as they hug them tightly.

"I did. That's the second reason I'm here. I need to tell you—*all* of you—what I found when I broke my curse."

Trystan takes a few steps back and sits on the bed. Aleksander exhales hard and takes a seat on the floor, looking mildly uncomfortable.

He snaps his fingers and the glass shards covering the ground disappear as the windows return to normal.

A useful spell.

Uri looks… hesitant.

"How did you manage to break the curse, Uriel?" Aleksander asks.

Uri's eyes meet mine again and they reach into their pocket. I didn't pay much mind to how they were dressed until this very moment. Their outfit is simple. Black pants and a black top that bares their muscular shoulders and arms, allowing for their wings to comfortably sit behind her.

I never expected, though, what they retrieved from their pocket.

Trystan makes an excited sound but all I can do is hold out my shackled hand as Uri drops two slimy, cloudy eyeballs in my bare hand, the cranial nerves still attached.

"I see how you broke your curse," Aleksander mutters.

"Just.. Just give me a little taste. I just want one bite." Trystan's pupils go wide as he focuses on the eyes. "Just one bite."

Nerethus slaps him on the back of his head and the Griffin flinches. "Not the time!" the Dragon hisses. Trystan pouts.

I blink. "That old meat suit is the one who cursed you? Seriously? That bitch?"

"Firstly, let me explain a few things," Uri says, backtracking. "500 years ago, I tried to steal some gold from what I thought was a harmless witch. I'm an Original, so a Witch cannot truly hurt me—no offense." I glare at them. "So consider my surprise when suddenly I'm hit with a bolt of the most concentrated magic I've felt since I was in the Divine Realm. The moment that magic hit me, I was locked in my raven form, unable to shift. The first thing I tried to do was find one of the Lesser Gods to try and explain. I went to Aegidus."

"Of course it was Aegidus," Trystan rolls his eyes.

Nerethus looks at me and whispers, "Aegidus is the God of Wealth. He's also the most annoying being to ever live. We've tried to kill him off many times but he's like a cockroach."

Interesting.

Uri continues, "When I found Aegidus, I couldn't even form the words to describe the Witch, or say I was cursed. I tried to tell him about how the three of you," they motion to the other Gods in the room, "were trapped here, and how I thought that Witch's magic had something to do with it. But the curse prevented me from sharing any details to anyone. I wasn't just locked in one form, I couldn't even tell anyone why, or the truth of it all."

"Wait, what?" Trystan asks.

"The sacrifices? They were never meant for us," they say, looking over their shoulder at him and then back to me. "The sacrifices were for *her*. Spilling innocent blood *powered* the curse. Most curses would have faded away over time."

"Tante Inga is an old hedge witch. She's a piece of work, but there's no way she could cast those curses. She's not powerful enough," I protest. "Besides, *something* ate the sacrifices. I—" I stumble over my words. "I've *seen* the remains."

"Yeah, I'll get to that. But after you fell unconscious on the night of your sacrifice, I kept watch. Worried that whatever being was consuming innocents for the sake of the curse was coming for you. Consider my shock when this dummy shows up and gently cradles you in his giant claws, whisking you away to the Aive?" Uri motions to Nerethus, who blushes in response. They continue, "For weeks, I tried seeing if there was any hole along the borders of the curse. I searched the skies and traced every centimeter, looking for a way in. But it was no use. I could get close, close enough to see you through the windows. But I couldn't get to you. So, I decided to finally do something about it. I went back to Interlaken, waited out the hag and when she wasn't looking, I dropped some wintarberries in her wine, poisoning her. I knew it wouldn't kill her, but it would knock her out for me long enough to peck out her eyes and get through the border. And it worked. But as I was leaving..." Uri breaks off, hesitant. "She... *healed*. Immediately."

Aleksander purses his lips. "Explain."

Uri bites their lip, giving me a look full of pity and fear. "That... isn't Tante Inga."

"No," I breathe. "No. That's impossible. That cannot be true."

"What? What am I missing?" Trystan asks, and Nerethus looks equally confused.

But Aleksander watches me, his eyes narrowed.

Uri continues and my world crashes to the ground as they say, "Tante Inga isn't real... nor is she a Witch. Which is how she was able to curse me—curse *all* of us, actually." I wait, unable to breathe as they go on. "Tante Inga's real name is Pertcha. She is the God of Magic and Witch-craft."

I cannot move.

Cannot think.

Cannot do anything but look at Uri as the final nail is hammered into my waiting casket.

Uri grabs my hand, squeezing it as they say, "Your Goddess is not who or what you think. *She* is the one killing the sacrifices, Elsie. She's the one torturing and killing *Gods*. The Mountain Gods didn't kill Daphne; *Pertcha* did."

Death, I think, would be easier than this.

the reaction

chapter 19

Pertcha is killing the sacrifices. She's... using Basilisks to consume them and get rid of the bodies.

Pertcha.

My Goddess.

"She killed Daphne?" My voice is hollow. I look up slowly and the only answer I need is the pity on Uri's face.

"Elsie—"

I interrupt them. "Don't. Don't you dare. You just told me the Goddess I've dedicated my entire life to, that my *family* has dedicated their lives to for centuries, is evil. Don't try and placate me and tell me everything is fine, Uri. Everything isn't fine."

Another tear falls down my cheek and I wipe it away, jostling the chains around my wrist.

Something occurs to me.

"How do I know you're telling the truth?" I ask. "You're the God of Tricks. Known throughout the entire world as the *least* trustworthy of the Gods."

Trystan snickers from the bed and Nerethus shoots him a glare.

Uri sighs. "Okay, you're not exactly wrong. All I have are Pertcha's eyes. The rest, I cannot prove."

"Wait, wait, hold on. Let me get this straight," Trystan says, standing up from the bed and pacing in front of us. "You," he looks at me, "thought we killed your friend. But you still fucked us because, what... You were bored?"

Nerethus grinds his teeth and Aleksander raises a brow as they all look at me.

I respond dryly, "I blame it on your charming personalities."

Trystan smirks. "Uh, huh. Right, so you meet us and then can't stay away, all the while you're plotting our demise to avenge your fallen friend."

I cross my arms, making the chains jingle and give him a tight nod.

"Right. And now that you know we didn't kill her, do you still want to stab us in our sleep?"

I sniff and glance at my nails, "If what Uri says is true, then no, I don't want to kill you anymore."

Aleksander scoffs. "Oh bullshit—"

Trystan interrupts. "No, no. Look at her. I've never seen something so pitiful and sad. She's like a kicked puppy."

"She tried to kill us, Trystan," Aleksander grinds out.

Nerethus clears his throat. "Yes but, it sounds like, in her shoes, that was the most logical thing to do. If one of you was murdered, I would be ripping throats out left and right."

Trystan pauses and they look at each other for a moment. "Oh my Gods," the Griffin says. "You totally love me, don't you?"

Nerethus hisses, "This is not the time!"

"You loveeee me," Trystan sings before turning back to me. "Does this mean I'm your treasure too?" The Griffin gasps, a manic smile on his face. Nerethus covers his face with one large hand, letting out a long-suffering sigh. "You know, gold *is* my color. It goes so well with my eyes, don't you agree, pet?"

"You're not wrong," I agree.

Aleksander blinks. "Can we *please* get back to the topic at hand?" he snarls.

"*Buzzkill,*" Uri fake coughs, causing Death to roll his eyes.

"Right, okay. So Elsing, you don't want to kill us? If Uri is right about all of this?"

I flick my tongue against my teeth. "If it's true… then I'm—" I break off, not used to communicating my feelings like this. "If it's *true,* then I would be very sorry that I blamed the three of you. I would," I force the words out, "feel *bad* about the whole poisoning and stabbing thing."

"Okay, great, problem solved then," Trystan says, coming to sit next to me. He leans over me and presses a kiss to my forehead, making Uri smile. But my jaw is on the floor and Aleksander's head is in his hands.

"What? Why do you all look so shocked?" The God of the Sky asks.

"Because. She," Aleksander points at me accusingly, "tried to murder us in our sleep!"

"Well, yeah, but it's not like it actually worked. A little stabbing never hurt anyone, eh?"

Nerethus pauses, cocking his head before turning to Aleksander and nodding. "As much as I hate to admit it, I agree with the bird."

"Because I'm always right," Trystan says. Death looks like he wants to fling himself off the mountain.

"Elsing lied about being a Witch, she lied about being attracted to us, she lied about every single thing. How the Hell can you trust her?" Death asks in disbelief.

Trystan pauses and looks away, scratching his cheek with wide eyes.

"Trystan." Aleksander's voice is laden with accusation. "Tell me you didn't."

Trystan shrugs. "Well, see, the thing is, I drank her blood the day she woke up. I just didn't say anything because, well, I thought everyone else knew she was a Witch too."

"You mother*fucker,*" Aleksander sneers.

Nerethus snarls, "Ryst, what the fuck!" The Dragon's anger quickly turns to a petulant pout, his lush lips pursing. "You didn't even share."

Uri rolls their eyes in exasperation. "Idiots. Every one of you!"

Nerethus looks away, chagrined.

"I didn't say anything because I didn't think it mattered," Trystan says pleasantly. "Who fucking cares of she's a Witch anyways? This just means we can have more fun."

"Fucking smite me," Aleksander curses, running his hand through his hair in frustration.

"I wondered for a while if Trystan would say anything. But you just *assumed* I was human. You never even bothered to ask, so this is your fault." I flash him a mocking smile.

Aleksander glowers.

Nerethus clears his throat. "I, uh... had a feeling you weren't human. You don't smell like one."

"Fucking Hell." Aleksander looks away, thoroughly disgusted.

Uri snickers at the irony in Aleksander's statement.

"Calm down," I chide Death. "I barely used any magic until today anyways. It's not like I'm a damn Vampir or something."

"Now hold on. You with fangs would be fucking *hot,*" Trystan says. Nerethus nods in fervent agreement. "Can we make that happen? Please tell me we can make that happen."

"So the two of you just forgive her? Even though she just tried to kill you?" Aleksander shouts. "You're insane. You're all fucking insane."

Nerethus and Trystan shrug, nodding.

The Griffin eyes Aleksander, raising a brow. "And we're just supposed to believe that her little stabby stabby moment didn't make you harder than mountain rock?"

Nerethus, Trystan, and Uriel all look down in unison, eyeing the outline of Aleksander's hard cock beneath his pants.

"Unbelievable." Death curses, muttering to himself about idiot beasts. "I don't believe her, for what it's worth. And you all love to forget, but as a reminder, this is my *home.* You are all guests here."

Trystan looks down. "Damn, that hurts."

Aleksander ignores him and continues, "Until I say so, Elsing cannot be trusted. She is now our prisoner. Got it?"

Nerethus grumbles and Trystan pouts.

"If Uriel can't prove her story, you'll never change your mind,"

Nerethus points out.

Aleksander crosses his arms, his tattooed arms flexing. I didn't realize some of his ink was real. I assumed each one was made of his shadow snakes, but even though they now sit beneath my skin, Death remains covered in black whorls.

"Why don't we ask Daphne?" Aleksander asks.

I turn and stare at Death in shock. My arms fall to my sides and everything goes quiet.

"I... *we...* can talk to her?" My voice trembles.

Death looks at me as if I'm missing something obvious.

"Elsie, he's the God of Death. He talks to the dead *all the time,*" Uri whispers.

Oh! *Oh.*

That... didn't occur to me. Not in this way, at least.

Aleksander watches me carefully, not missing a single moment.

"*I* can speak with her. The living, be they Witch or otherwise, are not permitted to speak to the dead."

My heart sinks.

"Right."

Aleksander clicks his tongue. "I'll speak with this Daphne person and determine if Uriel is being truthful. In the meantime..." He pauses and snaps his fingers. There's a weird pulling sensation and everything goes black as I'm sucked into the mountain, falling through the floor.

I hit hard, damp ground, my chains clanking loudly.

Groaning, I push up onto my hands, wincing at what I'm sure will be massive bruises on my ass. I'm no longer in Death's room.

I'm in some sort of dungeon.

The light, herbal smell of the hot spring is in the air. It's faint but it's there. This must be connected to it.

"You did try to kill us so, little Witch, you will stay here until I decide you can be trusted," Aleksander says, leaning against the bars of the cell I'm locked in. "I do not forgive easily, Witch. Say your prayers that

Daphne confirms your and Uriel's stories, otherwise this will be your home until you wither away and die."

Then he snaps his fingers and disappears, leaving only the remnants of his spicy scent in the damp cave air.

I lean against the damp stone wall, not even bothering to check out my surroundings and the horse-sized prison cell I'm locked in.

For the first time in decades, I feel completely and utterly alone.

the Familliar

chapter 20

The days pass slowly.

At least I think they do.

I do not know what time it is or how long I've been down here, but the more time I spend alone in the near-pitch black cave, the more lost I feel.

I could mark the stone wall with my sharp nails to try and track the time, but what's the point?

Everything I thought I knew was a lie.

My family has spent the past millennia pledging our lives to Pertcha. It's her name we cry when we kill the monsters who prey on the weak.

It's her name we give thanks to when things go our way, and we emerge from another battle unscathed.

There is no way to cope with the reality of her actions.

If it's true.

You know it is. You feel it in your bones, the voice in the back of my head whispers. *Pertcha betrayed you. Betrayed all Jägers. Everything you've done has been for nothing.*

"*Gottverdammt*, shut up!" I groan aloud.

But my conscience doesn't quiet.

It berates me, over and over.

I begin to wish Death *had* killed me. No matter how miserable soul consumption sounds, it would be better than rotting in my own failure and misery.

Food appears, brought by no one, just outside the bars of my cell twice a day.

Plenty to keep me full, but I'm not hungry.

There is nothing else to do, other than disappear into my own thoughts. I follow them, floating down the river of my mind, letting it wander wherever it deems fit to travel.

Mice and small bugs swarm the abandoned meals, and I spend my time watching them, wondering what God they pray to.

Is there a God of Vermin?

You know, I've always disliked that word.

Vermin.

Just because something looks different and speaks a different language, doesn't make it any less than. Such thoughts are only a sign of ignorance and greed.

Why do animals deserve to die, to be consumed for *our* survival, any more than humans do?

My family, of course, never agreed. My parents would laugh when I'd talk about it.

Then the lectures would begin.

"You're a monster hunter. You're a Jäger, for Pertcha's sake! We do not hesitate and we certainly do not pity. We kill to protect others. As is our Goddess given right," my father would say, while my mother would just shake her head and *tsk* in shame.

Even with their cruelties, I miss them.

As time passes, more often do I find myself wondering if I really miss *them,* or if I just miss feeling like I have a family. A community, friends.

When they died fifty-five years ago, I set off on my own. But every town I stopped in felt strange and unwelcoming, until finally, I wondered if perhaps there is no real place for me in this world. That maybe I'm too different to ever feel at home.

But then everything changed.

Then I met her.

It's not surprising how I always end up in the same place each time.

With *her.*

Daphne.

My Daphne.

I always end up back where I started. Thinking about Daphne.

My friend.

My *love.*

It's outlawed in the Republic, a woman lying with another woman.

I never got a chance to tell her how I truly felt. To tell her how I thought she was the most beautiful woman I've ever seen. To tell her how every time I saw the freckles spattering across her pale face, I wanted to follow the path with my lips.

I wanted to tell her the way being in her arms made me feel.

Like finally, after centuries of searching, I was home.

I'm terrified of the day the memories begin to fade, until I can't remember the shade of her blonde hair, or how she always left the faint smell of sweet lemon in the air.

Uri was the only one who knew my true feelings. There is a spell, passed down to the women in my family for generations, made of Witch blood and rare flowers, that can extend life.

It's not immortality... but for those of us who fall in love with a human, it's the ultimate gift.

Time.

More time.

Witches usually live 1,000 years, and with this spell, a human can live to be 800.

I was going to leave town to go hunt down the flowers required for the spell the day after Albrecht caught us.

The day I finally had the courage to kiss Daphne.

I wanted to kiss Daphne Bucher since the moment I first saw her, covered in sweat from carrying buckets of animal bones to be used for soup.

She was a mess. A beautiful, wonderful mess. I took one look into her pale green eyes and saw her great big smile and fell completely, head over heels, in love.

Her blonde hair was in a big knot on top of her head, with plenty of strands falling out. Some were plastered to her sweaty forehead. Her generous curves only enhanced her beauty.

I'm not a nice person, so socializing is something I've typically failed at. But we became fast friends when I offered to help her clean the bones if I could keep some for my potions and elixirs.

It was disgusting, but I got to be with her all day, and she helped show me around town as I got settled at the Apothe.

Eight years, we were friends. They were the best eight years of my life. We spent almost every day together. She visited me at work and I did the same for her, until our lives were so intertwined there was no separation. There was no me and no her, there was just *us*.

It took me eight entire years to make a fucking move. To be brave enough to do something about the feelings hiding away in my heart.

I'm not even sure if she returned it, or if she was simply too shocked to move. By the time she could react, it was too late. Albrecht walked in and saw us kissing, saw my arms around her, saw her hands on my waist.

It was all he needed. I pleaded with him to blame it on me, that it was *my* fault.

It was no use. He dragged Daphne to the town square and brought her to Willem's feet.

He hated Daphne and her joyful, free spirit. He wanted a subservient wife, and instead, he got her.

She was like the wind coming off the frozen tips of the Helvetas Mountains.

Fiercely full of life.

And then she was gone.

I tried to stop the trial, tried to do something.

But it was too late. Albrecht opened his stupid mouth and told them everything.

Just our luck, the wintar solstice was that night. Someone else had been picked to be the sacrifice, some young boy. Albrecht pleaded with Willem that the boy had so much potential.

Let the sacrifice be a useless woman instead.

I tried to get to her but Willem had his guards grab me. They locked me up while they took her out to the woods to get ready for the sacrifice.

I never got to say goodbye.

One last look was all.

Uri broke the lock cn the cellar, letting me out, but it was already too late.

The townsfolk were returning, on horseback and on foot, from the completed sacrifice. Their hands were full of lanterns as they laughed and smiled, comfortable in knowing that they were safe for another six months.

I stood there, hollow and numb as they passed me.

Nobody noticed or cared that I escaped.

I had no horse, so I walked all the way to Schollen Gorge, past Tante Inga's forest cottage. Uri flew above me in silence, joining me as we found the spot where she was left.

The Mountain Gods worked fast. Although now I know better.

All that was left of her was a pile of bloody bones, some stray pieces of sinewy muscle, and a few strands of her blonde hair within a puddle of blood and flesh.

With shaky hands, I covered my skin with her blood and pledged to finally take up the mantle of my heritage.

To kill the monsters of the mountain by any means necessary.

I would get my revenge and take Albrecht down with me. So I picked the most painful, slowest poisons possible, wanting to make him suffer.

I don't regret it either.

But if the Mountain Gods are innocent...

Then I do have some regrets, after all.

I doze off sporadically, since I cannot tell when it's day or night. The cave is cold but there's a thin blanket in the corner.

I dream of Daphne, but it quickly turns into a nightmare.

A soft wind against my face wakes me and Uri's blurry raven face appears.

"What are you doing here, Uri?"

There's a nudge against my magic and it's so familiar I don't even think before letting them in.

"I couldn't take another moment with those testosterone-laden heathens. If I hear Trystan complain about Nerethus singeing his tail feathers one more time, I'm going to hurl."

I snort, still half asleep. "Are they going to leave me down here forever, then?"

"Not sure. Death is projecting to the Below and we won't know anything until he returns. But that means I can sneak away to see you."

"Hmm." I pull the blanket around me, shivering a bit and still groggy with sleep.

"That fucker. I should peck his eyes out for putting you in this hideous dungeon. Let me make it more comfortable." Uri spreads their wings and there's a bright flash as something tingles along my skin.

I blink and the prison cell is transformed.

The stone is clean and bright flaming torches line the wall. Little lightning bugs crawl along the ceiling, making it look like stars.

The thin blanket on top of me is now a thick goose down comforter, and instead of laying on the cold wet floor, a soft, pillowy mattress with soft cotton sheets is beneath me.

"Better?" Uri asks.

Now fully awake, I turn to the side and see that they're in human form. Uri lays on top of the covers next to me, a wide smile on their face. Their head is propped on their palm and they face me, open and unjudging.

My dirty, smelly tunic is gone and I'm now clothed in a set of soft cotton pants and a clean black shirt.

The smell of sage wafts through the air and something occurs to me.

"Nerethus smells like sage... because he gets it from you."

Uri quirks their lips. "Smart Witch."

"I can't believe you helped create him. That you've created any being." I sigh, running my hands over the clean fabric. "Thank you."

Uri's shiny black curls brush against the thick pillows beneath our heads. The glimmering bugs above us play off their deep complexion.

"Of course, Witch. I would do anything for you."

I want to smile.

I want to hug them.

But instead, I hesitate, and I know it's not lost on them. This new doubt within me.

"Want to know a secret?" Uri smiles.

"Sure," I offer, mollified and very happy about the warm blanket and soft bed beneath me.

"Creation is *boring*. All of the Godly stuff is." They lean in, a conspiratorial grin on ther face. "I prefer being a bird."

I snort. "I doubt that."

Uri looks taken aback. "I'm serious! No responsibility, no rules. I can just... fly. It's wonderful, honestly. I was always the least committed out of all the Originals. I mean, look at Aleksander. The man will never get a day off in his entire existence. It has to be *exhausting!*"

I turn and look up at the lightning bugs on the ceiling, contemplating their words.

"I'd much rather be your familiar, honestly. As much as I wanted the curse gone, so I could tell you the truth, there was something freeing about just... being a raven. Not a God, not an Original. Just... me."

I glance to the side and our eyes meet.

"I'm sorry, Elsie," Uri admits. "The last thing I ever wanted to do was hurt you."

I bite my lip, still hurt from their years of lying.

But...

I look to the side. "You really couldn't tell me, could you?"

Uri shakes their head sadly. "No. I tried to every single day. Tried to figure out a way around the geas. But it never worked. Do you know how fucking relieved I was when Nerethus showed up instead of Tante Inga that night in Schollen Gorge? I was about to piss my feathers in terror when I saw his ruby eyes."

They look away with a pained sigh. "I don't think I've ever known true fear until that moment. The thought of losing you, after everything we've been through? I... I don't know what I'd do."

Without thinking, I grab their hand, amazed that it's skin and not a claw.

Uri follows my thoughts, and with a twitch of a finger, they shift their nails to become long, black, and pointed.

Mini talons. I trace them lightly before clasping Uri's hand lightly.

"I'm still here, Uri."

Uri snorts. "Yeah, and you've still got a damn death wish. We're going to talk about your little 'kill me, Aleksander,' moment. Don't think that's going to slide."

I look away.

"Elsie, I know," Uri whispers in my head. *"I know what it's like to want to die to join the one you love. To wish for death because the idea of living is too painful. How do you think I felt, waiting for you to die? For the first time in my eternal existence, I wanted to die, just so we could stay together."*

I turn on my side, facing them as my tears fall in earnest.

We lay like that for a while, gazing into each other's eyes, hands clasped, existing in each other's presence.

"I'm still hurt, Uri. I think I will be for a long time," I admit, and Uri's face falls. They take a deep breath and nod. "But," I continue, "I do have a question."

Uri blinks. "Of course. Anything, Elsie. Ask me for the moon and I'll give you the heavens."

I blush, fighting a smile. But something occurs to me just then.

"Did you... Did you visit me in my dreams? When you were looking for me? I feel like I've seen your face before somewhere."

Uri fights a smile. "Dreaming of me, Witch?

Something pangs within my heart.

Something warm and new and wholly unexpected.

"The first night I was here, I saw your face in my dreams. How is that possible?"

Uri winks at me, "Nothing is impossible for Originals, Witch. Tell me, was it a pleasant dream?"

My cheeks warm. "Yes, it was."

"Good. I'm glad to hear."

My jaw drops. "You *did* visit me in my dreams!"

Uri laughs. "I wanted to at least try it. I wasn't even sure if it would work with the curse keeping me out. I told you, Witch. I would do anything to find you. There is nothing, God or human-made, that can keep me away."

Oh.

Oh wow.

I take a deep breath and blurt out my next question, "I need to know if Gods can still be familiars. Because if you would still like to be mine, then I... I would like to be *yours*." I finish the words fast, nervous to say them.

Nervous they might say no.

But the smile that breaks out on Uri's face, it's brighter than the entire sun and makes me feel warmer than a sommer's day.

"There's no rule about it," Uri says. "I'm a God. I make my *own* rules. So yes, Elsie. The answer is always yes. As long as we're together, that's all that matters to me."

I'm unable to stop my own smile.

My heart is broken and torn, but at this moment, I feel a little more whole.

Uri's magic mixes with mine and I sigh happily at the feeling of closeness after so many weeks apart. The air begins to glow as our magics twine together, dancing in happiness.

I close my eyes and snuggle into the bed, suddenly exhausted.

A tiny bit of relaxation and the tension leaves me. I sigh and look at them, when a stray thought enters my mind.

"Do you prefer 'she' or 'they?' I called you 'they' when you were a raven, but this form is feminine. So, what do you like to be called?"

Uri smiles warmly. "Sometimes I feel like a woman, sometimes I don't feel like anything at all. This form makes me feel more feminine. When I'm a raven, I don't feel masculine or feminine. I am neither. Both 'she' and 'they' suit me just fine, Witch. It's my nature to be undefinable."

"That makes sense." I nod. "Do you want me to call you Uriel?"

She cringes. "Absolutely not. I prefer Uri. Being called Uriel reminds me of all the times Pennios would get upset that I tricked the Gods of Twilight and Dawn to switch places and briefly upset the entire balance of the world. They're still a bit mad about that, I think. You'd think the God of Light could take a joke!"

I snicker and we go quiet. My eyes grow heavy, falling closed as the glimmering lights on the ceiling fade.

"Sleep, Elsie. I'll watch over you."

I mutter, "You need to sleep too."

I nearly jump at the press of soft lips against my cheek.

"I'm a God, remember? I don't need sleep. But you, my pretty Witch, you need to rest. You look exhausted," Uri whispers, her breath fanning my face.

"That's a lovely way of saying I look like shit," I tell her.

She snickers. "Witch, you couldn't look bad even if you were covered in cow shit."

I wince, suddenly wide awake. "That's fucking gross. Take that back."

Uri smiles. "That, Witch, is *love*."

I blush and close my eyes, trying to focus on sleep. But my smile doesn't fade.

"Thank you, Elsie. Thank you for not giving up on me," Uri whispers.

"I will happily spend the rest of eternity making it up to you."

I murmur, reaching out a hand and wrapping it around their warm arm, "I know."

It's silent for a moment as I fade into a deep slumber, comfortable and content for the first time in days—weeks, even—when suddenly, a low, rumbling purr starts up, and the arm I'm holding onto turns into feathers, as Uri shifts and tucks herself underneath my chin, as if to sing me to sleep.

the heart

chapter 21

"**E**lsie, time to wake up."

I groan, smashing my face into the warm pillow.

Then the pillow *moves.*

I open my eyes and blink away the blur of sleep, realizing I'm using Uri as my own personal pillow. My face is smushed between her soft breasts and I'm cradled within her arms. She's so soft, and her skin smells like sage and the wild, salty wind.

Sleep has removed all of my walls, all of my hesitations and confusion.

Now, all I want is to be close to her.

"You're so comfortable," I murmur, scooting even closer and nuzzling Uri's neck.

The pillow beneath me chuckles, the sound vibrating my bones.

"Too bad, I guess I'll eat this lovely breakfast the Dragon prepared *just* for you and have it all to myself," Uri says wistfully.

My stomach suddenly rumbles, echoing through the prison cell.

I sigh. "Fine. For food, I'll wake up."

"Trust me," Uri says dryly, "I would rather say snuggled with you, little Witch. But you need to eat something, considering you've barely eaten for the past week."

A week.

I've only been down here for a week?

Without the light of day to track the time, I thought it might have been months.

"The Dragon made it?" I ask, sitting up and brushing my long black hair out of my face. It's a tangled, disgusting mess.

I'm a mess.

"Mhm. Brought it down here just for you. You slept through him staring at you for a good hour. It was fairly creepy. He sat on the floor and just... *watched* you. Like he's afraid if he blinks, you'll simply disappear."

I glance back at Uri, who is sitting up now as well. "He likes to do that. I think it's a Dragon thing. Trystan and the others mentioned that he, uh—" I clear my throat, looking up at the ceiling awkwardly. "Well, they said something about how I'm the latest 'treasure in his trove.'"

Uri chokes. "What? They said that? In those exact words?"

I look at her, alarmed. "Yes, why? What's so bad about that?"

Uri's eyes are wide. "Elsie. Dragons do not let go of their treasure... *ever.* They're greedy little shits."

I raise a brow. "You created them, remember?"

Uri purses her lips. "Are you suggesting he gets it from me?" I do not say anything. I simply watch her with knowing eyes. She sighs. "Fine, he might have gotten it from me. You know I like shiny things. But you have to know what this means."

I wait, clearly *not* knowing what she means. "I'm not a God, remember?"

"Right," Uri says, brow furrowed. "Well, let me put it more simply. Nerethus loves you and if you ever leave here, the Dragon is going to follow."

I freeze.

"What?" My voice is a few octaves higher.

Uri glances at the tray of delicious looking food next to us. I hadn't even seen it yet, but steam wafts from freshly baked biscuits next to sliced fruit arranged in an artful and complicated design based on color and texture.

"Oh. *Ohhhh,*" Uri says, clearly coming to some realization.

"Gods, what next?" I hiss.

Uri turns to me with wide eyes and a funny smile on her face. "Something for another time."

"Are you tricking me?" I hiss and Uri's face falls. "The Dragon does not love me. He can't!"

Uri gives me a sad smile. "You're the one being alive I will never trick, little Witch."

"But that cannot be true!" I protest.

Uri crosses her arms, showing off her toned biceps and shoulders. I briefly get distracted by the sight and have to shake it off.

"How do you know?" I ask in disbelief.

Uri nods. "He thinks you're his treasure *and* he feeds you. For a Dragon, that's love."

I fall back against the bed and press my hands against my eyes. "*Heilige scheiße*, how did this happen? They weren't supposed to *love* me, they were only supposed to *desire* me. And they weren't even supposed to be *men* to begin with. I thought they'd be raging, hideous monsters. *Gottverdammt*, I thought the Mountain Gods actually *did* kill me and that this was Hell and *they* were Demons. I never wanted them to be so fucking attractive and charming. Well..." I pause. "Nerethus is charming. It's questionable for the others. But still!"

Uri lays down next to me and props her head on her hand, listening as I continue word vomiting all of my worries from the past month.

"I mean, it's not like I came in here planning on sleeping with all of them. That's not my usual strategy."

Uri raises a brow and I roll my eyes. "Okay fine, but I didn't actually fuck Albrecht, so that doesn't really count. He only thought we were going to have sex."

Uri snorts. "Uh, huh."

I wring my hands. "But sex? Love? That was not a part of my plan."

"You made it a part of your plan, though," Uri points out. I glare at her.

"Yes, because they looked at me like they wanted to eat me. Their attraction was painfully obvious, and it was also the only clear path forward to achieving my goal. Was it ideal? No."

"But you enjoyed it," Uri says, a mischievous smile on her face.

I look up at the glowing bugs on the ceiling. "Yes. I did. But I'm 200 years old. I can do whatever the Hell I want, with whoever the Hell I want. I just... Well, I didn't want to kill them. I simply thought it was the right thing to do. For Daphne." I whisper her name.

Uri nods. "And if my words are true? If you learn that the Mountain Gods are innocent and it's Pertcha's fault—what will you do then?"

My head falls into my hands and I massage my dirty scalp, wincing at how oily it is.

I sigh and look back at Uri, feeling hollow. "Then I would need to make a few apologies."

He cannot love me.

He *shouldn't.*

Because I am the biggest monster of all.

I murdered him. And I felt no guilt. I felt nothing but rage as I watched the life fade from his stupid eyes.

I have killed many people in my life—most of them deserved it. But there is no guilt. No weight on my conscience, not until now.

If Uri is right, then for the first time in my long life, I will be *wrecked* with guilt.

And that makes me fear.

Uri watches me, reading my out of control emotions. "Why are you so scared of being loved, Elsie? I can feel your fear. But I can also feel your attraction. You like the Mountain Gods. So why are you trying not to?"

I sigh, exasperated and overwhelmed. The words are on the tip of my tongue, but I can't get myself to say it.

"You don't have to." Uri's voice is gentle as she reaches over and tucks a stray hair behind my ear, cupping my cheek. "I know what you want to say, remember? I'm in your soul, Witch. I know your heart. They will not end up like Daphne. Loving you isn't another curse leading only to an ugly end. It's okay to love."

Uri takes a deep breath, "For example. I love you. I would do anything for you, because we are two sides of the same coin."

My heart skips a beat at the way she's looking at me.

"*Anything* you need."

"Uri?" I ask, breathless.

She nods.

"I need you to be really fucking clear right now because I'm honestly not sure what you're suggesting."

Uri sighs. "Right. Give me a moment."

The God pauses, contemplating for a moment, before meeting my gaze again.

"If you wanted pleasure, I would happily give it to you."

My jaw drops.

"If you wanted merely friendship and companionship, I'm okay with that too," Uri says carefully. "I am not jealous of the other Gods, if that's what you're wondering. I would be more than happy to watch, if you would like that."

Uri's gaze turns hot and my skin tingles in response.

She would watch.

The thought of Uri's eyes on me while I'm taken by the others is enough to turn my legs numb.

"What do you want, though? You speak plenty of what I want, but perhaps I want to know what you want, my familiar."

Uri blinks, her pupils dilating. "That's simple. I want you. The how is inconsequential."

Uri goes quiet for a moment, before scooting closer to me, her hand landing beneath my chin. She tilts my head back so we're eye to eye as Uri leans down and brushes her lips against mine. So gently that I question if it even happened.

"All I want is *you,*" Uri pauses. "Though as a bird, I couldn't wax poetic about how beautiful you look when you smile. Or how I think the perfection of your body rivals all of the Gods combined."

I'm panting now, barely held together as Uri continues, "I couldn't tell you how, after so many centuries of nothing, looking at you makes me *feel* and *yearn,* when I'd long thought those feelings were impossible."

"Uri," I breathe.

"My Witch," she replies, brushing her lips against mine again.

"I don't know what's next, but I know I want you there with me," I whisper, reaching a hand up to caress her cheek. With a moan, her lips meet mine in earnest as the God of Tricks kisses me.

It feels like floating.

One single touch from Uri and I'm boneless, unable to do anything but melt into her touch.

She runs her hands through my hair as her tongue teases the seam of my lips, coaxing my mouth open. Uri makes a pleased noise when I let her in and our tongues tangle as the kiss deepens.

Her spicy sage scent grows stronger, mixed with the scent of juicy blackberries.

"That's us, Elsie. That's our magic," Uri whispers in my head.

We stay like that for a while, bodies tangled and lips locked.

But it never goes further. When Uri pulls back, her eyes are glassy and a small smile plays on her face.

We lay down next to each other, hands clasped.

Then I remember her earlier question and a lump in my throat rises. "Connections are vulnerabilities. Connections lead to loss and pain and *rage.* I don't want to feel that way ever again. I'm... scared of what I'll do."

Uri watches me without judgment. "Does that include our connection?"

I smile and raise a hand to caress her soft cheek. "No. We're different. You are the exception."

She smiles and there's a softness to it that tells me I surprised her.

"It's your life, Elsie—" She gives me a knowing look. "—but never forget that we *made* you to love and be loved in return."

I have to look away to keep from crying.

"Do you know why the Originals are so powerful?" she asks softly.

I clear my throat, looking back at her. "Why?"

Uri smiles. "It's not because we're older. Not really, even if the others claim that as the truth. What truly sets the Originals apart, is we are inevitable. Our power, our existence, it is unavoidable."

I try to comprehend but it's a struggle. "Who is the most powerful Original?"

A voice like liquid night but as cold as an ice storm flows through the dungeon, whispering in my ear, *"You already know the answer, Elsing."*

I nearly jump out of my own skin hearing Aleksander answer. He leans against the bars of the prison, arms crossed, listening to our conversation.

"There is no power greater than Death."

Uri rolls her eyes. "You wish."

Death raises a brow. "I came first."

I frown. "I thought Pennios came first."

Aleksander sneers. "They would like to think that. I simply didn't appear as early as they did, but I remember their creation. I watched it all, unable to move as my body was formed."

Aleksander uncrosses his arms and slides his hands in his pockets. "It's why I'm the most powerful Original. Pennios thinks they are, but when the world is over, I will be the last one standing. There is no power stronger than Death."

Uri makes a frustrated sound. "That is not the explanation I meant, you idiot."

Aleksander ignores her, his pale green eyes fixed on me. "However, the trickster is correct. We are *inevitable.*"

Goosebumps cover my arms at his words, but I don't look away. I don't give him a single inch.

He nods and something on his face softens. "Uri, bring her upstairs when she finishes eating."

"Oh, you're letting me out now? Is that it?" I snark, suddenly furious.

The corner of Aleksander's mouth twitches. "I do not yet forgive you, Witch. But you and I have somewhere to be. There is someone who wishes to speak with you."

Death waits, staring at me expectantly. I cross my arms and stare back, unsure what he wants and not at all pleased about being kept in the dungeon for so long.

"You have something of mine, huntress."

A play on my name. My true name.

I'm still unsure what he means, when his eyes slowly move down to my exposed collarbone, and the shadow beneath my skin peeking out from my shirt.

Oh.

Right.

I look up at him. "Is your magic broken or something? Are you so old that you've forgotten how to call back your little pets?"

"Burn," Uri says beneath her breath. Aleksander glares at her, but his gaze softens when it returns to me.

That softness terrifies me.

I look down and brush my hand over one of the snakes and it detaches from my skin.

I forgot they were here, to be honest.

"Time for you to go," I whisper and in my mind, I reach, using my magic to nudge them away. Their presence is faint and it's difficult not to hurt them, but after a few seconds, I feel the shadows detach, almost as if I woke them up from a deep slumber.

Perhaps moving hosts tired them out. They crawl lazily down my arm, and return to Aleksander who waits, palm up, where they burrow back into his skin.

I don't miss the way Death sighs, as if it's a relief to have his shadow companions back with him once more.

One shadow won't leave, though.

The one around my collarbone. The one he *ordered* to watch over me.

"Come on, go back to your daddy," I mock, and Uri has to look away to keep from laughing.

"I am *not* their father," Aleksander bites out, but I shrug.

"Sure looks like that."

He sighs in anger. "That one is yours. It doesn't want to return to me."

I look at him slowly, "The shadows... talk to you?"

He nods. "Of course. They're Rage Demons, actually."

I blink, taken aback. "Rage Demons?"

"Here we go," Uri sighs.

"What the fuck do you mean, these are Rage Demons?" I demand.

Aleksander shrugs, a glint of amusement in his eyes, "I thought you knew. You fed them your blood, after all. I wouldn't be surprised if you could summon them at will after that. They've never taken another host before. Not until now."

I want to cringe at the word "host," but I don't want to offend the little thing.

Then my heart drops.

"Wait. Wait a damn second. Are *all* of your shadows Rage Demons?"

Aleksander smirks and if I thought he was beautiful before, with all the scowling and grumpiness, seeing him smirk, even that tiny bit of a smile?

It's breathtaking.

But that arrogant shit knows exactly what I'm asking.

"Did you fuck me with one of your Rage Demons?" I snarl, ready to tear this cell apart.

Uri coughs and nearly chokes. "Excuse me, what the actual fuck?"

Aleksander doesn't answer, he simply smiles again and shrugs, "I have powers over all shadows, huntress. I fucked you with my shadows, not a Demon. Your precious morals are intact. Now, if you'll stop talking and eat the breakfast the Dragon made you, we have an appointment to get to."

Then he disappears, fading into the dark.

"Well, you've been busy," Uri says pleasantly.

I have to rub my temples to erase the last few minutes of that conversation. There's something more important to ask.

It hits me a few seconds later.

"What does he mean?" I ask Uri. "What appointment?"

Her eyes are sad and full of regret, which sets off my inner alarm.

"Oh. I see. It's his appointment to kill me. Well," I sigh. "I can't say I didn't see that as a possibility. I'm a little surprised but, all's well that ends well."

There's a sharp slap against my arm and I feel feathers against my face. Uri looks exasperated.

"He's not going to kill you, you ninny!" Then her face falls. "Well, kind of."

"*Verzeihung?* What the Hell do you mean, 'kind of?'" I ask in a high-pitched voice.

She bites her lip. "Well, uh, he's not going to kill you... but you *are* going to the land of the dead."

I blink and Uri coughs, wincing. "Aleksander is taking you to his realm. The land of the dead, which we call the Below. Otherwise known as the Underworld."

"Great. He's taking me there to kill me, isn't he?" I sigh, nodding.

That's gotta be it.

Uri slaps my arm. "He's not going to kill you. I told him if he even so much as injures you, I'll cut his dick off and trick it to never grow back."

Do not get turned on.

Don't you dare.

I clear my throat, shaking off the lust. "Why are we going to this 'Below' then? Why is Death taking me to the underworld?"

Uri's eyes are full of pity when she answers, "He's... taking you to speak with a shade, Elsie. He's taking you to see Daphne."

The food was delicious, I'm sure, but I couldn't enjoy it.

Not after Uri's announcement.

My limbs are numb, merely going through the motions.

Uri transports us back up to the Aive. It makes my stomach turn, threatening to reject all of the food I just gave it.

The gold stone floor beneath my bare feet is grounding.

But still, I am hollow.

I want to see her more than anything I've ever wanted, and yet I've never been so terrified.

I thought we'd see each other again when I joined her on the other side.

Now, I have to truly say goodbye.

I recognize the privilege, of course, but a part of me would prefer being down in the dank, cold dungeon.

The thoughts race through my mind, unable to settle as Uri brings me to the wing of the house with Aleksander's rooms, but we pass the large door that contains his bedroom. We continue past the library and I don't even take a moment to look wistfully at the books.

My fingers are cold and shaking.

It feels like I'm not in my own body as we approach a spiral iron staircase at the end of the hallway. The two of us ascend the staircase, climbing and climbing until my thighs burn and my lungs ache.

The pain helps.

It distracts me enough to allow me to take another step. The air gets colder until I can see my breath in front of me and my cheeks burn against the frost. The handrail of the stairs becomes covered with ice and I'm no longer able to use it to guide me.

Uri reaches back a hand and I grab it, thankful she's here with me.

"Me too," she whispers. "We're almost there. Remind me to yell at Death about this atrocious temperature. It's colder than a mountain goat's snowy balls up here."

The ceiling above the staircase suddenly gets closer and we emerge into a large, white room at the very top of the mountain. At first, I thought the ceiling was white, but now I realize it's actually snow covering see-through glass.

The clouds are far below us and I realize we're at the true peak of the Helvetas. I thought the Aive was high up, but this is... like nothing I've ever seen.

We're practically in the heavens. I can't even see the ground hidden beneath the clouds. Instead, it's endless sky and the occasional bird.

"Welcome to the Peak," Aleksander says. I turn and see him lounging on a large white bed. There are no bedposts or headboard. It's simply a thick mattress in the very center of the room.

"It's fucking freezing, Aleksander. Elsing is going to freeze to death!" Uri berates him, walking over and standing over him with her arms on her hips.

Aleksander stills. "Ah. I no longer feel the cold. My apologies." He snaps his fingers and the air warms. I sigh in relief as the feeling begins returning to my cheeks and my ears begin to thaw out. Death snaps his fingers again and a large blanket drapes over my shoulders. It's woven with fur, which is not my favorite, but in this moment I couldn't care less.

The warmth seeps into my bones and I sigh happily. "Thanks."

Death looks taken aback. His pale eyes wide and confused.

Oh.

Right.

He's not used to my kindness.

"Elsie, we've talked about being nice," Uri says in my head.

I sigh. *"Yes, we've talked about it, meaning you've told me to be nice, and then I consider and reject it!"*

"Sometimes it's okay to be nice, particularly when someone does something nice for you," Uri reminds me.

I glare at her. *"Until I know for sure the Mountain Gods are innocent, I don't trust him."*

"Mhm, sure," Uri says, not believing me.

"Are you two finished gossiping yet?" Aleksander sounds bored as he leans back on the bed, his arms behind his head. The movement highlights his muscles. His newly returned shadows slither beneath his skin.

It's haunting, and all too alluring.

"Yes, we're done," Uri says with a glance towards me. "Time works differently there, hence the bed. I'll keep watch from the skies."

I nod and there's a bright flash, nearly rendering me unable to see. When I can finally see again, Uri is in raven form. They caw at Aleksander and he waves a hand, using his magic to open a hatch in the ceiling.

Uri nuzzles me, their feathers silky against my cheek, before they take flight and disappear into the clouds with a squawk, leaving me alone with Death himself.

"Scared?" he asks.

I scoff. "No. I told you, Death is inconsequential."

He smirks. "Ouch. If I were mortal, that might actually hurt my feelings."

"Good thing you're not mortal."

Aleksander motions for me to sit beside him. I hesitate before joining him.

"You're not scared..." He cocks his head, trying to read me. "But you are nervous. I can hear it. Your blood is racing faster than usual."

I look him in his pale green eyes and say, "Let's get this over with."

He makes a humming noise. "You don't fear Death. I can feel the truth in your words. But you do fear something, don't you?"

I go still, crossing my arms as I stand before him.

He nods. "Yes, you don't fear Death, but you do fear the departed. You worry about what they'll say, or what state you'll find them in."

I grind my teeth, displeased at how he seems to see right through me.

"You said we have an appointment, so let's cut the chitchat and get going," I hiss.

"You work so hard to maintain control," he notes casually. "But while you might not fear Death, be warned, huntress. You will never control Death. No one can, no matter how hard they might try." Then he grabs my hand. I yank it away from him, alarmed, but he meets my gaze and slowly grabs it again, interlacing our fingers.

"Rule number one," he lectures. "We must touch at all times, or your soul will be stuck in the Below for all eternity."

I scowl. "Lovely."

"The Below is not meant for the living. It is the land of the dead, and if you don't do exactly as I say, the shades will kill you."

"I'm starting to see why you're such a grumpy old fuck," I mutter.

He squeezes my hand, not hard enough to hurt, but enough to tell me he is unamused at my snarky quips.

"Rule number two. When we're in the Below, you do exactly as I say, without question."

I scoff and suddenly he yanks my arm, dragging me on top of him so that I straddle his waist, with our faces so close I can feel his breath. Something hard grows beneath me, pressing against my core. It's hard to ignore but I try my best.

"Elsing," Death warns, "you must swear it. The Below is the most dangerous realm that exists. There is a reason only Originals are able to travel there. Lesser Gods cannot withstand the shades, even with their magic."

I'm shocked. "Nerethus and Trystan haven't been to the Below?"

Aleksander shakes his head. "No. They wouldn't survive it. Plus, trying to wrangle the two of them is near impossible. Uriel is the only other God here who has been to the Below, and when she returned, she swore to never visit again."

My heart races.

Not in fear, but from *him*.

"How many times do I need to tell you," my voice is low, "I am not afraid. You will not scare me out of this, Death."

"Fine," he snarls. "But we go no further until you swear to obey my every command while we're there. If you get stuck Below, Uri and the beasts will make my life fucking miserable."

I snort but consider his words. It's difficult to make myself say it, but I do.

For her.

For Daphne.

"Fine," I say slowly. "I promise, this one and only time, to obey your every command while we're in the Below."

"Good," he nods. "Rule number three. No magic."

I nearly fall off his lap. "What?"

He smirks. "You heard me. No magic must be used in the Below. Demons enjoy the taste. If you cast even the smallest spell, it will draw them near."

I huff and look away. "It sounds like you don't have control over your realm, Reapyr."

He grabs my chin and forces my face towards him. "The Below is my one and only creation, and like most creations, at some point it takes on a will of its own. So, huntress, you are correct. I don't have control over it. Which is exactly what makes it so goddamn dangerous."

Fear crawls into my heart.

I stomp on it, crushing it into dust.

"No magic," I promise.

Aleksander nods and releases me. I crawl off him, breathless. Death lays back and motions for me to join him.

I lean back against the mattress, looking up at the snow-covered glass. Death grabs my hand once more and ushers one final command.

"Sleep."

the below

chapter 22

*S*leep, *Sleep, Sleep.*

The command echoes around me, worming its way into my head like a parasite.

My eyes fall shut despite all efforts the contrary.

The feeling of floating is disconcerting.

Then we're falling.

All the while, I feel Death's cold hand in mine.

Everything halts and I realize we've stopped. We are no longer resting on a comfortable bed. Pebbles grind into my back. The air smells like frozen mint and just burnt trees.

It's cloying and intriguing, but distinctly off-putting. I neither hate nor love it.

As my eyes open, I take in the darkness above me.

We're in some wide open valley, a starless sky above our heads. Aleksander tugs on my hand as he stands, bringing me with him.

Dizziness hits me hard but I manage to keep my bearings as I look around at our new surroundings.

There is... nothing.

No grass. No plants.

No trees, no sunlight.

Just a gray wasteland, devoid of all life.

Barren mountains are in the distance and suddenly red lightning lights up the sky, making the realm tremble. I nearly jump out of my skin.

"The weather here is unpredictable," Aleksander mutters.

"Did you have to make your realm so…" I struggle for the right word. I don't know the equivalent in this language, so I switch to Almanni. *"Deprimierend and Trauig?"*

Death snorts. "It wasn't always that way, and the Below is not all depressing and sad. We're in the Between. There are no souls here. The Below is divided up into sections. The Between is for myself and my Demons to transport souls. It's meant for traveling. Then, there's the Beyond, which is where the good souls go after they face judgment."

"And the bad souls?" I ask.

Aleksander nods. "The Beneath, which is what the Republic would consider to be 'Hell.' Anyone who ends up in the Beneath is tortured for all time."

"Do they ever… earn their way out?" I ask, curious. I'm sure I'm headed right to the Beneath when I die.

Death smirks. "Very rarely. We put many of them to work, since it takes a lot of effort to maintain control over an entire realm. There have only been a dozen souls to ever earn their way out. But it is possible."

"Hm." I put this information in the back of my head for later. Glad to know I might only be damned for *part* of eternity.

"Let's go. We're headed to the Beyond," Aleksander says, taking off at a brisk walk. He tugs me along and it takes me a moment to catch up. His legs are so much longer than mine and his steps are larger.

"Slow down," I hiss.

"Ah, right. Sorry. I'm not used to anyone being here with me." He clears his throat. He looks around, surveying the landscape as we walk, like he's waiting for something to happen.

"You don't feel comfortable here, do you?" I prod for more answers.

Aleksander shrugs. "A long time ago, I did. The Below has become… different, in my absence. I used to spend most of my time here, but with the curse, I can only be here for a week at a time. Work has fallen by the wayside, and the Demons have grown more powerful. I am their king, but I fear the sight of you would cause waves of… distrust. Creation is dangerous. At some point, all creations take on a life of their own. The Below did the same."

"Because you're breaking the rules by bringing me here?" He nods. "Then why do it? Why go through all of this effort? You said you spoke with Daphne. Why not end it there?" I blurt.

Aleksander stops and turns, watching me with an unusual emotion in his eyes.

Almost like...

Pity.

"She told me you never got the chance to say goodbye."

It hits me so hard I nearly stumble to the ground.

"She told you," I breathe.

Death nods.

"Daphne wishes to say goodbye," he admits. "This is not about the curse, or finding the truth. Speaking with her for a few minutes told me all I needed to know. Uriel is correct, by the way. Their story is true. Pertcha has broken the rules."

"You must hate me," I say, swallowing the lump in my throat.

Aleksander raises a hand and brushes my hair behind my ear. "I should hate you. A part of me still does, but not in the way you think."

He doesn't expand on it any more than that as he tugs me forward again and we continue walking.

A man of few words, it seems.

I desperately want to badger him for more information, more answers, more anything.

But the wrongness in the air and the disturbing landscape keep me distracted.

As does the thought of seeing Daphne.

Of saying goodbye.

"I don't dislike you, Elsing," Aleksander says.

I nearly trip over myself.

"You just said a part of you still hates me," I remind him.

He squeezes my hand and it warms my heart, despite the chilly environment.

"Two things can be true at once. But I don't dislike you. I wouldn't have brought you here otherwise."

I huff. "Nerethus and Trystan could have pressured you into it. There's every possibility you're just doing this because you feel like you have to. Or, you could be planning to leave me here and be rid of me altogether."

Aleksander is silent as we continue on. But the Mountain gets no closer. Soon, my sides are burning as we navigate the increasingly steep terrain.

"Do you need a break?" Death asks.

I try to look menacing but I'm breathing too hard to be convincing.

"Sometimes I forget about mortal limits," he mutters to himself before turning away from me and lifting his free hand to his lips. He uses his fingers to let out a sharp whistle that makes my ears ring.

"Didn't you say we shouldn't draw attention?" I hiss at him.

"Yes, I did."

I wait for him to continue, but he doesn't.

"That's comforting," I mumble.

Still, my companion is silent.

A distant peal of red lightning hits the ground. The floor of the Below begins to shake.

"Earthquake?" I ask.

Aleksander laughs. "Not quite."

At first, all I see is a gathering dark cloud.

Then the shadows reach the ground, almost like a tornado. They grow closer and I pull Death's hand, wanting to get as far from the storm as possible.

But still, he doesn't move. Doesn't say a single word. He just *waits*.

"What are you doing? We need to hide!" I shout over the growing wind.

"It's fine, huntress," he reassures me, but I'm not in the least reassured.

As the storm approaches, it *shifts,* taking the form of a large, four-legged creature.

A creature with... hooves.

What approaches us is no normal horse.

It's at least three times the size of the horses I've seen, and its eyes are glowing red. But its body is made of shadows. Streaks of red lightning flash from beneath its cloudy gray and black skin, making the horse lit from within. The horse's mane and tail is a glowing, brilliant white.

It's the most beautiful, terrifying creature I've ever seen.

"This is Sälva, one of the guardians of the Below."

The shadow horse smiles, showing off a mouthful of sharp black fangs.

"She's a unicorn." Aleksander nods. "She's a unicorn in *Hell.*"

Death let out an annoyed sigh and nodded again. "She's a Demon."

I flash him a droll stare. "A Demon unicorn?"

Aleksander shrugs. "Of course. All unicorns are Demons."

I blink.

Okay then.

Facing Sälva, I take a deep breath. "Nice to meet you."

Aleksander reaches a hand up to pet Sälva's neck but the Demon-unicorn pins its ears, backing away from Death's touch.

Ah.

A mare, then.

"Temperamental females," Aleksander mutters.

"What was that?" I squeeze his hand and dig my nails into his knuckles.

He glares at me. "Sälva and I are normally on good terms. But she's been a bit upset the past few centuries in my absence."

"Well, of course." I'm not surprised. "You abandoned her. How typically *male.*"

Aleksander's eyes narrow further. "I did not *abandon* anyone," he bites out. "I'm cursed by, apparently, a meddlesome *God.* Which," he turns to Sälva, "I've explained to you many times."

Sälva sniffs and prances, hitting him in the face with her luminescent white tail.

I have to hold my breath so I don't laugh at the extremely unamused look on Aleksander's face.

"Sounds like you owe her an apology," I note. He sighs and lifts his free hand to rub his temples.

The shadows beneath his skin are more prominent here.

Red lightning travels along them, and bright red eyes dot many of the snakes along his toned arms.

Sälva pushes past Aleksander and stares at me, assessing whether I'm friend or foe. I have to crane my neck to meet her red eyes. It's difficult not to tremble as the horse leans down and sniffs my forehead.

Whatever the Hell-horse senses seems to mollify her, because Sälva lets out a huff and then kneels partially so we can get on its back. It's difficult to get on her without letting go of Aleksander's hand, but we manage, albeit ungracefully.

Once mounted, Aleksander settles in behind me and without letting go, he wraps his right arm around my waist. Then, in the absence of reins, uses his left hand to grasp her mane.

Sälva's hide, while made of shadows, is warm, soft, and very solid. The red lightning that flashes beneath her skin tickles lightly when it touches my legs. I reach down and rub my hand along her neck, admiring her.

"The Beyond, please, Sälva," Aleksander orders, and Sälva neighs, the sound full of booming thunder and screams.

I feel blood trickle from my ears in response. Aleksander lets go of Sälva's mane as the mare takes off in a soft trot, her gait floaty and smooth despite her large size. Death's hands cup my ears as he gently wipes the blood away, smearing it on his black pants.

We fall into a comfortable silence as Sälva picks up into a canter, and the Between fades into the background.

The terrain turns rockier as we make our way over the mountain, but still, there are no trees. Just black boulders. The steep route doesn't slow Sälva down. If anything, it speeds her up.

Soon, we're headed down the other side of the mountain. I have to lean back to keep from sliding off her. Aleksander's arm tightens around my waist and his large hand settles on my lower stomach, holding me in place.

We make it to the bottom in one piece and pick back up on the set path. A sprawling black river sits to the left. The water in it barely moved and bubbled, making it almost reminiscent of tar. Something moves beneath the surface, leaving telltale ripples, but I can't make out any distinct shape. It pulls me closer and I grow dizzy.

I can't look away. I need to get closer.

"Close now."

"Come close now," it sings to me.

A hand on my shoulder shakes me out of it.

"Don't look at the River," Aleksander orders sternly. "It comes from the Beneath."

"What's in there?" I shake my head, trying to brush off the compulsion within the river. "It's fucking powerful."

Aleksander huffs. "There are Demons beneath the surface. Kelpies, who love the taste of flesh. They torture some of the worst souls who land in the Below. You're hearing their hunting song. It means they're hungry."

I gulp.

"We chain the damned to the bottom of the river. The Kelpies consume them, only for the soul to reform. They're consumed over and over again, every day, without end."

I shiver and glance back at the passenger behind me. "Was that your idea?"

Aleksander smirks. "Perhaps."

"Sadistic fuck."

He laughs again and the sound makes my worries fade.

That's how I know I'm fucked in the head.

Death's smile makes me *relaxed.*

How much can be wrong with a person to create that sort of reality?

Berating myself, I refocus on the changing landscape, making sure to avoid looking at the river to our left.

A fork in the road appears, and we take the path to the right.

"The Beneath is to the left," Aleksander says, his breath against my cheek. My back is pressed into his chest and it's impossible to ignore. "If we took that path, we would eventually descend beneath the ground."

"Sounds lovely," I snark.

Aleksander doesn't respond, but I can feel his smile in the silence.

The landscape suddenly changes in a single blink, and a large, golden door suddenly appears out of nowhere. No walls hold it up, but there it stands, right in the middle of the given path.

I look down and gasp as the gray storm underneath Sälva's skin solidifies and her hide turns shiny and black. Any hint of her red lightning disappears.

A giant, red horn shimmers into existence on her forehead and I nearly choke.

I glance back at him, my jaw slack. He laughs again at the shocked look on my face. Sälva neighs and this time the sound is melodic and layered instead of painful.

Sälva comes to a gentle halt just before the golden door and kneels. We slide off and Aleksander deftly slides his hand from my stomach, trailing down my arm, and back into my own, interlacing our fingers.

I turn and reach my free hand back to rub her neck once more. Sälva stands and shakes herself off. Some stray shadows fade into the air at the movement.

"Thank you," I tell her.

"She will wait here for us until we're ready to return."

Sälva cranes her neck to look at him as she pins her ears.

I clear my throat. "He meant to *ask,* if you could kindly wait for us to finish? The road is steep and you made the journey so much more enjoyable. We would be honored if you could return us to the Between."

Sälva snorts and walks over to me, nudging my face with her velvety soft black snout.

She nickers lightly in my ear, the sound mellow and warm.

I smile and press a kiss against her nose.

"She never lets me do that," Aleksander mutters beneath his breath.

Sälva and I turn in unison and pin him with what I'm sure is a similarly exasperated glare.

"Perhaps if you weren't such a pushy asshole and exhibited some *manners,* females would react more kindly to you!" I snap.

Sälva stomps her foot in agreement and trots off to check out some of the surrounding trees, clearly tired of this conversation.

Aleksander sighs and pulls me towards the golden door. The edge of it seems to pulse with light, making the air shimmer.

With a tattooed hand, Aleksander reaches out and pushes the door open. I follow as he steps through. The scent of cool mint and herbs fades and is replaced with something sweeter, like sugared lemons.

Instantly I feel at ease. I come up beside Aleksander and stop. If it weren't for his hand in mine, I would drop to my knees. He has to hold on tight as I gaze out across the sparkling valley in front of us. A bright blue ocean sits to our right, with a pink sand beach. A golden moon sits in the purple sky beside the bright, burning sun that warms the air.

Impossible

And yet.

And yet.

It's perfect. I could stay here forever. Tears fall from my face as I behold the perfection of the Beyond, but none of it compares to the beauty of the woman standing in front of me.

A woman I thought I'd never see *again.*

My best friend.

And the woman I so desperately love.

Daphne smiles, dimples forming in her pale cheeks. "Hi, Elsie."

the beyond

chapter 23

The grass is soft beneath my knees as my legs give out underneath me. Tears stream down my face as I behold an impossibility.

Daphne is dead.

But now she stands before me.

"I'll give you two a moment." Aleksander nods to Daphne.

My head snaps to the side and I give him a confused look. "What about rule number one?"

He smiles. "I'm the God of Death. The rules don't apply to me, just you." Aleksander looks down and slides one of his silver rings off his pinky finger. It's a thick band of interwoven black and silver, with letters from another language. He lifts my hand and slides it onto my pointer finger. It's loose, barely staying on. The metal is cold against my skin as he pulls away, letting my hand drop.

"That will keep the Demons at bay for a short time. It contains enough of my magic that they will only see my signature. The longer you're here, the longer your magic and your scent are in the air. They will smell it eventually, and they will come for us."

I raise a brow. "Are you incapable of controlling your own realm?"

Death goes stiff.

"To a degree." His voice is tight.

Oh shit. Okay, that's not good.

"Right," I breathe, looking back at Daphne.

Her golden blonde hair cascades in perfect waves across her shoulder. Half of it is pulled away and I can make out the outline of a pink bow tying it back. Bangs fall artfully, framing her heart-shaped face, the picture of disheveled perfection. Full pink lips are tilted up in a gentle smile.

She wears a white, ankle-grazing lace dress. The sleeves fall from her delicate shoulders, showing off the smattering of freckles that decorate them.

Death didn't diminish Daphne's sparkle.

It *enhanced* it.

"You have one hour," Aleksander says with a nod.

"One hour?" I gasp. "No. That's not enough."

"I'm sorry, Elsie." Hearing my nickname on his lips for the first time is like a shot to the heart.

I want to hear it again.

But...

"It's not enough time," I breathe.

Aleksander sighs. "I know. I truly am sorry. I... cannot stop the Guardians of Hell when they come looking for us. Not anymore. All creations," Death pauses, "they eventually take on a life of their own. I can control most of the Below, but not all. And the time away all these years..."

He doesn't finish his thought.

I wish I didn't understand, but I do.

"One hour is better than nothing," Daphne whispers.

I nod but my heart continues to sink further and further into my stomach. It's not nearly enough, but I'll take whatever time with her I can get.

Aleksander lets go of my hand and walks away, heading towards the ocean next to the valley, giving us enough space to have our conversation in private, although I'm sure he can still hear us. He is, after all, a God.

"Hi," Daphne breathes.

My heart crumbles. "I'm—I'm so sorry."

I fall to my knees, my hands digging into the soft grass beneath me as the grief hits me in earnest. The tears come in full force, streaming down my cheeks.

A soft, delicate hand cups my cheek, brushing away my tears.

"Nope." She bops me gently on the nose. "Absolutely no blaming yourself. My death isn't your fault. Albrecht would have made up an excuse eventually." Daphne glances around. "Look around you. Look where I get to spend my afterlife, El. There's nothing to be sad about."

I hiccup, the pain in my heart not lessening any, despite the beautiful surroundings. "But you're dead. You're dead and I'm not. It should have been me. I'm the one who kissed you."

"That doesn't mean you deserve to die," she says gently. Her pale green gaze pierces through every wall I have erected around my cold, black heart. She's always seen right through me.

"I miss you," I cry, unable to stop the well of emotion overflowing within me. "I don't know how to do this without you."

Daphne smiles and kneels in front of me. Her hand drops from my cheek as she grabs both of my own hands, clasping them tightly. "Yes, you do. You've just forgotten."

She brushes the skin on my cheek. "I've never regretted meeting you. Not even when they dragged me to Schollen Gorge. My life was miserable before you. You gave me the greatest gift I've ever received: happiness.

I sob, closing my eyes and leaning forward to rest my head on her shoulder. She releases my hands to wrap her arms around me, rubbing my back lightly.

"Let go of your guilt, Elsie. The Fates decided it was my time. It was always out of your control," she whispers into my ear, pressing a kiss against my hair. I wrap my arms around her and squeeze her tightly. The scent of lilac and lavender make my tears fall harder.

She smells like home.

It used to bring me comfort, but now it reminds me that we have to say goodbye once more.

"I don't want to say goodbye. I want to stay here with you," I breathe.

Daphne pulls back and glares at me sternly, "It's not your time. You have so much life left to live. Don't give that up when you have so much goodness to offer the world."

"Will I ever see you again?" I ask, my voice hollow.

Daphne smiles, but there's a sadness to it. "Perhaps."

She pushes up to stand, the delicate purple flowers on her dress shimmer with the movement. "Come on, let me show you the orchard while we still have time."

Daphne tugs on my hand, helping me to my feet and pulling me along as we disappear into something that looks like a maze. It turns out to be a large garden area surrounded by fence-like bushes.

A giant tree sits in the middle, ripe with red and orange fruit. My breath stops as I look at the creature's grazing beneath the tree.

Baby unicorns nibble on the fruit, staining their perfect white snouts pink.

"Hello, friends!" Daphne calls. A few of the baby unicorns neigh and trot over to us. They're bigger than a foal, but clearly still younglings. Their hooves are coated in soft feathers and sparkling, small silver horns sit in the middle of their foreheads.

The unicorns have coats of varying shades of sparkling white, silver, and lilac.

They're beautiful.

Daphne kneels on the soft grass as they approach her, nuzzling her cheeks and nickering happily.

She glances back at me and reaches out a hand, signaling I should join her. "Come, I'll introduce you."

I hesitate. "I don't want to scare them."

Daphne rolls her eyes. "Just sit down with me, silly Witch."

I sigh and kneel next to her. The grass is like a plush velvet carpet beneath my feet.

The baby unicorns back away warily but Daphne whispers and coo's at them, reassuring them that I'm safe.

There's a loud neigh and a giant, all white unicorn pushes through the trees in the distance.

"That's their mom. She's the matriarch of the unicorn herd," Daphne explains.

The mare approaches me, pushing away her excited younglings. A soft, velvet snout comes within inches of my face, and I'm painfully cognizant of the sharp horn pointed at my head.

But the mare merely sniffs me. She huffs and retreats, nibbling on some fruit that looks a bit like a type of blueberry on a nearby bush.

The baby unicorns swarm me, licking my cheek and nudging me playfully. I pet their soft heads, marveling at their horns. Theirs are different, as if not fully formed. The texture is like nothing I've ever felt. It's both soft and hard.

"They're beautiful," I tell her. Several of the unicorns neigh and prance, showing off.

"You cannot hear them, but they speak to the dead. That one," she points at the baby unicorn who prances in circles around me, "his name is Theo."

My brows furrow. "Theo? That's not a very unicorn-like name."

Daphne shrugs. "They get to pick their names. He chose that one."

Theo neighs and approaches me again. Before I realize what's happening, he lays down on my lap, folding his delicate legs so that I hold most of his body weight. He's shockingly heavy as he rests his head on Daphne's legs.

I pet his soft coat, in awe at how soft it is.

He lets out a blissful sigh as the other baby unicorns lay down next to us. Some abandon us for the fruit tree, going back to their nibbling.

It's so peaceful here. Birds sing in the distance and frogs croak from within the forest, creating a natural symphony.

The warm weight of Theo emboldens me.

"Daphne?" I ask slowly.

She meets my gaze with a smile. "Yes?"

I take a deep breath, ready for the rejection, "Did you... Did you like it when I kissed you?"

Daphne smiles wider and looks down at Theo. A light pink blush settles over her cheeks.

She reaches over and squeezes my hand, eventually answering my question. "Yes, Elsie. I liked it very much."

The answer is joy and destruction.

My tears fall harder, dripping down my cheeks and onto the unicorn's fur.

Part of me hoped she would say no.

It would be easier to go on, that way.

To cope without her.

As much as I wanted her to say yes, it makes the pain that much worse.

"In a different life, we could have lived happily ever after," Daphne says gently.

I nod, unable to form words. "Right. A different life."

Daphne squeezes my hand. "Exactly. So don't waste the life you already have. The heart has infinite potential for love, Elsie. Don't close yourself off just because I've moved on. You deserve to be happy and cared for exactly the way you love and care for others."

I sniff and close my eyes, bending over and pressing my face against Theo's fur. He smells like milk and honey.

"Besides, I think, if you truly *look*, you'll find that love is all around you. Waiting, desperate for you to welcome it, to welcome *him.*"

I jolt so hard I wake Theo, who gets up and trots off. I stand, needing some space to breathe.

Daphne stands as well, crossing her arms while I pace.

"What do you mean by that?" I ask, although I'm terrified I already know the answer.

Daphne smiles and approaches me slowly, like I'm some scared animal who might bolt at the first sign of danger. She reaches up and brushes my hair behind my ear, just like Aleksander did earlier.

"You know exactly what I mean, silly Witch. Besides, loving you is the easiest thing in the world. Is it so hard to believe that others would feel the same?"

"Yes," I answer flatly. "Yes, it is. I'm... I'm mean, I'm cruel, I'm unfriendly."

A hand covers my mouth and I squeak. But Daphne simply watches me with a smirk. "I will hear no more of that absolute horseshit, Elsing Wylder. You shine brighter than the sun. Perhaps people are intimidated by how brightly you burn. But the self-hatred stops now. When you leave here, leave that too. See yourself as I have always seen you."

My tears fall onto her hand and she pulls away, only to wrap me in a tight hug.

"You are a wonderful, kind, loving person. Whoever convinced you otherwise deserves the Beneath, and I'm sure if you told your new beau about it, he'd make sure they end up there."

I choke and Daphne laughs, patting my back. I pull away and she smiles wryly.

"He's *not* my beau," I hiss.

Daphne doesn't look convinced. "Elsie, the man waxed poetic about you for hours the first time he visited me. He broke every rule in the book to bring you down here. He's *so* your beau."

I grimace. "I hate that word."

Daphne shrugs. "It's rather human, I'll give you that. Mate, then. He's your mate. That's what the Gods say."

My knees almost give out and I have to rub my chest, trying not to hyperventilate.

"He... He's not my mate. He can't be," I whisper.

Daphne shakes her head. "Nope, none of that. Throw the impossibilities away. It is very possible, and you know it. The God of Death likes you, Elsie." I sputter, but she continues, "Let me ask you this, do you like him?"

"I-I guess, but I mean, it's complicated—"

"Nope, it's really not. Are you attracted to him?"

I scoff and rub the grass with my foot, looking away. "Yes."

"Mhm," she says, "and do you think about him when you're apart?"

I wince. "Sometimes."

"There you have it. You like him and he likes you. Stop being such a stubborn ass about it."

"Daphne!" I hiss. "He's the God of Death. That's a bad idea."

"You're a powerful Witch, Elsing. It's not a bad idea. In fact, I'd say it's a good match. You're both so morose and grumpy."

My jaw drops, and I sputter some more, but Daphne clears her throat. "Anyways. Think about it, okay?"

The question enters my thoughts with a sudden intensity, because if Daphne is right, there's only one thing still holding me back.

"Daph, did they kill you? The Mountain Gods."

Daphne blinks, surprised. "It was a beast, but I do not know if it was one of the Mountain Gods."

"Was it a Dragon or a Griffin? Or, uh, a large shadowy person with a gray cowl?"

How else am I supposed to describe Death's beast form?

Daphne smiles sadly. "No, Elsie. It wasn't Death, and it wasn't a Dragon or a Griffin. I didn't see much of it, because I was drugged, but I know I didn't see either of them."

It wasn't them.

They were right.

"And... there was this person. I couldn't make her features out, but I could tell she had long hair and a dress on. I remember... the smell of rotten mushrooms, oddly." Daphne furrows her brow.

Fuck.

It was Pertcha.

The Mountain Gods are innocent.

I tried to kill them over something they never did.

Daphne grabs my hand and we walk back to the door.

It hasn't felt like an hour.

Aleksander did say time passes differently here.

It hasn't been nearly enough time.

I don't think it will ever feel like enough time with her.

"He's waiting for you on the beach. Theo's mom can give you a ride," Daphne says, lifting two fingers to her lips and whistling lightly.

A neigh sounds in the distance as the unicorn matriarch gallops out of the forest, approaching us.

"Please take my friend to Death," she asks, and the unicorn nods.

"I don't want to say goodbye," I whisper as my heart breaks all over again.

"I know." Daphne smiles.

Then her lips are against mine, warm and soft. I gasp and she catches it, swallowing my surprise. I wrap my arms around her soft waist and fall into her gentle touch.

It's perfect.

It's everything I've ever dreamed of.

She tastes like lemon custard and I can't get enough.

But I know what this is.

I know what she's doing.

"This can't be goodbye," I whisper against her lips.

She smiles and flicks against the seam of my mouth with her tongue, gently coaxing my mouth open as her hands raise to trace the panes of my cheeks.

"We'll see each other again someday. I know it."

I let out a broken sound and she presses one last kiss against my lips. I savor it, desperately hoping it could last forever.

I want to scream and beg for her to never let me go.

But she does.

"Be good, Elsie." She kisses my right cheek. "Be happy." She kisses my left cheek, before pressing her forehead against mine and bruising her lips against mine. "Be alive. Live, El. Live," she whispers, before pressing another kiss against my mouth. I sink against her but my hands grip air.

There's nothing.

Just the lingering taste of her on my tongue and her sweet scent in the air.

Her laughter follows the breeze.

"Daphne? DAPHNE?" I scream, looking around. "No, no. Please come back. That can't be it."

The wind brushes my cheek as a soft voice sounds in my ear, "Be happy, Elsie."

"Please don't go," I beg.

But the wind dissipates.

Leaving me alone once again.

The unicorn mare ignores my tears as she kneels, allowing me to get on her back. I can't stop looking around. Seeing if Daphne is there.

Wishing to see her again.

That can't be it.

It wasn't enough time.

I want to scream.

I want to rage.

I want to *stay*. Here, with *her*.

Yet her words repeat over and over in my head.

Aleksander cannot like me, let alone love me.

He... He shouldn't.

The mare trots slowly over to the beach. A soft, minty breeze brushes against my cheeks. As we get closer, the sound of waves gently lapping at the shore becomes louder. It's so beautiful.

Something gray jumps out of the water in the distance. Some aquatic creature with a long nose and fins. It giggles happily as others of its species join in on the fun.

Aleksander sits in the pink sand, watching it all.

As the unicorn approaches him, he glances up at me, his elbows resting on his raised knees.

He looks relaxed. I've never seen him this way. It's unsettling and curious.

"I see you made another friend," he notes, taking in my tear-soaked cheeks and what are, I'm sure, my swollen, red eyes. "Are you alright?"

The unicorn stops. I grab her thick silver mane and slide off, landing in the soft pink sand.

She nickers and nudges my shoulder with her lips. I give her head a pat, pressing a kiss against her cheek. "Keep an eye on my friend, please."

I swear the mare nods before neighing and cantering off, pink sand spraying the air in her wake.

"No," I answer finally. "I'm not okay. I'm not sure I ever will be."

The weight on my heart is still heavy. But it's lifted, slightly.

Daphne isn't alone.

She's not suffering.

She's not in pain.

That knowledge is a gift. I know it is.

Sinking down until I'm sitting next to Aleksander, I process in silence.

We say nothing.

We simply watch the frolicking sea creatures.

Something joins them and I squint, trying to see what it is.

It has... hair.

And a human face. But where there should be legs, there is a beautiful set of orange and pink fins.

"A Mer?" I ask in wonder.

"Mhm," Aleksander murmurs. "Her name is Lythe."

Something about the way he says her name.

It's... It's how I sound when I talk about Daphne.

"Oh," I whisper. "You... *loved* her."

He shoulder bumps me gently, eyes still on the ocean. "Yes. She doesn't remember me now. Pennios made sure of it."

"How long has it been?"

"Nine centuries, give or take."

I reach down and run my fingers through the soft sand, the pink grains tickling my palms.

"I'm sorry."

Death sighs. "Don't be. It was a long time ago. But sometimes I... I come here. To see her. To remind myself it was real. When you live as long as I do, it all becomes a bit of a blur, and I find myself questioning what was real and what was just a dream."

I look out at the blue ocean. "It sounds lonely."

Death is silent for a moment. "It sounds like you understand the feeling."

I smile, but there is no happiness within it.

Just hollow acceptance.

"I do."

Aleksander glances at me, his face unusually earnest. "Daphne loves you, you know. She thinks the world of you. Only a few minutes into our conversation and that was very apparent."

I look up at the glowing moon overhead with a sigh. "The feeling is mutual."

We're quiet as we watch the waves, both of us sitting in our silent grief.

"It never gets any easier, does it?" I ask.

Aleksander looks at me finally, his pale green eyes so clear and earnest it makes me lose my breath.

"No. It doesn't. But life goes on. The world continues to spin. The pain never leaves. It never grows smaller, but over time, we grow *around* it. The sharpness of grief will dull as the years pass. Never gone but, softer, somehow." Death reaches over and grabs my hand, squeezing it.

"I wish I could stay," I admit quietly.

Aleksander nods. "I do too. Though, I think I would miss the constant annoyance of a certain Griffin and his looming, red-eyed scaly boyfriend."

"Right," I say the word slowly.

Where do I fit? I want a home too. I want to scream the words but they die in my throat, suffocating on my embarrassment.

"I'm allowed to come here as much as I want. Often... my 'work' here is simply an excuse to visit Lythe. She never comes to shore, which is for the best, really. Shades aren't supposed to interact with anything living, and although I am a God, I am technically *alive.* But I come and I..." He pauses, hesitating. "I watch her. Seeing her grounds me. She reminds me of what I stand to lose, should I love the wrong person again."

Am I the wrong person?

I try to think of the right words to say in return but there are none. He looks at me, pale green eyes full of frustration. "I do not hate you because I dislike you, Elsing Jäger. I hate the way I don't hate you at all."

Everything else disappears.

It's just us.

Death and me, on the shores of an eternal sea.

For the few seconds we look at each other, time and reality cease. Maybe this is the true power of an Original. To feel the weight of their full attention is like becoming a rock within the raging river of time.

Aleksander glances down to the ring on my pointer finger, but I can't look away from his beautiful face, at the sharp planes of his cheekbones and the light shadow of facial hair.

"Keep it," Death says, nodding to the ring. He opens his mouth and hesitates, something I've never seen him do. Whatever he was going to say, he changes his mind on. Clearing his throat he announces, "We've lingered too long. We need to get back."

Aleksander snaps his fingers and suddenly we're standing in front of the gold door.

I take one last glance at the Beyond, my heart aching for one final look, hoping to see a flash of golden hair.

There's nothing. No sign Daphne was ever there. But her scent remains in the air, and that's enough.

It was real.

Every second of my time with her was real.

No matter how the years pass, her memory will never fade.

"We'll see each other again," I push the vow into the wind, and I swear, some phantom fingers brush against my cheek in return, but Aleksander is there, pulling my other hand as he drags me through the golden door, and we begin the journey back to the Between.

the return

chapter 24

T he trip back to the Between is quick. The landscape is a blur as I disappear into my mind, lost in my own thoughts. Sälva is so fast, I barely even notice when we ascend the mountain. Aleksander has to squeeze my hand when we go down the other side, reminding me to lean back when I almost fall forward down Sälva's neck as she descends the steep cliff.

Her coat has turned back to its shadowy state, but I swear she controls the bolts of red lightning beneath her skin so as to not bother me. There are no telltale tingles of her power like there were last time.

Death, however, hisses a few times, and out of the corner of my eye, I see a few stray bolts of red lightning hit him in the ass.

"Sälva, cut it out," he snarls.

She neighs and flicks him hard with her tail.

We get to the bottom of the mountains and Sälva breaks into a fast gallop.

"Why are we rushing?" I shout against the wind. I never noticed any breeze before, but at this speed, the air blasts me in the face. Aleksander bats my black hair away as it mimics Sälva's actions, hitting him in the face again. He grabs it and twists, securing it into a rope that he tucks into the back of my shirt.

The feeling of his fingers at the nape of my neck sends goosebumps across my body.

This man has seen me naked, has tasted me, but the innocent, casual touch of his fingers makes me unable to form coherent thoughts.

How weak I've become!

"Look behind us," Aleksander says, his voice dark.

I crane my head and look over his shoulder.

The sight that greets me sends my stomach into knots.

A monstrous cloud darkens the landscape and suddenly the wind picks up. The storm sweeps closer and closer to us.

It reminds me of Sälva, but there is an evil to this storm that makes me shiver.

Shapes begin to take form: a group of riders and their horses. But nothing about them is normal. Flesh hangs off the horse's bodies, revealing decaying organs and bony skeletons beneath. The riders are in similar states, half rotten and wielding black, bloody swords. The dead horses spit blood as they let out horrible screams that make my ears bleed again.

"Hurry, Sälva. The Horde cannot get Elsing," Aleksander urges.

I force my gaze away, looking forward as I grip the mare's mane tightly.

"Who are they?" I shout.

"The Guardians of the Below. They hunt souls who attempt to escape and consume them. They're powerful Demons. Their bodies are not like mine, so the consumption of souls has rotted them from the inside out, the evil bleeding into their bodies."

I scoff. "Your realm is such a joyous place."

Aleksander ignores me and urges Sälva forward. We approach the spot where we first arrived and Sälva slows down.

"Jump," Death orders and I slide off Sälva's back, barely landing on my feet. The gravel digs into my hands as I catch my balance but Aleksander's hand is on my back, pulling me up and dragging me close to a large boulder.

"Fuck, they're too close," he snarls, whirling to the mare who watches the approaching Demons with wary eyes. "Sälva, go!"

The mare neighs and takes off in the other direction, shifting back into shadows as her material body dissipates.

But the storm she becomes does not travel far. Instead, it grows bigger. Peals of thunder rock the ground, vibrating down into my very bones.

The storm suddenly moves fast, hovering over us. The Horde approaches but bolts of red lightning stop the skeletal horses in their tracks.

"Sälva must like you," Aleksander notes. The lightning creates a cage, protecting us from the Demonic entities.

One of the rotten Demons snarls and lifts their sword, using it to break through the lightning barrier.

I've had just about enough of this day.

Grief is a funny thing.

How quickly sadness can turn into *rage*.

"Fuck this," I snarl, pulling away from Aleksander. I lift a finger and unleash my own lightning at the Demon, yanking it down from the heavens.

But something is different this time. Maybe it's this place, maybe it's me, I'm not sure.

I point at the Demon. "Leave or die."

It's not white, nor is it red like Sälva's.

It's *black*, and when it hits the main Demon, the one who raised its sword, the Demon explodes, covering everything with rancid black blood and pieces of rotten, decayed flesh.

There's nothing left of it. The other Demons roar in anger and charge.

Aleksander curses and his shadows shoot out of him, suffocating one of the Demons.

"You just had to start a fight!" he snarls.

"You love it," I pant, pulling more lightning down as it blasts out of my fingertips. Demon parts go flying—rancid, oozing pieces of flesh covering the ground.

The smell is so rotten I gag.

Two Demons left.

I take the left and Aleksander takes the right. I direct my lightning into the Demon's chest with a scream. My hands are so hot, I'm surprised they're not on fire. The lightning tugs at my core as the magic streams out of me.

The Demon is left with a massive, gaping hole between its chest. It falls to the ground, disintegrating into a pile of liquified flesh.

Aleksander finishes off the last one and we stand there, panting.

"More will come. We need to leave *now*." He grabs my hand and pulls me so we're facing each other, palms clasped.

He leans forward, wrapping me in his arms, his voice in my ear. "This will feel strange."

"Do it!" I shout and the next thing I know, something *sucks* my body into the air. Into nothingness.

I'm floating, going nowhere yet being pulled in every direction all at once. The sensation is painful, but Aleksander's hand remains firm in mine. I cannot see him, but I know he's there. He squeezes my palm and something hard hits my chest as I'm flung back into my body.

"Breathe!" Aleksander orders, his hand slamming down on my sternum. Air is forced into my lungs as I open my eyes, back in the Aive.

I gasp violently, writhing against him as my body readjusts.

Then I proceed to hurl up every bit of food in my system all over the God of Death, covering him in green bile and bits of half-chewed fruit.

He doesn't flinch.

Embarrassment floods me but my stomach turns again and I moan, leaning into him. He wraps his arms around me despite the sick on his shirt and arms, rubbing my back in slow circles.

"I'm sorry, usually the process is slower. The disorientation will pass in a few minutes."

I groan. "No offense, but your realm fucking sucks. The Beyond excluded."

Aleksander snorts. "Thank you."

The sound of wings approaches and Uri drops into the room, shifting from raven to a woman in an instant.

"You're back!" She yanks me out of Death's arms, but he maintains a firm grip on my arm. "Gods, you were gone for so long. I considered going down there myself to get you."

"How long were we out?" I croak, allowing her to hold me and check me over. Uri pulls back and examines me, her dark eyes missing nothing.

"You were there for two weeks, Elsie. Do you know how difficult it's been to keep the beast Gods entertained for two whole weeks? Do you know how many times I've considered tossing both of them off of this godsforsaken mountain?" Her voice is high-pitched with strain and I laugh, kissing her cheek.

Uri stills. "You laughed. Are you okay? Gods, Aleks. What the Hell did you do to her?"

Death shrugs. "I did nothing. The huntress can tell you of our time in the Below, but before that, a bath is in order. For all of us."

Aleksander snaps his fingers and my stomach flips as we reappear next to the hot springs. The two Originals lead me into the hot water, clothing and all.

I sigh at the warmth as my mind and soul defrost.

"I am not getting my hair wet," Uri says, and shoots Aleksander a hard look. "Be nice or I'll peck your eyes out again." There's a flash as they turn back into raven form, shaking the moisture off their feathers and flying over to the edge to watch us while they preen.

"Again?" I ask and he sighs, rubbing a hand down his face.

"I do not want to talk about that particular incident," he mutters.

I glare. "Fine. But you will tell me the whole story sometime. Not now, but later."

He nods noncommittally and drags me deeper into the water. "Let's get you out of these clothes. We're both covered in vomit."

I want to cringe. "Technically that's your fault."

He makes a general noise of partial agreement. "Enough distracting me, arms up."

I'm frozen at his kindness, at this new, gentle version of Death. I've grown accustomed to his prickly nature and snarky comments.

"Why are you being nice to me now?" I ask, lifting my arms and allowing him to pull the ruined tunic off. He reaches down and runs his fingers beneath the hem of the shirt, tickling my thighs, before peeling it off me slowly.

The cold air hits my stomach and breasts and I shiver, my nipples growing cold and hard.

Aleksander tosses the shirt onto the walkway near the springs before pulling me further into the water.

Then he's below the surface, his fingers brushing the waistline of my panties.

He peels them off with careful precision, lifting one foot and then the other until I'm completely naked before him. He emerges from the water and I realize his clothes are gone now too.

"You could have done that to me, you know. Magicked my clothes away," I note. But why the fuck am I saying this?

What is happening?

"Be happy, Elsie." Daphne's voice sounds in my memory and I shiver.

I... I'm not sure I know how to be happy anymore.

"Maybe I wanted to take care of you, little huntress," Aleksander murmurs softly. "Come, your hair has bits of Demon flesh in it and as beautiful as you are, it really is quite disgusting to look at."

I snort and allow him to dip me down, rinsing my hair. A bar of soap appears in his hand. It smells like lavender mixed with his own spicy, black pepper scent. He creates a rich lather in his hands before applying it to my damp hair, massaging my scalp with slow ease.

"Neither of us are particularly nice," he notes. "But that doesn't mean we're incapable of kindness."

I want to glare at him but the head massage feels too good. My body floats as I relax into his touch and consider what he's said.

"But," I start, opening my eyes and glancing up at him, "you did admit you still hate me. So what is this, Aleksander? No more word games, please."

He nods and takes a deep breath, going silent as he rinses the soap out of my hair. Another bar of soap appears in his hand and he applies it like a lotion to the ends of my long black hair, careful to massage it in. Some sort of solid oil, perhaps.

"I do not hate you, Elsing. I hate what you do to me," he admits slowly. My heart thuds as I wait for him to continue, terrified of his next words. His pale green eyes meet mine, his blond hair damp from his journey beneath the surface of the springs.

"From the moment I found you in my kitchen, wearing nothing but that ridiculously sheer shirt, you have been embedded in my soul. As hard as I might try, I can think of nothing else but you. I hate how much I need you, how much I want you, and I do want you, huntress. Every fiber of my being craves you from the moment I wake up until the second I fall asleep at night. The power you have over me drives me insane, because the last time I felt this way, I lost *everything.*"

My tongue goes dry and my jaw drops as he proceeds to rinse the solid oil from my hair.

He pulls me to the edge of the hot springs, giving me another whispered order. "Stand up."

My feet touch the warm stone beneath the surface as I stand and face him. The water comes to my waist, leaving my breasts bare.

Aleksander uses his muscular arms to lift himself onto the edge.

His tattooed cock is hard, the barbell shining in the warm light of the room. It makes me salivate.

I want to taste it. Taste *him.*

His hand grabs my face as he cradles my cheek, his eyes fixed on my lips. "Save that look for later, huntress. My control is in tatters and you've been through quite an ordeal, both physically and emotionally. We have all the time in the world to play, but for now, relax."

I suddenly want to slap him.

Then kiss him.

Then fuck him.

But I sigh and nod, putting my fate in his waiting hands.

The exhaustion is beginning to set in as the adrenaline of being in the Below finally fades from my body.

"Just this once I'll follow your orders," I mutter.

He smirks. "Just once?"

A different soap appears in his hand, the bar the same shade of green as his eyes. This one smells exactly like him: spice and incense and Death.

He creates a thick lather in his palms and grabs my hands gently, massaging the soap into my skin, traveling up my arm slowly, cleaning every inch of my body.

I have no words, all I can do is watch and *feel* as he takes care of me the way a lover takes care of the one they cherish most.

Making his way to my shoulders, he switches to my other arm and repeats the motion.

"Leg." In one swift movement, we've swapped places and he's placing me on the edge.

I lift my leg, placing my foot in his tattooed hand. He massages the soap into my calves and I moan. My muscles are tight and it's painful in the best way possible.

It also leaves me completely exposed. The air hits my throbbing pussy and all of the sudden the ache is too much to handle.

I need him. I need him like I need my next breath.

He doesn't change course though, continuing to massage up my legs.

"Switch," he orders, dropping the foot he held as I lift the other, placing it in his waiting palm.

He continues his slow path up my body, the pleasure making me sway and my eyes fall shut. Despite the heat of his touch, exhaustion weighs heavily on me.

There's a flash and soft arms wrap around my waist as Uri brushes my wet hair with her fingers. "I've got you," she whispers. "Just relax. I can feel how exhausted you are."

I mumble something incomprehensible as she begins brushing and braiding my hair. It feels so nice.

I can't remember the last time someone took care of me, let alone two people.

Death makes his way up my legs, his fingers brushing against the outer lips of my cunt. I shiver, jerking at his touch.

His eyes meet mine as he begins cleaning me there too. I moan, leaning back against Uri. The God of Tricks hums pleasantly, some song I've never heard of before.

"We wouldn't want you to be dirty *anywhere*," Aleksander notes, his fingers sliding inside of me. His eyes shutter as he feels how wet I am.

He massages my inner walls slowly, so slow it's indecently hot. The orgasm comes on fast as he rubs me inside and out, his other hand reaching back to clean between my ass cheeks.

I cry out, my voice hoarse, as I fall apart in the hands of two Originals. My pussy muscles clamp down on Death's fingers as I ride his hand. "Good girl," he murmurs. "Such a good girl."

"My sweet Witch," Uri whispers in my ear.

It's too much.

The second the orgasm passes, twitches still traveling through my body, I nearly collapse.

Uri floats to the side of the pool, pulling me so my back is to her bare chest. Her small breasts press against my bare skin and I suddenly need more contact.

Aleksander slides off the ledge and comes to my front, using his soap to massage my breasts, collarbone, and neck.

Still, his actions are slow, concentrated, as if he's afraid I'll shatter.

He finishes cleaning me before leaning close and pressing an achingly slow kiss against the corner of my mouth. At the same time, Uri kisses the nape of my neck.

I'm unable to move, caught between the two of them, but I've never felt safer.

Sleep beckons and suddenly my eyes grow heavy.

Uri says something I don't catch and Aleksander snaps his fingers, transporting us to his bedroom. They wrap me in a thick white towel, drying me off, before carrying me to the bed.

It's a blur as they set me on Death's bed, tucking themselves in on either side of me. Uri at my back, brushing my now braided hair, caressing my neck and arms, while Aleksander wraps his arms around my waist, tucking me so our legs are intertwined and his chin rests on my head.

"Sleep, Elsie. Just sleep," Aleksander whispers. I try to nod, but slumber wraps me in its waiting talons as the world disappears.

the truth
pt. II

chapter 25

A voice breaks through my dreams as I wake slowly. "Control your progeny."

"That word is *gross*," someone responds.

"You know what's gross? The way you *prefer* to call him your *spawn!* It's sick!"

"I think I'll peck out your right eye this time. In your sleep too."

"Try it and I'll drop your ass in the deepest level of the Beneath. See how you like it then," Aleksander replies.

I'm fully awake now, thanks to the bickering Gods on either side of me.

"Please, I can handle the Below better than your sorry ass can." Uri scoffs.

Aleksander goes to reply but I slap my hand over his mouth, forcing my eyes open.

Even if they were arguing, his pale eyes are filled with mirth.

"You woke me up," I complain.

Uri snickers. "He started it."

I glance back at her, removing my hand from Death's mouth. "Somehow, I doubt that."

Uri's jaw drops in faux horror. "How dare you! I am merely an innocent bystander."

Aleksander lets out a bellowing laugh so hard it shakes the bed. "That is the biggest load of bullshit I've ever heard. Innocent my *ass.*"

Uri reaches over and smacks him in the head. I glare at her. "I'm the only one allowed to smack him."

"Oh dear, are we feeling a bit possessive, huntress?" Aleksander whispers, his breath against my cheek.

I shove his chest and he topples off the bed with an alarmed sound.

"Mostly annoyed, actually. I was having a *lovely* dream about some unicorns, and you both ruined it, so now I'm *cranky* and it's your fault."

Uri giggles. "Oops. Sorry Elsie. But also, good shove!"

Aleksander stands, now clothed in a pair of black pants, but his chest remains bare, showing off his ripped physique and the shadows beneath his skin.

"Actually, it's good you're awake. We need to talk," he says, and instantly I grow nervous.

"Yeah, we sure fucking do," a voice booms as the door bursts open. Trystan and Nerethus shove into the room and move so fast I can barely track, but suddenly I'm in the Dragon's arms and Trystan is shouting in Aleksander's face.

Uri watches it all with amusement, her arms behind her head, still in bed.

She's in a sleeveless top that shows off her toned arms, and pants similar to what Aleksander wears. Nerethus, as usual, is also shirtless, and his chest is burning hot.

He's also growling so loud it vibrates my jawbone as I lean against his pecs.

"Tone it down, lizard," I mutter, still shaking off the deep sleep I had been in.

"No," he snarls. "I will *not* tone it down. Not when we thought you were still in the Below! These two assholes didn't even tell us you were back!"

"Yeah, fuck that," Trystan agrees. He's shockingly wearing a shirt, but he rips it off, his wings exploding into existence. "You kept her from us?"

Nerethus growls louder and Aleksander shrugs. "It wasn't the time."

"Training room.NOW." Despite being a Lesser God, Nerethus's order leaves no room for disagreement. He blurs and we reappear in the all-glass room.

"I really don't like it here," I mutter. Nerethus, at least, has the courtesy to look sheepish.

"Sorry," he mutters. "Stick to the edge. I'm about to beat Aleksander to death."

I snort and he glares. "Sorry. It's just... You're going to beat Death to death? It's a little funny."

"God, what did he *do* to you?" Trystan asks in disbelief. "I'm the one who cracks the jokes. Now you're buddies with Death? Nere, this can't stand!"

Nerethus drops me and cracks his knuckles. "Agreed."

Aleksander walks into the room with Uri in tow, the latter of which is now carrying a basket of snacks. My familiar joins me at the side of the room and passes me some apple slices.

"This is gonna be so good," she whispers with glee.

"You want them to beat each other up?" I ask, my brows raised.

She shrugs. "Not really, but it's been a long time coming. Like, centuries long. Best they get it out of their system."

I huff. "Fine. Pass me some of that bread, will you? I'm fucking starved."

"Well, yeah," she comments. "You didn't eat for two weeks while you both were in the Below, and you slept for a good forty-eight hours after getting back. Take the whole loaf while you're at it."

She hands me a loaf of bread and I tear into it like a wild animal. Uri smiles happily, tossing some berries into her mouth.

"What the fuck, Aleks? Why did you keep her from us?" Trystan demands, cracking his neck.

Aleksander slips his hands into his pants pockets and shrugs, the picture of disinterest.

Nerethus on the other hand is practically *vibrating* with rage.

"If you want to talk about truths, *bird,*" Aleksander drawls, "then let's talk about how you knew Elsing was a Witch the *entire* time, but coincidently 'forgot' to mention anything?"

Trystan scoffs. "Oh please. We've covered this already."

Nerethus turns slowly and faces Trystan. "No, no we haven't actually. What the fuck, Tryst? We said she was human *dozens* of times. You had every chance to correct us and you intentionally chose not to."

The Dragon's voice is full of betrayal.

Trystan raises a brow. "At least I didn't throw her in a dungeon for two weeks."

Nerethus growls. "Fine. But you still lied."

"Blah, blah, blah, you all lied. Move on from it, spawn!" Uri calls, making me choke on the bread I'm still shoving down my throat.

She pats my back hard, keeping me from choking in earnest.

Nerethus shoots Uri a look. "You know I hate when you call me that, Uriel."

My familiar smiles at him and lifts her middle finger, giving him the universal hand signal to "fuck off."

Nerethus sighs but Aleksander smirks. "Why don't you go take a flight or something, lizard? Your emotions are getting the best of you."

The Dragon goes still and my heart stops as the air turns hot. The rage in his ruby eyes is out of control. He steps towards Aleksander and cracks his neck and jaw, allowing his fangs to lengthen as scales begin to glow beneath his skin.

"You've been a dick to us for four centuries, but this? This is too far, Aleks. You put Elsing in the fucking dungeon for two whole weeks!"

"She was never in any real danger," Aleksander says calmly and I snort. But he's not wrong. After seeing the Below, the dungeon is luxurious in comparison.

"I don't give a shit. You do not treat her that way!" Nerethus snarls.

"Calm down—" Death attempts to diffuse the Dragon, but Nerethus interrupts him with three words that change everything.

"SHE'S MY MATE! Don't tell me to calm down!"

We all freeze.

I look down at my open palms, seeing only breadcrumbs.

Strange. I could've sworn my heart fell right out of my chest at the Dragon's words.

My ears ring, my heartbeat thudding so hard I won't be surprised if it leaves a bruise.

"Wait," Uri starts, "you didn't know?"

Every head in the room swivels to her. My jaw is on the floor as I look at Uri.

"Fucking *birds,*" Aleksander groans.

"Hey, rude," Trystan cries. Our eyes meet and he sends me a cheeky wink.

Then a giant ball of fire explodes in the middle of the room as Nerethus charges into Aleksander, ramming them right through the glass window at the far edge of the training area.

The Gods plummet, quickly disappearing from our sight.

"Oh, shit," Trystan curses, sprinting after them. He makes a vertical dive, wings tucked tight against his back as he follows.

"Men," Uri says, sounding disgusted. "Come on, let's go make sure your mates don't kill each other."

I choke. "What? Mates? I.. No. No they can't *all* be my mates. That's not possible."

"You seem to have a habit of making the impossible *possible,* sweet Witch. Because it's true. I can feel the bond hovering around your magic. You smell like them. Sage, sky, and spice hidden behind your blackberry magic. It's delicious," she sends me a wink, "and the sage is my signature too."

I'm speechless. "Wait, are you saying you're my mate too?"

Uri laughs and in that moment, she's so beautiful it robs me of my breath. "No, pretty Witch. But familiars are just as close, if not even closer."

"Oh," I breathe. "Right."

"Now," she starts, "let's go. I really don't like the taste of roast lizard. It's so stringy."

Uri grabs my hand and pulls me up. I follow her, unsure what else to do.

My mind is stuck on that word.

Mates.

Mates, mates, mates, mates.

Yes, yes, yes, my magic calls from within me, happy at the thought.

"Shut the fuck up," I scream at it.

But the word still pelts me.

Mates. Mates. Mates.

"Jump on my back," Uri says. I do as she says, awkwardly jumping on her back and securing my arms around her neck, with my legs wrapped around her waist.

"Hang on tight." She laughs and dives out of the window.

"YOU BETTER HAVE A FUCKING PLAN," I scream at her out loud and in my head.

Her laughter is the only response I get as a bright light flares from within her and suddenly something silky is between my legs and beneath my hands.

"Heilige scheiße, you can get big?" I scream against the wind and the giant raven beneath me cackles with glee.

"Now that the curse locking me within my smaller form is lifted, yes! I can get as big as the Dragon if I want to."

Woah.

I laugh into their silky feathers, marveling at the inky black color and how soft they are. I tuck myself down, using the thicker feathers around Uri's neck to block the wind, and to hold on. She dives, falling with grace as we chase the three Gods.

Even against a Griffin and a Dragon, my familiar is faster.

Soon we're at their backs. Uri reaches out and pecks Trystan's feet, making him squeal in surprise. He careens to the side, hitting a mountain.

Uri cackles again.

Nerethus is below us now, a giant black cloud within his claws. The black cloud changes forms every few seconds, making it impossible for Nerethus to truly trap it. But the Dragon bellows, unleashing a torrent of flame right in the middle of the darkness.

"I've had just about enough of pushy, emotional men!" I hiss and Uri nods in agreement.

Hm.

An idea hits me.

Lightning is usually my go-to, but it's not my only affinity.

"Freeze their asses," Uri suggests.

"Get me closer to them. I need both hands for this."

Uri squawks and speeds up, diving faster and faster, the wind making my eyes water. But in seconds, we're beside them. Nerethus's fire nearly singes Uri's feathers and my familiar lets out a bone-curdling caw, making her anger heard throughout the Helvetas.

It's enough that Nerethus blinks, pausing for a moment.

Which is exactly when she banks, going horizontal so that I can raise both of my hands, fingers flexed and palms flat, as I slam them together and summon an arrow made of black ice that shoots Nerethus in the forehead.

It hits him right between his eyes and his fire goes out.

The Dragon blinks in shock and coughs.

Aleksander takes advantage of his hesitation and shifts back into a man, but huge wings made of shadows extend from his back.

"ENOUGH!" Death booms, his eyes piercing and pure black. Aleksander bares his sharp teeth. "You are not the only one to whom she is mated, Dragon."

The Dragon snarls but we all slow until there's no falling, just hovering. Nerethus breathes heavily as Aleksander slips behind me, wrapping his arms around my waist as he joins me on Uri.

"Okay, now I'm the one who's hungry, and my head kind of hurts from hitting that mountain. I think I dented it," Trystan shouts from above as he descends.

Aleksander nods at the Dragon, "We are not enemies, Nerethus. I apologize for my actions. I was wrong."

"He never *apologizes,"* Uri croaks in my head.

Nerethus sighs and nods, the rage leaving his eyes.

The winged God's begin the journey back to the Aive and we fly in silence. It's a calmer journey. No death dives or shocking revelations.

Shock courses through my system. Perhaps it's the cold addling my thoughts, or what happened in the Below, but... I'm not *as* shocked as I should be.

As I would have been.

"Be happy."

For you, I will try.

The five of us stare at each other in silence.

It's horribly awkward and makes me want to rip off my skin.

"Alright, someone say something. This silence is killing me," Trystan says. He's seated to my right, with Uri on my left, trapping me between the two bird-shifters.

Uri nods. "Agreed. This is weird. There's so much staring."

Nerethus sniffs. "Fine." He sits across from me, with a hefty amount of space between him and the God of Death. His ruby eyes land on me and he stands, coming to kneel at my feet.

My palms are sweaty but he takes my hands anyways.

"Elsing," he starts, "I don't care if you're a Witch or a human with a murder streak. You are my *mate*."

"*We* are your mates," Aleksander adds. "It seems we all figured it out at different times. I didn't realize this to be true until we went Below."

"I always knew," Uri says happily. "Because I'm right about everything, always."

Aleksander glares at her and Trystan snorts.

"Yeah, I *also* knew from the beginning," the Griffin adds.

Nerethus has to close his eyes for a moment, sighing. "I... suspected. But I didn't know until you left. Being separated from you was horrible. My kind only gets protective over our families," he pauses, *"or* our mates."

"I'm not human, but considering how much the Republic has lied about the history of the Gods, explain this mating thing to me."

The Dragon nods, blurring and pulling me into his lap as he squishes between the two avian Gods. Uri squeaks in anger but allows it, elbowing Nerethus as he gets settled.

"Of course," Aleksander says, nodding. "Mating is like marriage, only there's more magic involved. If you accepted the mating bonds, you would get pieces of our magics, and we would get some of yours in return. Your life expectancy would become infinite. You would, in many aspects, be a Lesser God." Death licks his lips, his black eyes meeting mine. "Which is appropriate, considering you are becoming one."

"I'm sorry, what?" I explode as the others do the same.

"She's not a God," Nerethus says indignantly.

Trystan stops. "Oh shit. She drank my blood, Nere. Death is right."

"It's okay, Witch. Calm yourself." Uri consoles me mentally but I'm frozen in place.

"What the *fuck* do you mean by that?" I demand. Aleksander nods.

"The Griffin is correct," Death says. "But your power was already there. Tell me, the last few times you've used your magic, have you casted?"

I pause.

I…. I hadn't. I thought I did but I don't remember saying the cast, even in my thoughts.

"My family casts differently," I protest in denial. "We don't have to verbalize the spell aloud. We say it in our heads."

"And did you?" he asks gently. "Did you cast in your head, or did you simply *will* the magic into existence?"

My heart stops.

"No," I reply numbly. "I didn't cast at all. I just imagined the result and my magic did the rest. But that's not witchcraft."

"Perhaps it's a new kind of witchcraft. A mix of divine power and casting. But what are you describing? That's how our power works."

"Yeah," Trystan replies with a nod. "When I control the air, I just think of what I want and it happens."

"I doubt this is just from Trystan's blood. The Griffin is powerful, but you used black lightning in the Below."

Now it's Uri's turn to look at me with a slack jaw and wide eyes. "You used black lightning? Are you… Are you sure?"

"Quite," Aleksander responds and I nod.

"Why does it matter?" I ask her.

"Because it doesn't exist. If you can summon black lightning, it means you're *creating.*"

My hands start to tremble and Nerethus reaches around my waist to clasp them between his. The warmth is so nice.

"Creation is something only an Original is capable of," Aleksander says slowly. "Something you shouldn't be able to do."

"But I can," I protest.

Uri's jaw is on the floor. "That fucking *whore.*"

We all look at her, confused.

She gets up and paces around the living area, "That raggedy old hag did this. I know it. Pertcha has been meddling in Witch and human affairs for too long. Somehow, she's behind this. Somehow she elevated Elsing's power. Pertcha *created.* That's why everything is fucked up. She broke the only rule that truly matters."

Aleksander curses and Trystan cringes.

"That can't be allowed. It will upset the balance of the entire world. Lesser Gods cannot ascend and gain the power of creation. She's upset the balance," Aleksander snarls.

"So we reset it." They all turn to me. I lift my chin, refusing to cower. "If she's the reason everything keeps going wrong, then we kill her and reset the balance of power."

Trystan nods. "Yeah, alright."

The Gods turn to him with varying levels of disgust and confusion.

"So weak." Aleksander rolls his eyes.

"I'm with Elsie. Fuck that bitch. We break your curse, we find Pertcha, and we blast her into smithereens," Nerethus growls, making my whole body vibrate.

"How is your curse broken?" I ask.

The Gods go still. Aleksander looks to the ceiling. Trystan plays with his fingers. Nerethus sighs deeply. But it's Uri who answers. "Well, coincidently, the only way to break their curse is to blast it with a huge wave of power."

"Well, that's easy. We use our magic at once and blast the border, breaking the curse."

Uri clears her throat. "Well, I don't think that would be enough. The magic needs to... be combined. This needs to be subconscious power. Every God has a well of power, so to speak. We can access most of that well, but there is a portion of it that simply cannot be used consciously."

"Okay," I reply, "So what would access the rest?"

"Completing the mating bond would," Aleksander answers, staring at me, his eyes back to pale green.

Fucking great. Of course it would.

"When a mating bond is completed," Nerethus explains, "it generates a huge explosion of power, both conscious and subconscious. It's why mates are so rare, and so dangerous. Mating allows us to access our subconscious power."

Aleksander picks up where the Dragon left off, "If we all accept the bond, the magic generated would be so powerful it would instantly destroy the curse. "

"But we'd be bonded forever," I attempt to say, but it's hard to make my mouth form real words.

"Yes," Uri says. "You would. You and I are already bonded, but there would be no getting rid of these idiots."

"Hey!" Trystan protests.

"Rude," Nerethus mutters.

Aleksander smirks, his eyes sparkling. "Mates are for life, Elsing. You will be connected to us until the end of time."

I shove off Nerethus's lap and take a few steps away, facing the windows. My chest is so tight it feels like it's going to collapse and crush my lungs.

My hands tremble.

This can't be real.

They can't be my mates.

I can't be a *God*.

"Why don't we take a few days to think about it. Elsing has been through a lot," Aleksander says carefully.

Nerethus makes a reluctant sound of agreement.

Turning to face them, I cross my arms and take a shaky breath. "The last time we were all together," I start, "I tried to kill most of you." The Gods all freeze. "Yeah," I drawl. "I'm gonna need some time with this."

"But—" Trystan protests, and I stop him.

"Without any of *you,*" I finish slowly. Their faces are a mixture of hurt and confusion. But Aleksander nods.

The Below changed everything between us.

An understanding is there that wasn't before.

We are the same, I realize.

He realizes it too. I can feel it. Like a change in the air. Where there used to be fear and anger, there is love.

And that terrifies me.

Uri clears her throat and I snap out of it. "I'll watch over you."

"No."

Uri goes still, her shining black eyes going wide as her smile falls.

"You… You don't want me to watch over you?" she asks quietly.

"Not this time. You knew my plan this entire time, Uriel. You knew what would happen when Nerethus found me, that I would try to kill them. You suspected they were my mates, and yet you never said a single fucking word. Were you going to let me kill them and enjoy having me all to yourself?"

Uri rocks back like I slapped her. It's the first and only time I've used her real name. The others are silent, their eyes wide, like they've never seen the God of Tricks get put in her place before.

"Elsie, you know that's not true," she protests, her voice shaky.

I snort. "Do I? Because it sounds like everything I thought to be true is actually a carefully planned lie. Most of it by Pertcha, but each of you," I look to each God in the room, "are culpable."

Facing Uri once more, I say, "In the past two months, I've watched my best friend die, murdered her abusive prick of a husband, went on trial for his murder, watched as the whole town turned on me in an instant, never questioning my guilt—then I was poisoned, strung up, beaten, left for dead, kidnapped, seduced by said kidnappers, thrown off a mountain, taken to the land of the dead to speak with my now dead best friend, and oh yes, my familiar of the past *decade* isn't even a raven, they're a God. An *Original,* for fuck's sake. On top of this, the Goddess my family has dedicated their entire lives to is actually a psychotic asshole who has somehow changed me into a God, and now you all are claiming to be my mates so we can live happily ever after."

The room is so silent, my own breath seems loud.

"Are you all out of your fucking minds?" I shriek. The emotions I keep locked away explode out of me, unable to hold back any longer.

"Elsie," Uri chides but I shake my head.

"No! No more 'Elsie this, Elsie that.'" I turn to Trystan. "No more 'pet' either. I need to think about this because frankly, all I want to do right now is run as far away from all of you as I can. You once told me that if I pushed you too far, you wouldn't ask for permission. Well, same to you. Push me on this and you *will* lose me."

Nerethus and Uriel look terrified. Trystan looks shocked and mildly turned on by my outburst.

"I just... I need some space. I need to think and breathe. It's all too much—and I miss Daphne." My voice breaks.

Aleksander stands and approaches me. "You're right. We might be Gods, but we are still fallible. I'm sorry, Elsing. We've been here for four centuries. We can wait as long as you need. I can speak for myself," his voice gets low and soft as he presses a kiss against my forehead, "but time will not change my feelings."

Trystan nods. "Mine either."

"Nor mine," Nerethus adds, his ruby eyes blazing.

I look into Aleksander's clear green eyes and hate how badly I want his arms around me.

Instead, I take that hate, that anger, that swirling storm of emotions within me, and I use it.

"Thank you." I nod. "So I'm only a *little* sorry about this next bit..."

There is magic in everything, including the stones and glass making up the Aive. If I truly am becoming a God, if I can create, then I can break the rules. So with all of my strength, I imagine my intent and push my magic out into the world.

The Aive shakes.

Several of the Gods startle, jumping to their feet, but Death isn't concerned. He watches me carefully, not out of fear but more curiosity and... contentment, perhaps.

The rumbling stops, and something brushes against my magic.

Something *old*.

The Aive.

I long suspected it's made of magic. If it's magic, then it's somewhat sentient. All old magic is.

If it's sentient, why not ask if it would like a new master?

The Aive enters my mind and attaches itself to my soul. I can taste the bitter limestone and sharp glass, waiting for me to mold it in whatever image I see fit.

I hold the picture clear in my mind and the Aive rumbles again.

"Oooooooh, *Witchy.*"Trystan smiles with unhinged glee, rubbing his hands together in anticipation.

Then the Aive quiets, the only sound a soft hiss as a new door shimmers into existence in between the two existing wings of the mountaintop castle.

I meet Aleksander's pale gaze. "The Aive is under new ownership. This is my home now. You will find it will no longer respond to you."

Nerethus's jaw hits the floor and Trystan hollers with laughter.

But Aleksander's eyes twinkle with pride.

"Did you steal my home from me, huntress? How monstrous of you."

I glare, angry that he's suddenly being so goddamn charming. "Yes, I did. So I'm going to *my* room, and I don't want to be bothered. I need to think, and I make no guarantee of how long that will take me. Do what you will." I turn on my heel, walking across the room on trembling legs as I open the newly made door.

With a thought the door clicks, locking behind me. I can hear arguing break out immediately but I tune it out.

My hallway is similar to Aleksander's, but there's a soft brook winding along the floor, allowing just enough room to walk next to it. The sound of the water running along the rocks and stones underneath it is calming. The carpet is lush and vibrantly colored, with amethyst and azul patterns.

Soft candle-lit sconces line the wall alongside beatific paintings of flowers and meadows.

At the end of the hall is an open door.

I didn't actually make a new room. The door and the hallway are new, but I changed and moved a room that was previously there.

I wonder how long it will take them to realize their library is now my bedroom.

As I walk through the open door, I enter the newly minted library. A large bed is against the far wall, with books lining the walls, crawling up to the ceiling. Now there's a skylight at the top instead of endless darkness.

The fire roars, crackling and infusing the space with warmth.

It's all jewel tones and lush fabrics. The daybed is still there but now it's the same shade of green as the trees near where I grew up.

The bed is covered in dark purple and red blankets, with white pillows and sheets. Tiny glowing bugs wrap around the bedposts, creating the effect of a light string.

Something moves and a wooden tree arm emerges from the wall, creaking and groaning with each inch it grows.

A soft pair of pants and a fresh shirt are handed to me. I reach down and pet the branches, murmuring my thanks.

It shakes with happiness and suddenly one corner of the room creaks as a tree emerges. A Helvetas spruce. It shouldn't be able to grow inside, but my magic seems to have given the Aive new energy.

The smell of the forest travels through the room and calms my scattered spirit.

I change clothes, tossing my old ones in a pile on the floor.

Without thought, I crawl into bed and burrow under the covers, relishing the silence as I close my eyes and pretend the world, and my new problems, no longer exist.

"I wish you were here, Daph."

the dream

chapter 26

My sleep is deep and dreamless.

I wake sometime later in the exact same position I fell asleep in. Every muscle in my body cries in stiff pain as I stretch and turn over, flopping down on the soft pillow.

Then I freeze.

There's a shadow snake, curled up on the pillow beside me. My fingers brush against my collarbone, but there's no telltale tingle. This is the shadow that was around my neck.

For some reason, it left me.

"Why are you on my pillow?" I ask the lesser Demon.

I'm not sure why I ask, it's not like it will respond.

But the snake uncoils and shifts, dissipating for a moment before reforming into a different shape.

A cat.

It stretches, red eyes blinking into existence as whiskers form on its tiny cheek.

The shadow cat pads over to me, rubbing against my face.

There's a weird vibration.

I pull back, looking at it curiously "Are you purring?"

"Friend. Friend. Friend. Friend. Nice. Nice." It's not a voice I hear, but more of a feeling that it projects. So they do communicate, then. Just differently.

The shadow's magic smells like sweet lemons and freshly picked lavender.

Wait.

"You're from the Below, right?

"*Yes. Yes. Yes.*" I feel the confirmation.

"I met a creature Below, a unicorn named Sälva. Aleksander said she was one of the guardians of the Below. You remind me of her."

"*Friend. Friend. Friend. Yes. Both Demon.*" It jumps and prances on the pillow next to me, almost like it's pretending to trot like a horse.

"Are you the... same kind of Demons?"

"*Yes. Yes. Yes. Shadow Demon.*"

"You can't quite speak to me, but Demons can still talk to each other, then. Sälva must have told you about me, I assume?" The shadow flops over, its feet in the air.

A small shadow mouse manifests next to it, and the shadow cat proceeds to fling it around, playing with it.

Hmm.

It can divide itself.

Interesting.

"Will you be reporting back to your Master on my status, then?" I ask, rolling over on my back and looking up at the dark sky above me.

It's nighttime.

I wonder if I only slept a few hours, or a whole day. I slept deeply enough that I don't know the answer.

"*You. Yes.*" The shadow pushes the two feelings at me.

I glance over at it. The shadow has abandoned the mouse and now sits comfortably with its legs tucked beneath it. It sees me looking and gets up, approaching and walking over my pillow.

"*You friend. Me yours.*"

Wait. "You mean I'm your master now? You no longer answer to Death? Is that what you're saying?"

The shadow cat nods. "*Yes. Yes. Friend. Friend. Nice friend.*"

"Friend. You mean you're my friend?"

"*Nice to friend.*" It tries to communicate.

Nice to friend.

Hm.

Hold on—

"Do you mean Sälva? The shadow unicorn I met in the Below? Is she your friend?"

"Yes. Yes. Yes."

Oh, wow.

"You decided to stay with me... because of Sälva. Because I was kind to your friend." My voice betrays my shock.

The shadow cat nods again.

"Thank you, friend," I whisper, raising my left arm to try and pet its head. "I am glad to have you. If you can, please find a way to thank Sälva as well."

The shadow curls around my head, and for a moment, it almost feels real. There's a pressure and a warmth where it's pressed against me. Not quite solidified but definitely there.

It begins vibrating again, trying to purr. This time the sound is louder.

There's a tingling on my shoulder, and I watch as it kneads against my skin. It doesn't hurt. In fact, it feels soothing.

"What am I supposed to do?" I ask it.

There's no answer, but the comfort the shadow creature brings also brings a wave of emotion.

"I have no idea where to go from here. *If* they really are my mates, that means I almost killed them. I stabbed my mates. Slit their throats, tried to burn them to death with lightning," I say to the room.

The shadow is quiet.

"They'll never trust me again. How am I supposed to have a mate—*any mate,* let alone four of them—when they don't trust me? That sounds like a miserable life."

"Love. Love. Love. Love." The creature projects the feeling. I can't discern if it simply means the shadow loves me, or love in general.

But it's not wrong.

"I don't know if they really do love me, though. Even if they say they do. Lying is easy. Trust me, I know," I admit with a weary sigh.

Then I remember Daphne's words.

"Be happy."

I guess I finally found something I'm scared of.

I'm scared of giving the Mountain Gods a chance.

I'm scared of... being happy *without* her. Because if I am happy, doesn't that make me cruel? It seems wrong to feel happiness within a world she's no longer living in.

"Love. Love. Love. She. Love."

"She?" I ask, glancing back.

"She happy. Say you be happy."

Oh my Gods.

"You speak with Daphne," I gasp.

The shadow squeaks happily, tucking in closer against my head.

"Yes. Short. Only short. She want you happy," it projects to me.

I thought I'd finished crying, but emotion wells within me nonetheless.

"Thank you," I whisper to my new shadow friend. "Thank you for being my connection to her. You are a true friend."

I sniffle. "Friends need a name. What would you like your name to be? Do you prefer being a cat over a snake?"

The shadow nods and I blink. "Okay, then what about... Noctis. Since you're as dark as the night sky."

"Like. Like. Like. Yes!" Its happiness is overwhelming.

"Okay. Noctis it is then. I know I said I wanted space and to be alone, but I'm glad you're here."

A feeling of agreement brushes against me in response.

If I'm a God, if I can *create*, perhaps I can make the shadows solidify.

"Noctis, I'd like to try something if it's okay with you. I'd like to see if I can make you more corporal, the way Sälva can become real. Would you like that?" The shadow nods eagerly. "Okay, stay still. I'm not exactly sure how this will work, but we can at least try."

I let my eyes fall closed as my breathing deepens. My magic unfurls from within me, leaving my body and swirling around the room. Everything feels so alive.

The coolness of the stones, all layered on top of each other beneath the warm earth. Every gust of wind against the windows is a breath straight into my lungs.

Every pane of glass vibrates through me, a brand-new living organ.

There is no separation. I feel it beneath my skin as we merge.

This.

This is *divine.* For there is no other word to describe the feeling but to call it divinity.

The magic slowly settles over me and I breathe it in.

Something brushes against the edge of my mind and I remember the shadow cat beside me.

I picture my desired result, and instead of casting, simply *will* my magic to make it so.

There's a crackling noise and a small white flash. I wince, closing my eyes against the brightness.

"Meow!" I blink and turn to find a velvety black cat with red eyes sitting above my pillow on the headboard.

"It worked," I breathe. "Which means... Fuck. Which means the Gods are right. That wasn't casting. That was something else."

My head falls back on the pillow as I look up at the night sky above.

"Divinity," I whisper to the stars. "I have... *divinity.* I am *divine.*"

It sounds wrong.

But it feels right. My magic *feels* divine.

"How the fuck did I get here?"

The stars don't respond.

Noctis meows again and leans forward, licking my cheek with its rough tongue, making me laugh.

"You're real for a few seconds and I swear your breath already smells like fish," I say to him. He purrs loudly, headbutting me and rubbing against my cheek before settling in.

This time, when he goes to knead my shoulder, sharp black nails dig into my skin.

"None of that now that you're real. That *hurts.*"

I feel the apology.

"It's alright," I say to the cat. "You didn't know."

My thoughts stray.

Would it be so bad? Letting the Mountain Gods love me?

Before I can answer my own question, the exhaustion hits and my eyes fall shut once more as I fall into a deep sleep next to my new companion.

The dream is peaceful.

I'm by a beautiful pond on the outskirts of a large forest. It looks like the Helvetas. It's sommer, judging by the warm sun that reflects against the surface of the pond. I find myself sitting next to a pond, my feet bare.

The water looks so inviting.

So refreshing.

Scooting forward, I dip my toes beneath the surface.

Sighing at the refreshing feeling of the cool water against my warm skin, I lay back in the grass and close my eyes, listening to the birdsong.

That's when two slimy, clawed hands wrap around my ankles and yank me under the water.

Water fills my nose but I can't scream or I'll drown.

The creature pulls me down away from the surface and the water grows darker.

The pond is so murky I'm unable to see much. We hit the bottom and sediment explodes upwards, darkening the water even more.

A grotesque, rotten face appears in front of me.

The face of Tante Inga.

Now I know better.

Pertcha.

"Hello, malificer," a voice calls in my head.

I try to respond but I can't. Something is nulling my magic.

My lungs burn with every second that passes.

"Poor, poor Witch. No one to save her. No one to love her." She sneers, leaning in and licking my cheek with her rotten, black tongue. I try to pull away but her grip is too strong.

But her eyes have me gagging.

Tiny blue eyeballs the size of my pinky sit in the middle of bloody eye sockets. It's horrific to look at but with every blink, her eyes are just a bit bigger.

They grew back.

Her tattered clothes sway in the water. I nearly escape her grasp but curled yellow nails dig into my arms, holding me in place. Her strength betrays her identity.

"You taste like evil," she says, licking her lips.

My lungs burn. I can't last much longer.

Panic hits and I flail, fighting against her hold but it's no use.

I gasp and water floods my lungs and my body begins to spasm and jerk.

"Let it happen, malificer. Let Death come. The world will be better without you. You should thank me. You went to the Mountains to die, and now you can get your wish." She laughs, showing fully rotten brown teeth.

Everything goes dim as my organs die. My heart beats slower and slower.

Thump, thump.

Thump... thump.

Thump...

Then Tante Inga stabs her hand into my chest nails first, grabs ahold of my still-beating heart, and rips it out.

Everything fades to black as the pain takes me over.

I cry out, sitting up in bed as I clasp my chest, frantically shoving my shirt aside to see if there's a wound. My breath comes in giant gasps as I realize my heart is still there.

But all around it are red, raised puncture marks.

My nightshirt is practically see-through, and little droplets of water fall from my wet hair.

It was real.

Pertcha invaded my dream and tried to kill me.

"Meow!" Noctis cries.

A wave of emotion rushes over me from the shadow Demon. *"BAD. BAD. BAD. NOT FRIEND."*

Shaking, I turn and look at the cat. "That fucking *hag* tried to kill me."

Something clicks into place in my mind and suddenly everything makes sense.

"She pushed me to kill them," I realized with a calm kind of horror. "She wanted me to do something that would get me killed. To get me out of the way."

Noctis meows again, agreeing with me.

Heilige scheiße.

The cat crawls into my lap, headbutting my chest. I caress its silky fur, the weight of the creature grounding me, calming me.

Fear dissipates, and in its place, fury rises.

No one controls me.

Not anymore.

I *refuse.*

I will not die today. Not for her, not for anyone.

Nor will I allow some insane God to decide my life.

Which means, once more, it's time for me to kill a God. Only this time, I'm going to make it *stick.*

And... I'm going to need my mates help to do it.

the revelation
pt. II

chapter 27

"**A**re you holding a *goat?*"

The Gods whirl, looking at where I stand at the edge of the kitchen area.

Trystan smiles. "Pet! You're back—"

I stop him with a raised hand. "No. Absolutely not. Don't try to be cute. Answer my fucking question. Why in the actual fuck are you holding a baby mountain goat?"

"Um." Trystan pauses, pursing his lips and looking away from me.

Nerethus starts, "Well..."

Uri is surprisingly quiet. She watches me, her eyes hesitant. Aleksander, who sits atop one of the tall chairs at the counter, is who answers.

"They were going to eat it," Death confirms.

"Dude!" Trystan cries. "Way to throw me off the mountain,"

I turn to Nerethus, his red eyes gleaming. "The bird, I understand. He clearly has self-control issues. But you? Really?"

The aforementioned mountain goat bleats, its fur white and fuzzy. Trystan holds it carefully, but I don't miss the occasional glance down in hunger.

"We are predators, Elsing," Nerethus says, his eyes guilty. "Trystan found this one abandoned... and baby mountain goat is a delicacy. So tender." His eyes unfocus as he looks at the goat, licking his lips. "So sweet."

So I kick him in the shin. *Hard.*

"What the fuck," he snarls, hopping onto one leg. So I kick the other shin.

"We—" *Kick.* "—are not—" *Kick, kick.* "—eating the mountain goat!"

"Alright, alright! No more kicking," Nerethus hisses. "That hurts!"

"This is very entertaining. Elsing, do feel free to continue kicking him." Aleksander sounds pleased.

Nerethus glares at him and flashes his fangs. "Fuck off, Soul Eater."

"Come on, pet. It's natural!" Trystan protests.

I whirl to him and summon lightning with a thought. It flares into existence, wrapping around my arms with a sharp crackling sound. "Eat the goat and I will fry your ass and eat your roasted drumstick for dinner!"

Uri chokes and Nerethus blinks.

Aleksander looks shocked and then quickly has to cover his mouth with his hand at the absolute look of *horror* on Trystan's face.

"That was *mean*, Pet," he says, looking aghast. "Fine! Fine. No eating this lovely... delicious looking little goat."

"You're damn right you won't." Like a dam, I turn off the flow of magic and my lightning disappears, leaving only the faint smell of something metallic in the air.

The Griffin sighs and looks to Nerethus. "Well, let's just take it back down the mountain where we found it. I'm sure it will survive... somehow."

I sigh. "Congratulations. You now have a pet goat."

The four of them stare at me with various looks of disbelief and confusion.

"That means we're keeping it. *You* caused it to become abandoned by scaring the living Hell out of the poor goat's mother, so now it's our responsibility." I lean down and pick up the baby goat, cradling it in my arms. It snuggles into me, sensing safety. I caress its head gently, unable to help my smile. I glance back up at the Gods. "We're keeping it. *Her* actually." I check with a glance to verify. "Isn't that right, little one?"

Uri and Aleksander smirk at that, but the beast Gods both have varying looks of shock and disgust on their faces.

"Fine," Trystan sighs petulantly. "But I'm still hungry."

"Figure it out," I say, caressing the mountain goat. "But no eating the goat. *Ever.* Or else we will be having roast Griffin for dinner next."

"It's so hot when you threaten me," Trystan mutters, before letting out a piercing shriek when something brushes against his leg. He blurs, jumping in the Dragon's arms, trembling out of fear. Nerethus blinks, shocked, but holds onto Trystan with a gentleness that speaks to the love between them.

"Trystan," Aleksander says calmly, "is afraid of cats. Do you care to share why you suddenly have one, huntress?"

I smile. "I don't, actually. But thanks for asking. Meet Noctis." The aforementioned cat meows and approaches me, jumping up to sit on my shoulders. Uri looks affronted.

"Noctis?" Aleksander asks in amused disbelief. "You gave it a *name?*"

"Noctis approved of it," I responded primly. Uri looks at the cat with disgust. "He's not my familiar," I reassure her. "But he *is* my friend. He's also not on the menu. *Ever.*"

Nerethus sighs and sets Trystan down.

Uri sniffs. "Fine. Fine! But I don't like it."

The Griffin looks disgusted. "I agree! It's going to try to kill me. Mark my words. Look at how it's staring at my perfect feathers. Look! It wants to *eat* me!"

Nerethus gives Trystan a knowing look.

Trystan shrugs. "It's true. You remember what happened with Falla!"

I must make a face because Uri whispers in my head, *Falla is the God of Twilight, who prefers the form of a winged panther. Great wings, but very temperamental. She, uh, tends to get a little bit peckish whenever she sees Trystan in his Griffin form.*

"Fucking cats." Trystan grimaces. "They never leave me alone. Look at it! What kind of cat has red eyes, anyways? Clearly it's a Demon!"

Everyone pauses, looking at me suddenly.

I shrug. "We're all a bit evil anyways."

Aleksander's brows raise slightly as he connects the dots. "The shadow isn't around your neck anymore. You... made it corporal."

I smirk. "Noctis chose this form and I used my magic to give him a solidified form. Sälva was my inspiration."

"A Demon cat?" Trystan hisses. "Are you fucking kidding me, pet? It's definitely going to try and kill me. First the goats, and now this? Is nowhere safe anymore?!"

Nerethus elbows him. "Stop being such a baby bird. The cat isn't going to hurt you."

Trystan glares and mutters under his breath about evil cats.

Nerethus sighs and rubs his temples. "Let me rephrase. I will not *let* the cat hurt you. Besides, if it's bonded at all to Elsing, it will know that you're not to be harmed."

"The only thing we need to be worried about," I start, "is that rotten flesh suit, Pertcha."

Aleksander is in front of me a second later, his eyes looking at my chest, his eyes narrowed, like he's looking beyond my skin, into my soul. "I can feel... strange magic on you." His head cocks, processing. "You're wounded too." He's nose to nose with me a second later, his breath tickling my cheek. "Pertcha hurt you?" Death whispers. "She hurt you in *my* home?"

"Technically it's *my* home now," I respond, but Aleksander doesn't smile.

"Tell me, Elsing. Say the words."

I sigh, trembling at the way we're *almost* touching but not quite. "Pertcha entered my dreams and tried to kill me. I thought it wasn't real but when I woke up, the wounds were still there."

Aleksander inhales sharply, his eyes going black as the room darkens. His shadows writhe and the snakes beneath his skin detach, red eyes appearing within the darkness.

Death leans in and presses his cheek against mine. He lifts his hand and places it on my upper breast, just on top of the raised wound on heart. I gasp silently at his touch, unable to help the way I lean into him.

This is real.

He is real.

"I'm real," he says. Aleksander doesn't need to be able to read my thoughts to understand what I'm feeling right now. He knows this feeling. This confusion of dream versus reality.

"You're real," I repeat back. He nods against my cheek, clutching me tightly against him.

"I thought I was going to die," I whisper so quietly, I'm not sure I make any sound. But he inhales sharply and I *feel* his fury.

There's a warm tingle against my chest and I feel the wounds close.

Aleksander is... healing me.

"Oh shit," someone says in the background.

"That's new," another god comments before they're shushed.

I can't pay attention to anything besides Aleksander's hand on my heart.

He presses a slow kiss to my cheek, moving down to kiss the side of my mouth, and then the other side, before ending back at my mouth. His lips press against mine, soft and warm despite his cold hands. Death inhales, taking in every second.

I'm lost in it.

In *him.*

Aleksander pulls back and wraps his hand around the back of my neck, tilting my head to look into his eyes.

"Understand this, huntress." His voice is full of fury. "Pertcha's fate is sealed. She will have no afterlife. I will tear her soul apart piece by piece until there's nothing left. When the world falls and Gods perish, I will be left standing. I am *infinite. No one* touches what's mine and lives to tell the tale."

The air rushes out of my lungs and my jaw drops.

"Damn," Trystan mutters in the background. "That was hot. Scary, but hot."

Uri snorts.

"What the fuck was she doing here?" Nerethus snarls, barely in control. "How did she get pass the border?"

Wait.

I turn to look at the Dragon. "Are you saying the curse *also* keeps the other Gods out? It doesn't just keep you in here?"

"Correct," Aleksander says, still in front of me.

I turn to look at Uri. "Then how are you here?"

The God of Tricks gives me a soft smile, her eyes sparkling. "Well, I *am* the God of Tricks. When Pertcha was weakened from losing her eyes, it weakened the border curse just enough that I was able to trick it into thinking I was already within. Nothing is beyond the power of a good trick." Uri smirks briefly, then her smile falls.

"There is no rule I will not break and no curse I will not bend to be with you, Witch," Uri whispers in my head, making me blush. I shoot her a small smile.

"The curse is hers, then," Aleksander ponders. "This confirms it. Only the one who casted it would be able to bend its rules, Uri not included."

I turn to the Dragon and take a deep breath, readying for the explosion about to occur. "Pertcha was here to kill me. She even tried convincing me to finish the job, should she not succeed."

All of the Gods hiss violently.

I hesitate and the words come slowly. "If she can access my dreams, I think she's been... pushing me to hate you. For decades, centuries, even. If you can sense her magic on me," I say to Uri, "then it confirms I'm right. She's been messing with my mind. She wanted me to try and kill you, not to actually get rid of you, but..." I swallow around my dry mouth. "But to get rid of *me.*"

Uri's eyes narrow and Aleksander stares at me, his face furious. Trystan and Nerethus look equally angry, albeit a little more confused.

The words are on the tip of my tongue and I have to physically force myself to speak. "She—She told me that no one loves me. That the world would be better off without me."

Uri's hand grabs my jaw, turning my face towards her. "Don't you fucking *dare* listen to her. Don't *ever* think that's the truth. I have loved you ever since you saved my life. No one gives a shit about a dying, hurt raven. But you did, Elsie. *You* gave me a chance. I will peck out Pertcha's nasty eyes for this, I swear it."

"I call dibs on the right eye," Trystan says, coming behind me and pressing a kiss to my shoulder. "Her words couldn't be farther from the truth, pet."

"He's correct," Nerethus says. "The fact that she tried to hurt you, that she's spent so long trying to convince you of these horrible feelings?" The Dragon bares his fangs, roaring, "I'll rip her to pieces for it. *No one* touches my mate."

"She fears you," Aleksander says and we all look at him.

He doesn't look upset. He looks *pleased.*

But his words ring true, despite how strange that would be.

"Think about it. Why are *you* her target? Why not one of us?" He smiles. "Because she thinks *you* are the biggest threat. That means you *can* kill her, huntress. Somehow, this strange magic of yours can hurt her. She's scared of you, so she's trying to remove you from the game."

I sigh and Noctis rubs their head against my cheek, purring. The baby mountain goat bleats and I set it down. It runs over to the living area and jumps in one of the soft chairs, curling up around a blanket.

"I think you're right," I say, turning to look at Uri. "All of you are right. Which means, I owe you an apology." My heart races. I have to reach one hand up to pet Noctis to keep from trembling. With a deep breath, I continue, "I'm sorry... for all of it. I wish I had known the truth from the beginning, but no one here is at fault for that. Only Pertcha is. But, I'm truly sorry. When I think of hurting the four of you now, after everything I've learned over the past few weeks... it makes me sick to my stomach."

Uri grabs my free hand and wraps it within hers, a soft smile on her face.

"It seems, I'm finally afraid of something." I look at Aleksander, who watches me carefully. "I'm afraid of losing all of you. Because for the first time in a long while, with you…" I look to each God in the room, meeting their gazes for a few seconds each. "With *all* of you, I feel like I belong. And that *terrifies* me."

I take a deep breath. "I cannot promise perfection. I'm fucked up, I've been under Pertcha's suggestion for centuries. I have anger problems and trust issues. But I…" I swallow the lump in my throat, "I would like to try this mate thing… *if* you're still willing to have me."

Aleksander's face is stony. He takes a few steps forward until he's just in front of me once more. Death cracks a small smile as his eyes turn back to pale green. "Eternity doesn't seem quite as boring if you're there next to me." I bite my lip, blushing, but Aleksander is there, pressing another kiss to my lips. "I figured out why I can't get you out of my mind, huntress."

"Hm?" I mumble.

Aleksander smiles as he kisses me again. "You don't fear me because for the first time since the beginning of days, I've found my equal."

I pull back, eyes so wide I'm surprised they don't fall out of my skull.

Death smiles and it's the end of all things—

—and the beginning of something new.

"You're going to regret saying that," I say, fighting a smile. It doesn't work. We stand there smiling at each other like idiots.

"They never smile. I'm kinda scared," Trystan whispers to Uri who nods, clearly disturbed by the rare sign of happiness.

Nerethus appears next to Aleksander and shoulders him out of the way with a cough. "My turn."

Death snorts and steps aside, his eyes never leaving me.

Nerethus wraps his arms around my waist and lifts me off the ground until we're face to face. His muscles aren't strained at my weight.

The sign of strength turns my insides molten.

"There is no question," he murmurs, pulling me tightly against his chest. "I will *always* have you, Elsing, and you will always have me in return. Dragons mate for life, and it is my greatest desire to spend the rest of it with you."

I smile. "I never knew Dragons were such romantics."

He blushes. "We can be if we so choose."

Trystan approaches from behind, his hands wrapping around my waist so they're squished between my stomach and Nerethus's chest. The Griffin settles against my back, leaning up to press a kiss against my neck. "You didn't even have to ask, pet. A murderous, powerful Witch-God as a mate? I couldn't ask for anything more. Besides," he laughs, "I haven't had this much fun in ages."

"I'm going to get you back for throwing me off the mountain, you know. Can you trust me, even then?" I poke at him, testing his loyalty.

He smiles against my neck and kisses me again, his tongue darting out to taste the sweat on my skin. "Oh, pet, it's your murderous side I trust the most. The thought of you sliding that knife across my skin as you ride my cock has been seared into my mind for weeks."

"You're fucked in the head," I respond, my voice breathy and low, betraying how turned on I am.

He chuckles darkly. "Haven't you realized? We all are, and you, my pet, are at the top of the list."

"Am I?" I gasp as his hands travel up my chest, cupping my breasts.

Nerethus starts vibrating, that low purring sound shooting straight to my core. The Dragon's nostrils flare.

Then he smiles at me. "Do you smell that, Ryst?"

"Mhm." The Griffin laughs, licking up my neck to suck on my earlobe, making me squirm. "You smell wet, pet."

"Liar," I protest but he pinches my nipples at the same time and it comes out as a moan. "Fuck you, bird. You're not in control here."

"Oh? I'm not? And let me guess, you think you are?" He pinches my other nipple as Nerethus lowers me slightly, his cock pressing against my throbbing pussy.

"Oh *fuck,*" I breathe and my head falls back against Trystan's shoulder.

"I think you're in control all the time, but this? This is where you get to let go of it all. This calms you, the lack of control. It frees that needy little slut inside of you, doesn't it, pet?"

Nerethus grinds his cock into me and leans down to kiss me, devouring my lips in a hot, open-mouthed kiss. His tongue flicks against mine before sucking my lower lip into his mouth. Trystan releases my breast and reaches down to rub my clit. One flick against it has me crying out.

"Bastard," I moan. "You're a fucking *bastard.*"

"Is that why your cunt is soaking wet, Elsing? It's soaking all the way through my pants," Nerethus comments, pulling back from our kiss. His hair is mussed from where I've been running my hands through it, and his ruby eyes are gleaming with need.

He's so fucking gorgeous.

Nerethus smiles. "See something you like, Witch?"

"Yes," I gasp. "Your face. But I'd much rather see it between my legs."

Trystan groans. "Oh my Gods, yes. Nere, we're moving this to the couch."

We all blur and something cold meets my back as they set me on a soft leather couch. The cold material is shocking against my back. I don't know where my clothes went but I'm completely naked, and so are the Gods in front of me.

Aleksander and Uri are sitting in two chairs across from me, each with a glass of amber liquid. They watch me as Nerethus pries my legs open. He doesn't have to work hard. I eagerly spread myself for him, knees falling to the side.

Nothing is hidden. The Mountain Gods see all of me.

Nerethus lowers himself before me, pushing my legs apart further. He brushes a thumb across my entrance, playing with the liquid gathered there.

Trystan appears at my left. "Lean forward," he whispers, lifting me so he can slide in behind me. His cock presses in between my ass cheeks. I'm stuck between them.

The Sky and the Deep.

The Griffin and the Dragon.

Completely and totally at their mercy.

"Taste her, Dragon." Aleksander says, taking a sip of his drink. "Our mate is needy."

Oh God.

Hearing him say that.

My emotions explode and I almost cry.

Our eyes meet and time pauses. He sends me a knowing smile.

Then Nerethus is pulling my pussy lips apart, opening me up and leaning down, licking up every drop of cum.

"Yes," I moan, back arching and hips thrusting. Trystan grips my hips harder, preventing me from moving.

"I want a taste," the Griffin says, his voice gravelly.

Nerethus takes another few licks, pausing a moment to suck on my clit hard enough that I see stars. He gathers my cum in his mouth and sits up, face shining and coated in my pleasure.

The Dragon leans forward, pressing a kiss to my lips. My tongue darts out and I taste myself, moaning.

But Nerethus pulls back, leaning to the side where Trystan waits.

The Griffin parts his lips as Nerethus descends, kissing him with abandon and spitting all of the cum he gathered into Trystan's waiting mouth.

Trystan moans and Nerethus fists the Griffin's hair.

Nerethus pulls back, panting. "You can taste her next." Then he's back to kneeling, yanking me close so he can grind his mouth into my core. I yelp and it quickly turns to a moan as he shifts his tongue, spearing it inside of me.

"Oh my Gods," I cry out. Trystan is there a second later, one hand going down to rub circles against my clit, and the other wrapping around my neck, holding me in place.

I fight against it, unable to stay still.

His hand tightens until I can't breathe.

I cum instantly, moaning and grinding against Nerethus's face. He moans into my pussy, loving the way I'm riding him. "Fuck yes, Elsing. Give me more. Cum for us again." He thrusts two fingers inside of me a second later, curving them to hit right against my most sensitive inner walls. I jerk, twitching and out of control. The orgasm returns and I scream as he inserts a third finger, stretching me just enough that it hurts in the best way.

Nerethus smirks. "Has Uri seen your little trick, Elsing? Does she know just how talented our mate is?"

Uri is next to him a second later, kneeling on the floor. She's topless and I can't look away from her perfect body. Her breasts are small and supple, with dark brown nipples that I instantly want in my mouth.

Her black curly hair cascades over her shoulders, gleaming in the moonlight above us.

"A trick, you say? Elsie, are you trying to steal my job?" She winks at me before turning her gaze to my open pussy. Nerethus fucks me with his fingers slowly, the wet noise of it echoing throughout the room.

"Yes," the Dragon purrs, his gaze landing on me. "Our mate is very special. Show her, Elsing."

He inserts a fourth finger and I nearly explode. "Fuck you."

Nerethus chuckles. "Not yet, little treasure. First, you need to squirt. I want to be covered in your perfection."

Uri's eyes widen, turning fully black the way Aleksander's can. But the black of his eyes is like an empty void. Uri's eyes are shiny, reminding me of how they appear in her raven form.

"Show me," she demands, her voice low and scratchy.

"I'm sorry," I whisper. *"I'm sorry I pushed you away."*

A tiny seed of anxiety suddenly sprouts within me.

In a blink, Uri is beside me. She cocks her head to the left and the room goes quiet. I feel her magic explode outward, covering the room. It tingles my arms and makes my tongue go numb.

I blink, looking down at the still fingers inside of me.

"Uri?" I ask, confused.

"I could never hold this for long, but I felt it. You're anxious. Are you okay?"

My jaw drops. "You—You stopped time for me?"

Uri smiles. "Of course, Witch. Now, what's wrong?"

I go to answer and stop, suddenly nervous.

Uri sighs. "Ah. I see I haven't done a good job at making my feelings clear. So let me make them clear to you now, my sweet Witch." Uri blurs and Nerethus's hand is gone.

Instead, Uri is between my legs.

But she doesn't touch me. She just looks, laying her head against my thigh.

Her deep onyx eyes meet mine, and my heart skips a beat.

"Elsing Jäger." My name rolls off her tongue. "I love you. I have loved you from the moment you saved me. I love you and I want you with every fiber of my being. There is nothing you could do to make me feel otherwise." She pauses. "But, if you would rather just be familiars, I'm okay with that. No matter our relationship, Elsie, I am yours. Okay? This doesn't need to happen with me if you don't want it to."

I'm breathless at her words.

"Kiss me," I order and Uri freezes, shocked.

Then a wicked, wicked smile breaks out on her beautiful face.

"Where do you want me to kiss you, Witch?" she purrs and my eyes shutter.

"Everywhere," I breathe. "I want you to kiss me and touch me *every-where,* Uri."

I blink and her lips are against mine as she cradles my face with such warmth and care, I nearly cry.

Then Uri blurs and Nerethus's fingers are back inside of me, just the way they used to be.

"Shh," Uri winks. "Our secret." And time restarts.

It's so fast I can't react but oh my *Gods.*

"They don't know you can do this!" I gasp and Uri's answering giggle is the only answer I need.

The God of Tricks always has something up their sleeve.

Thoughts quickly abandon me as Nerethus inserts another finger inside of me, thrusting and curling his fingers to hit me right where it feels best. My back arches as I whine, panting and quivering from the feeling of intense fullness.

"Come on, pet. Come for us again. Drench them," Trystan orders, rubbing his thumb against my clit so fast it causes a vibration. I'm shaking and incoherent as Nerethus increases the speed of his fingers and the wet slapping sound increases.

Something hot and tingly spread across my lower abdomen. I tense but Trystan is there, whispering in my ear, "Relax, love. Don't fight it. Relax into it and let it happen. You're safe."

The sincerity and care in his words is what does it.

The warmth increases and I relax my muscles. Liquid shoots out of me. Nerethus and Uri lean down, mouths open, catching all they can.

Uri's laugh in my head is dark. "You've been holding out on me, Witch. It's my turn to play."

She waves her hand and the room changes.

I'm now on all fours on the short glass table in the middle of the living area and Uri is behind me, pulling my ass cheeks apart. Aleksander is right in front of me, kneeling on the rug. He tips my chin up and captures my mouth in a searing kiss right as Uri swipes her mouth across the rim of my ass. I squeak, leaning into Death. He fists my hair, preventing me from moving. "Take it, huntress. Take the pleasure. Let us savor you."

"Do you want this, Elsie?" Uri runs her fingers across my ass, tickling me lightly with the gentle touch. *"Do you want... me?"*

I glance behind me, meeting her gaze over my shoulder. *"You're my friend, my familiar, and my soulmate. Yes, I fucking want you, you silly raven!"*

Uri shudders, her eyes falling closed. *"I've waited a decade to hear you say that."*

Then she's between my legs, dragging her tongue from my ass to my pussy and back again, sucking up all of my cum with an indecent sucking noise.

"Oh fuck," I cry, as her fingers spread me open and plunge into me. It's so different from the others. Her fingers are so delicate and soft, her movements slower but with lazy precision.

She pumps in and out, massaging me and stretching me, adding another finger, then another, until all four of her fingers are inside of me.

"Can you take one more?" she asks, her voice low.

"Yes. Fuck yes. I want your whole fist inside of me." Even in my thoughts, my words are a moan.

"Greedy Witch," Uri laughs.

Then her thumb is joining her other fingers. It burns for a moment as she passes my pubic bone, but then her whole fist is in me.

My legs shake and I fall into Aleksander. He holds me up by my hair, with his other hand around my neck.

Uri's other hand reaches around to rub my clit and I scream against Aleksander's lips, my orgasm approaching yet again.

"Going to cum again for us, pet? Such a needy cunt." Trystan comments from the side, but I can't even open my eyes. It's too much.

Suddenly another mouth pushes Aleksander's aside. Death snarls and pushes back. I peek my eyes open to see Nerethus, his lips going back and forth from kissing me to kissing Death. I lose track of whose lips belong to which God.

Everything becomes pleasure and white noise as the orgasm fully hits and I scream, gushing around Uri's hand. She thrusts in and out harder, flicking her forefinger against my clit, causing my squirt to spray all over her. Then her hand pulls out of me and her mouth replaces it, licking and cleaning up every last drop.

I'm a moaning, quivering mess.

Aleksander laughs against my lips, taking my mouth back from Nerethus. "Oh, we're just getting started. This is the appetizer, and you, huntress, you are the *dessert.* "

the witch's mates

chapter 28

Death snaps his fingers and we reappear in his room.

"So, how does this curse-breaking work?" I'm breathless and still panting from Uri's touch.

Death smirks and sets me on the bed, caressing my cheek.

Some of the shadows embedded in his skin lift away from him, forming into snakes.

"They're not all Demons," I realize. Aleksander winks.

That lying bastard.

I thought he used one of his shadow Demons to fuck me last time. But it makes sense, if he has power over shadows, that not all of them are actually Demons. Some are simply manifestations of his power.

"Evil as I may be, I'm not in the business of traumatizing lesser Demons," he whispers. "Now, close your eyes."

Before I can respond, shadows wrap around my eyes, blacking out my vision. These are cool to the touch, but I can't see anything.

"Be a good girl for us and wait here, little mate," Death murmurs, kissing my cheek. Something wraps around my wrists, lifting and anchoring them above my head, causing my back to arch. My hard nipples are pushed into the air and someone groans at the sight. The shadows wrap around my ankles, all cold and tingly. Then they're pulling my legs apart, baring my throbbing cunt to the waiting Gods.

"Perfect," he utters with reverence. Then he goes quiet. I feel them moving around me, but I can't track who is who.

I don't know how much time passes, but it feels like an eternity.

A mouth suddenly lands on mine and I moan. The God uses their lips to pry mine open, flicking their tongue gently against the seam of my mouth. They swallow my sighs of pleasure, fisting my hair and tilting my head back for better access.

The kiss turns frantic and I whine, unable to get close enough. Our teeth knock together and I bite their lip, needing more.

They chuckle, but the voice is modulated, not giving away who it is.

The walls holding my emotions back shatter, and what's left in its wake is *need*.

So. Much. Need.

All at once, it hits me. I need all of them more than I need my next breath.

"More," I snarl. "Enough of this waiting bullshit. Give me *more.*"

"You are not in charge," someone says. Hands grab me, kneading my breasts and pinching my nipples. Then I feel a mouth on my clit. They suck, teasing me with their tongue.

I don't know who is who and it's driving me insane.

My restraints release for a second and I'm flipped over. Someone grabs my hips and pulls me back so I'm on my hands and knees. A hand lands on my lower back, pushing down. I expect my face to hit the covers but I hit hot skin instead.

A hard cock pushes against my neck and I open my mouth automatically, needing to taste it.

"Suck it." I can't tell who is saying it. I can just lick and taste their salty precum. I jump a little when a hot mouth lands between my legs. They lick up my slit before sucking on my clit. My cries are muffled. The God fucking my mouth begins thrusting, going deeper and deeper into the back of my throat.

Fingers join the lips at my core, pushing inside of me as the mouth continues to work my clit.

I'm so overstimulated and it's fucking amazing. I reach that place where you zone into the pleasure, giving fully and completely into it.

That place you can only reach when you're truly *relaxed* with your partners.

I love them.

I love this.

I love being theirs to use, because I use them right fucking back.

Cool liquid suddenly drips down my ass. The fingers swirl it around, massaging my rim before gently pushing one in.

It's already so much, but then the mouth at my clit disappears and is replaced by the warm head of one of my mate's cocks.

As they slide inside of me, I catch the feeling of a cold, metal piercing.

I moan at the knowledge that Death is the first to take me.

It makes me feel unhinged and suddenly I need more. I go from overwhelmed to frantic with need as Death pushes in all the way.

Between my cheeks, the fingers multiply as they explore my ass. The feeling of tightness is so much. Everything feels heightened.

I scream against the cock between my lips.

The God fucking my mouth thrusts faster.

"Swallow," they order, right before hot cum shoots down the back of my throat. I swallow every drop with a greedy moan, loving the taste. Loving the feel. Loving every second of what's happening. "Such a good slut," they murmur. "Such a perfect mate."

"More!" I scream as Death fucks me harder. "Yes, oh my Gods, yes."

The hand in my hair shifts and I'm yanked up, Aleksander's front pressed against my back.

"Not God," Aleksander says. "*Death.*"

"Ego problems?" I tease and he shoves me down against the bed. There's a different body beneath mine this time.

"Hello, my Witch," Uri whispers, nuzzling my cheek as she wraps her arms around me.

I don't know why, but suddenly, I'm crying.

"Don't cry, Elsie. No tears," she mutters, kissing the sides of my mouth before pressing her soft lips against my own. "Enjoy this. It's all for you.

Now, you need to release your magic."

Aleksander slows and withdraws, and I whine in protest. "No! Don't stop."

"Hold on, huntress," he orders, sliding the wet tip of his cock down past my lips. The fingers pull out and Aleksander slides in, replacing them as the cold liquid makes the movement effortless. I scream into Uri's neck at the sensation.

"Release your magic!" Death commands.

I whimper, the sensation so intense I'm unable to think.

Uri kisses my cheek, murmuring in my ear, "I'll help you."

I feel her enter my mind as her magic mingles with mine. It feels like her fingers are caressing my soul. She nudges and coerces my magic to the surface.

The air turns hot and my hair stands on end.

"Oooooh, *Witchy.*" Trystan laughs.

"Keep going," Uri whispers. *"Pull as hard as you can."*

It's slow going until Aleksander leans down and kisses my neck, whispering in my ear.

"I didn't expect you to give up so easily. How disappointing."

My eyes flash open as anger explodes within me, and with it, my magic. Through my shadow mask, bursts of white signal the arrival of my lightning. But this time, the glass doesn't break.

Uri shifts, making way for another body to slide beneath me, but her hands never stop caressing me, making sure I know she's right there.

Aleksander goes still, waiting for something.

"Relax, pet," Trystan whispers beneath me, wrapping his arms around my waist. He kisses me, devouring my mouth as he slides his thick cock into me, swallowing my moans of pleasure.

"Oh my Gods," I groan, sounding like some wild animal at the feeling of having both of them inside of me.

Trystan thrusts a few times and slows, pausing. "That's a good girl. Now, this might sting a little. Don't focus on the pain, focus on relaxing your muscles."

Suddenly I feel something else press against my core.

I stiffen and Trystan leans down, pressing a kiss against my cheek as Uri cuddles me from the other side. Even Aleksander caresses my back; each of them treating me like something precious.

"Relax, my treasure," Nerethus's low voice fills the space. His lips suddenly crash against mine, all of my mates crowded around me like a shield.

The Dragon's tongue teases me, sucking on mine as he makes love to my mouth.

His cock presses in and I pant, trying to keep my muscles loose despite the intense sensation.

"It's so much," I gasp, tears starting to form.

"You can do it," Aleksander murmurs as he rubs my back. "You're a goddamn *God*. You can do anything you want."

I pant even harder, my heart racing as Nerethus pushes in further.

The shadows around my eyes dissipate as Aleksander removes the makeshift blindfold, and I blink against the light in the room. Death's room is dim against the moonlight. Candles are spread throughout the room, casting everything in a subtle, shimmering glow.

Trystan and Nerethus are below me, their bodies intertwined, their glowing jewel-tone eyes watching me. Uri lays next to them on Trystan's side, her head on his chest as she wraps her arms around us. She leans forward to suck on my breast. The sight makes me instantly soaked.

It's like something unlocks in all of us.

Nerethus thrusts all the way in, joining Trystan, and we all go wild as the pleasure becomes too much to handle.

"Please," I whimper, not even sounding like myself. "Please, please, please."

"Please what?" Aleksander's voice trembles at my back. I glance over my shoulder and nearly combust.

Sweat coats his body, turning his pale skin resplendent. His shadows are darker than usual, decorating his skin in swaths of midnight.

Eyes of pure black watch me as more shadows coat the air around us.

Death undone.

Seeing that, seeing that this affects them as much as it affects me?

I am undone as well. All of the walls around my heart collapse, turning to dust as I let them in.

"Please, fuck me," I whine. "Mate me. Make me yours."

Nerethus snarls so loud I'm surprised the windows don't shatter once more. Then he begins to thrust.

The God of the Sky cries out, "Oh fuck. Oh my Gods. It's so tight and your cock feels so fucking good."

"Don't come yet," Nerethus growls. "We need to merge our magic and complete the bond."

"I don't know how much longer I can last. I can—" Aleksander groans, breaking off. "I can feel both of you inside her. Her ass got so much tighter. It's so fucking good that I'm already close."

"Then make sure our mate is close too. Elsing, are you ready?" the Dragon asks. I moan and nod. At my affirmation, he withdraws slightly and thrusts, rocking against me. The pain is sharp but enough to send me over the edge. I'm trembling and sweating as Nerethus and Trystan alternate.

"Now!" Uri shouts, and Death joins their thrusts.

All three of them, pumping in and out, filling me and stretching me until I'm just a suit of flesh and bone.

Then their magic hits me. My screams shake the windows. This entire mountain could come down, and I wouldn't care.

The sensation of their magic slamming into me is otherworldly. My stomach twists and turns as my pleasure triples. I cum hard and in that moment, they all lean down and bite me. Death is at one side of my neck, with Nerethus at the other. Trystan bites my breast and Uri...

Uri slides her fangs into my heart.

I am undone and I am remade.

There are no thoughts.

Only pleasure.

I free fall into that lake of magic inside of me and everything goes quiet, the bonds snapping into place, anchoring us to each other.

The surface is still as I dive into its depths, unleashing the full weight of my magic.

The magic responds eagerly, as if it's been waiting for me to learn how to use it.

Which is when I explode.

Someone screams. Everything goes white as a shockwave hits me and I'm knocked unconscious.

the aftershock

chapter 29

There's a ringing in my ears as I slowly drift back to myself.

I blink, clearing away the gunk in my vision.

I'm in... the library?

Oh yeah, this is my room now.

Hmm.

My body is stiff as I roll over, coming face to face with a baby mountain goat.

"Hello," I whisper, my voice scratchy.

It bleats, making me wince. The animal's loud call hurts my head and sensitive ears.

"Meow!" A cat suddenly weaves through the goat's legs.

Noctis.

They brush against my face, purring loudly and curling up below my chin, rolling on their back. Noctis licks my chin, and while the gesture is sweet, their tongue has the most awful, grating texture.

"Thank you," I say, gently leaning away. They don't take offense and continue purring.

I sigh, sitting up and putting Noctis in my lap. "How long have I been asleep?"

"A full day," a voice next to me sounds. I don't need to look to know who it is. I know that voice within the depths of my soul.

His black pepper-scented magic makes me smile as I turn over and meet Aleksander's pale green gaze.

My mate.

He's my *mate.*

I can feel my heart beating within his chest, and his mine.

"We need to stop meeting like this,"

Death cracks a smile. "Hello, mate."

"Hi," I whisper, suddenly shy. With a shake of my head, I shrug off the embarrassment.

"How do you feel?" he asks. "I don't sense any injuries on you."

"I'm stiff, but fine. What happened?"

Death sits in a chair next to the bed but he stands, coming over to sit on the bed next to my knees.

"When our magics combined and the bond snapped into place, it caused an explosion of magic. It knocked out Nerethus and Trystan as well, and Uri could barely walk."

I raise a brow. "And you?"

Death smirks. "I told you. I am *infinite.* All you did was give me a headache."

"Bastard," I mutter. "What happened next?"

"Nerethus and Trystan woke shortly after. They were only out for a couple of hours, but between the insane sex and the magic, you were knocked out for a whole day."

Flashes of all four of them fucking me assault my thoughts.

Aleksander's smile turns wicked. "Are you sore, mate?"

At his words, my muscles clench and my pussy floods with creamy wetness. In a less than a second, I went from half asleep to turned on and ready.

Heilige Hölle.

But... a thought makes me pause.

"Are you watching over me, Aleksander?" I ask with a smile, and the sight of the slight blush on Death's cheeks is too much to handle.

"Maybe I like watching my mate sleep."

I snort. "Creep."

"You didn't answer my question. Are you sore? That was a lot, even for a God, newly made or not."

I am, but not painfully so.

"Yes, but I like it," I admit and Aleksander's eyes turn onyx immediately.

"I don't want to... push you," he says carefully.

"Take the goat elsewhere," I order Noctis and nudge them off my lap.

The Demon isn't the smartest creature, but they're smart enough to understand when they're not wanted around. They meow at the goat and lead it out of the room.

I meet Aleksander's darkened gaze and admit, "I can't stop thinking about you."

Suddenly I'm panting as my heart races, and my skin starts tingling.

I'm so wet it's dripping down my thighs. I rub my thighs together, desperate for friction. "I don't—I don't know what's happening but I need you inside of me. Oh Gods, what the fuck is happening? I feel like I can't *breathe* unless you fuck me."

As long as I live, I'll never forget the sound Aleksander makes in response to this.

The snarl rivaled the Dragon's, but it was infidelity colder. He gripped the post of the bed so hard the entire thing creaks. "That, huntress, is the mate bond."

I want to cry. "Is it going to be like this all the time?"

He crawls onto the bed, hovering over me with a dark smile. "It will fade slightly after our magics settle, but yes, Elsing. This is what it's like being mated to four Gods."

"Gottverdammt," I curse. "Touch me. I need you to touch me."

"You sound needy, huntress."

"Yes," I cry. "Fucking *do* something about it!"

"Hm." He leans back, thinking, and it makes me want to punch him in the face. "Show me. Use your hands and show me exactly how you want me to touch you."

"I hate you," I snarl, sounding feral.

Death smiles. "Good. Now slide your panties off and touch yourself. Show me that wet pussy, huntress."

My hands are moving before I can make a decision. I slide my underwear down, shucking my T-shirt with a quick, clumsy movement.

Then I'm naked before him.

I wish I could save this image. If I had any skill as a painter, I would paint this.

Death.

Shirtless.

Kneeling at my feet.

I nudge his magic and will his wings into existence. Aleksander's mouth goes slack as two huge wings made of shadows emerge from his back.

"You might be a bastard," I say. "But you're beautiful, Aleks."

Death blinks at the nickname.

He's on top of me in the next moment. "Calling me a cute name," he pauses, kissing me, "is cheating." I moan into his lips, his taste on my tongue. My back arches and I struggle to press my core against him with a frustrated whine.

I throw his own words back in his face. "I'm a God now. Rules don't apply to me."

He laughs against my lips.

I pause, pulling back. My chest rises and falls quickly as I pant, needing him more than I need to breathe.

"No games." I caress his cheek. "Please. I—Gods, I need you."

Something about that moment breaks me down.

Tears fall from my cheeks in the next second, my need growing.

Maybe it's the vulnerability of knowing he sees me fully. Not just because I'm naked but because, thanks to the bond, he can also see my magic.

Still.

He chose me.

I must have said the words aloud because he gives me a soft smile, leaning forward to brush his nose against mine. "Yes, I did. It seems, though, that I need to convince you, so just this once, you can get out of my punishment."

He drops down to kiss me again, moving slowly.

I whine, wanting him to speed up, but he traps my wrists, forcing the slow pace.

Then the kiss deepens as he flicks his tongue inside my mouth, tasting me.

Death devours me whole.

Only once he's sure I won't fight the pace, he lets go of my wrists, cupping my face.

"My mate," he whispers reverently. "You are my mate."

"And you're mine," I respond, gasping when he kisses me again. His hands wander my body, cupping my breasts and massaging them, his fingers tickling my nipples.

Aleksander swallows my moans and gasps, trailing his fingers down my stomach. But still, he doesn't speed up.

He tortures me, slow and steady, his finger dipping down to circle my clit. Close, but never on it.

"Please," I pant. "Please, Aleks."

His chuckle sends goosebumps up my arms. "You look so pretty when you beg."

He drags his finger down, through the outer lips of my cunt. I'm so wet, it's dripping down to the rim between my cheeks. Death spreads my cum around, using it to soak his fingers.

"You're always so wet," he murmurs. "I need to taste you."

Death blurs, reappearing in between my legs, my feet over his shoulders. He lifts my ass, which puts my core right in front of his mouth. A pillow slides under me, keeping me comfortable and putting my pussy at the perfect height of access.

Aleksander chuckles, "Oh, huntress. You're absolutely *dripping*. Poor little mate. Your pussy is crying for touch."

His pale green eyes meet mine, the color leeching out, turning completely black until the whites of his eyes are completely gone.

"Get comfortable. This isn't going to be quick." Then he descends, using one hand to spread my lips open as he licks all the way up my pussy. I moan, fisting his hair and pulling him closer. He laughs against me, sucking on my clit with a level of wanton abandon that has me nearing orgasm already. Hearing the wet sounds he makes as he consumes my pussy is too much. Then two of his fingers thrust inside of me.

"Always so tight," he murmurs. "Ride my face harder, huntress. I'm a God, I do not need to breathe. Suffocate me with your pussy." Then he curves his fingers, hitting my walls where it's most sensitive.

"Aleks!" I cry, grinding against his face until his nose is smushed into my clit. He grips my hips, lifting me and pulling my pussy harder against him. Aleksander's eyes open and he moans happily as I start to tremble, cumming so hard I see stars. My hips thrust of their own accord as I clench down on his fingers.

Liquid gushes out of me with a warm burst, drenching his face, but he doesn't pull back. Instead he *sucks,* swallowing every single drop with greedy abandon.

"Say my name again," he breathes, retreating. His eyes are pure black and shadows darken the entire room.

"Aleks," I repeat, and his eyes shudder.

"I can't get enough of you. It's never enough," he mutters, lowering my legs.

He climbs on top of me, his tattooed biceps flexing as he holds himself up so as to not crush me. I'm not sure when his pants disappeared but I'm not about to complain. Not as he drags his pierced cock through my wet folds, teasing me with that cold barbell.

I wrap my arms around his back and pull him closer, one hand reaching up to brush through his hair.

"Please," I whisper, pressing a kiss to his lips. "Fuck me, please."

I will never forget the sound he makes.

Death undone.

With a moan he kisses me, pushing his cock inside at the same time. I gasp and he swallows the sound. My legs wrap around his waist automatically, wanting him deeper.

He laughs against my lips, pressing kisses to the side of my mouth.

"Say my name again," he demands.

I whine, wiggling against him to push his cock deeper inside me, but he stays still.

"Say it, Elsing."

"Aleks," I cry. "Aleks, *please.*"

Death sighs. "I am the God of Death, but you, my mate... You're going to be the death of me."

Then he thrusts all the way in and I scream, but he kisses me again, drinking down my moans of pleasure. Now I can feel the soreness left over from the other night, but it doesn't stop me. If anything, it makes me wetter at the reminder of having them all inside of me.

"My mate," he whispers. "Mine."

"My mate," I repeat, claiming him as my equal.

This isn't fucking.

This is more.

I fall into him, our bodies intertwined until I begin where he ends. Every time he exhales, I *inhale* him deeper and deeper into my soul.

In between moans and sighs, we whisper those words.

Those three magic words that change everything.

And together, my mate and I, we *shatter.*

I scream into his lips as our souls completely merge.

We become one being.

One entity.

His hips jerk and Death groans, cumming inside of me. The hot splash of liquid coats my walls.

Still, it's not enough. He goes to pull out but I stop him, panting.

"Stay," I whisper as our eyes meet. Reaching up, I caress his cheek before pressing my face against his. "Stay."

"I'm not going anywhere, mate."

I smile and kiss him again.

We stay like that for a while, him inside of me, even as he grows soft, our limbs tangled, lost in each other's kisses.

He murmurs soft affirmations, but my need never lessens.

"This might be a problem," I admit.

Death chuckles, pulling back and pressing a kiss against my sweaty forehead before tucking me against his chest so that his chin rests on my head.

"I rather enjoyed it," he says with a warm laugh.

I huff. "Oh? Is that why your cock is suddenly getting hard again?"

"You're not the only one feeling the mating frenzy, huntress."

I smile and press a kiss into his chest. "Is that so? How terrible."

"How do you feel?" he asks, leaning back and cupping my cheek. My head tilts back, meeting his gaze. His eyes are back to pale green.

"You're very pretty," I tell him.

Death laughs. "Thank you. The sentiment is mutual."

I raise a brow. "You *also* think you're pretty?"

"Well, yes. I've always been the prettiest Original, even if Pennios disagrees." He shrugs, his eyes sparkling with mirth. "But I meant I feel the same way about you. You're the most beautiful creature I've ever seen."

He slides out of me finally and I whine in protest, but he quickly rolls to the side and takes me with him, keeping me cradled in his arms.

"Every time I'm in the Beyond, I'm in awe of its beauty." Death pauses. "Until I went there with you."

I prop my chin on his chest and look at him, confused.

Death smiles, his thumb brushing against my lips, "The Beyond pales in comparison. It didn't seem as vibrant. Not with you by my side."

"Liar." I scoff, but he shakes his head.

"It's the truth." He smiles.

"Such a romantic," a voice says from above. I squeak and Aleksander yanks the covers over us with a snarl.

"URIEL!" he shouts. "What the fuck?"

"What?" she says, dropping down from the ceiling. "I've seen you both naked. Don't play coy, Aleksander. It doesn't suit you."

Death growls and the shadows return, darkening the room.

Uri bats them away like naughty schoolchildren and the shadows squeak, which is shocking considering I didn't know they could make sound.

"Always so showy with your magic." Uri rolls her eyes.

"Hi, Uri," I say, waving. She jumps on the bed and rolls next to me, propping her head on her hand.

"So, the mating frenzy hit you. How's that going?"

I choke. "Um. It's fine, thank you."

She winks at me. "I can see that. Good thing Aleksander was here to help you."

"You can always call me, Elsie," she says in my head.

"I will," I reply. *"I'm still adjusting to the fact that you're real and not just a bird."*

Her eyes twinkle. *"I'm very real, Witch, and I have ten years of pent-up desire, so the next time you feel needy, I want to be the one to give you what you need."*

My cheeks heat at her words.

She winks again. "Now, onto business."

I cough. "Right. Yes. The curse, did we break it?"

"First, why don't you call your other mates? We have much to discuss."

Call my mates?

Hm.

I reach within me, looking for the strings of their magic threaded between my own.

I tug hard and there's a shout somewhere in the distance before two giant bodies come barreling into the room.

"Are you okay?" Nerethus shouts, blurring and scooping me up from the bed. Aleksander snarls as the Dragon takes the sheets with him.

"Oh, it's this kind of meeting?" Trystan says, rubbing his hands together. "Calm down, lizard. Time to get naked."

Uri sighs so hard I'm surprised she doesn't fall over.

"I felt you call. All of a sudden it felt like something was yanking my heart out of my chest," Nerethus says, cradling me carefully.

"You can put me down, I'm fine," I console.

He sniffs and sets me on my feet.

I cross my arms and look at them all, trying to keep my cool when really, flashes of the other night keep bursting into my thoughts. Images of their naked bodies, their murmured words.

"Fuck," I look up at the ceiling with a deep breath.

"You're aroused. I can smell it," Nerethus says, his voice low.

"Spawn, that's a very weird thing to say," Uri chastises.

The Dragon snarls. "I've told you not to call me that."

"Too bad I don't care," she says happily. "Now, the curse. Congratulations, Elsie. Whatever the fuck happened was so powerful it blew right through the curse."

"My magic is stronger too," Aleksander says, grabbing one of the blankets to cover his quickly hardening cock. "I don't need to project to the Below to manage it."

Uri sits up, her eyes wide. "Fuck. Seriously?"

"Mhm," Aleks hums, raising his arms to rest behind his head. The action shows off his muscles and all of my thoughts empty from my head as I stare, entranced. He smirks, well aware of what he's doing to me.

Uri slaps him on the head. "Stop that. She needs to concentrate!"

"You're being *very* annoying today, trickster." Aleksander glares.

"Again, I don't care! Back to the curse."

"So it's gone?" I ask her.

They all nod and it's Trystan who answers, "You blew it into smithereens when our magic combined. While you were asleep, we checked the border and it's completely gone. We're free, pet. You did it."

The Griffin sprints over and lifts me, twirling me around and making me shriek.

"Put me down, you menace!" I screech.

He kisses my cheek and whispers in my ear, "I'm going to fuck you so hard later."

My body trembles at his words and my mouth goes dry.

"Oh my Gods, not you too." Uri scoffs. "Males! Get your cocks under control! We have more important matters."

"Like what?" Nerethus asks. "Our mate has needs. What's more important than taking care of those?"

I bite my lip and look at Uri, who appears on the edge of stabbing her progeny.

"Well, while Elsie and Death were getting busy beneath the sheets, my unkindness has brought news. Yes, the curse is gone, but—" Uri pauses, her eyes rolling at Nerethus's raised hand. "Yes, spawn?"

Nerethus grinds his teeth so hard I'm shocked they don't break, "Don't use that word!" He clears his throat. "But, what's an unkindness?"

Uri and Trystan look at him with disgust.

"Fucking lizards," Trystan scoffs.

Uri shakes her head. "I'm so disappointed in you."

"Gods, just answer him!" Aleksander roars from the bed, fed up with their nonsense.

Uri sighs. "It's a group of ravens."

Nerethus blinks. "You can... talk to them?"

She glares. "Of course, I can talk to them, you idiot. Can you speak with other Dragons?"

Nerethus cocks his head. "Yes?"

"So why would you think I couldn't speak with other ravens?"

"I can talk to any bird," Trystan adds unhelpfully.

Uri glares at him. "No shit. I can too. I was making something the humans call a 'metaphor.'"

"Sounds boring," Trystan replies.

Uri closes her eyes and takes a deep breath.

"She's considering beating the bird out of you," I tell him. Aleksander tries to hide a smile.

Trystan shrugs. "I haven't had a fistfight in a while. Sounds fun."

Uri pins Nerethus with a glare. "I genuinely can't believe you like him."

Nerethus scoffs, his cheeks going red. "I do not *like* him."

"Yeah, you *love* him," Aleks adds.

Nerethus blushes harder and flashes his fangs. "None of you are getting any treasure from my hoard, *ever.*"

"Oooh, how awful," Uri mocks. "Now! Back to the fucking topic at hand!"

She takes a deep breath. "Birds are everywhere, so I have a huge network of spies that report back to me should anything happen I need to know about. A few hours ago, some of my unkindness arrived and brought word…" Uri pauses and looks at me, her eyes hard. "Interlaken is under siege. The Republic is *here.*"

"Do you want to let it happen?"

Aleksander's question takes a moment to hit me fully. He asks it so casually.

But he's not wrong.

"Those assholes sacrificed me, pelted me with rotten fruit, cursed at me, humiliated me, all of it." I pace across the room, pulling away from

Nerethus with my arms crossed.

"Yes, they did." Uri's voice is laced with fury.

For a few moments, I stay silent. Considering my options.

I turn and face them. "I can't let them die just because they're stupid."

Nerethus blinks and Trystan cocks his head. "Explain," the Griffin demands.

"They believed the Shauptmann because they didn't know any better. They were easily manipulated into believing whatever those in power wish them to believe."

I take a deep breath and continue, "Which is why we can't let them die. I hate them, but I hate the Republic more. The Primatori *relies* on their stupidity. He takes advantage of them, using it for his own political gain. He thinks because people follow him, believe him to be some fucking prophet, that he's above the law. Above morality." I spit on the ground with a viscous hiss. "It's about time someone taught the Republic a lesson."

"Can we fuck up that bitch Pertcha while we're at it?" Trystan asks.

At her name, lightning bursts to life in the room, wrapping around my arms.

Something else guides me in that moment, and I envision a giant lightning bolt with blades like a sword. It appears in my hand with a thunderous clap as my hair begins to stand on end.

"God, she's so fucking hot," someone mutters.

I look up, the room alight with the blue glow of my lightning, as I bare my teeth. "Pertcha is *mine.*"

"Care to share, mate?" Aleksander asks, stepping into my lightning. It burns him, the smell of cooked flesh and burnt hair in the air, but he doesn't even wince. "She hurt you. She entered my *home.* But how many souls were sent to their death, with long lives still ahead of them, because of her?"

"Thousands," I snarl.

"Death is my domain, not hers. Let's teach her a lesson too." Aleksander says, letting go of my arm as he slaps his arm down, a giant scythe appearing in his hand as a black cowl appears, covering him in shadows.

"Fuck, he's hot too," Trystan groans. Uri slaps him on the back of the head.

"He's not wrong though," Nerethus adds.

Uri rubs her hands together with glee, cracking her neck. "I get her eyes."

Trystan scoffs but I shoot him a look.

"They're yours," I promise my familiar and her eyes light up. "Let's go save the assholes in my town, and show the Republic why all should fear the Mountain Gods."

Uri's whispers in my head, *"The new Mountain Gods, Elsie. You're a Mountain God now too."*

"What am I a God of, then?"

Uri cackles, the sound scratchy and fully raven. "You haven't figured it out? You're the God of Chaos. My chaos Witch."

Chaos Witch.

I like it.

"Let's show them the meaning of *chaos.*"

the siege

chapter 30

We land at the edge of the forest near the outskirts of town, in between Pertcha's hut and Interlaken, using the trees to cover our entrance.

I rode on Nerethus's back with Aleksander, while Trystan and Uri flew beside us. Uri kept pecking Trystan in the ass. It was very amusing.

As soon as I announced we'd be going to Interlaken, all of the Gods had jumped into motion. All disappeared and reappeared a few minutes later dressed in intricate, shining armor. Nerethus' armor is the same shade of black as his scales, with small red accents throughout. Two giant swords hang on his back. When I inquired how that would be helpful if he was a giant Dragon, he simply smirked.

Later, as he shifted, I got to see why he was so damn pleased with himself about it. The swords shifted *with* him, becoming so big they're taller than my whole body.

Not much shocks me anymore, but my jaw was on the floor.

Aleksander returned dressed in all-black armor so dark, I can't look at it for too long without feeling like I'm falling into an empty pit.

His shadows are completely separated from him, writhing around his black cloak. But beneath his armor is chainmail made from what appear to be bones. It's painted black, but the shape is clear. His scythe is secured against his back, painting a macabre picture.

Death unleashed, indeed.

Trystan's armor is bright silver, reflecting off the feathers in his brown hair. On his right hand was some sort of glove, and as he gleefully showed me, when he shifts his nails, the claws become pure metal. What I didn't expect was that they also became so long they can almost touch the ground.

Uri needs no weapon or armor.

With a thought, she shifted her plain tank top and pants into an outfit of pure black leather, covering her from neck to toe. Thick black boots lace up her legs. But no weapons.

If I didn't know her so well, I would have asked why. I know better. My familiar is a weapon unto herself.

Then the Gods took one look at me, dressed only in a sheet, and sighed in unison. Aleksander snapped his fingers and clothes suddenly appeared on my body. A black halter top made out of a shiny fabric is tight against my breasts, pushing them up and nearly out of the neckline. A gauzy black skirt with two tall slits on either side sits on my waist, with black leather leggings beneath.

Thick, heeled boots with silver toes appeared on my feet and matching silver gauntlets materialized on my forearms. Inlaid on them are designs depicting Dragons, Griffins, ravens, and a scythe.

All of my mates. A reminder that I'm no longer alone.

We quickly made our way into the training room and set off.

No plan. Just centuries of pent-up rage.

The Republic will learn to fear the Mountain Gods once more.

I inhale, putting my emotions aside and trying to ignore the now constant lust burning deep within.

The others seem to be equally affected. Hands keep brushing against my back or my arms, grabbing my hands, caressing my cheek.

Every time they pull away and their touch disappears, I want to weep.

Part of me loves it, and part of me is terrified.

Me.

The one who swore I'd never fear anyone ever again. Things have changed so quickly and it's overwhelming.

And yet, it feels so incredibly right.

I can feel each of my mates around me, feel their magic, tasting the flavors on my tongue.

I want to get this over with so we can go back to the Aive. I need them inside of me. I need their skin against mine. I want them to fill the hollow, empty holes in my body and in my weary soul.

"How do you want to handle this?" Nerethus asks, cracking his knuckles. The Dragon's words shake me out of my lust-filled stupor. I take a deep breath, exhaling slowly out of my mouth.

Uri sends me a knowing glance, winking as a mischievous smile appears on her face. I refuse to blush but God.

Gods, actually. I want my Gods. I want my *mates.*

We're on the north side of the forest. The Republic began in the south and it remains their seat of power, so they'll take the other road. The easier road.

"Uri? Can you scout ahead?" I ask over my shoulder. She nods and shifts so fast it's over within a blink.

"Good idea. Hang back while I check things out," they say, shaking out their feathers. Then they pin their dark raven eyes on the three Gods beside me. *"Nothing happens to her, or it'll be your eyes I peck out next."*

Trystan sighs, his hand landing on my shoulder and massaging lightly. "Such a warm and loving family we're all becoming. It's lovely, really."

"The huntress is always safe with us." Aleksander is stony as he replies. "We will never do anything to hurt our mate."

They make a displeased bird sound but nod. *"Give me a few minutes. I'm going to scout out the southern entrance too. We need a count of how many legions the Republic sent."*

A shrieking cackle echoes in my thoughts. Trystan smiles and Nerethus winces.

It goes silent and I lose myself in the quiet peace of the forest.

It used to make me very sad that I was unable to venture deeper into the woods. I believed the fearmongering. Believed I really would get eaten alive.

Now that I know better though, there's a calm sort of peace the tall trees bring me. The scent of old trees and morning dew after the rain calms something within me. It settles me, grounding me into reality, as if the branches are anchoring me to this plane.

"I'm loving this outfit, pet." Trystan surprises me, interrupting my thoughts, his breath at the back of my neck. "I want you to wear it for me later. I need to fuck you in these boots."

I shudder at the need in his voice.

"Uri is fast, but in their smaller form it will take a few minutes to check the area," Aleksander notes, leaning against a tree, arms crossed.

I blink and then Trystan's arms are around my waist and he's pulling us back against the tree, putting Aleksander beside me.

Nerethus prowls towards my front as Trystan reaches his hand down my skirt and into my leggings.

Within seconds, he has a finger inside of me.

I go to moan but he slaps his other hand over my mouth. "Quiet. Not a single sound."

He chuckles darkly. "Our mate's cunt is soaking wet already. So needy. Such a greedy little pussy. Let's make it nice and happy while we wait."

He thrusts his fingers inside of me, curling them in a way that has me groaning against his hand. "God, you're so fucking tight, pet. Now be a good girl and ride my hand."

My body answers before I can agree. Hips thrusting, I work myself on his fingers.

"You like this, don't you?" Trystan whispers. "Our slutty mate loves that anyone could show up and see you, here, completely at our mercy. They could see every inch of you, pet."

My inner walls clench around him as pleasure batters away at me, sweat dripping down my sides.

"Her heart rate increased when you said that," Nerethus mutters, a dark smile growing on his face. "You *would* like that, wouldn't you? Dirty, wicked thing. You want everyone to see as we fuck you. You want them to know you're *ours.*"

"Perhaps," Aleksander adds, "it's the other way around."

I clench around Trystan's fingers again and he laughs, "Pet, are you feeling possessive over us? Do you want the world to know it's your pussy we crave?" Trystan licks up my neck, making me shiver. The Griffin sucks on my earlobe before whispering, his breath against my cheek, "Sometimes I crave your cunt so badly, my lips twitch. Do you know that, pet?"

I exhale hard, moaning against his warm hand. My tongue darts out and I lick his salty sweat. The Griffin's pupils turn huge as he starts to lose himself in the mating frenzy too.

Nerethus surprises me when his hands land on my collarbone. He pulls my top down and kneels, taking one of my nipples into his mouth with a greedy moan, like he's been missing my taste. Then that wiley Dragon opens his ruby eyes, winks at me, and *bites.*

I squeak and pleasure hits me with the weight of the entire Helvetas. My hips thrust of their own accord as I ride Trystan's hand and get myself to an orgasm. It hits hard and fast, drenching the Griffin's fingers. He groans in my ear as Nerethus moans around my breast.

Then Aleksander leans over. "Quiet, mate, or I'll bend you over in front of the entire Republic and spank you, your wet pussy on display for all to see." Then he's tearing into my neck with a snarl, sucking my blood with a wet slurping sound.

I scream against Trystan's hand as I keep cumming. My knees give out, but they hold me in place. Aleksander chuckles against my neck.

Clearly rules aren't my strong suit.

Tell me to do something, and I'll do the opposite, just because.

"Move," someone snarls and Nerethus is shoved out of the way. My nipple leaves his mouth with a wet *pop.*

Trystan's hand is yanked out of my pants as Uri appears before me, back from her scouting mission.

"My turn," she hisses. Her hand dips into my pants and she curses when she finds how wet I am. "Be a good Witch and cum for me again."

She inserts another finger and I tighten against her. Trystan's hand remains on my mouth and he raises the other to massage my breast as Aleksander sucks at my neck.

Then Uri shoves two more fingers inside of me, scissoring them, stretching my sore pussy walls.

I shatter, screaming against the hand that silences me.

Aleksander pulls away from my neck, biting his tongue and using his blood to heal the wound. But he leaves the blood smeared all over me.

Uri blurs and my pants are down, her head between my legs as she dives into my pussy, swallowing every drop of my pleasure with a pleased moan.

I cry out as she inserts four fingers inside of me once again, curling them and hitting my sensitive spot. Heat spreads through my abdomen and suddenly I'm squirting all over her face. She pulls back and flicks her fingers against my clit so fast it makes my pleasure spay everywhere. She raises the back of her hand, wiping it against her wet mouth as she cleans my pleasure from her skin like a happy cat lapping up a treat of milk.

Trystan removes his hand with a kiss to my cheek. His other hand cups my pussy with a satisfied groan.

"*Ours,*" he growls. "This pussy is *ours,* pet."

I reach back and grip his hard cock, making him hiss. "And you are *mine.* All of you are."

For a moment we all stand there, breathless. Uri helps me pull my leggings back up and I right myself, stumbling slightly when I try and walk.

Trystan chuckles and I flash him a rude gesture with my hand. I crack my knuckles and take a deep breath, getting my shit together. A quick glance down ensures all of my clothes are in place once again. Well, besides the addition of blood smeared all over my arms and chest.

I shake my head, facing Uri. "What did you find?"

Uri blinks. "There's no one there."

"Then we have more time until the Republic arrives. I saw a smooth patch of moss back there that we can use," Trystan says. "I need to fuck our mate."

We all look at him and he shrugs.

Uri rolls her eyes, then they turn oddly serious. "No, I mean... there's no one there."

I pause. "Not just the Republic?"

"Elsie, the town is empty. There's no one there at all."

the chaos witch

chapter 31

A leksander stills. "That's not possible. I would have felt their spirits pass."

"Well, they're gone. Every single person in town is gone. Come on, let me show you," Uri says, turning and walking into town under the light of the late wintar sun.

We follow, confused.

As we enter the town, we pass by empty houses and silent buildings.

There's not a single person.

No distant chatter, not even the sound of footsteps.

"What the fuck?" Trystan swears.

"Something is wrong," Aleksander adds.

Nerethus's nostrils flare as he scents the air. "I don't smell any bodies. Entire towns don't just disappear. What the Hell happened here?"

"I don't know," I choke out, a rock in the pit of my stomach.

Something is very, very wrong.

We reach the town square and I come face to face with the pillory I was chained in only a few months before.

The wood is a bit rotten and moldy, and there's dried blood on the wrist clamp.

"You okay?" Uri asks, sensing my discomfort.

I nod tightly. *"I'm fine."*

We turn around, looking for any sign of life, but there's nothing.

"Uri, your unkindness said the Republic was coming. How could they get this wrong?" Aleksander asks with suspicion.

Uri exhales shakily. "I don't know. This... This has never happened."

"Well, well. The Witch bitch isn't dead. How unfortunate," a voice calls. The sound of metal follows as the Gods draw their weapons. "I was so hoping to gnaw on your bones."

"You," I growl, sounding deadlier than the Dragon next to me.

Willem Tell walks slowly into the town square, a pleased grin on his face. He's dressed in fine clothes, as per usual. His silvery-white hair is longer than it was when I last saw him. Now it hangs down to his shoulders. If anything, it makes him look even more handsome than before.

Bastard. I really hoped I'd never have to see him ever again.

"Do we know him?" Trystan asks not at all quietly. "I don't know him but I have this feeling like we should kill him. We should kill him, right?"

Trystan steps forward but Uri slaps a hand against his chest, baring her fangs. "This is the fucker who sentenced Elsing to die. This is the man who tried to kill our *mate.*"

Willem smiles and some strange, green-looking substance drips down the side of his mouth.

"It's a good thing he had help," a feminine voice calls.

I watch in horror as Tante Inga steps out from behind Willem, her eyes fully healed and a shockingly bright blue.

But the voice that spoke, it doesn't match the withered old crone now standing before us.

Pertcha shakes and her skin, the skin of Tante Inga, falls off. Trystan gags as chunks of wrinkled flesh are flung about, one piece hitting him in the face. Her tangled hair falls off in white clumps, taking pieces of flesh with it.

The horror continues and even I become nauseous as she turns into a blob of bloody muscle and white bone. Rotten teeth fall out, bouncing off the ground.

Uri has to look away with a wince.

Then Pertcha shakes herself again and the remaining flesh is strewn about as blood sprays everywhere.

The only thing left are her eyes.

It's the most horrific thing I've ever seen. Even more so when new skin emerges with a sick, squelching sound. It grows at such a fast rate, I can see it binding together. The sound of the new skin traveling over her bleeding muscles and bones makes me want to throw up.

I have to hold my breath so I don't.

New, unblemished pale skin forms as white-blonde hair grows from the freshly made scalp.

A figure takes form. slowly and painfully.

A beautiful figure.

Pertcha.

The God of Magic shakes her head, a thin mesh shift appearing on her perfect body. It doesn't do anything to cover her nakedness. But all I can look at is her beautiful face and her perfect red lips.

"You're disgusting," I declare, surprise in my voice. "All that work and you're even more disgusting than you were before. How pathetic."

"You *dare*," she utters, her eyes narrowed, cheeks reddening.

I make a look of disdain. "I *do* dare actually. I liked the withered crone look more than this horrid flesh suit."

"You little bitch," she snarls. "I'll tear you limb from limb and curse your rotting remains so your soul is stuck here forever. No afterlife, nothing." Willem places a hand on her arm and she glares at him, composing herself with a stiff sniff.

A voice like midnight echoes through the empty town.

"No, I think not." Aleksander's shadows explode, dimming the sun as the world becomes awash in shades of gray and shadows.

"This is a trap," Uri whispers in my head, but there's an echo to it.

"I know," Aleksander says. I almost jumped hearing his voice in my head. It's only been Uri's voice and mine for so long. *"I guessed it would be."*

"Damnit, Reapyr. Maybe you could share with the class next time?"

Trystan replies, furious.

"*I guessed it would be a trap too,*" Nerethus admits.

"*Well fuck you both then!*"

"You did so well, my wayward child," Pertcha says to me. "Bringing the Mountain Gods all the way down from their little glass castle, just for me."

I raise a brow. "I am no child of yours, hag."

"But you are," she says primly. "And you followed my instructions to the T. Failed creation you may be, you're so easy to compel. Never once did you guard your mind, you stupid girl."

I look her dead in the eyes. "Touch my mind again and I'll kill you."

"Oh, you're hilarious." Pertcha laughs. "My dear, your whole family are my pawns! It was so easy to convince your mother to kill herself once your father died. And you! One push sent you to the Mountain Gods hidden away within their sad little castle. Bravo!"

"*Don't let her get to you,*" Aleksander whispers.

I brush against his magic. "*She's not getting to any of us ever again.*"

"Are you done with the monologue? What did you do with the people of Interlaken?"

"Oh, it wasn't me." She smiles, her lips bloodred against the white of her teeth. Pertcha looks up at Willem. "It was him. My golden child. My best creation."

Wait, what?

A flock of birds caws overhead, fleeing the forest.

"*Uh, Elsie?*" Uri whispers frantically. "*Something's coming. Something big... Many somethings actually.*"

Their hair.

It's the same odd shade of silvery white.

Something... There's something I'm missing.

Something I should have seen.

"You didn't actually think he was human, did you?" Pertcha cackles and my blood goes cold. "Gods, you're stupid."

The forest rumbles and the trees shake.

"You and your family were a test, little witch. A test of what I can do with my power. Centuries ago, I convinced one of your ancestors to drink some of my blood. Within it, I sent a tiny seed of my magic. Unfortunately it took centuries to manifest into much of anything at all other than thought-casting and a long life. But, your kind... Their will is too strong. I needed something easier to manipulate. Something more... animal."

"She doesn't know I'm a God now too. She can't feel my magic," I whisper to Uri. Her face is stony, but I feel her inner shock.

"And then to convince the Primatori that I was his long beloved God. Well, that was child's play. Now I have the prayers of the entire Republic at my back."

What?

"What the fuck?" Trystan asks.

"Funny," Pertcha smirks, "how the Republic never describes their God in too much detail. It was pathetically easy to put on a male guise and convince them to worship me. They were practically waiting for it. Now, they conquer the world in my name."

"Holy shit," Uri says. "You're insane. *You're* the Republic's God?"

Pertcha makes a dramatic bow. Then her figure... shimmers. Before us now, is a God that is neither male or female. They are all and none of it. Their clothes are plain, a simple white shift with a gold sash over it. A bright, gold crown floats a few inches above their head, and their skin glows as if lit from within.

The image shimmers again and Pertcha turns back to her other form.

"Like it? They really should have called me the God of Tricks, not you, Uriel. The idiots took one look at me and fell to their knees, sobbing about how I'm here to save them." She chuckles.

"You're going to die, *cousin,*" Willem says suddenly, his purple eyes fixed on Nerethus.

We all turn and look at the Dragon in shock.

"Excuse me?" The Dragon looks aghast. "We're not related, you psychotic ingrate."

Willem smirks. "Oh, we are. Distantly. But we *are* related, fire-breather."

"Elsing, are you sure this one is right in the head? He seems quite stupid." Nerethus looks at me, his face passive. But there's a glint in his ruby eyes.

He's goading Willem on. A tactic I rather appreciate.

"What did you do, Pertcha?" Aleksander asks, his voice dark as night.

"Wrong question," Pertcha responds with a smile. "The better one is, what did I *create?*"

"That power was never yours to take!" Aleksander bellows, slamming the butt of his scythe into the ground. The ricochet causes the ground to shake. "There's a *reason* there are only five Originals."

"Why are the Originals the only ones allowed the gift of creation? You have your own realm, Aleksander. How is that fair?"

"Creation is a curse," Aleksander says darkly. "But it was never your power to take. Don't you understand the repercussions this will have? You're breaking the world, Pertcha. There is no coming back from this."

Pertcha pouts. "You've gotten so fucking boring. Mighty Death, how you've fallen." The God of Magic smirks, glances at Willem, and utters two simple words.

"Kill them."

Willem smiles and instead of teeth, he has huge white fangs. "With pleasure," he lisps, then skin starts to shift, bubbling as he grows larger and larger. Scales appear, merging together to create thick, impenetrable plates.

"Oh *scheiße*," Trystan curses. "He's a fucking basilisk. I thought we killed them off long before the curse!"

Nerethus looks like he just got punched in the gut.

"It's not just him," Uri says, furious. We all whirl, backs to each other as more giant scaled beasts slither out of the forest, their fangs dripping with green venom. Everything the green liquid hits sizzles, burning smoking holes into the ground.

The creatures roar. It's a high-pitched sound that bursts my eardrums. I slap my hands over my ears to protect them but it's too late. Hot blood drips down from my ears, coating my hands.

"All I had to do was kill a few Dragons and curse their eggs, and I made my own little army," Pertcha says happily. "Thankfully for me, they love the taste of flesh."

Oh my Gods.

I look at Nerethus with horror. "Dragon eggs?"

"Yes," Uri replies in my head. "Basilisks would have grown up to become Dragons... but their eggs were cursed before they hatched. Willem was right. He and Nerethus are related, albeit very distantly. If Pertcha hadn't gotten to him, Willem would have become a Dragon."

Heilige scheiße.

Pertcha looks at them with a proud smile. "Through them, I found perfection, and thanks to them, I will complete the final step of creation. Sometimes you have to kill your children, and you, my child," she nods to me, "are going to die."

The basilisk that is Willem Tell towers over us, roaring and spraying venom everywhere. I cover my face with my hands but someone throws me to the ground, rolling us so they land beneath me.

I blink, coughing at the dust the landing created. Aleksander appears beneath me, the right side of his face covered in venom. His skin falls away, bearing a white skeleton.

"Oh my Gods," I cry.

He smiles, a thing of horror and beauty.

"Are you worried for me, huntress?"

I shove his chest with a scoff. "Of course not. I'm merely worried for your ego. I know how much you love that pretty face."

He snaps his fingers and we're back to standing. My center of gravity shifts, turning my stomach into knots. I exhale it out, refusing to think about it as I focus on Pertcha once more.

I shove a burst of magic down the bond, healing his cheek. The skin was slowly starting to reform but with my magic, it's instantaneous. One second he's half skeleton, the other, he's back to normal.

Death glances to the side at me with a raised brow.

"No one hurts you," I hiss, my fury rising.

Death smirks, unsheathing his scythe. Nerethus takes a few steps back and I hear the crunch of a building crumbling to pieces as he shifts, taking half the town with him. The mighty black Dragon lets out a roar so loud, it shakes the trees.

It brings me endless joy to see how Pertcha blanches, fear momentarily overtaking her at the sight and sound of my mate, the God of Dragons.

Then the ground starts to shake.

"Earthquake!" I call into Uri's mind. I've never experienced one before but I've heard of them plenty.

A cawing laugh returns. *"That's no earthquake, my Witch. Did you forget? Your mate is the God of Deep Earth. He can bring this whole mountain down on our heads, should he wish."*

Giant boulders roll into town, crushing houses and knocking down trees. They run into the basilisks, smushing them against the still standing trees. The forest turns into a battlefield as Nerethus roars and more boulders appear. The ground shakes so vigorously I can barely keep my feet.

Trystan shakes his head and transforms into his Griffin form. Now, his talons are silver and sharp as the edge of a blade, thanks to his unique armor.

A harsh breeze hits us and I'm nearly lifted off my feet. It follows Trystan as he jumps into the air, easily executing a perfect vertical ascent. When he joins Nerethus, a wave of wind hits the basilisks, catapulting two of them into the air. They come down hard, crashing atop the others. The basilisks have giant horns in the same way the Dragons do, so when the two airborne basilisks land, they're skewered and stabbed to death.

Uri cracks her neck, drawing my attention back to Pertcha.

"This time," my familiar says, "when I peck your eyes out, I'm going to pull your brain out with it, you fucking bitch."

"Not if I get there first," I promise.

Uri laughs.

"Unlikely," Pertcha says. "I'm an Original now. I can create, so I can no longer die. Besides, you'd have to get past my beasties first."

Basilisks crowd us into the town square, coming from every angle.

Nerethus launches into the sky with a mighty roar, ascending enough that he can unleash a torrent of violent flame at the basilisks. They startle but don't stop. The fire doesn't hurt them.

Trystan unleashes a mighty shriek and joins Nerethus, diving down and raking his silver talons through the basilisk's scales. Black blood sprays everywhere as the first one goes down. Nerethus swoops in and grabs the body in his huge claws, ripping it in two.

"Willem! Kill them now!" Pertcha screams.

There's a sharp sound and Aleksander raises a bloody wrist to my mouth.

Pertcha blinks, confused.

I look at Death with a smile and lean down, drinking his blood with greed.

It hits my system and my magic explodes, blasting Pertcha into the air. She flails before red magic envelops her, allowing her to land on her feet like a cat.

I pull back and glance at Pertcha. Her eyes are wide with confusion as she pushes to standing.

"You drank their blood?" she hisses, horror painted on her features. "Are you insane?"

I give her a bloody smile. "You know what? I don't think sanity is for me. *In*sanity is much more fun. You miscalculated, Pertcha. Your plan did work. What you did to my bloodline worked. It just needed a little divine blood to activate it. Now who's the idiot?"

With a scream I slap my hands to the side, summoning giant lightning bolts into my waiting palms.

Pertcha's jaw drops.

"Congratulations," I mock. "You created a *God*."

"That's not possible," she cries.

"Meet the newest Original," Aleksander says, his voice dripping with wicked delight. "The God of Chaos."

"NO!" Pertcha sprints at me, unleashing a wave of red magic with the swipe of her hand.

I whisper the words like a spell. "You will control me no longer."

Pertcha's red magic races towards me like a wave and I take a deep breath, slapping my palms together and slamming the combined lightning bolt into the ground.

Her magic meets mine with a giant *boom*. Houses are torn to pieces and doors fall off their hinges as the entire forest shakes.

A wall of lightning protects Death, Uri, and me from her onslaught. Pertcha screams in anger and continues battering me.

There's a pained cry and I risk a glance back to see Trystan falling from the sky, venom burning holes in his wings.

My stomach drops and my hands turn cold in horror.

"GO HELP HIM!" I scream at the others. Aleks hesitates but Uri grabs him, dragging him away. Uri shifts into her giant raven form and joins the melee, attacking the basilisks with glee. Aleksander swings his scythe from the ground, his shadows wrapping around the basilisks and choking them, pinning them in place. Death swings, making scales and blood fly.

I don't see Trystan though.

Let him be alive. *Please.*

There's something that happens inside of a person, be they God or otherwise, when their loved one is threatened. It's hot, that specific brand of fear and rage. It burns through me with a reckless intention.

"I love you," I realize. Without knowing it, I connected to the magic inside of me, sending the words to each of my mates. *"I love you. You're not allowed to die. Any of you. I refuse it. I won't lose* anyone *else."*

Before they can reply, I cut the connection.

My head goes quiet.

All that's left is rage.

"It's you and me now, girl. Drop the shield and let's handle this like ladies, hm?" Pertcha taunts.

I eye Pertcha, not trusting a single word that comes out of her red-painted mouth.

If this is a game, then I need to get the upper hand.

I thought revealing my divinity would do it. It threw her off, certainly. But it didn't stop her in any way.

Time for a different strategy.

"Fine," I acquiesce, dropping the shield. "But no magic," I add, my giant lightning bolt dissipating as the remaining lightning crawls up my arm, burrowing into my skin the same way Death's shadows behave. I can feel the lightning in my muscles, all the way down to the bone.

Pertcha steps towards me with red magic swirling around her hands. "No magic?" she *tsks.* "My dear, I *am* magic. No, I don't think that rule suits me."

I shrug and look to the side. "Your new creations are dying. Everything you create *fails,* Pertcha." Several basilisks cry out as they're ripped apart, mutilated bodies collapsing against the ground, dead. I whistle as they topple over, the life leaving their eyes. "Pity. Not so perfect after all, then."

Willem has entered the fray, facing off with Nerethus. The Dragon tries to flap his wings but Willem is too fast. The basilisk bites Nerethus in the leg and my mate cries out.

Pain rips through my calf and I scream.

Pertcha laughs. "The only failure I see here is you, Witch. Enough of the attempts to distract me. Now, you die."

The screams of my mate unlocks that pool of magic deep within me. Magic surges out and my hair begins to float in an invisible breeze as the air around us turns hot and electric.

Pertcha's hair stands on end and she bats it down.

"You are not the only one who can create," I remind her, quickly forming a half-assed plan. "I just do it *better*."

She scoffs, her eyes narrow, but for a brief second, she hesitates.

That's all the time I need.

"I need you," I whisper down my bond with Death.

"Always," he responds, and in a second he's on the ground next to me. He bends his knees and jumps, his shadow wings flapping. I quickly connect to his mind and show him my plan, and he nods, understanding what I want.

Side by side, we face Pertcha.

Death and Chaos united.

"Do you know how I figured out I'm the God of Chaos, Pertcha?" I ask, lifting a hand and summoning a peal of lightning bolts that blast around her in a perfect circle, trapping her. "I don't follow the rules. I *make* them.'

"Let me out!" she screams, blasting at the cage with magic. Distantly, I feel my head begin to throb from her onslaught. My nose begins to bleed but I don't pull back.

Nothing will stop me now.

"Here's a new rule for you," I say, pushing my will and my magic into the world, all the way into the heavens themselves.

"All Gods can die!" My shout reverberates through the forest.

"What?" Pertcha shouts. But there's a sharp crack heard across the world as my rule falls into place.

A rule that contradicts *everything*.

My vision goes white and I fall, but Aleks is there to catch me, gently setting me on the ground. He keeps his arm around my waist, holding me steady.

I take a deep breath and nod, pulling away.

Now is not the time for vulnerabilities.

Then I drop Pertcha's cage.

Another wave of red magic, this one brighter and faster than the rest, is slung towards me again.

Death raises his scythe and the magic ricochets off it with a bang.

Pertcha is thrown into the air, toppling head over heels as she hits the ground with a hard thud. Blood drips from her nose as she pushes onto her hands and knees, struggling to stand.

"You can't kill me," she pants. "I'm magic *itself.*"

"About that," Uri appears behind Pertcha and punches a fist through her chest. Pertcha gasps, blood bubbling out of her mouth. Her still-beating heart is in Uri's fist. My familiar yanks her hand back through the hole she just made, breaking more of Pertcha's ribs on the way. The sound is wet and crunchy.

Pertcha gasps, her eyes wild, and then she lets out a shrieking laugh. "Do you," she says, breathless, "think that will stop me?"

Already, her bones snap back into place as her flesh reknits, growing and healing at a rapid pace.

Uri takes a bite of the raw, still-beating heart and grimaces. "Rotten to the core. I'm not surprised." She tosses it to the ground and stomps on it with a horrid squelch. Uri glances at Pertcha with a wry smile. "Here's the thing. When we made you, we said you were magic itself. Your job was to bring magic to the world, allowing the humans to advance and thrive. Well," Uri cringes, "the thing is, Pertcha, the others *thought* that was true. But, how do I put this?" She pauses, pretending to think. "Right, *I lied.*"

"What?" Pertcha's mouth gapes open like a fish, her eyes going wide in disbelief. "What the fuck are you talking about?"

"You're the God of Magic," Uri reassures her mockingly, "that much was true, but you weren't the first, nor did you bring magic into the world. You've always been a bit sensitive and nobody really knew what to do with you, so we made up some bullshit job to keep you occupied. But magic in no way hinges on your existence."

"That's impossible!" Pertcha screams.

Uri laughs. "*I'm* the reason the world has magic. I stole it from Pennios because I was really fucking bored and released it into the world."

My familiar winks at me as my jaw hits the floor.

"Surprise!" They cackle in my head, the sound wholly raven.

"No," Pertcha stumbles back. "No, that can't be true."

"It's true. I was there," Aleksander says, confirming Uri's words. "You were made to manage that magic, nothing more. The simplest job out of every single God and you still fuck it up," Death says with disgust.

"I AM THE GOD OF MAGIC!" Pertcha shrieks, the sound hurting my still injured ears. **"I AM AN ORIGINAL NEWLY MADE. I CREATE! YOU WILL NOT TAKE THIS FROM ME!"**

"See?" Uri caws. *"So sensitive! I'm gonna peck out her eyes again. Without the cataracts, they'll be nice and tasty."*

"Be my guest," I tell her. *"But first..."*

"I don't need to take anything from you," I say aloud, nodding to Pertcha. "I've done my part."

I step to the side, allowing Aleksander to step forward, the shadows around him writhing. He's terrifying with his wings behind him.

Terrifying and completely and utterly *mine.*

"Gods can die now, Pertcha," he says with a wicked smile. "You're in *my* domain. No one is above Death. Not even an Original."

Pertcha hisses, "You're not the first, Pennios is."

The first, meaning the first God.

The first being.

The beginning.

I smile, knowing what's coming.

"I'm not," Aleksander confirms, raising his scythe. Pertcha creates a shield of magic, raising her hands. "But I will be the last. Gods and man will die, and still I will stand. I am the ending. I am *your* end—and I've come to collect."

His scythe slices down, severing through her shield. Pertcha jumps to the left but the blade comes down on her arm, severing it. The limb falls to the ground as blood sprays everywhere. Pertcha screams.

Muscle and bone are already growing back.

But not fast enough.

Aleksander sticks the staff of his scythe into the ground and drops his wings. He shrugs off his cloak, letting it fall into the blood and dirt.

In only black armor, with no weapons, he blurs, grabbing Pertcha around her neck.

Then he inhales.

The sound it makes causes blood to drip down my eyes. I squint, trying to see around the red liquid burning a path down my face. The screams of a thousand, agonized souls echoes throughout the destroyed town, as frost appears on the ground, turning dirt into pure ice.

Pertcha screams and writhes against Aleksander but it's no use.

Out of nowhere, the screams stop. Death pauses, blinking with a look of confusion. Then he drops to the ground, stumbling and falling on his ass with an agonized groan.

No.

NO.

All of that pent-up rage bursts out of me as I rain lightning down upon us. Pertcha scrambles away but she's not fast enough. My bolts hit her with terrible precision, burning her new skin all the way down to the bone, muscle and nerves appearing beneath it.

Aleksander groans again, rolling to face me, which is when I see the dagger in his chest.

"Poisoned," he gasps, yanking it out with a wince. "The blade. It's poisoned."

"I'm dying," he whispers to me. *"The venom is burning my skin faster than I can heal. She stabbed me in the heart. It's spreading through my system."*

"NO!" I scream, sobbing and furious.

"I wanted more time," he whispers. "But if this is my end, I'm glad yours is the last face I'll see."

He cannot die.

He can't.

I throw my head back, my arms out at my sides, and *pull* on the combined magic of my mates. With a scream, the magic explodes out of me and my vision goes white.

I fall into an abyss, not fully unconscious but not conscious either.

My mates need me.

I can't give up yet.

Fighting tooth and nail, I climb and scratch and battle my way back to consciousness.

I will not let them die.

With a gasp, my eyes open and I inhale violently.

The bright white coating the world in light is gone.

Now, the world is silent.

No birdsong, no cries of pain.

Just the soft sway of the Helvetas trees in the calm wind.

With a cough, I push up, my hands cut and bleeding.

I don't even feel the pain.

All I feel is terror as I stumble over to the body lying on the ground.

"Aleks?" I ask, frantic. "Aleks, wake up."

I turn him over and cry out when I see his eyes are closed. They flutter lightly, like he's trying to stay awake, but he can't even open them.

A glance tells me Pertcha is gone.

Another clump of flesh with pieces of white hair is all that remains.

We won.

But at what cost?

Aleksander groans in pain. My hands tremble as I look at his wound that gets bigger by the second.

"URI!" I scream, my voice hoarse.

She's next to me a second later. "What do you need?"

I sob as she places her arms around my shoulders. "He's poisoned. He can't die. He can't. I can't lose him. Help me, please."

"Fuck," she curses. "Elsie I…" She hesitates and that's all I need to know.

She can't fix this.

"FUCK!" It's a scream and a sob as I hyperventilate, my hands never leaving Death's.

An idea forms in my head. I don't know if it will work but I can only hope.

"Rip open my wrist," I demand to Uri. Her eyes go wide. "Bite me!" I demand. My familiar doesn't hesitate, doesn't even ask why, proving all the more why I love her.

Unleashing her fangs, Uri gently grabs my wrist and bites a large wound. I don't even notice the pain.

Nerethus appears, limping, with his arm around Trystan. Both are back in mortal form but in bad shape.

Hurrying to press my wrist against Death's mouth, I lean down and whisper in his ear. "Swallow. You have to swallow.

He moans, but his mouth stays closed.

"Don't be a fucking martyr, Aleksander," I hiss. "Drink my blood, goddamnit!"

He coughs and I shove my wrist into his open mouth, taking advantage of the moment. He chokes as my blood floods between his lips.

I disappear into my mind, envisioning my blood entering his body and pushing the poison out of his system.

With every ounce of will in my body, I force myself and my lifeblood to be immune.

It cannot hurt you. You cannot be poisoned ever again. I whisper as each drop of blood trails down his throat.

I feel the resistance of the poison, but I concentrate harder, shoving every bit of magic at it, *forcing* my words into reality.

Green liquid seeps out of Aleksander's stab wound, dripping onto the ground. I reluctantly pull my wrist away now that I know he's not going to die. Blood drips down the sides of his mouth, coating his lips.

"I was enjoying that," a voice murmurs.

Uri scoffs and slaps him in the head. I'm about to yell at her for hurting him while he's injured, but his pale green eyes open and he smiles at me with a rare wink.

"You're a bastard," I curse, unable to help my smile.

"I love you too," he says, pulling me down for a bloody kiss. I moan into him, my tears falling in earnest. "I thought you were dead," I sob into his lips. He swallows my sadness, turning it into something sweeter.

Aleksander pulls back, cupping my cheek, "I was never dying, huntress. Of all the beings you need to worry about, I'm not one of them. But, I was very upset at the thought of losing my mortal body and being separated from you." He smiles. "It seems I've become quite attached to my new mate."

I slap his now healed chest. "I hate you again."

"Promise?" he purrs in my head.

Nerethus drops Trystan to the ground next to me. The Griffin moans, his wings burnt to shreds. I crawl over him, the dirt digging into my palms, my blood smearing all over the ground.

"Hey, you need to drink," I whisper, pressing my wrist to his mouth. He moans but accepts, his pupils blown out.

"Bite me," I order Nerethus. He hesitates for a second. "Nerethus! Stop worrying about me and just do it!"

With a shallow nod, he leans forward and bites my neck gently.

My will is enough.

Venom soon seeps from their wounds.

As soon as I know they'll live, the exhaustion hits.

"She escaped," I curse. "Fuck. I can't believe she escaped."

"You wounded her greatly." Aleksander coughs, sitting up with a wince. "For now, she's lost her mortal form. Not just the outer suit but what's inside too. It's going to take her a long time to recover from that."

"Define long," I sigh.

"A few months, at least. Maybe a full year."

"Great, so we get to do this again," Trystan mutters, pulling away from my wrist. His face is smeared in my blood and it makes me all warm inside at the sight.

"It means we get smarter. We train, we continue growing our magic. We do not let her win. However long it takes, we take her down. We change the rules of the game."

"You made all Gods mortal," Uri mentions. "That shouldn't be possible, but I can feel it, Elsie. The weight of mortality hangs over our heads."

They all stop and look at me, eyes wide.

Uri laughs. "I can see the horrified look on your face. No, my Witch, you didn't turn us mortal in the way you're currently thinking. We will live for a millenia and then some. But I think... our ability to regenerate is hindered. I suspect only a God with Original level abilities could heal from a life-ending injury, thanks to you."

I glance at Nerethus and Trystan as my horror increases.

The Dragon smiles at me, my blood all over his face. "Our mate is an Original, Elsie. That means unlike the remaining Gods, we *will* heal. And I suspect you would be able to heal us, should anything go wrong. You don't need to worry," he repeats my own words back to me. "We're not going anywhere."

"Damn, I think I feel it too, Uri. There's a weight on my chest," Trystan breathes. "It burns a little. Like I have to burp."

Nerethus glares, sighing with anger. "That not mortality, idiot. That's from all the basilisk flesh you ate. It's extremely acidic. You're not *dying,* you have *indigestion.*"

Trystan burps. "Oh, whoops."

Nerethus glances at me. "Speaking of. We do have another problem."

I sigh, my head falling back. "*Scheiße,* what now?"

"That." Uri points and I follow her clawed finger to where Willem Tell sits on the ground, staring at nothing, covered in bits of flesh and blood.

the new
mountain gods

chapter 32

"When Pertcha disappeared, her compulsion magic wore off. We killed every basilisk but him because, well, as soon as she was gone he shifted and collapsed. He's been like this ever since."

My brow furrows. "Alright. Let's see what he knows then."

"Willem!" I shout, he jerks and looks at me with wide eyes. "Come here!"

For a second he doesn't move. I sigh and snap my fingers, zapping him with a bolt of lightning.

There's a high-pitched shriek and he quickly stands, walking over to us.

"Damn," Trystan mutters under his breath.

Willem is completely naked and... Wow.

The man is quite well-endowed. His cock isn't even hard but it's thick and long, swinging against his legs with every step.

"What do you want?" he asks in a hollow voice.

"Why did you surrender?" Trystan asks, pushing to stand. He and Nerethus cross their arms and look at Willem with distrust.

Willem stares at the ground, his face emotionless, "I just spent the past century under Pertcha's compulsion. Why the fuck do you think I surrendered?"

"You were compelled?" I ask, not sure I believe him.

Willem nods. "Do you know what it's like, to see, feel, and hear everything around you, but not have a single ounce of control over your body? Over your decisions and words?"

"I have a bit of an idea," I scoff.

Willem nods. "I know. I knew the whole time, but I couldn't fight back. She's compelled me since the day I hatched. Hers was the first face I ever saw. She's more than my creator," he says, his voice full of numb grief. "She's... She's my *mother*."

Oof.

"Can you say mommy issues?" Uri cackles in my head. I mentally roll my eyes at them.

"It's so quiet now," Willem croaks. "Her voice was always in my head and now it's silent."

He sounds lost.

"You had no control over your actions?" I ask again and he nods. "Alright, then we won't kill you."

Trystan and Nerethus look at me with disappointment.

"Damnit," the Griffin mumbles. "I'm still kinda hungry."

Aleksander rubs his temples.

"What happened to the town?" I ask.

Willem sighs. "It's an illusion. Most of them are still there. She wanted you to think I ate them. I did eat some of them. The ones that fought back, at least."

"Lovely," Death scoffs. Then we all pause and look around at the destroyed houses.

Aleksander sighs and waves his hands. Uri does the same and together their magic rebuilds what was broken.

Houses reform as glass unbreaks and wooden panels reattach to walls.

"Won't some of them be crushed to death?" Trystan whispers, voicing my own thoughts aloud.

Uri smirks. "Let's just say, I always have a few tricks up my sleeve."

"You mean your mate is also mated to Death," Nerethus notes plainly.

Uri glares at him. "Yes, that's what I mean. Don't be a dick, spawn."

Nerethus looks like he wants to gag at that name, which makes Trystan laugh with glee.

The houses finish reforming and Uri claps her hands twice, a wave of magic washes over the village with touch of her palms.

The sound of distant voices waking up is music to my ears.

"We should go," Aleks says. He nods toward Willem, "What are we going to do about this one?"

"We're not killing him, as much as I would relish that," I reply and stand. My muscles protest as I brush the dust and blood off my dress. It's so stained it doesn't even matter, but I do it anyway.

"Willem Tell, I hereby exile you from the town of Interlaken and the Helvetas region. Find a new home somewhere else. Find yourself too. But not here. You've lost that privilege."

He nods, his face impassive. "Fine."

"And if you ever eat another innocent person again?" I smile. "Well, then I will kill you, and it'll make what Pertcha did seem nice."

Trystan smiles and Nerethus looks pleased.

The townsfolk start leaving their homes and a few let out shouts of shock as they see us.

Time to go.

"Willem, leave. Now," I order, before turning to Uri. "Can you magic him some clothes at least?"

She sniffs. "If you insist." Uri snaps and a plain black shirt with matching pants appears on the basilisk. He doesn't say a single word, he just turns and walks out of town, disappearing into the forest.

"Are you okay to fly?" I ask Trystan, placing my hand on his arm.

"Of course, pet. Good as new, thanks to you" he replies with a wink. "Want a ride?"

I pretend to think it over and his jaw drops.

"Yes, alright," I admit and he smiles, shifting in a flash. I climb onto his back.

"That means you get to ride the Dragon." Uri laughs, looking at Aleksander. Death sighs but acquiesces. Nerethus shifts and Death climbs onto his back.

Shouts sound behind us as the villagers come out.

"Wait," I tell my mates. They hesitate before going airborne, allowing my former neighbors to get a good look at us.

"Tell all who pass through here," I project, using my magic to make my voice sound throughout the entire village, "that the Helvetas are under new management."

"The Mountain Gods!" Someone gasps in horror. "They're free!"

I expect them to shout, to riot, to call me names.

Instead, they all drop to their knees, heads bowed in reverent prayer.

"Protect us, Mountain Gods!" someone calls.

"Protect yourselves," I respond. A few of them cry out in horror but I continue. "Let it be known far and wide, the Mountain Gods are back, and we will kill anyone who makes threats of violence—be they God, Witch, magical being, or the might of the entire Republic."

"What do we do?" someone sobs. "Willem is gone!"

I shrug. "I don't give a shit. You sent me to die. Govern yourselves and figure it out."

"What about the sacrifices?" another person screams. "We will give you all the sacrifices you need—"

"THERE WILL BE NO MORE SACRIFICES!" My voice booms. Several people scream and the smell of urine floods the air as they lose control over their bladders, the fear overriding their ability to function. "There will *never* be a sacrifice ever again. Do you hear me? Anyone who tries to break this rule will be fed to my mates."

"I get the eyes," Uri says quickly.

"Damnit!" Trystan roars. "Then I get the liver AND the kidneys."

"Take it. The rump is the best part."

I cringe. *"That's disgusting. All of you are absolutely disgusting."*

"You love us," Trystan croons.

"I do," I admit, happiness lifting my heart. "If you cook it right, meaning all the way through, Uriel," I give her a pointed look, "then I claim the heart."

Uri cackles and Trystan cranes his neck to glance over his feathered shoulder with a wink.

"Absolute heathens," Aleksander chastises. "All of you are heathens!"

"Don't worry, honey," I say sweetly. "You can have the soul."

He huffs, but I feel his wry happiness.

"Let's go," I tell them, and the beast Gods take flight as we leave Interlaken and the rest of the world behind.

Uri follows close behind me in their smaller raven form. The flight is calm, like the quiet after the storm.

It's not the end though.

Not even close.

It's the beginning of a new age. The old rules are gone, and I will write them anew. I am the God of Chaos, and if anyone crosses me or tries to hurt my mates?

Well, they won't survive long enough to tell the tale.

Beware the forest—that way *chaos* lies.

we're all monsters

on the
inside

epilogue

Something is wrong.

"Do Gods get stomachaches?" I ask, wincing as my stomach cramps while Uri braids my hair. I'm sitting on the floor, wearing Aleksander's shirt as Uri sits behind me, their legs tucked against my back, as they braid my wet hair.

The second we got back, the scent of dead basilisk flesh became too much to handle. We all scrambled to the springs and rinsed off.

Which lead to Aleksander fucking my mouth while Nerethus devoured my pussy under the water.

Trystan took my mouth next, while Uri rinsed their feathers off, still in raven form, in the shallows.

"Clearly they get indigestion," Aleksander murmurs. He and Trystan are playing a game of chess, and based on the Griffin's furrowed brow, it isn't going well.

Or it could be that the goat had crawled into his lap and fell asleep.

"Whatever. So who's sleeping where?"

Aleksander glares. "My room, of course."

"That bed is not big enough," Nerethus says. "Besides, I have the better view."

"Well, my bed is the most comfortable, so fuck all of you," Trystan says, placing his knight with a smile. "Ha! Check!"

Aleksander doesn't even blink as his next move knocks out Trystan's knight. "Checkmate," Death purrs.

"What the fuck, man?" Trystan swipes the board off the table and the pieces bounce across the living area.

"Ignore them," Nerethus says, massaging my feet. I moan happily but then my stomach cramps again. I press a hand to the area and wince.

Nerethus is face to face with me seconds later and I blink.

"Are you alright, treasure?" he asks with concern. His ruby-red eyes survey me. "Are you injured? Why do I still smell blood on you, Elsing?"

There's a pause and he sits back, "Did you stab someone again?"

I roll my eyes. "No, I didn't stab anyone."

Then it occurs to me. I glance back at Uri. "How long has it been exactly, since the sacrifice?"

"Uh, seven or eight?" she guesses. "Why?"

"My cycle has arrived early, apparently. I forgot all about it. I thought this whole God thing would—" I pause. The hands on my feet have gone still and the room is completely silent.

My mates watch me with wide eyes and blown pupils. Nerethus's scales glow beneath his skin, like his beast is hovering just beneath the surface. Aleksander's shadows writhe and sway, agitated... or expectant.

"What?" I ask. "Why the Hell are you looking at me like that?"

"You..." Nerethus's voice is low and trembling. "You get a cycle?"

I blink, furrowing my brows. What the fuck is wrong with them?

"No shit."

"I thought Witches weren't mortal enough for that," Trystan says, watching me with his glowing yellow eyes. My gaze drops to his lips and his tongue darts out as he flashes pointed fangs.

My skin heats and all of the blood in my body rushes to my core. I become hyperaware of the way they're staring at me.

Like they're starving, and I'm their dinner.

"You bleed," Aleksander says in a voice so wicked, I'm wet merely at the sound of it.

"She does," Uri adds, finishing my braid and tugging on it lightly. Then she winks at me and presses a soft kiss to the sensitive spot where my neck meets my shoulder. I shiver at the feeling and she wraps her arms around my waist. I melt into her touch.

"Would you like a taste?" Uri asks and I freeze.

There's a loud groaning noise as Trystan grips a chess piece so hard it shatters. Aleksander watches me with need in his eyes and it has me panting, ready for him in an instant.

But it's Nerethus's furious snarl that makes me gasp. It echoes through the room, settling in my bones until I feel it in the depths of my soul.

"I'm going to taste your blood first, treasure. Crawl over here—*slowly*—and sit on my face."

Oh *fuck.*

I moan and rock forward, not even thinking about my actions. My body moves automatically as I'm pulled towards my mate. I crawl on my hands and knees.

"Slower," Aleksander orders. I slow down even more, swaying my hips with the movement. It makes the shirt I'm wearing ride up, giving them a view of my bare cunt.

"Oh fuck," Trystan curses.

Aleksander just makes a low groaning noise, like he's barely holding it together.

Uri just sighs with appreciation.

I'm so wet I can feel that it's starting to drip down my legs. Although...

I glance between my legs and watch as a drop of blood slowly travels down my thigh, followed by another.

Shit.

"I didn't say you could stop," Nerethus snarls. He blurs and suddenly I'm airborne. When we land, Nerethus is on his back and I'm straddling his chest.

The Dragon lets out a wild snarl as I smear my blood across his abs.

Two dark moans sound in the background as my mates watch. Then the sound of chairs being shoved back echoes as they come closer.

Trystan hovers over us. "Sit that bloody cunt on our Dragon's face, pet."

My eyes shutter and a hand fists my hair as I'm lifted by the waist and placed on Nerethus's waiting mouth.

One lick and I'm screaming. Nerethus's answering moan as my blood hits his system is so loud, it shakes the glass windows.

"Fuck it, I have to taste you," Trystan curses and then I'm gasping for breath as I feel him kneeling behind me as he licks my blood off Nerethus's chest. The Dragon groans again and it only makes me wetter.

My eyes close but a tight hand around my neck makes them burst open. Aleksander—one hand in my hair, one hand around my neck—stands above me.

"Eyes on me. I want to watch you fall apart for them."

"Oh my Gods," I gasp, my words breathy from the pressure around my neck. It's not tight enough to hurt or cut off my airway, but the small pressure is enough to enhance my pleasure tenfold.

Nerethus palms my asscheeks, spreading them wide as he devours me whole.

I want to glance down and see his bloody face, but Aleksander doesn't let up. He smirks, his pale green eyes turning obsidian.

"Poor mate," he coos. "Do you want to watch our Dragon eat your bloody cunt, huntress? Would that turn you on to see his tongue spearing into you, swallowing your cum and blood?" I cry out, and he *laughs,* and fuck, he's so beautiful when he smiles. "Such a fucking whore for us, aren't you?"

I nod, needing to come so bad it's making me see stars.

"Please."

"Please what?" Nerethus snarls beneath me. I gasp, my back arching, as my moans fill the glass living area.

"*Please* make me cum." Aleksander hisses.

"Beg for it." He leans forward and presses an open mouth kiss against my lips. I moan into him and he swallows the sound.

"Please." I'm no longer held back by guilt. These are my mates. I trust them.

I trust them. Gods... that's still surreal to think.

But I do.

So instead of feeling bad about it, I embrace the slut and I fucking *beg* for it.

"Oh God, please. Please let me cum," I cry against Aleksander's lips. "I need it so bad."

"Better," Death says.

Then I'm being flipped around so that I face Trystan, who waits with an open mouth. The Griffin latches onto my clit and *sucks*. At the same time, Nerethus shifts his tongue and thrusts it inside of me, licking *inside* the walls of my cunt.

It's too much.

I twitch and shake, falling apart in their arms.

"Good girl," Aleksander says with a final kiss. Then he lets go and I slump against Trystan, allowing my full weight to sit on Nerethus. They catch me, and wrap me in their arms. But their hard cocks rub against me, signaling that we're not at all done.

"My turn," Death says, the orgasm haze making me sleepy and pliant. Aleksander easily plucks me out of the beast Gods' arms, cradling my body as if I'm some fragile flower.

Trystan pouts but then we *both* get a good look at Nerethus, whose face is covered in my blood.

We groan in unison. The latter curses.

Nerethus smirks and looks at the Griffin, motioning him to come closer.

"Clean me up," Nerethus orders and I moan, watching as Trystan dives at Nerethus with a sharp curse. Their lips meet and they each groan, my blood and cum mixed in with their own saliva.

"Fucking perfect," Trystan sighs, licking the blood off of Nerethus's face. Nerethus closes his eyes as his mouth falls open, his hands on Trystan's waist. Soon, their hips are thrusting lightly as their cocks rub together. Trystan pants and Nerethus kisses the Griffin's neck.

"Watch them while I fuck you," Aleksander orders and my attention snaps back to him just as he sits down in a lush chair, giving us the perfect view of my other mates. As Aleksander sits, his pants disappear and I land right on his hard cock.

I moan as he thrusts into me without preamble. The stretch burns in the best way possible. My thoughts blur, going quiet as he spreads my legs wide to straddle him. One of his hands reaches around to cup my clit and play with my lips, touching me *and* himself with each thrust. The other grabs my breast, kneading and pinching until I'm crying out.

On the floor in front of us, Nerethus has flipped Trystan so that the Griffin is on his back.

"I need lube," Nerethus snarls. Then he's between my legs, his tongue licking my entrance and Aleksander's cock. We both moan at the sight.

"Pull out for a second," the Dragon orders, and surprisingly Aleksander acquiesces. Nerethus slips two fingers inside of me, fucking me with his hand as he gathers my bloody pleasure, scooping it out of me until it's dripping down his hand. Then he presses a soft kiss to my clit and pauses to suck Aleksander's cock into his mouth, making Death tremble, before going back to Trystan and smearing my cum and blood all over the rim of his ass.

It's the most obscene and erotic thing I've ever seen.

Trystan shouts as Nerethus thrusts inside him. Trystan relaxes, sinking against the Dragon's cock with a moan.

"Oh fuck, you feel so good," Trystan groans. "Her blood is making me so hard."

"I'm going to fill you with my cum until it's dripping out of your ass," Nerethus snarls, before picking up his pace. He thrusts faster, his hands on Trystan's thighs.

They're so fucking beautiful like this.

Raw. Undone.

It's perfect.

Aleksander and I watch, but my attention is divided as he too thrusts faster.

"I'm going to cum inside you and use my shadows to hold it inside your pussy all day. I want you to feel me with every step you take, and then tonight, I'll use it as lube to fuck you again."

My curses turn nonsensical as I begin begging for release, begging for more, for anything and everything he desires.

Because I desire it too, and he knows it, that asshole. He can feel what turns me on and what turns me off. He knows how much I love when he and the others talk to me like this.

"I'm yours," I gasp. "Use me, mate. Take what's yours."

Aleksander curses and thrusts harder.

"Come with me," he orders, and I'm already there.

I shatter in his arms. Death follows, shouting his release as ropes of thick, hot pleasure coat my insides.

I watch, in a daze, as one of his shadows pulls away from his skin and travels down my stomach.

Aleksander pants, pulling out after a moment, and I whimper at the loss.

"I want to spend the rest of eternity inside of you, little mate. Your cunt was made for us. So, so fucking perfect." He whispers praise in my ear until my cheeks are burning red.

Then his shadow moves over my pussy. I think that will be it, but as Aleksander kisses my neck, the shadow pushes in further. I gasp and Death chuckles.

It pushes in even further and I moan.

"Keep that pussy plugged and ready for me, mate."

Oh my Gods.

I'm going to be crazed for the rest of the day.

"I can't—" I gasp. But Aleksander tsks.

"You can. Or else I won't let you come later."

"You motherfucker," I curse, but the shadow pushes in further and my curse becomes a moan. "Oh God."

"I do love when you pray to me, huntress."

I only make it an hour before I'm on my knees, begging him for release. He gives in eventually, unable to help it. Particularly when I start grinding against his cock and sucking on his neck like the whore that I am.

Death it seems, is a pushover

My feet are in Trystan's lap and I moan happily as he massages the sore soles. It's been a few days since we got back, and we still haven't sorted out the sleeping situation. Because, well, so far there hasn't been much sleeping happening.

The Aive smells of sex and blood. I only bled for three days. This morning, I could feel that it was over. All of my mates look exhausted because of it, but they all have pleased grins on their faces.

"I've told you," Nerethus grits out. "Stop calling me spawn."

"I can do whatever I want, but fine. I'll stop... *if* you say please."

Nerethus rolls his eyes and lets out an angry sigh. "Fine. *Please* stop calling me spawn. I don't like it."

"Such manners," she taunts. "You definitely didn't learn that from me."

"It's a Dragon thing," Aleksander says. He's reading a book about some ancient war and honestly, it sounds extremely boring, but it terribly cute. "They all have horrible superiority complexes."

"We do not," Nerethus snarls.

Aleksander peeks out over his book, his eyes unamused. "Uh, huh."

"Yeah," Trystan nods, "He's kind of right. Remember your cousin Ahren? She almost decapitated me with her wing just because I made a joke that alchemy is fake magic."

My head snaps to glare at him. "It is not *fake* magic, you ass. No wonder she almost killed you."

"It wasn't that. It was because you slapped her ass before you realized she was my cousin," Nerethus reminded him.

Uri and I give Trystan mutual looks of disgust.

"Males. Absolutely disgusting. Are you sure you're attracted to them?" Uri asks.

"Yes," I laugh. *"I'm quite sure."*

"Ugh, fine."

Trystan furrowed his brow. "No... I would never!"

"You slapped my ass this morning," I added unhelpfully.

Suddenly his foot massage turns sinister as he tickles me. I squeal so loudly Noctis and the goat both shriek and run away from their position, sleeping at our feet.

I summon lightning with a thought and reach my arms up. With a yanking motion, I grab two giant bolts and send them into him.

Trystan is thrown across the room, leaving the scent of roast game bird in the air.

"Would now be a bad time to say I'm a little hungry?" Uri asks.

"You're horrible." I laugh.

Uri snickers. *"You love it."*

"You're damn right I do."

My head is in Nerethus's lap as he massages my head and brushes my hair. It's incredible and I told him I want him to do this for fifty years straight.

"You're in so much trouble for that, pet," Trystan calls. He's already on his feet and striding over as the burns on his skin heal.

We've all been healing even faster than normal. Well, any fast healing was still new for me, but all of my mates agreed they felt more powerful than they did before.

Our mate bond made us all level up magically, it seems.

"Oh no," I mock. "I'm so scared. The big bad Griffin might get me!

Everyone run!" That only makes Trystan more excited.

He's almost to me when a loud snapping sound goes off, followed by a white flash that makes my vision go blurry.

The Gods all jump to their feet, alarmed.

"Fucking Hell. Not him again!" Trystan bemoans.

"Who the fuck is in my house?" I ask, getting to my feet.

I stop and blink at the tall, gorgeous man standing in our kitchen.

Astoundingly gorgeous, actually.

With dark red hair that curls around his ears and eyes of bright amber. His skin is a few shades darker than gold. He's dressed in a high-neck black shirt, with long sleeves that go down to his wrists. The shirt is tucked into form-fitting black pants that cling to his lean but muscular legs. He's taller than Aleksander but not by much, only a few centimeters or so.

"Your house?" he asks in a low voice. "My lord, have you been robbed?" The man speaks with an accent I've never heard, but it sounds like something from down south near the coastal kingdoms.

But there's a presence to him.

A weight to his gaze.

Wait a second.

"My lord?" I ask, confused. But the man stares at me as if I'm an idiot.

Is he a God? I send the question to Uri.

She drops down from the ceiling, landing with grace. "Theron isn't a God," she answers aloud. I glare at her. "Theron is a Demigod, but his first form isn't human, it's Vampir. He was the first, actually."

I frown. "But the first Vampir died a long time ago. Even I know that."

"It's a long story," Aleksander says. "And no, I have not been robbed. The Aive is now under Elsing's control."

"That sounds like theft," Theron points out. "Shall I kill her for you and remedy the situation?"

For a moment, it's silent. Then a low growl fills the space as my mates close in on Theron.

"Touch my mate," Nerethus snarls, "and I'll figure out a way to make you die permanently."

"Yeah, you boring little shit. In fact, don't even look at her," Trystan adds, glaring at him.

But Theron doesn't look concerned.

He actually looks a bit... well, bored.

"Terrifying," Theron says flatly. Aleksander has to look away. Based on the way one side of his mouth is twitching, he's fighting laughter.

If Death is struggling not to laugh, Theron isn't a true threat.

"So, *Theron*," I start, shoving my mates aside, "tell me why you're in my house."

"Do I have to?" he asks. Aleksander nods.

"Yes," I respond. "Or else I'll kill you."

He just crosses his arms. "Yeah, that's the thing. You can't."

Nerethus's arms are around me in the next moment. The move pins my own arms against my sides, preventing me from pulling more lightning bolts.

"Try me," I snarl, fighting against the Dragon's hold. "Fucking try me!"

"I'm so hard right now," Trystan mutters somewhere behind us. Aleksander makes a noise of agreement.

Theron rolls his eyes. "I mean, I'll regenerate. I'm the first Vampir, after all. I did die, for the record. I've died hundreds of times, because for a long time, I was a prisoner of the Below."

I go still. "Wait what?"

Theron sighs. "Now is not really the time. Your mate can tell you my sob story."

Aleksander glares at Theron. "My mate wants an explanation *now*, so just stand there and shut up." Death looks at me. "Theron is my regent and the first and *only* soul to ever earn his way out of the Below through some very impressive deeds of good behavior. For a thousand years, he worked the stains off his soul, and the Below let him out. Needless to say

I was quite surprised when he walked into my castle."

"Which is mine now," Theron adds.

Aleksander lets out an angry sigh. "Yes, which is yours now. I named Theron as regent not long after and I gave him some divinity. He's not a full God, but he has some of the powers of one. Theron has kept the Below running for the past four centuries. This is actually the first time I've seen him since before the curse."

I blink. "Do you need a moment to hug or something? Is this going to be some emotional moment? Because those make me uncomfortable."

"No," Theron says flatly. "This isn't a reunion. I'm here on official business anyways."

The air changes as all of the Gods turn serious.

Something's wrong.

"What is it?" Aleksander asks, stepping forward.

Theron bows his head. "Uh, well. I'm not quite sure how... but a prisoner has escaped the Beneath. An extremely dangerous prisoner. A berserker."

Uh, what?

"Excuse me?" Aleksander's face is the picture of fury. "What the fuck do you mean a berserker is loose in the Below? How did they escape?"

Theron sighs. "That's the thing. I don't know. But I personally over-saw her sentencing. She's bad news, boss. A God killed her, too. She must have done something really evil to deserve that."

"She?"

"A God?"

"Okay, hold on, what the fuck?"

All of my mates begin speaking at once, but I raise a hand and they go quiet.

"Explain. All of it. Starting with which God killed this... beserker."

But my heart is racing.

"You're scared," Nerethus says suddenly, and my mates all turn to look at me. "Why are you scared, treasure?"

I make an exasperated hand motion at Theron, "Just tell me which God killed her."

Theron looks at Aleksander in confusion, "Do you all not know? I thought you would have felt it. Pertcha has personally sent dozens of mortals down recently. She's on a killing spree."

I look at my mates and I know we all share similar looks on our faces.

"What was the victim's name?"

Theron blinks at my word choice. "It's a strange name. An old one. Almanian, I think." I'm not breathing as Theron pauses before finally answering, "Jäger, I think. Hella Jäger."

It's like being hit with a knife in the chest.

The pain of grief is a physical thing.

All of the Gods look at me in shock as I look Theron in his eyes, tears already falling down my cheeks, and ask, "My baby cousin is *dead*?"

There's a beat of silence as Theron stares at me in shock.

"Yes," he finally says. "And she's escaped."

"This is a problem," Aleksander mutters, but the Gods all stare at me, waiting for some sort of reaction.

They all jump when a peal of shrieking laughter explodes from me.

Nerethus's red eyes go wide, while Trystan just looks confused.

"Oh wow," I wipe the tears from my eyes, unable to stop laughing. "Oh, you're so fucked."

"Explain," Aleksander demands.

I snicker. "Let's just say I'm known as the nice cousin."

Trystan's jaw drops. "Nice? You are known as the nice one?"

"This isn't good," Nerethus swears.

I snicker again and look at Theron, "Yeah, best of luck, but you're never going to catch Hella."

Theron smirks. "We'll see about that."

Read Hella's story in the next installment of the RH universe...

there are
monsters
beneath
Republica Helvetorum #2
coming 2025

acknowledgements

Publishing a book is a group project, and I consider myself so lucky to have an amazing team at my side, helping me get these stories out into the world.

Mom and Dad, for always supporting me, even when I decide to write smutty dragon books for a living. For the **entire Garrett/Wolski/Schaeffel/Pearson family;** thank you for never balking at my career path. Your support of my art is the greatest gift. I am so proud to be a part of this family and a part of your lives.

To my best friends. **Tiffany, Corrine, J, Lyss, Becky, Rachel, and Beth;** thank you for showing me the meaning of friendship. I don't know where I would be without you all.

To my amazing Alpha & Beta readers. **Julia, YarnWyvern, Jane, Ashley, Molly, Lindsay, Jessica, Jess, & Reina;** your support and feedback is a lifeline. I am beyond grateful for all of you.

To my incredible editor, proofreader, and sensitivity reader, **Havoc Archives.** You elevated HTBM with your keen eye and crucial feedback. Unfortunately, this means you're stuck with me forever so get ready for book 2, because Hella's story is WILD. Thank you so much for your hard work on this; you made HTBM a better book, and you have made me a better writer.

To my fabulous PA **Molly.** Thank you for being my literal ride or die, and for keeping me on track with all of these deadlines. I would actually be lost without you. I'm so honored to be able to have you on my team.

To the authors and writers who are constant inspirations: **Harper**

Ashley, Paula Lafferty, CK Beggan, River Bennet, Marilu Moser, Azalea Crowley, Ashley Michele, and so many more. This list could genuinely go on forever. I am in awe of all of you and look up to you all so much. It is an honor to call you all my friends.

To my amazing street team & inner circle, **The Scale Society.** It's your kind words and your constant support that keeps me going. Every single day, I am overwhelmed with gratitude because of the impact you've had in my life.

To the authors who taught me that pleasure and romance are nothing to be ashamed of; **Sierra Simone, Gena Showalter, Larissa Ione, Kresley Cole, Trilina Pucci.** Yet another list that could go on and on. Thank you for teaching readers everywhere that pleasure is beautiful.

To the **University of Nevada, Reno, and the College of Liberal Arts.** The History, Philosophy, and English classes that I took molded me into the person I am today. Liberal Arts degrees are incredible and I hope to see more funding for Liberal Arts colleges in the future. Thank you for fueling my desire to learn and how to ask the right questions. To the professors and teachers who molded me, I owe my success to you. Thank you for your patience with my endless questions.

To the whole **Under The Cover** team, thank you for the constant stream of support and for championing all authors, regardless of publishing style. It's such an honor to be on your shelves.

And **you, dear reader. Thank YOU** for making it this far and for giving my book a chance. I hope you loved it, and I can't wait for what's next.

XOXO, ECG

the author

EC Garrett is an Alaskan transplant now living in Kansas City, MO who writes fantasy/sci-fi speculative fiction. She received her Bachelor's Degree in English Literature with a focus in Early Modern and Medieval Literature and a minor in Medieval History from the University of Nevada, Reno in 2016. EC hopes to get her Masters in English Literature as well. In her spare time, she's either reading or watching the latest fantasy releases, riding horses at the barn, spending time with her family, or playing with her very cute but extremely ornery dachshund mix, Frankie.

She dreams of becoming a dragon rider.

Follow ECG on social media to get all the latest updates.

www.authorecgarrett.com
Instagram: @authorecgarrett
Tiktok: @author.ecgarrett
Threads: @authorecgarrett
Facebook: @authorecgarrett

Join ECG's exclusive reader membership **The Scale Society f**or bonus content, bonus artwork, behind-the-scenes sneak peeks, and more!

Scan or click to join today! Trust me, you don't want to miss this.

Loved Here There Be Monsters? Don't forget to leave a review on Amazon and Goodreads.

also by ec garrett

REPUBLICA HELVETORUM
gothic monster romance
Here There Be Monsters (RH #1)
There Are Monsters Beneath (RH #2) – *coming 2025*

THE DRAGON QUEEN
dark epic fantasy
The Forgotten and The Feared (TDQ #1)
The Broken and The Brave (TDQ #1.5) – *coming early 2025*
The Defiant and The Damned (TDQ #2) – *coming 12/10/24*
TDQ3 – *coming late 2025*

THE HOME FOR WAYWARD CREATURES
paranormal romantic sci-fi
Vol. 1 – *coming 2025*

Midnight Pages

indie publishing house + bookish candles

midnightpagesemma@gmail.com